MURDER
AT THE
PORTE DE
VERSAILLES

MURDER
AT THE
PORTE DE VERSAILLES

CARA
BLACK

Published by
Soho Press, Inc.
227 W 17th Street
New York, NY 10011

Library of Congress Cataloging-in-Publication Data

Names: Black, Cara, author.
Title: Murder at the Porte de Versailles / Cara Black.
Description: New York, NY : Soho Press, [2022]
Series: The Aimeé Leduc investigations ; 20
Identifiers: LCCN 2021043173

ISBN 978-1-64129-455-3
eISBN 978-1-64129-044-9

Subjects: LCGFT: Novels.
Classification: LCC PS3552.L297 M7825 2022 | DDC 813/.54—dc23
LC record available at https://lccn.loc.gov/2021043173

Printed in the United States of America

10 9 8 7 6 5 4 3 2 1

For the ghosts

Disorder, we are in full disorder . . . sketches, drawings . . .
and a genius split like a peach . . .
—"The Atelier," Blaise Cendrars

The ink on the soft banknotes quickly fades . . .
—Georges Brassens

Other things may change us, but we start and end as family.
—French saying

The truth is rarely pure and never simple.
—Oscar Wilde

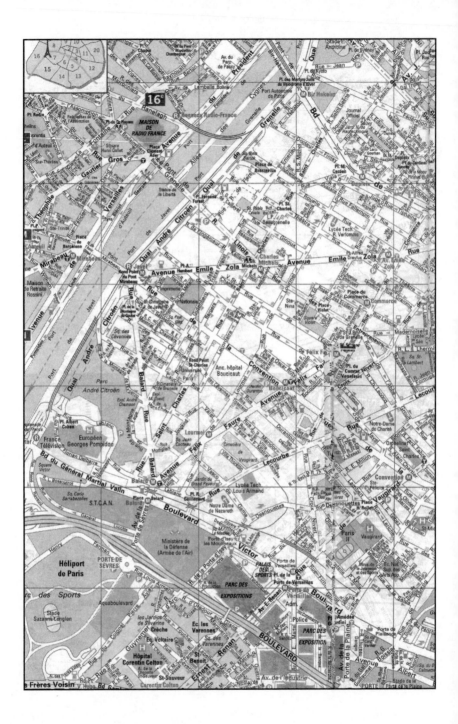

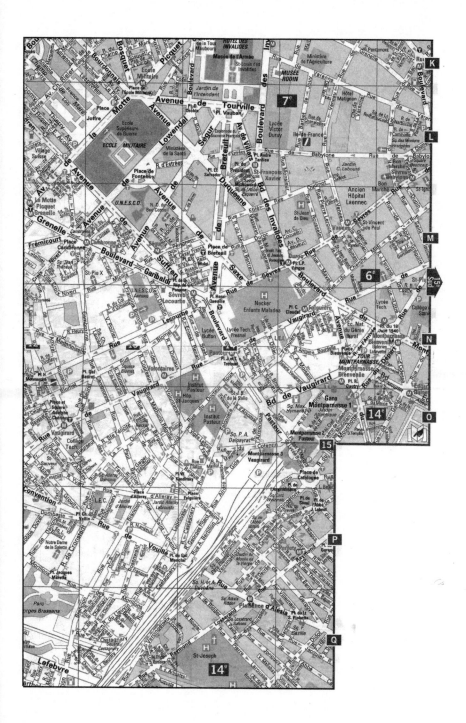

MURDER
AT THE
PORTE DE
VERSAILLES

November 2001 • Sunday • Late Afternoon • Paris

DIRECTRICE BÉCARD'S WORK phone vibrated on the crowded café's zinc counter in a frenetic burst. On the blaring *télé*, sports fans shouted "10 . . . 9 . . . 8 . . ." in the championship game's last seconds just as she answered.

She strained to hear, her wine glass still in hand. Silly idea to come here for peace and quiet after a long day of meetings at the anti-terrorist unit. Cigarette smoke spiraled to the ceiling. People jumped and cheered. She pressed the phone tighter to her ear.

"Hate to bother you, *Madame la Directrice*, but you said you wanted to know the latest."

Her stomach clenched. Had the threat level been raised since she'd left work?

"Of course. What's happened?"

"Police reports of stolen explosives, possibly military-grade or industrial, just crossed my desk. Purportedly taken last night. We've been kicked into high alert."

She almost choked on her wine. *Merde.* She'd feared those words since 9/11.

Protocol kicked in. Trained for emergencies—as if one could ever really be prepared—her brain scrambled to the next step. She dropped a five-franc note and rushed out into the late afternoon.

Once outside, she gulped the chill fresh air and hit redial. "Give me more on the threat level status."

"What's your ETA?"

"I'm across the street. Is this confirmed? Do you have a location?"

"Confirmed." Castel, her department colleague, sighed. "But no location."

She ran on rue de Dantzig past the wall plaque—a memorial to a local *résistant* shot here in the war. A faded bouquet tacked onto it shriveled in the shadows. Through the tall metal and glass Deco door, she entered the building complex home to the bomb squad, the laboratories and scientific police, and arson investigation. She crossed the lobby, nodding to the duty clerk, who gestured her upstairs.

Fluorescent lights flickered on the scuffed vanilla walls and brown tiled stairs as she padded to the top of the building to what they used for a situation room.

Panting, she looked down the glass-windowed hallway reflecting the ribbon of the Seine, backlit by a sky lush with burnt orange.

"Here's the latest," said Castel, handing her a printout from the ministry. Five or so desks occupied by techs sat near hastily mounted wall maps.

Just as she'd feared.

CREDIBLE INTELLIGENCE INDICATES IMMINENT EXPLOSIVE ATTACKS—DUTY PERSONNEL MAINTAIN HIGH ALERT.

Sunday • Late Afternoon • Père Lachaise Cemetery

AIMÉE LEDUC'S EYES misted under the lead-grey sky in the Père Lachaise cemetery columbarium. She placed white chrysanthemums at her father's niche. Filled with the lingering ache of loss, she kissed his name etched in stone: JEAN-CLAUDE. Aimée helped her daughter, Chloé, do the same; the child's kiss landed with a slobbering effect. Three years old on the anniversary of her grandfather's death. The bitter and sweet of life.

"I can't believe it's been twelve years, Mademoiselle Aimée. But I know he'd be proud of you." Martin, the only other mourner, had been an informant of her father's. Every year on this day Martin had mass said for her father. Martin's oversized glasses, silver pompadour, and leathery tan—even in November—gave him the appearance of a seventies-era film producer at Cannes. He dabbed his nose with a handkerchief. "I miss him."

Aimée squeezed his arm. "I miss him, too." Half the time she still expected her father to walk through the doors of Leduc Detective, flash that lopsided grin of his, and sling his coat on the hook. Following his death, Aimée had taken over the agency, focusing on computer security, earning good money. Fed up with field investigation, she'd recently gone into consulting and qualified as an expert witness for court testimony. It gave her more time with Chloé.

A mosaic of yellow and orange leaves crisped into gold over the cemetery's charcoal cobbles. On a mausoleum, damp oozed from moss on an angel's wing, the cracked stone frozen forever in flight.

Aimée opened her umbrella to the patter of drizzle. A broom scraped as a bent old woman, her scarf tied under her chin, swept leaves off a gravestone.

Martin ruffled Chloé's blonde curls as she tottered on the slick stones and grabbed his leg for support. "*Bon anniversaire, ma petite.*" He held out a Printemps box as big as Chloé.

Chloé's laughter numbed the welling sadness. Time to move on, Aimée told herself—she had a daughter to raise. At that, her phone chirped. The message was from her partner, René—a reminder that she had a business to run, too.

"*Voilà,*" she said, scooping Chloé up in her arms. "Now it's time for your birthday party, *ma fille. Grand-père* would like that."

Martin nodded. "He's watching over you, his two beautiful *mesdemoiselles.*"

They embraced goodbye among tombstones freckled with mold and lichen. Aimée wondered, noticing Martin's age and faltering step as he walked away, if it was for the last time.

Sunday Evening • Ile Saint-Louis

FUCHSIA HELIUM BALLOONS and pink streamers bobbed in Aimée's high-ceilinged seventeenth-century Ile Saint-Louis flat, the place warm for once from the body heat of partygoers and the sputtering tapers in their silver candelabras. Chloé ran past in her furry leopard-print boots, an early gift. She wouldn't take them off, had even slept with them on.

Already a *petite* fashionista.

It was a circus, Chloé chasing little Miles Davis, Aimée's bichon frise, and preschoolers trailing streamers and squealing in delight. The birthday party would end soon.

Not soon enough.

Martine Sitbon, Aimée's best friend since lycée, a writer for *Libération* and a party animal, had conned her into not only throwing the birthday party but also having it catered. With her hair dyed pink for the occasion, Martine danced into the salon holding a chocolate-raspberry *gâteau* with three candles.

At last, Aimée thought. Not only were the three-year-olds restless, but their parents had been glancing at their watches for the past twenty minutes. It was, after all, a school night.

Aimée pinged a wine glass with her fork. "*Attention!*"

She nodded to René, Chloé's godfather, to capture the moment with his video camera. René struggled to climb up on a chair, brusquely refusing help from a parent who'd offered him a hand.

A dwarf at four feet tall, he prided himself on being self-sufficient. His black belt in karate helped in that department.

"Let's sing 'Happy Birthday,'" said Aimée.

René panned the video camera as Chloé's puffed cheeks blew out the candles to rousing cheers. Lifting her up was Melac, her biological father, whose grey-blue eyes she'd inherited. Beside them hunched Morbier, Aimée's white-haired godfather, his basset-hound eyes crinkled with laughter as he pulled out the candles for Chloé. Michou and Boris Viard, a gay couple who were René's neighbors and close friends of Aimée's, blew her kisses.

Yet Chloé's grandmother, Sydney Leduc, was a no-show. Typical. Aimée's American mother, a seventies radical who had once been on Interpol's Most Wanted List, had taken a therapeutic "cure" at a salt spa outside Kraków. But a check with several zeros drawn from a Swiss bank account had arrived for Chloé's "education."

Aimée wiped the crumbs off her *bébé*'s cheeks, moved by the candlelit faces shining with love for her daughter.

Michou, his eye makeup perfect, popped a cork; vintage champagne flowed. Boris, in black leather with streamers in his hair, lifted Chloé into the air and kissed her. "I can't believe my favorite *fille* is so big!"

Chloé kissed him back, grinned, and raised three chubby fingers. Aimée was so proud that her daughter attended the *école maternelle* around the corner, Aimée's own alma mater. She took in another glimpse of Michou and Boris, etching this picture of them into her mind. She loved these two and often relied on them as backup babysitters.

As Martine sliced the cake, Melac took Aimée's hand—his thumb catching on the gold bracelet he'd given her—and leaned into her ear. "Next year, we'll have her birthday on the farm in Brittany. Everyone will come. Chloé will love it."

Not this again. A former *flic*, Melac ran a corporate security business and wanted to be more than a part-time dad. He also wanted to leave the city. Aimée's thoughts ricocheted. Live on Melac's farm, work remotely, and look out her window to see goats, not the Seine?

Her?

"It's healthier by the sea, out in nature. What do you say, Aimée?"

If only this appealed to her. Was it selfish not to think of how it might benefit Chloé? She had to stall.

"Not now, Melac."

"Don't brush me off again." Hurt edged his voice. "I'm tired of waiting."

"I told you, I'm thinking about it. Seriously."

Wasn't she?

His gaze read her indecision.

"You need to decide *now*." His tone notched up in irritation. "What's so difficult about this? It should be an easy choice."

Pack up and go just like that? What about Chloé's friends? Her school? Not to mention Aimée's whole life and her business were here. Her relationship with Melac had been fraught after Chloé was born; he'd disappeared, then returned at her christening with a new wife, wanting custody. They'd finally come to an arrangement, then the wife left and Melac became more of a constant in their lives.

Could she trust him?

As usual, he'd picked the worst time for an ultimatum. She needed to hurry the party along.

She stood, summoned a smile, and raised a champagne flute. "Time to open presents."

Boris clapped his hand over his mouth. "*Quelle horreur!*"

Everyone turned and looked at him.

"I had Chloé's present sent to my office," he explained. "It's sitting on my desk at the police lab."

Michou stomped his high-heeled foot. "*Mais zut alors*, how often does Chloé turn three?"

"*Désolé*," Boris said, shamefaced. "I feel so stupid for forgetting."

"Don't worry," Aimée soothed. "Just pick it up another time."

But Boris, after downing a flute of champagne, had piled into a taxi at quai d'Anjou.

After the ensuing flurry of presents and the departure of the children and their parents, Aimée swapped Chloé's sticky, sugar-smeared polka dot dress for pajamas. Done, she returned to the salon with Chloé on her hip to say goodnight. She took in the scene before her. On the floor, the stuffed bunny from Morbier, his replacement for the one dropped in the Seine. Laughing Martine, blowing Chloé kisses from across the room. Morbier in the Louis XVI chair next to Melac, deep in conversation, relaxed for once, talking *flic* to *flic*. As she'd often seen Morbier do with her father, his first partner.

How could she have ever thought herself an orphan? Even if her mother was nowhere to be seen, here was family.

Her family.

She gathered up the ribbons, fashioned a bow and tied it around Miles Davis's collar.

"Poor Miles Davis," said Morbier, pronouncing it *Meelz Daveez*. "And catering a kiddie party? Really, Leduc?" Morbier grunted as he got out of the chair.

Always a critic. She wouldn't let him fault her nonexistent culinary skills. The next minute he'd accuse her of spoiling Chloé, something he did shamelessly.

"You seemed to enjoy it," she said, brushing specks of foie gras off his jacket sleeve. "Or should I have left the baking up to you?"

Melted Berthillon ice cream dribbled on the table next to

empty Veuve Clicquot bottles, a Bordeaux from Chateau Figeac in St. Emilion, and remainders of hors d'oeuvres. Sputtering decorative candles dripped wax. Pah—it could wait until tomorrow.

Everyone kissed a sleepy-eyed Chloé goodnight and bid adieu. When Melac took Chloé from her arms to put her to bed, Aimée realized Boris hadn't returned.

Concerned, she joined Michou in the kitchen, where he stood at the sink, washing champagne flutes. "*Merci*, Michou. Heard from Boris?"

Michou pouted. "He rarely answers his phone."

"*Dommage*. Silly for you two to fight over this."

"*Non*," he cut in. "We're fighting over something else." He put the glasses on the shelf. His pinched lips quivered. "He's having an affair."

"*Comment?*"

Aimée thought of their recent anniversary party. They'd seemed like the perfect couple—Michou, a former seaman and current cross-dressing cabaret singer, and Boris, a manager at the police biology lab.

Michou squeezed lemony dish detergent onto the already clean flutes and scrubbed furiously. "How could he forget Chloé's gift unless his mind's on someone else?"

A lovers' spat? The last thing Aimée wanted to deal with right now.

As if on cue, Michou's phone rang from his jacket pocket.

"Finally! He'll spout some story, act contrite." He thrust his hip at Aimée, indicating for her to dig into his pocket. "Here. You talk to him."

"*Moi?*"

"I can't."

Reluctant, she took the phone from Michou's rhinestone-embroidered pocket. Didn't feel like added drama, but maybe she could avert a disastrous conclusion to the evening. Smooth things over.

"*Allô*, Boris?"

Sirens whined in the background.

"Boris?"

"*Et quoi?*" came a man's gravel-tinged voice.

Whose voice was this? Why didn't Boris answer?

She looked at a frowning Michou, who mouthed *I won't talk to him.*

Her skin prickled. "*Attendez un moment,*" she said.

She left the kitchen and opened the glass door to her balcony. The glimmering Seine ribboned below her, the quai-side lights a pale yellow in the dark November night. Swollen clouds nearly obscured the low-hanging moon.

Anxious, she kept her voice low. "Who is this?"

The only answer was a clanging noise. Then a man's voice rose amid shouts. "Identify yourself."

She should identify *herself?*

"Where's Boris Viard, the owner of the phone you are speaking on?" she said, louder.

No answer. Crunching footsteps. What was happening?

Then another voice erupted in the background. "The robot is activated. Stand clear."

That meant one thing.

A bomb.

Aimée's blood went cold. She reflexively held the phone away as if she could protect herself from the explosion. Stupid.

Michou found her like that. "What excuse have you come up with this time, Boris?" he shouted at the phone in Aimée's outstretched hand. His jean jacket draped over his broad shoulders; his hands dripped with soapsuds.

Over the line came a squawking staccato from a police radio, a voice saying, "Suspected bomb at Laboratoire Central de Police on rue de Dantzig . . ."

Aimée caught a flash of light from the corner of her eye, causing her to look up. It flared in the distance, reflecting yellow on the cloud bank. A moment later came the thundering crump of an explosion.

She looked at Michou, standing rigid beside her, his mouth open, aghast. For a split second, she was back at Place Vendôme, running toward her papa.

Midnight • Rue de Dantzig • Paris

THE EXPLOSION KNOCKED Hugo Dombasle out of bed. He awoke on the floor and frantically reached for his cigarettes to hide from his mother. Like his *grand-père* always said, *You must grab what's most important when you're under attack.* Besides, his mother would slap him and more if she knew he smoked. Lung cancer had taken his father.

He tore a pant leg of his striped pajamas while struggling to stand. His astronomy textbook had tumbled to the floor. Horrified, he saw that his telescope, which he'd mounted securely on the tripod next to his desk, had slanted.

Hugo rubbed the sleep from his eyes, righted the telescope, and tightened the screws. Thank God it hadn't cracked or broken. He peered through the eyepiece, adjusting the telescope's angle. Hugo flinched at the sight. Shooting yellow flames and smoke billowed across the street on rue de Dantzig.

Someone was running away on the street. A man. A man who darted in and out of shadow and kept looking behind him.

"Hugo, we must get to the bomb shelter!" his grandfather shouted, hopping into his room on crutches. "It fills up fast. Hurry."

"Who's been smoking?" said his sleepy-eyed mother, wrapping her robe around her.

Hugo shoved the cigarettes in his pocket.

"Something exploded, *Maman*," Hugo said. "The police lab's on fire."

"*Mon Dieu*," she said, panicked. "The whole block could go up. Help *Grand-père* get his leg on."

"It's the Germans. We're next," his *grand-père* said, strapping on his old peg leg. His grandfather always thought the Germans were attacking. "Get your coats, shoes. There could be more bombs."

Just then a thunderous roar rocked their ears. Another explosion?

For once, his grandfather was right.

Midnight • Ile Saint-Louis

"*Allô, allô?*" AIMÉE said, but the phone had cut off. The stars shone, a hard glitter in the night sky.

Michou's hand gripped the railing. "Was Boris there? Is he hurt?"

"I don't know. Someone wanted to know who I was. Who's been calling. Then—"

Her throat caught. She imagined the worst and almost dropped the phone. Roaring flames, burnt concrete blocks strewn like Legos, Boris's body . . .

She put her arm around Michou and herded him off the balcony into the warmth of her flat. "You know he loses his phone all the time," she said with more confidence than she felt. "He probably dropped it. I bet he's on his way back right now."

Inside, she looked around for Melac, then remembered he'd read Chloé a story and put her to bed. René was sprawled with Miles Davis in his lap on the Aubusson carpet. He sat beside a champagne bottle, looking glum. It occurred to Aimée that his girlfriend, Leila, hadn't shown up to the party. *Merde*. This night.

"*Non*, there's something terribly wrong." Michou's words slurred and she realized he was drunk. "Boris could be dead." He burst into tears, his mascara streaking his face. "I have to go there. Kick the ass of the *salope* who did this."

She couldn't let Michou go in this condition. He was a mess. What if things went as she feared? No one deserved to see the person they loved in charred pieces.

"René and I will go clear this up at the police lab," she said.

"*Non*, it's not your problem," Michou said. "You've got Chloé."

"You're in no shape to leave, Michou." She needed to hurry up before she changed her mind. Turning to her partner, she said, "René, let's go."

"What?"

Aimée caught René's eye and flashed a *just-go-along-with-me* look.

"Got your keys?" she asked.

He stood up unsteadily and brushed off his tailored black velvet Le Smoking jacket. Burped. "*Excusez-moi.*"

Lovelorn and tipsy. Great.

"I'm driving," she said.

Tearful, Michou started to object. Aimée dried his damp hands with a cloth napkin and set the phone in his hand.

"We'll find Boris." She hesitated, wishing she hadn't promised that. The first thing that popped into her head just had to come out of her big mouth. Michou had always wanted to be a PI, so she decided to play to that. "I need you to stay and be the point person"—she caught herself before she said *if*—"for when Boris comes back. It's vital during an investigation. Keep your phone on."

She grabbed her leather jacket, pulled a trench coat over it, and stepped into her knee-high agnès b. boots.

Before heading out into the night, she paused at Chloé's door and peeked inside. Melac lay asleep curled in a chair, a picture book on his knee, Chloé blowing whistles of sleep in his arms. His jawline was silhouetted in the moonlight, his face in shadow. Aimée's chest tightened. If he put down roots here instead of in Brittany, she could see them as a family. United. Whole.

A tinge of guilt filled her. She'd been lazy, letting the relationship coast as *amis avec bénéfices* to avoid moving in with him. She shoved the thought away. Now wasn't the time to think about all that.

"WHAT THE HELL'S going on, Aimée?" René said, helping her adjust his Mercedes driver's seat and controls to her height as she removed the pedal extenders. "We shouldn't get involved in whatever's going on between them." He frowned while adjusting the seat belt, the strap of which hit his chin. "They've been fighting a lot. But it's not our business."

"Drink this." She handed him a bottle of Badoit from the glove compartment. The fizzy water would do him good. "There's been an incident where Boris works."

"At the police laboratory? This time of night?"

He sounded as cranky as Morbier had.

"The bomb squad's there with an activated robot."

"Do you think Boris is involved?"

"Someone called from his phone. I heard an explosion."

"We shouldn't get involved," he said. "Let the *flics* handle this."

Every part of her wished this hadn't happened. Whatever it was. Maybe he was right.

Still, she couldn't let it rest.

"Someone picked up Boris's phone outside the lab and called Michou," she said.

René pulled out his phone. Dialed. Let it ring.

"Boris never answers," she said.

Would he ever?

MORE SOBER NOW, René turned on his police scanner—a birthday gift from Aimée—and fiddled with the frequencies while Aimée focused on navigating the rain-slicked streets among late-night buses, taxis, and darting bicyclists. Outside the car window, wavelets crested with foam from passing blue-lit *bateaux-mouches*.

She clenched the steering wheel as she drove by Notre-Dame and the inky wash of the Seine; past Saint-Michel's splashing spot-lit fountain. She cut through Saint-Germain. Nerves jangling, she shifted into third up rue de Vaugirard, Paris's longest street leading to the Porte de Versailles, along the dark expanse of the Jardin du Luxembourg, its fence tipped by gold.

She strained to hear the crackling scanner. No more explosions. So far.

Skirting Montparnasse, they entered the fifteenth arrondissement, its population the size of Bordeaux's. The second largest in Paris. A real pain to drive through at night. Once it had been the villages of Grenelle and Vaugirard. Aimée knew it well, from the seventies quai-side high-rises near the former Citroën factory site to the working-class neighborhoods laced by narrow lanes and sporting views of the Tour Eiffel, to one of her favorite street markets on rue Saint-Charles, where she got Miles Davis's horse meat.

Residential. Quiet and boring on the surface. But another side lay beneath the fabric of the *quinzième*.

"What are they saying, René?"

Rain pattered on the car's roof.

" . . . rue de Dantzig . . . explosions . . . one casualty . . ."

Only one casualty? Did that mean Boris had survived? Had he been there at all? Tense, she burned with the need to find whoever had his phone.

At Métro Convention, she downshifted, made a sharp left, and sped by shuttered shops and the Café du Marché, open even at this late hour. She barely avoided a knot of laughing fans in sports jerseys by the graffitied bus shelter, drunk and staggering into the glistening-wet crosswalk. Sucked in her breath sharply: she had forgotten rue de Dantzig was a one-way street; she was going the wrong way.

Merde.

René fiddled with the scanner dial, getting more static. Two blocks later, she took another sharp turn onto rue Brancion and sped by Parc Georges Brassens, wreathed in a dark mist of shadowy trees. The Art Nouveau wrought-iron roof of the old abattoir loomed in matte shadows. The wipers scraped the fine drizzle beading the windshield.

At the corner, flashing red lights pierced the night. Car alarms sounded in whooping wails along the street.

"*Mon Dieu*," René said, a catch in his voice. "I don't like this."

He pointed. Barricades were strung up rue de Dantzig, fronting the L-shaped brick complex that encompassed the old car impound, the Objets Trouvés—Lost and Found—and the thirties-era Laboratoire Central de la Préfecture de Police headquarters and laboratory buildings.

Her shoulders tightened. Here, just last week, over the canteen's dirt-cheap lunch on the Objets Trouvés's fifth floor, Boris had called in a favor. He'd asked her to perform a simple background check without involving his police colleagues. *Why?* she'd asked. *Long story,* he'd replied, complaining how the different police laboratories rarely worked with each other and the workers only ran into each other in the gym across the street. Or in the canteen.

At the time, she'd thought nothing of it. Now his request struck her as odd. Could it have to do with tonight?

"We'll get closer if you go up to rue Olivier de Serres," René said, reading from the street map, "then left and another left."

She downshifted. Made it to rue de Dantzig in two minutes.

Diamond-like splintered glass carpeted the rain-pelted road. It crunched like gravel under their tires. Firemen steered residents from the apartments across the street to safety while a few bystanders huddled on the pavement.

A wrench in Aimée's gut plunged her back in time to the Place Vendôme explosion. To the moment her life had changed.

"Aimée—watch out!"

René grabbed the steering wheel with a jolt and turned the car to narrowly avoid a policeman. The car stalled with a shudder.

"You almost hit him, Aimée."

Shaking, she restarted the car, took the steering wheel, and paused. She had to get a grip. Concentrate on Boris.

Alert now, she powered down the window.

"Can't you see the street's closed?" The angry *flic* motioned for her to turn. Up rue de Dantzig, she saw the flashing lights of an ambulance. "Turn around or I'll have you towed."

She showed her fake police ID, her father's old identification, which she'd doctored with the latest stamps.

"I was called here by the crime scene manager. Move the barricades," she said, mustering a false bravado.

René pinched her leg. He hated when she did this.

The *flic* leaned in the window, his blue anorak dotted with rain. "No one told me."

The police scanner crackled, as if in answer to her prayers. Aimée caught a name. Toureau.

Was it the same Toureau who'd been a *brigade criminelle* detective?

"Take it up with Toureau," she said, knowing she had to move fast before the *flic* checked. René's S-Class Mercedes, booty from the son of the ex-president of France, now in prison, still had government plates. "It's crucial I see the victim before the ambulance departs."

A fire truck pulled alongside her, the firemen shouting for him to move the barricade.

Then the *flic* was waving them both through.

René tugged his goatee, something he did when nervous. "They'll throw us in jail."

"Not before we find Boris," she said.

She gritted her teeth, shifted, and drove up rue de Dantzig—once again the wrong way on the one-way street—trying to avoid the glass and winding around two emergency vehicles.

A charcoal cloud of dust hung in the drizzle above the bio lab. The building had been sliced in half, exposing offices and laboratories to the sky. Concrete rubble and iron beams spilled onto the parking lot. All of it looked like a bombed-out war site.

Ahead, she saw a gurney with a white body bag beaded with drizzle. Her heart fell. She slammed on the brake, stalled the car. Helpless, she felt helpless. Unable to face the fact that the body bag might contain Boris. The man who'd hugged her daughter just hours earlier, who'd left the birthday party to come here for her present.

Why had she thought she could do this?

René switched off the ignition and cast her a long look. He put a warm hand on her knee. "Stay here." He buttoned his trench coat, popped a mint, and got out.

Apprehensive, she watched René speaking to the firemen, gesturing. Waiting, seeing the destruction ahead, she couldn't help but remember Boris's office, full of his prized orchids. His pride and joy.

Then it clicked. Boris's office wing was under renovation. He'd been temporarily relocated to the building next door to the lab.

He wouldn't have been in the lab. He would have gone to his temporary office. Possibly dropped his phone in the confusion.

Praying that was it, Aimée looped her scarf over her head, hopped out of the car, and ran in the cold drizzle toward the crowd.

As she made her way through, Aimée recognized Directrice Bécard, one of the police bomb unit Directors Boris had introduced her to. Dark-haired and in her early forties, she stood, pale and rod-stiff, under a dripping umbrella. A stench of burnt flesh hovered.

Someone was asking, "Can you identify him?"

Directrice Bécard nodded to the fireman who'd unzipped the white body bag. She took in a breath. "Noiro," she said. "He's the homeless man we discovered sleeping in the lab cellar."

The fireman shook his head. "Sleeping in the lab cellar for how long?"

"Noiro seemed harmless, and the staff . . . well, it's cold," she said, averting her gaze. "We've turned a blind eye for a while."

A hapless victim? Or involved in the explosion? Aimée pushed that thought away and stepped forward.

"*Excusez-moi*, Directrice Bécard, where's Boris Viard?"

"Boris? The lab's closed." A confused look crossed Bécard's drained face. "But I know you. What are you doing here?"

"I know Boris came to the lab earlier tonight."

"Why? I don't understand."

As she was about to answer, three men from the bomb squad emerged from the mist, *démineur* written across their blue jackets.

"This area is off-limits. Public's not allowed," one of them said. "Move on. It's unsafe."

Aimée couldn't back down. Wouldn't. She had to find Boris.

"Who's in charge here?" she asked.

"This is an active crime scene. There could be other explosives. You need to go behind the barricades."

Before she could protest, another ambulance wedged forward, forcing everyone behind the blockades. A few onlookers gathered under umbrellas. Gawkers, the curious, or those unable to return to their apartments. She recognized the police lab building's guardian along the barricade and wound her way toward him.

"Hold on. Who are you?" asked a distinctive, gravel-tinged voice. The one she remembered from Boris's phone.

She turned. A lean, fortyish man in a rain-dotted anorak

showed her his police badge. BRI, the Brigade de Recherche et d'Intervention, responding to heavy-duty incidents. He gestured her forward to the front of the barricade.

"*Bonsoir*, I'm Boris Viard's friend," she said, knowing time was of the essence. "Aimée Leduc. Are you in charge?"

"For now. Denis Toureau."

Up close, she recognized him. She also remembered his reputation. Less than stellar.

"Wasn't it you who called me from Boris's phone?" she said.

"Wait." Toureau blinked. "That was Boris's phone?"

So he knew him.

"Of course." Her voice rose. "Why didn't you identify yourself when I asked who you were? Protocol requires you to identify yourself."

But Toureau had turned away to confer with the *démineur* squad. Someone jostled Aimée from behind. *René*, she thought, scanning the crowd, looking for him. Where had he gone?

The rancid odor of burnt plastic and wet stone mingled with the crowd's fug of wool overcoats.

"Start searching, Toureau," she said. "You need to find Boris. He was here."

Toureau exchanged a look with the bomb squad and the Directeur. He motioned Aimée forward and let her past the barricade. His eyes flickered alert. His attitude had changed.

"When?"

"Maybe thirty minutes ago. More." Frantic, she rummaged in her trench pocket—papers, keys, her phone—for the photo in her wallet. Chloé in Boris's arms, taken at his anniversary party. She lifted it up for the *démineurs* and all to see. "Have any of you seen him?"

A shaking of heads.

"What are you waiting for? You found his phone. Find him!"

Toureau exchanged a look with the *démineurs*. A look that sent a shudder down her neck.

"Get the dogs," said Toureau.

BANISHED BACK BEHIND the cordon again, Aimée felt a cold stone of dread in her stomach. Moisture fringed her eyelashes. She belted her damp coat.

Two minutes turned to three. To five. Seven.

This was taking too long. Michou kept calling, but Aimée had nothing to tell him. She'd jumped into this and doubted she could handle the outcome.

She didn't want to be here.

From the mutterings of the bomb squad, it sounded like they were treating this as a terrorist attack. After 9/11 two months ago, everyone was on edge.

A political statement? But by whom? And why?

Boris had only realized he'd forgotten Chloé's birthday present less than an hour and a half ago. Forget him as the target. Was the homeless man, Noiro, somehow involved?

Bright portable arc lights now illuminated the sheared-off building and rubble, half of an office lit nakedly in the night. She saw a desk and chair, a wall calendar, a coatrack, intimate and exposed.

However it played, Boris had stumbled into this—the wrong place at the wrong time. She looked around again for René. Where was he?

Tensing, she heard the crunching footsteps of the hastily assembled rescue team tramping on shattered concrete. They formed a chain, lifting and sifting through the rubble.

The Mercedes headlights flashed. Aimée picked her way back through the crowd. René huddled in the driver's seat.

"Get in the car," he said. "Listen to this."

She climbed in the passenger side, her wet trench sticking to the leather seat. Her legs tangled on trailing wires.

She heard crackling. "Precision bombings . . . professional . . ."

"Who's saying that?"

He lifted a walkie-talkie. "Not sure."

"Are you recording this?"

René nodded, his face pensive. "Remember the bugs from our last job? I hooked one up to my walkie-talkie, which feeds into a digital recorder. They're treating this as terrorism."

"I know," she said. Standard procedure these days. But this was out of character for René, always a law-abiding citizen. "You're always complaining about me breaking rules," she whispered.

"Easy. No need to whisper, mine's a one-way channel. They can't hear."

"I'm impressed," she said, but he'd put on headphones.

A dog's repeated barking drifted through a thick mist as palpable as wet wool.

Shouts.

"They found Boris, Aimée," René said softly. "Someone's saying proof of life."

She bolted out of the car. Grey needles of rain pelted in the arc light beams. Peering over the heads of the bystanders at the cordon she saw a body, shielded by a policemen's jacket.

Her heart beat double-time.

The body was slid onto a gurney, then into the back of an ambulance. A siren whooped, its flashing lights casting a blue glow over the rescue team's faces as it sped away.

She ran back to the car and got in.

"Follow the ambulance, René."

FOUR BLOCKS AWAY, René parked at the emergency entrance of Hôpital Vaugirard. The modern white building bordered a park and the run-down eighteenth-century limestone building housing the Sorbonne law school.

"Proof of life can still mean bad news, Aimée."

He didn't have to tell her that. She nodded anyway. "First we find out."

She called Michou. He sounded semi-hysterical until she promised to give him updates and asked after Chloé. Asleep. His frantic questions had unsettled her because she had no answers.

Police grouped at the nurse's station. She overheard a harried emergency nurse reveal that Boris Viard had been taken for tests prior to imminent surgery. It could take hours.

Aimée hated hospitals—the antiseptic smells and despair in the waiting rooms. Her shoulders sagged. Without warning, she felt the weight of the night. She spotted René in the waiting area, his legs dangling from the bench in the scuffed green linoleum hallway, and made her way to him. She needed to return home to Chloé. Reassure Michou, somehow.

She also needed an espresso.

"Want anything, René?"

He shook his head.

At the vending machine, she pushed buttons for *café express, noir sans sucre*, and slid her francs in the vending machine.

Nothing. She pressed the buttons again. And again.

"Trouble?" Toureau asked, appearing suddenly behind her, holding his damp anorak over his arm. "Here, let me." He pounded the side of the machine twice with the palm of his hand.

Plop. A white plastic demitasse cup fell. Steaming brown liquid dripped into it, a lacy froth on top.

"Magic touch, eh?" she said.

He shrugged. "Experience."

She needed info from Toureau. "Where did the first responder find Boris?"

"Why?" Before she could answer, Toureau picked up the plastic cup and turned as if to hand it to her. "Let us do our job."

"You still haven't answered my question. Why didn't you identify yourself when you answered Boris's phone? I asked who you were, but you never answered."

He looked her up and down, then let his eyes rest on her face. "Now I get it."

"Get what?"

"You're old Leduc's daughter."

Aimée's spine stiffened. Her father had been kicked out of the force for corruption; set up and taken the fall. Years after his death, she'd exonerated him, uncovered the chokehold of the criminal network of high-level police and political corruption. To say the least, this had not endeared her to some on the force.

"You knew my father?"

He stared hard into her eyes. "I know you're a troublemaker."

"I'm a private detective, Toureau," she said. "Investigation's my job." What she didn't say was that this wasn't a case—this was her friend.

He leaned over the cup, held it precisely between his thumb and forefinger, and spit in her coffee. Handed it to her.

"Enjoy."

RENÉ SIGHED. "ANOTHER member of your fan club?" he asked her.

She tossed the cup in a bin and shook her head in disgust. Wanted to kick Toureau. The insult bit deep.

"Boris is having brain surgery, they're saying," René whispered. "No guarantees he'll come out of it."

She couldn't take the sitting, waiting. Impossible.

"I'll be right back," she said.

Determined, Aimée scanned the hospital floor plan—a diagram

on the wall with all the exits marked. She had to find out what had happened.

While a medical team ran to receive an incoming ambulance, Aimée stepped inside the double swinging doors into the emergency wing. She had to hurry; eyes would be on her in a minute. She darted down a hallway, opening doors. A closet with cleaning supplies. Another with linens, sheets, towels. Useless.

She needed cover. Could she pass for a medical orderly?

Aimée concentrated on what she remembered from the floor plan. She found the X-ray station across from a nursing station and headed toward it.

Outside the X-ray room door, a nurse wheeled a gurney from across the hall.

Boris.

She felt someone pulling her arm. Another nurse had discovered her. "The public's not allowed here. You need to leave."

"Please let me talk to him. Just one minute."

"Impossible. Please go now."

"Boris," she called out.

Even at a distance, Aimée saw him turn toward the sound of her voice. She tried not to gasp at Boris's swollen, lacerated face. She caught Boris's eye briefly before the gurney continued down the hall.

"I'm calling security right now," said an orderly the nurse had summoned.

Hands shoved her back. The double doors to surgery—where the surgical team in scrubs was assembled—pinged open, and the gurney's rubber wheels whooshed across the linoleum. She sent another silent prayer for Boris before she was kicked out the emergency room door into the lobby.

Melac was striding across the lobby toward René. Beside him

was a red-eyed Michou, dressed in a sober blue suit Aimée recognized as Melac's.

Aimée's eyes searched Melac nervously. "Did you bring Chloé?"

"She's asleep," Melac said. "Madame Cachou's watching her."

Relief flooded her. Madame Cachou, her concierge, loved Chloé.

"Answer your phone sometime," Melac said, eyeing her. "*Attends ici*, I'm going to find out what's going on."

Always Monsieur Macho.

"I just did," she said. "Boris went into surgery." She looked up at Michou. "He's strong, Michou. He heard my voice and turned. That's good. I think he saw who set the bomb."

"What do you mean, Aimée?" asked Michou.

She described seeing Boris's face and began to tear up.

"You're sure?"

She wasn't sure of anything, but she nodded. The explosion had rocked her to the core, bringing back every old fear she had locked away.

Melac put his arm around her. "*Désolé*, it must remind you of your father," he said. The anguish in finding her father's charred remains on the cobblestones must have shown on her face. "Don't worry, Aimée."

She couldn't hear him. All she could hear was her own voice, saying it was her fault. If only she'd insisted Boris stay at the party. That he should fetch Chloé's gift another time.

"Now all we can do is wait," said René.

"Michou says no one at the lab knows about his and Boris's relationship," Melac whispered. "We're keeping it that way, *comprends?*"

"Even now?"

The force was run by dinosaurs. A code of silence cloaked sexual orientation.

"Michou's worried their relationship could cost Viard his upcoming promotion," Melac said.

"Go along with it, Aimée," said René.

"*Bon sang!* Promotion? He's fighting for his life. I just saw him wheeled into surgery."

Toureau passed into view as an irate nurse pointed at Aimée.

Sunday Night • Hôpital Vaugirard

OUTSIDE HÔPITAL VAUGIRARD's brightly lit emergency entrance, Aimée pulled her trench collar up against the chill. Madame Cachou answered on the first ring, oozing sympathy. Chloé was asleep, and there was no need to hurry back with poor Monsieur Boris in the hospital.

If there was ever a time Aimée needed a cigarette, it was now. She riffled in her coat pocket. Not even Nicorette gum. Only her wallet, keys, her photo of Boris and Chloé, crumpled receipts, and a Carambar—her childhood favorite.

Merde.

She opened the crinkly paper. Read the cartoon and joke. Silly. She was too old for candy.

About to toss it and the crumpled receipts in the bin by the ambulance bay, Aimée noticed something. Among the receipts was a limp article from *Le Parisien*. When had she stuck this in her pocket? And why?

She paused outside the entrance and scanned the piece. The article detailed the arrest of Johan Selles, an Action Directe member and eighties radical who'd turned himself in at long last for involvement in a 1986 bombing attack.

One of her mother's old friends? The friends Sydney Leduc had abandoned Aimée and her father for? She had only been eight years old at the time, and her father had never recovered.

The newsprint felt slightly soggy. Smudged black Sharpie at the bottom read: *WE HAVE STRUCK AGAIN*.

Who was *we?*

She looked around. Saw only an orderly smoking. Her feet rooted themselves to the concrete. Images flooded her mind: the glass-splintered street twinkling sapphire as the blue lights flashed, the sheared-in-half lab building open to the sky, rain-drops glistening on the white body bag, Toureau's intense stare, the bystanders jostling around her.

Fear twisted her gut. Someone in the crowd had put this in her pocket; of this, she was sure. She scrounged in her pockets for an evidence baggie. Nothing. She wished she'd brought her secondhand Vuitton—that thing carried her whole life. She made do by folding and sticking the article into one of Miles Davis's unused doggie bags.

The rain left a fresh dampness hanging in the air. Aimée looked around. Only that weary-faced orderly, still smoking. She cadged a cigarette, thanked him, and inhaled the smoke. The nicotine filled her lungs. She took another drag. Felt it rush to her head. Dizzy, she stubbed it out with her toe.

She pulled out her phone. She should inform Toureau of what she'd just found in her pocket. But she dreaded dealing with him again and dialed Melac's number instead.

Voice mail.

She tried René.

"Can you see Toureau or Melac?" she asked, just as a cough racked her.

"Are you smoking?"

"*Mais non,*" she lied.

"No one's here but me and Michou," he said.

"Where did they go?" She hadn't seen them leave.

"Who knows? Listen, they're going to put Boris in a medically induced coma."

She gasped. Had they done all the scans, lab tests, and exams so quickly? Rushed the procedures since he was one of their own?

No more talking with him now. Or . . . She put the terrifying possibilities out of her mind. Heard voices in the background.

"Michou's upset. Got to go," René said, and clicked off.

THE POLICE LAB was a few blocks away. Maybe she'd find Toureau there. A quick walk would do her good anyway. Give her a chance to clear her head.

Near rue des Morillons, she grew aware of footsteps behind her, keeping pace with hers. Heard the click of nails, the rustle of damp leaves. Aimée stopped dead.

A wet nose sniffed the top of her boot.

"*Arrête*, Sami," said a man wearing glasses, a wool scarf, and a dark cardigan. He pulled the dog's leash back. Sami, a basset hound with eyes that reminded her of Morbier's, whined.

"*Excusez-moi, mademoiselle.*"

Aimée smiled. "He smells my dog."

"No doubt," he said. The man leaned down and ruffled Sami's ears. "He's such a bundle of nerves after the explosions."

Aimée's ears perked up.

"You live here, monsieur?"

"In the quartier."

Sami sniffed her pant leg and got another tug on his leash.

"Did you see what happened?" she asked.

"I heard it," he said. "The police won't say anything."

"Did you look out your window? See anything strange?"

He buttoned up his cardigan. "Sami woke up and pawed the door. Unlike him, mademoiselle. He's well trained, but tonight . . ." His voice trailed off.

She nodded. "What about anyone acting odd? Out of place before the explosion?"

"Not that I remember," he said. "You think it's terrorists? Like 9/11 again?"

That sent a shiver through her.

"No idea, monsieur," she said.

Excitedly, Sami barked at the search-and-rescue German shepherds entering the police canine van ahead.

"Better go. *Bonsoir*." He gently pulled Sami's leash, ruffled his ears again, and coaxed him away down the street.

Large white canvas tents had been erected over parts of the explosion site. High barricades now encircled the area and closed the street. The response time had been almost immediate, but then, it would be—the police bomb squad HQ was only a few doors down. She wondered if the HQ had been the actual target.

Everything was veiled in soot, and the acrid tang burned her throat. The fire trucks were pulling out and making way for the *démineur* squad.

No Toureau. Several uniforms stood guard, in conversation with the building's *gardien*, a man she'd met last week in Boris's office.

The *gardien* wore a navy parka. He pointed something out to the *flics*, a cigarette between his fingers, the orange-gold tip arcing in the night. He seemed to know the officers. The next minute, he stubbed out his cigarette with his toe and headed toward a side barricade.

"*Excusez-moi, monsieur*," she said, catching up with him.

He turned.

She took in the sight of him. Forties, with beetle-thick eyebrows. Dark, intense eyes stared back at her. His sharp cheekbones and pitted complexion—the telltale scars of adolescent acne—gave him a severe, hunted look.

"Monsieur, we met last week in Boris Viard's office when you"—what was it?—"fixed the electrical switch."

"What of it?" he said, wary.

Bring down his defenses.

She smiled. "I'm Aimée, Boris's friend. We spoke briefly. You're . . ." *Zut*, why couldn't she remember his name?

"Feroze Hooshnan."

"That's right."

He waited, a tense stillness about him. She wasn't handling this well. "Boris forgot my daughter's birthday gift in his office."

"What do you mean?"

Cold, damp wind carrying odors of burnt plastic and wood gusted around them. She stamped her boots in the chill to warm up.

"That's the thing, Feroze," she said, stalling as she figured out how to enlist his aid. *Simple and direct works best*, her father always said. "He came back here for it. A silly, spur-of-the-moment decision. Did you see him before the explosion?"

The chill wind rustled leaves in the gutter.

"Not tonight. You should talk to the *flics*."

Not helpful, this Feroze. She remembered how he'd joked with her and Boris just days ago. Where had that friendliness gone?

"Look, Boris is in the hospital in critical condition."

He shook his head. "Terrible."

"They're putting put him in a medically induced coma."

"I'm sorry." A muscle in Feroze's cheek quivered. "I like Boris."

He was thawing a little—and she needed to make the most of it. "Think back. Didn't you see him tonight, Feroze?" she asked. "Or do you know where the medic found him?"

Feroze tugged the zipper of his parka up. His body language said he wanted to leave—and for her to stop asking questions. He was the second one tonight.

"Medic? I don't know, but I found a cracked phone in the rubble where the stairs used to be. I passed it over."

Good. That was how it had ended up with Toureau.

"You mean the stairs near his office? Where we first met?"

"You have a lot of questions. Why?"

She didn't want to reveal the hunch she was following—a gut feeling that Boris might have seen who planted the bomb or gone to get help.

"Don't you want whoever did this caught?"

A look almost of pain crossed his face. He nodded. "I thought it was odd."

"What do you mean?"

Feroze pointed. "I found the phone in the next building, over there. But not near Boris's office."

"Did you see anyone besides Boris?"

Feroze glanced at his watch. "I was on my break when it happened."

A convenient coincidence.

"I heard an explosion. Then another. There were two. That's it."

"What?" A second explosion? "Are you sure? Couldn't the next noise have been the building collapsing?"

"I was right there. It was a bomb. I got out of there as soon as I could, in case there were more."

Aimée made a note to look into this. "What about Noiro, the poor homeless man?"

"Him? Poor?" No compassion on his face. "*Mais non*, I reported him. Twice. But *la directrice*, she's a softie."

"She let him camp out in the cellar, right?"

Feroze nodded.

Aimée shook her head empathetically at the lax security. "Did you ask him to leave?"

"*Bien sûr.* The other night, he cooked down there on a camp stove. You know how dangerous that is? Especially where he was in the basement."

Wasn't the basement where the refrigerated evidence was kept? She tried to remember what Boris had told her.

"So I escorted him out. That's it." Feroze looked at his watch again. "*Pardonnez-moi.* Time for me to see what assistance the team needs."

She handed him a card. "Please call me if anything else comes to you."

"You undercover?"

Aimée nodded. Let him think so. "But it's more than that. Boris is my friend." She'd been struggling to recall Boris's words last week about Feroze. Now she placed him. An Iranian who'd fled to France when Khomeini took power. Not just a *gardien*, she sensed. As Boris had said, a man with secrets.

AIMÉE DEBATED RETURNING to the hospital, but ultimately decided to go home and relieve Madame Cachou of her babysitting duties. She caught a taxi that let her off at quai d'Anjou in front of her dark-green double doors. She overtipped, as usual, to garner rainy-night taxi karma. After paying Madame Cachou and topping up Miles Davis's water bowl, she kicked off her boots.

She leaned down and kissed Chloé. A little flutter of her eyelids. Still sound asleep. She pulled the blanket up on her "big-girl bed," as Chloé insisted on calling it.

Aimée called the hospital to inquire about Boris. A curt nurse informed her that only family were permitted patient information. She knew that but figured it had been worth a try. René, who answered on the first ring, had no new information on Boris's condition. Then she tried Melac. Voice mail. Again.

She tossed and turned, unable to sleep. Her mind spun with questions. She ached with guilt. Why had she let Boris go?

Monday Morning • Ile Saint-Louis

AIMÉE WOKE TO an orange dawn spreading outside her window and Miles Davis licking her toes. She'd eventually fallen into a fitful sleep, rocked by nightmares of her father's death.

Not a peep out of Chloé. Nor from Melac, whom she'd expected to find spooning her. Instead, she found only cold sheets.

Where was he? She reached for her phone. Dead.

Merde. She hadn't charged it. What if there had been an update on Boris? His condition could have taken a turn in the night.

Hurrying, she pulled on cashmere socks, jeans, and her silk YSL tunic—a treasure from the Porte de Vanves flea market. Thank God dry cleaning had erased Chloé's crayon stains from the collar.

She plugged her phone into the old porcelain outlet at the kitchen counter, hoping it wouldn't blow a fuse when she made espresso. She felt another stab of guilt noticing Michou had cleaned up the party mess; the trash was put away, the glassware washed. Everything gleamed . . . except a set of suspicious pink paw prints on the Aubusson carpet.

"Meelz Daveez!"

His furry head—pink, now, with frosting-tipped whiskers—skulked around the corner.

"No wonder my toes feel sticky."

He disappeared.

Her charging phone beeped with two messages.

Both from Toureau at BRI, the Brigade de Recherche et d'Intervention, instructing her to come in and make a statement first thing this morning. Like hell she would. Hadn't she tried to talk to him last night?

Visualizing Toureau's lean face and panther eyes, she whacked yesterday's coffee grinds into the bin. Ground the fresh beans and pulverized them into a fine powder as she imagined his skinny frame. How could she cooperate with a vengeful unprofessional who hadn't followed protocol during an emergency?

A man who'd spit in her coffee.

What was he hiding?

She sipped her steaming espresso. Frustrated, she sponged off the carpet before Chloé woke up. Last night's happiness rushed back: Boris hugging Chloé, the pop of champagne, the smiles and warmth, the feeling that she'd formed her own family. All that love, until the sound of the explosion over the phone.

Her phone beeped. René.

"How's Boris?"

René gave a long sigh. "He's in a medically induced coma. *C'est tout.* I took Michou home a little while ago."

The image of that damp newspaper article in her pocket kept coming back to her.

WE HAVE STRUCK AGAIN.

"Something strange happened last night, René."

"You bet it's strange," he said. "At least, I thought so until I opened my eyes. The crisis teams and bomb squad jumped up faster than fleas on Miles Davis."

She gazed with suspicion at her fluff ball, who now waited near his chipped Limoges bowl. "Are you saying Miles Davis needs a flea bath?"

"*Pas du tout,*" he said.

"René, the bomb squad's headquartered next door. Of course they'd respond immediately." Yet the feeling that she'd missed a detail or overlooked something dogged her.

"Right. But why target the biological lab with bombs in the first place? And only half of it?"

Good question. Had something gone wrong? Perhaps the first bomb had misfired?

"I overheard Toureau at the hospital," René was saying. "Now it's a murder investigation because of Noiro. He mentioned something about the biological lab's evidence kept in a refrigerated underground storage room."

"Overheard, René?"

"Fine, I made it a point to eavesdrop," he said.

Aimée started scrubbing at the floor again as she thought. "You mean the bombs could have destroyed the lab's evidence?"

"No clue," said René. "That's all I caught."

Could it link to the Action Directe claim—if it was true—on the wet copy of the article from *Le Parisien*? But how? Their goal would have been to make a political statement.

So why had that been placed in her pocket?

She heard the key turn in the door, her nanny Babette's cheery "*Bonjour.*" Stood up. Her Terabyte-Teal lacquered nails tapped the counter.

"*Un moment.*" She turned to Babette, a nursing student she adored. "*Bonjour*, Babette. I've got an early meeting. Can you feed Chloé and take her to school?"

"As long as I hear about the birthday party later." Babette winked.

Such a jewel. Aimée was fortunate to share childcare with the family living in the building's coach house.

Babette's eyes widened as she walked further into the kitchen. "Whoa . . . everything's spick-and-span! Good job, Aimée."

"I'd like to take credit, but it goes to Michou."

Babette took off down the hallway and Aimée returned to René. "You're getting devious, René. I like it."

"Learned from the best," he said.

Monday Morning • Rue de la Saïda

"HURRY UP, HUGO, or you'll be late for school."

Hugo worried that the firemen's hoses could reach their apartment windows. Worried that he'd left his bedroom window open. Worried that his telescope had gotten ruined by the elements.

He sipped the bowl of café au lait at his aunt's kitchen table. Amber light filtered over the red-and-white checked plastic tablecloth and the chipped blue enamel coffeepot. A fly buzzed near the jar of raspberry confiture. Aunt Mimi, his mother's older sister, shooed it away.

"When can I go home?" he asked.

"Who knows?" She scrubbed a sponge over the tablecloth, then opened the window to a brisk November morning. "Your mother went to work, Grand-père's asleep, and you need to get ready for school."

His mother always said Mimi's kitchen was a sixties time capsule. It had neither a full-sized refrigerator nor a proper stove, just two gas burners. Everything about Aunt Mimi was old-fashioned, Hugo thought, from her resoled shoes to her old coat and frugal use of heating.

"I need my notes and books for school," he said.

"Tell the teacher what happened. He'll understand."

"It's she. Madame Sisich is strict, and we've got an exam prep today," he said, stretching the truth. "She won't care that we were bombed out."

"Quit being dramatic, Hugo."

Dramatic? "You heard the explosions, Aunt Mimi," he said, dipping his buttered tartine in the café au lait. "You saw the smoke from here."

Aunt Mimi lived around the block in the HLM social housing projects on rue de la Saïda. Built during the First World War by a sugar magnate and intended for workers to experience healthy living, the communal showers and baths were one to a floor. Hugo didn't know how his aunt survived bathing in December.

"The radio said they got the fire under control almost immediately," she said. "The damage was limited to one building."

The building directly across from Hugo's window.

"That's God's blessing." Aunt Mimi pulled her glasses from atop her grey hair. "Now hurry, Hugo. Get dressed."

"In what? My clothes are at home."

"Never mind, you'll fit into your uncle's pants. Just . . ."

Hugo didn't want to wear his dead uncle's clothes, which his aunt refused to throw away. They carried a metallic odor. His uncle had butchered horses in the old abattoir, which was now Parc Brassens. Later he'd worked in the butcher shop on rue Cambronne.

Still, Hugo couldn't go out in his pajamas.

Aunt Mimi tutted. "If you played sports, you'd lose that weight, you know. Instead of sitting in your room all the time like your mother says you do."

Not this again.

Before leaving, he cozied up to his aunt for extra lunch money. Ten minutes later he'd skirted out the back and through connecting courtyards, up the rear stairs into the back of his building. The spare key was where it always was—under the doormat. He let himself in.

Hugo sniffed the faint, smoky odor clinging to the walls. Once in his room, he binned his uncle's clothes, got dressed, and checked his telescope.

He found it tilted out of alignment. No damage, thank God. The Sony video camera was still hooked up to his telescope, but he'd forgotten to turn it off.

The battery had died, so he slotted in a new one. He powered on the camera, wondering if it had caught the woman he had named Chantal, who undressed nightly in her window. He'd gotten an eyeful over the past week, when he'd discovered her during his astronomy assignment recording the moon's phases.

Forget school today.

He hit rewind and lit a cigarette, keeping one eye on the time counter and one on the horrific remains of the police lab: charred grey metal rods, with half the building collapsed. The video camera provided a clear view of the park behind.

At 11:55 P.M., he paused, then played the video. Somehow he hadn't adjusted the telescope properly, so it had caught the street in front. Dumb. Noiro, the homeless *mec*, was talking to someone at the lab's door.

Just his luck.

The person gave Noiro a bag.

Boring.

Minutes passed. About to fast-forward, he saw the person walking out. Now the man was running up the street. A bright flash of a thundering explosion followed.

The man he remembered seeing after falling out of bed.

Stunned, Hugo ground out his cigarette in his pencil sharpener. Was it what it looked like? A man giving Noiro a bag and running away just before the explosion?

"Hugo!"

Merde. His mother. Why wasn't she at work?

"Why aren't you at school?" She opened his bedroom door without knocking. Her eyes bulged in shock. "And smoking, too!"

"*Non, Maman*, it's the apartment that smells of smoke."

"If you weren't sixteen, I'd spank you. I'm confiscating your telescope and that camera right this second."

Monday Morning • Ile Saint-Louis

A BRIGHT ARC of autumn-orange ginkgo leaves fanned the cobbled courtyard as Aimée rocked her scooter off its kickstand. She maneuvered it under the pear tree, crooking the phone between her neck and shoulder. She was fuming at the way the conversation with Morbier was going.

"I can't believe you don't know the liaison to counterterrorism these days, Morbier," she said. She'd asked, and he'd evaded her question.

"Why should I?" he said, clearing his throat.

"Don't tell me it's you."

"You won't get a rise out of me that way, Leduc."

She slid the key in the ignition. Turned it to hear the engine's soft putter.

She'd caught Morbier, supposedly retired, supposedly confined to a wheelchair, up and about on an undercover mission. He'd kept the truth from her, and she hadn't fully forgiven him yet.

"Melac caught me up on what happened," Morbier was saying.

Of course he had. And he hadn't come back last night.

"Boris went there on his own. This wasn't your fault." Morbier's voice held a softness she rarely heard. "Give Toureau your statement. Get it done and move on."

"You know I don't play well with types like him." She hated the idea of going to Toureau with the newspaper article. It was all she had. He would deal her out, and any investigating she could do for Boris would be over. She'd get no answers of her own.

A voice inside said, *Why not let this go?* No one would think less of her.

But she couldn't necessarily trust the *flics*. Boris might be one of them, but what if what had happened to him was tied up with someone else on the force?

What would her papa do? Advise her to tread carefully, quietly, and find out as much as she could on her own? If she gave up info, she'd be discarded. Or kept away in case she scared off the big game. Maybe even neutralized—the very thing they had done to her father.

Or could she give the *flics* just enough to stay in the game, use their manpower, and figure this out?

"*Et alors?* It's routine, Leduc."

"What I have is too hot for Toureau. He's low-level."

"Pull my other leg, Leduc."

"Action Directe's claiming responsibility."

There. Now he knew.

"Those old codgers? Who'd spread such a rumor, eh? Most are in prison or dead." A pause. "Be careful pointing fingers, Leduc."

"What do you mean, 'careful'? What don't I know?"

"Let's meet at Café du Soleil by the *préfecture* before you give Toureau your statement," Morbier said, not answering her questions.

The whole thing unnerved her—the explosion, the vivid memories of her father, the message in her pocket. Boris. Instead of lying to Morbier as she usually did, she recounted what had happened, starting with the call from Boris Viard's phone. Gave him every detail, including the note on the newspaper shred in her pocket.

Silence. A crow's shrill caw in the background.

"Like I said, leave this alone, Leduc."

"Boris is in a coma, fighting for his life. I need to report this to the right people."

"The *flics are* the right people," said Morbier.

"Just cover for me."

"What you want is justice for Boris, *non*? Why does it matter if it's you or the *flics* who find the answers?"

It didn't—in theory. Yet Toureau had actively warned her off and would actively work against her. Discredit whatever she turned up. He'd been clear as glass.

She needed to use her own channels for this.

"Look, Morbier, what if it's someone grabbing attention, deflecting the real reason for the bombing? There has to be more."

"So hand over what you've got."

"Stall him and I will." She clicked off.

She'd gotten things wrong before, but none of this felt right. She went with her gut. She recalled the rumors about Toureau: a scandal, divorce, corruption. This screamed cover-up, and Boris was a victim of the wrong time and place.

Aimée flipped through her Moleskine and found the number for Loïc Bellan, her only ministry contact in counterterrorism.

He answered on the first ring. "Are your ears burning?"

Her stomach lurched. "Why would they?"

"Your name just came up in a meeting."

No doubt Toureau had been badmouthing her. The *flics* were like gossipy old ladies. Her father's stain resurfaced no matter how many times she scrubbed it away.

"I've got something you need to see, Bellan." She hoped he didn't register the false bravado in her voice.

A pause. She heard a crinkling as his hand muffled the receiver.

"Café du Commerce," he said. "Twenty minutes."

Monday Morning • Rue de Dantzig

IN THE RUE de Dantzig apartment, pale sunlight slanted through Hugo's window over the video playing on the screen. He'd had to convince his mother he needed the camera, and she'd demanded to see the video. He'd tried to fast-forward the Peeping Tom part.

"Don't you believe me, *Maman?*" he asked.

"That your school project involves a woman undressing? Your teacher will have something to say about that."

Hugo chewed his thumbnail. Everything he did was wrong.

He pointed to his notebook. "The video backs up my observations for an astronomy paper."

"Hugo, the priest will call this a mortal sin at confession."

"Do you want me to fail the class, *Maman?*" She wouldn't guilt him with religion this time.

"Now it's my fault?" His mother checked her tortoiseshell comb clipping her wavy hair up. "Didn't I raise you to respect God?" Her tone was one of despair.

His *grand-père* came in. He laughed when he saw the video. "Calm down. Hugo's becoming a man. You coddle him; he's too naive. In my day, we'd already gone to the bordello."

"Forget your day," his mother said. "That was last century."

His *grand-père* winked. "Some things never change, *eh?* Anyway, the *flics* are here."

"Why?" Hugo asked. His stomach clenched. What if he was arrested as a Peeping Tom?

"Why do you think? They want to know if we saw anything suspicious. It's routine," his *grand-père* said.

Hugo remembered a girl who'd recently committed suicide in the park. Wouldn't questions about that have been routine, too? But no *flics* had come around then.

As if on cue, a voice rang out from the hallway. "Madame?"

His mother smoothed down her skirt. "We were all asleep, remember that."

His mother feared police almost as much as hell and cancer. Orphaned and raised by their uncle, a prison warden, she and her sister had spent their childhood raised in prison staff lodgings, causing her to develop an unhealthy fear of the law.

Grew up in prison, the classmates had taunted her.

"We can't be sure it's routine, *Maman*," Hugo said, his voice quavering.

But her heels had already started clicking away down the hall.

"Play that again," his *grand-père* instructed, nodding to the video.

"Which part?"

"You know. The man who's running away."

Hugo stiffened. "Why?"

"Go on."

He advanced the tape.

"Stop." His *grand-père* pointed to the man running up the street. "Him. I've seen him before."

Monday Morning • Rue du Commerce

AIMÉE WALKED TOWARD the café across from the Métro to meet Loïc Bellan. Her last contact with him had been when he was just an analyst at the Ministry of Interior. A desk job.

After 9/11 sent shock waves around the world, followed by the Toulouse explosion ten days later—the biggest explosion since World War II—the counterterrorism and related branches had been folded under the Ministry of Interior's umbrella. Rumor circulated that terrorists were responsible for the Toulouse bombing, while the government set the blame elsewhere to avoid panic.

Now, Bellan—mid-thirties, clean-shaven, with his hair in a modified quiff—looked less like ministerial material. Aimée figured he'd gone operational. He wore a khaki green jacket with a knotted scarf under it and black jeans. He was smoking under a heat lamp at a table on the *terrasse*.

Undercover counterterrorism at GIGN, Groupe d'Intervention de la Gendarmerie Nationale, most likely. Aimée's father had called Bellan the most promising *flic* he'd worked with. Instinctive and born to the job, he'd said.

Bellan had idolized her father until he was kicked off the force for supposed corruption. Bellan couldn't forgive Jean-Claude. Years later, even after Aimée had proven her father's innocence, Bellan still hated her guts—until she'd cracked a case for him. By then, he'd grown up, once even admitting he felt guilty after her father's death. Bellan was divorced, she knew, and cared for his daughters and his son with Down syndrome. The divorce had shaken him. It had taken a while to bounce back.

Aimée didn't know the chain of command, or the new protocols after 9/11—only that Bellan was someone she somewhat trusted. Face it, she told herself, he was her only contact there, and he got things done.

Besides, he owed her.

Two espressos, each in a demitasse on a white porcelain saucer beside a square of chocolate, sent curling steam into the cold air. She sat down, thankful for the coffee, unwrapped a sugar cube, and plopped it in the cup. Stirred.

"Why here, Bellan?" She sipped. Strong and sweet, as she liked it. *Parfait.*

"You're welcome." He winked. "It's convenient. My ex inherited her aunt's place right there." He pointed to a nineteenth-century Haussmann-style building. It looked just like every other building that ringed the narrow park by the Métro: mansard roofs, iron-fenced balconies teeming with red geraniums, façades of limestone. Aimée eyed it. Too bourgeois for her style.

"Not bad. *Très domestique ici.* But I never figured you for the bourgeoisie *quinzième* type."

"I'm not. I live in my ex's *chambre de bonne*, the maid's room in the attic with a WC down the hall." He half grinned. "Too old to live like a student, *n'est-ce pas?* But at least I'm part of my kids' lives this way."

Strange divorce agreement, thought Aimée.

"My daughters go to Manuel, the bilingual school nearby, and I'm on dinner-homework-duty this week."

She'd heard good things about the school—prestigious and public. Maybe a good fit for Chloé one day. But right now wasn't the time to discuss that.

Bellan had flipped his wallet open to a photo. A proud look shone on his face. "You remember my son, Guillaume?"

Aimée nodded.

"He's twelve. Loves art."

She smiled at the photo of the child, who was holding a colorful origami crane. It was sweet, to be sure, but this wasn't a social call. Her friend was near death, and she had a mission.

"I need help, Bellan."

Bellan stubbed out his cigarette with his toe. "Help? What's so important?" he asked, his tone suddenly businesslike. "I'm due at a ministry meeting."

She'd annoyed him. Had she been tactless, as René so often accused her?

"Someone put this in my pocket last night at the bombing on rue de Dantzig." She handed him the plastic bag with the article from *Le Parisien*. Gave him an overview of last night's bombing, pointing out the phrase at the bottom:

WE HAVE STRUCK AGAIN.

"The Sharpie smeared here, see, from the rain," she said. "The whole piece of newspaper was damp."

"What's to say it wasn't in your pocket before? That you didn't write it yourself?" Suspicion was his stock-in-trade.

"That's not my handwriting. And my subscription to *Le Parisien* lapsed a couple of weeks ago. This is from yesterday."

"You know I need more than that, Aimée."

"Why would I make this up? It's my friend, Boris Viard, head of a department in the police lab, who got stuck in the bombing." She filled him in on Boris being in a medically induced coma.

"You're the one to look into this," she told him.

He looked interested now. "Who else knows?"

"Toureau wants my statement," she said, ignoring his question. She took out her Moleskine, searched in her bag. Only a kohl eye pencil. Still, she sketched him a rough diagram of the street,

the crowd, the *démineur* squad going through the rubble, the barricades, the apartments opposite.

"I'm asking for your help because I don't trust Toureau."

"Why?"

"It's complicated." She shrugged. "Plus, I helped you before,
and I need a favor."

She'd done Bellan's group a service in Saint-Germain by
catching the terrorist targeting NATO league members from the
Serbian conflict. Even let the military take the credit.

"That was what, two years ago, Aimée?"

"You're still in the counterterrorism business, *non?* Long memories drive your world's work."

He sniffed. "All that's to say what?"

"What if this message isn't really from those old radical members of Action Directe?"

He grinned. "Still your father's daughter, eh?"

And he was still a *flic* deep down, saddled with ghosts and loy-
alties.

Aimée downed her espresso. Unwrapped the chocolate square.

"These days, I'm an expert witness on computer forensics at
court, mostly," she said. "But Boris is a good friend. He's fighting
for his life." She remembered what Morbier had said. "Isn't Action
Directe old news?"

"You'd think so. Yet a fugitive member in hiding for years
turned himself in last week. He's got cancer and wants a deal."

"So he's got information on the bombing? Alerted you?"

"I can't talk about it."

Still, that put a new spin on it. Explained Bellan's interest.

"Then why wouldn't Action Directe make a public claim
taking responsibility?"

"Good question," he said. A black car approached and halted
at the curb. "By the way, Sharpies don't smear."

She blinked.

"The better question is, why would they leave this note with you?"

"What if the bomb was meant to destroy lab evidence?" she said. "Can I see the bomb squad's findings?"

"You're not cleared for that," he said, putting out his hand for her Moleskine. "But I'll use this as your statement—the investigation is under our jurisdiction."

Her brand-new red leather Moleskine, shiny and with pristine lined pages.

"Use your portable scanner."

"Like I carry one with me?" said Bellan, amused.

"I usually do." *Zut*—she'd left it at work.

"You want my help, Aimée? A favor? Give me something to work with."

Reluctant, she handed the notebook over. "I want this back."

Bellan got in the car. The door closed, and it pulled away, then stopped, reversed, and its window rolled down. "Action Directe claimed responsibility for bombing Interpol's old HQ nearby in 1986."

She knew Bellan was telling her this for a reason.

"*Et alors*, you're implying last night's bombing relates to the eighty-six bombing? Some piece of that puzzle, then? The same signature?" She shrugged. "That's your field. Not mine."

BELLAN GLANCED AT his buzzing phone, then at her, his eyes darting. A conflicted look, as if battling loyalty versus duty. "*Entre nous*, you do know that your father consulted on that investigation in eighty-six, right? Don't discount revenge."

The window rolled up and the car pulled away.

Dry leaves crackled and spiraled around her like the thoughts in her head. Aimée didn't know what to think.

Monday, Midmorning • Rue de Dantzig

"STOP IT THERE," his *grand-père* said.

Hugo's finger pressed the pause button on the video camera. Click. It froze a frame of the man on the dark thread of pavement.

Thankfully his mother hadn't revealed the video footage to the *flics* and had left for her secretarial job at the Institut Pasteur, forgetting to confiscate his video camera. Still, his nerves tingled.

"How can you say you know him, *Grand-père?* He could be anyone."

Anyone caught at midnight, mid-run, right leg extended, left foot raised, arm bent in a swinging forward motion. The image showed him half in shadow, wearing a black outfit—a suit or jacket, Hugo couldn't tell. The toe of his right shoe glinted in the streetlight. So a dress shoe, not a sneaker.

Outside Hugo's apartment window, crews worked on the lab's wreckage. Arson and bomb experts, along with the *démineur* team, sifted through the soot and charred rubble. The churning bark of a small bulldozer dulled to a low roar.

"Keep going," said his *grand-père*. "But not so fast."

Hugo pressed the slow-motion setting. Click.

Before their eyes, the man moved as if underwater, his legs and limbs in a gel-like stride.

"Stop. There. See, he's tall."

Hugo paused the video.

"You can't tell that," he told his grandfather. "Can't judge how tall he is from the camera's vantage point, looking down."

"Don't you have eyes to see, Hugo? His head bobs but there, his head's level with the notch on the gate post."

"*Et alors?*"

"I know him."

"You keep saying that, but you can't be sure. The video's too dark." The man's gait, stance, and furtive pivots of his head had imprinted on Hugo's mind. He'd recognize him if the man ever ran ahead of him on the street. Not much use now.

"We'll tell your mother I had a doctor's appointment. Let's go."

"Go where?"

"To talk to him. I need a replacement leg, don't I? Damned insurance won't cover a new one after I lost the old one. Let him pay, or I'll report him."

Just like that?

"A man was murdered. Buildings blown up."

"That's right. It's war, Hugo. I lost my leg at *la Libération*."

According to secret family lore, he'd fallen drunk out of a jeep and gotten pinned against the *préfecture* wall, his leg crushed.

"If you think you know his identity, you've got to tell the *flics*," Hugo said. But how? Make an anonymous phone call, send a note—anything to avoid showing the video with Chantal taking off her lingerie to others. His mother seeing it was bad enough.

"Who says we won't? Later."

"*C'est fou.* Too dangerous."

"In war, you do what you must. If you won't come, I'll go myself."

Why couldn't his grandfather get out of that time warp? Always back in the war.

"You can't."

His *grand-père* grabbed his wheelchair. "Watch me."

Midmorning • La Préfecture • Ile de la Cité

IN TOUREAU'S OUTER office, the *tap tap tap* of Aimée's high heels on the worn parquet floor competed with the myriad other sounds of 36 quai des Orfèvres: doors shutting, suspects shouting, handcuffs clinking. She couldn't wait for this to be over. A million things waited for her at the Leduc Detective office. She'd already had to cancel her meeting with Morbier, and still needed to prepare for a pre-trial meeting with her top client, Dutot.

And, according to the glance she took of herself in the bathroom mirror, she also needed to apply more undereye concealer. Her lack of sleep was showing big-time.

Toureau, rude again after a *hurry up and wait*, had disappeared to attend a meeting. He'd summoned an officer to take her statement instead. No doubt he'd lost interest in her the moment counterterrorism had claimed jurisdiction.

Could Morbier have stalled him? She doubted it. Wouldn't put it past Toureau to use this as a tactic, circling back like a coiled snake before attacking her.

Frustrated at this wasted time, she studied the middle-aged female police officer, who finally clicked the print key on her keyboard. Something about her—perhaps the black hair going grey?—looked familiar.

The printer whirred and spit out several sheets of paper, all with the department letterhead and *procès-verbal* printed at the top.

"Read, sign, and date, please."

The pen didn't have any ink. Nor did the second pen the officer handed her. Their taxes at work, René would say, and the *flics* didn't have a single decent pen!

By the time she scrounged one from the bottom of her bag, signed the page, and slid it back across the woman's desk, Aimée remembered why the officer looked familiar.

"Didn't you work at the *commissariat* with my father, Jean-Claude Leduc?" She paused, found the name. "Are you Florence?"

A nod.

She'd aged. Fine lines webbed her mouth.

"Took your time remembering that one," Florence said, pinning the sheets together and handing Aimée a copy. "I'm retiring next month. Not soon enough."

Not a happy camper, this Florence. But who would be, working with Toureau?

"You made a *galette des rois* for the team." Aimée grinned. "Every year at Epiphany. One time, I found the charm and wore the crown."

That wonderful almond-filled tart with flaky, buttery crust in the wintertime at the *commissariat*. Her father wiping the crumbs from his mouth.

Florence smiled and the corners of her eyes crinkled, making her look younger.

"Good days. Different times."

Aimée smiled back.

"Your father was a good officer. Knew how to work with his team. What they said about him wasn't right."

Aimée's chest constricted. She nodded in agreement. "Even now. Just last night Toureau was flinging mud on Papa's name."

She hadn't meant to say that aloud. Her fingers rotated the button on her silk shirt. But Florence had known her father.

Aimée summoned the courage and leaned over the desk. "How is it working with Toureau? I've heard some . . . rumors."

Florence filed Aimée's *procès-verbal* in the out tray. Took a breath and looked around.

"Which ones?" she whispered.

Before Aimée could answer, a sergeant beckoned Florence from an adjoining office.

She stood and showed Aimée out.

Paused at the door. "Word to the wise, eh?" Florence said under her breath. "Watch out for him."

AIMÉE REVVED THE scooter across Pont Neuf in the blustery wind. Florence's words replayed in her mind. Cloud wisps skated across the lint-grey sky, framing the zinc rooftops and pepper-pot chimneys.

Turning off busy rue de Rivoli, she parked in the garage on rue Bailleul. She bought her daily *Le Parisien*—despite her home subscription, which she'd lied about to Bellan—from Marcel, the one-armed Algerian vet who ran the kiosk. Then hurried through the Second Empire blue door of her office building. Instead of heading up to Leduc Detective on the third floor, she descended to *la cave*, the ancient cellar and her storage space.

She had to find her father's 1986 files detailing his work on the Interpol bombing. He'd never mentioned the case, but then, she'd been in school studying for her *baccalauréat* exams. Several years ago, she'd organized Leduc Detective's files, digitizing many of them, and now she hoped to God they were still where she remembered storing them.

The coved door, wooden with wormholes, scraped open on the packed dirt floor; the whole place exuded cold and damp. She pulled the cord, and the hanging bulb sent dim yellow light flickering over the piled boxes and files. Cobwebs everywhere.

Half an hour later, after hunting through papers, spiderwebs in her hair, Aimée found what she was looking for.

Old-paper smells assailed her as she opened the cabinet drawer labeled 1986. Her father's faint scent lingered in the cabinet's corners, too. Suppressing a pang of grief, she studied the much-thumbed files. How she missed him.

No time for that now, she thought, and hefted the contents into a cardboard box before dousing the light and tramping up the worn stone stairs.

The Art Nouveau birdcage elevator groaned, creaked, and gave up on the second floor. Would their landlord ever fix the thing? She lugged the box upstairs, her bag swinging against her hip. At least she no longer had to lug around Chloé's diaper bag. Her little girl wasn't so little anymore.

Dumping the box on the hallway floor, she keyed in the security code and opened the frosted-glass door etched with LEDUC DETECTIVE.

A pile of mail on her desk and strains of Radio Classique greeted her in the pale custard light from the office window. On the wall, black-and-white photographs of her grandfather, Claude, in his police uniform on the running board of an old Citröen; her grinning father wearing a cap, fishing on the quai.

"Fashionably late, comme toujours," said René, not sounding happy. He was reaching into the low file cabinet next to his desk.

Like it was a conscious choice?

"Désolée."

René turned back in his ergonomic chair, specially designed for his height. He pumped the lever, raising it to face the three screens on his desk. Given the dark shadows under his eyes, she figured he'd been up all night at the hospital.

In the corner, she saw Saj's empty tatami mat. Their permanent part-time hacker was due back from his ashram in India any day now. With all their work, she needed his help.

"Any update on Boris?"

"No change," he said, his voice harried.

Her phone blipped with a message from Morbier.

Merde.

She set the cardboard box on her desk, then dialed Morbier.

"*Allô,* Morbier?"

René shook his head and put on his headphones.

"Turns out you didn't need my help," said Morbier. "Got your bases covered."

"Look, let me explain," she said.

"My old colleague works with Toureau. Last time I try to help you."

"Wait, what?"

"Last time, like I said, Leduc."

"Don't be like this. It's not fair." How childish that had come out. She hated the eight-year-old she reverted to when they argued.

"It's handled already, so leave it alone," he said.

"I don't know what you've heard, but what if there's more to it? Last night's bombing signature could match the bombing at Interpol in 1986 that Papa worked on."

But he'd clicked off. She slammed her bag down on her desk, knocking the stapler to the floor.

"Another tête-à-tête with your godfather?" René had taken off his headphones. "And you were so grown-up last night."

Could she help it if they had a problematic relationship? If she didn't always trust him? And when he came through, which it sounded like he had, she often unintentionally hurt his pride.

"Sometimes you two mix like oil and water."

"Oil and water don't mix, René."

"Exactly." He glanced pointedly at the wall clock. "We've got that security report due."

"You look exhausted. I'd take over, but I can't." She pushed the report aside on her desk.

"What?"

"I need you to finish it."

"What are you hell-bent on doing besides our business? Tell me what's more important than our livelihood, eh?"

"Finding out who set the bomb. *Désolée*, but that's my priority. Like doing this is yours."

"Life doesn't just stop, Aimée."

"Do I act like it does?"

"I'm invested in helping Boris, too."

"But you're almost done with the report. Please, can you just finish up?"

So far today she'd ticked off two people and been warned off by another two, and it wasn't even noon.

René relented, but she was immediately waylaid. Fumed through three important client calls in a row. René had gone to a meeting by the time she was finally done.

She slipped off her heels. Rubbed her ankle. Barefoot, she padded to the espresso machine, powered it up. While she waited for the thick espresso to drip, she turned the radiator knob to high. No response. Took the stapler, banged it. Again. The radiator sputtered to life with a dribble of heat.

Demitasse in hand, she sat down cross-legged on the Aubusson carpet. Sipped and relished the jolt of caffeine. After lifting out the box's contents, she arranged everything into piles. Most of the files were labeled in her father's angular handwriting; a few in her grandfather's distinctive hand.

She heard her father's voice as she read his reports. Saw him at this desk that was once his. Pain flooded her again.

Why couldn't she deal with her feelings and move on like all those self-help books she'd read told her to?

Right now, she needed to focus. Forget the past, forget the memories. She had to scan these dates.

Five minutes later, she found a file labeled *May 1986: Resolved.*

Clipped inside was a newspaper article dated May 17, 1986, reporting a terrorist attack on Interpol headquarters at 10 P.M. the previous evening. Gunfire and explosives had resulted in damage to the Interpol building in Saint-Cloud on the outskirts of Paris. Several security guards were wounded. Leaflets found at the scene were signed by the left-wing radical group Action Directe. Conflicting first reports by the police attributed the explosions to grenades and later a bomb.

But how did this connect to her father, who'd left the force by then?

Taped to a small sheet of cardboard was a cassette labeled *Witness Account, May 21, 1986* in her father's hand. Good thing she hadn't thrown away her old Walkman. She ejected an old Madonna tape and slotted the cassette into the player. Dead. After finding batteries in René's drawer, she powered the Walkman to life. She heard whirring, muted background noise, a door closing. Then her father clearing his throat, like he always used to.

"Monsieur Chatham," said her father, "your position at Interpol for the past two years has been assistant to the Interpol deputy director, correct?"

"Correct."

"Please tell me what happened as you experienced it on the evening of May 16, 1986." Her father was speaking English, and his fluency surprised her. It shouldn't have, since he and her mother had spoken English together. The tape hadn't degraded, thank goodness; she could still hear her father's clear voice. As if he were here in the office.

She grabbed a notebook to catch his words in her rusty English vocabulary.

"We'd had dinner at La Coupole after a long day of summit meetings," said Chatham, his accent American—flat, with a hint of a Southern twang. "Myself, the director, and two of our staff were eating when my beeper went off, indicating an emergency at HQ. We took the director's car, equipped with a telephone, and were able to reach one of the security guards. The guard said they were under attack and he'd managed to call the police."

"Did he give any specifics of the attack?"

"Before he could, we heard gunshots and then an explosion, glass breaking and such, and then the line cut off. It happened so fast. Maybe within a minute, I'm not sure." Chatham took a breath. Paused. "By the time we got to Interpol, the police and ambulance had arrived. The building resembled a war zone."

Aimée paused the tape. She paged through the file and found a photo of the Interpol building. A war zone all right—half of the fifties-era, five-story concrete-and-glass building overlooking the RER station had crumbled. Jagged concrete teeth pointed to the sky.

She hit play.

"How do you mean, Monsieur Chatham? Would you like some water?"

The sound of liquid, a pause, then the clunk of a glass on a table.

"I mean smoke, soot, broken glass everywhere, the door bent in and strewn wreckage. Later we learned a car had pulled up, then engaged in a gun battle with the guards."

"Does Interpol employ the security guards?"

"They're independently contracted."

"So did the attackers have access to the building at any point?"

"No. One guard was wounded in the arm but was able to close and barricade the steel doors. Thank God for that," said

Chatham. "The next day, we were told they'd left a twenty-five-pound satchel charge in front. It blew a hole in the concrete floor, reaching to the garage below. It blew the steel doors in, the elevators off their tracks, traveled through the heating system, blew every window in the building out. The implosion sucked the glass back in. Every window in the neighborhood got blown out, too."

She heard crinkling, a rattling, and the scratch of a match. An inhale.

"Pass that ashtray, please," said Chatham.

A scrape as the ashtray slid over the table.

"Monsieur Chatham, on the following day when you entered Interpol headquarters, can you describe more of what you saw?"

"Yes, the next day our team inspected the damage. Extensive. And we supervised operations to secure sensitive documents."

"And the guards, monsieur," her father continued. "Did you know the two involved that evening?"

"Involved?" he said. Paused. "Ah, you mean the ones guarding the building?"

Aimée paused the tape once more. The way her father had said "involved" jarred her. It had thrown Chatham, too. In her father's inflection, she caught the nuance she knew so well. Her father's question implied the bombing was an inside job by the guards.

She wrote INVOLVED in her notebook. Hit play.

"One's in the hospital and . . . the other, who was uninjured, made the call. Yes, whenever I worked late, they were on the night shift. Good men, responsible, consistent with security procedure."

The tape ended.

Riffling through the papers, she found the contract. Her father had been hired by Alliance Insurance to do a skip trace on Nazir, one of the security guards at Interpol. Standard work for him. Nazir, the injured guard, had claimed extended disability, then moved and, according to the last report, had been found by her father. That ended the investigation. A total of three days' work. Nothing unusual, and a nice payout to boot.

So what did Bellan's remark about revenge signify? According to her father's contract, he'd located the guard and verified his disability. Done and done.

She'd figured her father's name had popped up on a counterterrorist database cross-referencing all terrorist attacks. After 9/11, any connections to terrorists were red-flagged. But in her bones, she felt her father had investigated more than an insurance company claim here.

What if he'd also been contracted by the ministry and worked off the books?

HUGO SWEATED, PUSHING his grandfather in the wheelchair past the crime scene vans on rue de Dantzig. His grandfather used the chair for sympathy; he walked on his wooden leg just fine.

Hugo had wanted to tell the police about the man running away. But that would mean giving a statement and calling his mother a liar for saying they were all asleep. It would also mean that his video camera would be taken away.

Still, his grandfather's idea stank.

A voice came from the rubble site. "You and the family manage all right last night?"

Startled, Hugo looked up and recognized Stéfane, a stocky *démineur* who worked in the police lab. A friendly *mec*, Stéfane worked out in the gym by la Petite Ceinture, the old rail line. Hugo often saw him there after school.

"We manage in war," his grandfather said. "Don't we, Hugo? Coats over pajamas and huddling in the shelter."

Stéfane was working from a tech box filled with vials and tubes. He paused as he swabbed a soot-stained cinderblock for evidence.

Embarrassed, Hugo shook his head. "We stayed at my aunt's around the corner. We're back home now."

Stéfane wiped his brow with the back of his gloved hand and looked up at their building. "You're lucky the windows didn't blow out. These terrorists, well, who knows where or when it will end."

Hugo's heart jumped. "Terrorists?"

"Three attacks this year," said Stéfane. "No one's safe these days. We're still analyzing the evidence from the Toulouse bombing that happened ten days after 9/11."

"Are they connected?" Hugo asked.

"We've got a huge backlog to test and analyze," he said. "But it's not my job to theorize."

Part of Hugo wanted to confide in Stéfane. Another part screamed he had to get away, to think this out.

Stéfane left to rejoin the team scouring the rubble.

His grandfather had released the wheelchair brake. "Hurry up, Hugo, we don't have all day."

Hugo leaned down. Whispered, "Did you hear that? The man's a terrorist. Maybe he's with Al-Qaeda."

"Not on your life." His grandfather snorted. "What does that Stéfane know about it, anyway?"

"He's a pro. It's his job. We have to report this."

"If you want to keep that video camera away from your mother, you'll let me handle this. *Compris?*"

SEVERAL OLD-TIMERS STOOD at the zinc counter inside Café de Dantzig. His grandfather bet on horses here every day. His mother hated it—complained it was flea-infested and last remodeled in the fifties, even though the family who'd owned it were millionaires.

After the Great War, the café's patriarch had fed hungry artists—Chagall, Léger, and Modigliani, to name a few—from the nearby artist colony of La Ruche, "the beehive," an octagonal building leftover from the 1900 Exposition. He'd accepted their pieces as payment. The family sold the café and now owned the famous La Coupole. Nowadays, his mother said, these artists' works were in museums and collections.

Hard to tell it had all started here. Who would have guessed?

His grandfather placed a bet, clutched his PMU ticket, and walked over to hang with his cronies. A few reporters and cameramen who'd reported from the bomb site ambled in for coffee.

Hugo needed to fix this. He'd make an anonymous call from the public phone downstairs. Disguise his voice, describe what he'd seen.

"Let's go, Hugo." His grandfather beckoned him, smiling. Tonio, a gap-toothed old crony of his grandfather's, wearing suspenders and an old duffel coat, had opened the café door. "Tonio's joining us."

"What do you mean?"

"Your grandfather and I reached an understanding." Palm up, Tonio rubbed his thumb and forefinger together.

Hugo leaned toward his grandfather's ear. "You're crazy, getting Tonio involved. We need to report what we saw."

His grandfather pulled the small videotape out of his pocket. "I've got the proof now."

But he'd hidden the tape. How had his grandfather found it? Crestfallen, he reached for it. "You can't keep that."

"Eh, why not?" His grandfather stuck it back in his pocket.

"Don't make a scene," said Tonio. "Go along with us or you're in deep trouble, my boy."

Monday, Noon • *Hôpital Vaugirard*

RENÉ HATED HOSPITALS as much as Aimée did. More, even. The antiseptic smells, the dirt in the corners, harried nurses and stiff-lipped doctors, the drama of life and death in bland waiting rooms—it was all too much for him.

He'd trembled seeing Boris Viard hooked to machines in a room that resembled a freezer.

"They're hopeful, Michou," he said, fighting back his fear. "He's tough. Strong."

Michou looked haggard in the fluorescent light. "Don't patronize me, René."

René wanted to be anyplace but here.

Michou shook his head and gave René a rueful smile. "*Désolé*. I didn't mean it that way. But I'm a realist. His chances look bleak."

"Boris survived, Michou," said René. "If he'd been closer to the blast, we wouldn't be here. The doctor says he's lucky. That luck can hold."

Michou nodded and wiped away tears—a disconcerting sight, René thought, the tears of a tall former merchant marine. "Forgive me. I'll stop the defeatist talk. *Mon Dieu*, I've got to get ready for work."

"Can't you get out of work, Michou? I mean . . ." René's words caught in his throat.

"I'd go crazy if I did, René. Fall apart and make more big scenes. I need to work."

René nodded.

"Got to keep busy," Michou said. He leaned down to hug René. "You're the one who's strong. *Merci*, my good friend."

BY THE TIME René made it to his car, his phone was chirping. Aimée.

"How's Boris?"

"No change. Michou's gone to work."

"*Bon.* I'll visit later." She paused. "Counterterrorism's handling this now."

"Meaning?"

His phone chirped again—a message. Leila, at last. She wanted to meet at a café near Institut Pasteur, where she worked in the lab. *We need to talk, René*, the message read.

"Wait, if counterterrorism's handling this, why aren't guards stationed outside Boris's room?"

"How's that, René?"

"If Boris witnessed something, he could be a target."

He got out of the car, struggling with his aching hip, and locked the door.

"I'm going to find out, Aimée."

He clicked off.

René backtracked down those fluorescent-lit hallways, weaving among the scurrying hospital staff and visitors. His pulse thumped as he stepped inside.

Boris's room was empty.

AIMÉE RANG BELLAN at the GIGN. Got his voice mail. She left her callback number and a concerned message over the lack of security for Boris at the hospital.

Revenge, my foot. If her father had done contract work for the GIGN investigation in 1986, why didn't Bellan just say so? Unless he hadn't.

Was that Bellan trying to reel her in? Even better. She wanted in on this investigation. She'd use her edge into GIGN to investigate. She couldn't start soon enough.

Melac answered on the third ring. "Don't worry, I'm picking Chloé up from school."

She'd completely forgotten Babette had the afternoon off and she'd drafted Melac for school duty. She had an appointment in twenty minutes with the attorney to prepare expert testimony for their upcoming court case.

"Listen," she said. "Security's lax at Hôpital Vaugirard. There's no police presence guarding Boris."

Pause. "They've moved him."

"The man's in a medically induced coma. It's unsound to move a patient in that condition."

"There's more to it, Aimée."

"Like what?" she said, packing a dossier and papers into her Vuitton bag, throwing in concealer and mascara. She reached for her Chanel jacket and leather coat. With her phone crooked between her neck and shoulder, she closed the office door and set the alarm.

"I'm waiting, Melac," she prompted.

"Boris is a possible suspect," he said. "So certain parameters—"

Anger rippled inside her. "A suspect? That's insane. You were at the party when Boris left."

"You know it's a standard line of questioning in an investigation. Boris needs to be ruled out. Technically, he could have set the bomb."

She wanted to scream. Controlled herself. Good God, what *lunatiques* ran this investigation?

But she knew.

"*Non*, it's Toureau," she said. "He's pushing this."

Her line clicked. Call waiting. The attorney.

"Got to take this," she said. "Check the corruption rumors on Toureau. I'm sure he's spit in other people's espressos."

She switched lines. The attorney said, "I'm running late."

"No worries," she said, taking the stairs down two at a time. "Take your time. I'll wait."

With that she waved at a taxi depositing a passenger on rue du Louvre and jumped inside as he was paying.

"Someone's in a hurry," said the taxi driver, an older man with a ponytail. The news station blared: a rehash of last night's bombing and an announcement of an ongoing bomb alert.

"More bombs?" the taxi driver continued. "*Zut alors*, what else is new?"

She pulled out her makeup kit. Dabbed double concealer under her eyes and noticed a faint line. A new one.

"Double fare if you make it to la Motte-Picquet in ten minutes."

Aimée jumped out of the taxi in front of the Belle Epoque building, then ran up the wide marble staircase to the stately law firm on the second floor. The bored receptionist showed her into her client's empty office. She caught her breath with just minutes to spare before his arrival. She checked her phone. No message from Bellan.

Merde.

Where had they transferred Boris?

Asian antiques filled the large, high-ceilinged office. The plush interior always pleased her with its black-lacquer wooden chests and scrolls with calligraphy, all tastefully offset by matte-red walls and white carved moldings.

Her client, Dutot, who had financed a personal charity for Cambodian land-mine victims, was suing a board member who had sabotaged the endeavor, milking the charity's funds to pay the back taxes on his family's château. A financial mess. Her fees and the court costs all came out of Dutot's pocket.

When he finally rushed in, suave in his tailor-made suit, they got straight to business. Throughout the entire meeting, Aimée suppressed the urge to check her phone.

Even though she was curious, she'd avoided asking about her client's commitment to this charity. Her new philosophy was to stay *discrète* and maintain professional footing as a legal expert. Avoid her tactlessness, as René would call it.

"For the trial, I'd like to bring in another verifiable piece of evidence," Dutot said. "The discrepancy on page nineteen where it's obvious the deposit amounts were changed."

Aimée followed along in her file. Made a note. "Not a problem." She'd already culled more than enough and had only given him a sample. "I'll prepare that for court."

Dutot's phone rang.

"Must take this, excuse me."

She gazed around the office. Took in the photos on his desk. One of them was of a smiling couple—Dutot with his arm around a striking Asian woman before overgrown temple ruins, banyan trees in the background. A black ribbon framed the photo.

Dutot hung up and followed her gaze.

"Seven years ago, my wife, Lin, died in a landmine explosion," he said. "The jungle path was marked as cleared of land mines, but in Cambodia . . . mistakes happen."

"I'm sorry," she said. Another bombing. Such a horrifying way to go.

"No doubt you were wondering at the raison d'être for my charity. It's in her memory, so that others don't suffer the same."

"You'll have the evidence this evening," Aimée said.

She stood and shook his hand.

Outside his office, persimmon-hued leaves fluttered from the tree-lined avenue de Suffren. The Tour Eiffel poked its iron girders beyond. Street cleaners swept cabbage leaves from the now-empty aluminum-framed morning market stalls at la Motte-Picquet. Riders disgorged from the Métro, flittering back and forth like the yellow and brown autumn leaves in the wind.

On the street, she heard the blare of a siren. An ambulance sped by.

She glanced at her phone. Still no word on Boris.

Monday • Noon • Near Porte de Versailles

LÖIC BELLAN ENTERED the safe house on rue Léon Dela-
grange, a dead end at the edge of the fifteenth arrondissement by
the Porte de Versailles. Bellan had chosen it himself.

In his mind, it was perfect. The fourth-floor Haussmann-style
apartment was situated in a cul-de-sac, and he paid a lookout who
was already employed in the Dehillerin cookware repair atelier
at the street level of the building. The cul-de-sac was bordered
by the abandoned Petite Ceinture rail line. Behind the apartment building on the left stood a semi-ruined factory, giving it a
remote, village-like ambience.

Bellan ignored the Art Nouveau wire-cage elevator. Hiked up
to the fourth floor, keeping alert for anything out of the ordinary.
Nothing.

He knocked twice, then once more. Sarah, the middle-aged
woman who managed the safe house, opened the door and whispered, "He's restless today."

Bellan nodded, hung up his coat in the hallway, and entered
the small salon. A muted television played the news. An Ikea
bookcase held paperbacks under bright countryside prints from
Monoprix.

"Why haven't you taken me to the doctor?" Johan Selles
was hunched on a brown leather sofa in the salon. His hands,
with their cracked fingernails and bitten cuticles, never stopped
moving.

Round-shouldered and looking older than his fifty-six years, Johan reminded Bellan of shriveled leaves in a gutter. The former eighties radical and Action Directe member had recently given himself up, but it was hard to imagine him lobbing bombs anymore. He had a nervous expression on his pasty face. A twitch in his neck.

"The doctor's coming this afternoon," said Bellan. "I told you."

"Why not now?" he said. "I'm ill. Can't keep anything down."

"Safer for you, Johan. We discussed this, remember?"

Johan snorted. His restless hands picked at the buttons on his shirt. "You mean to keep your shoddy investigation quiet. No one's after me but my ex-wife's bill collectors. I'm doing you a favor."

A favor?

"You came to us because you want treatment, Johan. Not the other way around."

"We made a deal."

"Right, so keep to it. Pancreatic cancer's tough. Let's talk."

Bellan thrust a sheet with photographs showing the members of Action Directe. The photos were old, from the eighties; in one, Johan looked young, strapping, and rock-star sullen.

"Tell me where the members are now."

"We split in 1990. Félix went to prison, Melanie overdosed in Istanbul, Raymond got caught five years ago in Italy, and the other two—"

Bellan interrupted. "You mean Anna Soulages and Nicolas Pantin?"

He nodded. "They scattered. Imagine they're dead by now, or I'd have heard."

Alert, Bellan leaned in.

"How?"

"Word gets around," Johan answered after a ragged coughing spell.

"Gets around how, Johan?"

"I've got nothing to do with that anymore. Not for years."

"No one's accusing you." Bellan sat down next to him. "Yet."

Johan spit phlegm into a tissue he took from his pocket.

"How do you get word, Johan?"

"I just hear things."

Of course he did. This was why Johan had approached them. He had something to trade.

"Not good enough," Bellan said. "We need your cooperation. Every detail, however small."

Another hacking, coarse cough. Winded, Johan lay back and closed his eyes. His breathing grew labored and his chest heaved.

Alarmed at the man's condition, Bellan realized he needed the information Johan had before it was too late.

A faint knock sounded on the door. Sarah beckoned him. "Doctor's here. Also, you've got a special message from the boss." She showed him her phone.

Commander Tingry. He was late.

HUGO HAD FELT sheepish pushing his grandfather's wheel-chair into the crowded studio. Grew more embarrassed with his grandfather obsessing on some "Paul" fleeing the bombing in the video. A "Paul" with ties to this artist.

He was introduced to Rasa, the Lithuanian sculptor, who stood in her glass-doored atelier, the space cluttered with plaster molds of naked female torsos. Plaster bits clung to Rasa's long black braid and spattered overalls. Sweat beaded her neck. Hugo tried to look away, but his gaze kept going to where her T-shirt clung to her chest.

This was *his* Chantal. His breath caught.

Rasa, along with fifty or so artists, worked and lived in the artist colony at La Ruche, in a rotunda designed by Gustave Eiffel for the 1900 Universal Exhibition. Hugo's apartment looked over the building and its gardens.

"You're looking for Paul?" Rasa said. "Hasn't lived here for a month, maybe more."

"That's not what I heard," his grandfather said.

"You heard wrong, old man. *Bien*, I'm preparing for my exhibition, so if that's all . . ."

"Does Paul still work at the butcher's?"

"Don't know," she said, "and don't care."

"He was here last night," Tonio said. "Don't cover for him."

"And why would I do that?" She used a wooden stick to stir a thick white mixture in a plastic tub. Powdery traces of the plaster on the floor made for white footsteps. "Watch out. If I mess up this pour, you're paying."

She shoved past Tonio, hefted the tub, and poured the thick, milk-white contents into a metal mold. It reminded Hugo of rich crêpe batter. Made him hungry.

"There's something in it for you if Paul gets in touch," said his grandfather.

Rasa skimmed off the excess with a flat ruler. "Get lost. And don't bring the kid around unless he models for me." She looked up and grinned at Hugo. "You and your telescope, eh?"

Blood rushed to his cheeks. Good God, she knew he'd spied on her. He'd get arrested, sent to juvenile prison or maybe "the big house," like they called it in films.

AIMÉE'S PHONE RANG as she reached the Métro's Art Nouveau–style station entrance. An unknown number. Her thoughts flew to Chloé. But the *crèche's* number was already saved in her phone. Was it the clinic, a doctor calling in the wake of a playground accident?

"*Allô?*"

"Turn to the right."

Bellan. But where was he? She scanned her surroundings, not seeing him.

Stupid of her to worry. Her cheeks flushed in anger.

"Quit the games. Why's Boris Viard being moved from the hospital?"

"Good afternoon to you, too," he said. "I'll tell you on the way."

"What?"

"I'm in the Renault to your right."

She looked up, startled to see a blue Renault double-parked on the curb ahead. Bellan waved from the driver's seat. Unease filled her.

Aimée ducked in and slammed the door. "Answer my questions or I'm getting out. How did you know I was here, and how—"

"One at a time. Your partner René told us. The rest I'll answer en route."

Her scarf tangled in the ragged seat belt. "I've got a trial coming up. Work to do."

"Of course you do. And we're offering you a new job, too."

Thought so, she almost said.

He checked the rearview mirror, shifted into first and released the clutch. "Hold on."

"FORGIVE ME, RENÉ, I didn't mean to be late," Leila said, stowing shopping bags under the café counter and perching next to him on a stool. She leaned over, giving him *bises* on both cheeks, friendly and passionless. Her rosewater scent lingered in the air between them.

"Just got here," he lied. He'd waited fifteen minutes in the suffocating café with its steamed-up windows and the *télé* newscaster spouting new theories on 9/11 montaged with the Twin Towers' destruction. He'd gotten Aimée's message that Boris was a suspect, and roiled in frustration that she hadn't answered his repeated calls.

"It's my grandmother's birthday, and she loves halvah. So I rushed to that shop," Leila said, catching her breath. Her dark eyes glimmered under perfectly arched eyebrows. "We went there once, remember? I told you, it's famous for halvah."

He nodded, remembering a small, crammed shop on rue des Entrepreneurs, full of Persian food, DVDs, pomegranate syrup, and clientele speaking Farsi. Leila, who was of Iranian descent, lived with her parents in this area, known as Téhéran-sur-Seine.

Leila caught the waiter's eye. Signaled for the same tisane as René. Rose-cheeked from the cold, she rubbed her hands.

"They offered me the job," she said. "I'm so excited."

Only now she was telling him? No wonder she hadn't made it to the party last night.

"You got a promotion at the lab?"

She squeezed his hand. Hers was cold, her nails painted with light-pink lacquer. "My project at Pasteur's finished. My colleagues say this is an amazing opportunity." Glowing, she poured hot water from the teapot into a cup. Sipped. "Why the face? Can't you be happy for me, René?"

He'd thought she'd wanted to meet up with him to make up for last night.

"I thought your lab needed a brilliant researcher like you."

"Not until there's a new project. My union rep would have fought for me, but why wait? This position opened up in Abu Dhabi, and the timing's perfect."

René's insides tightened. He tried to manage a smile.

"Abu Dhabi?"

"As blood lab supervisor. It'd be a big step for me." Her face brightened, then fell. "You said you'd understand."

Had he? His hip ached, and his leg, dangling from the café stool, throbbed. Did Arabs and Iranians get along?

"I thought we'd talk about the future," he said. "Our plans."

"You're special, René. You deserve someone to share your future with *here.*"

His heart seized. "We're breaking up?" He was such a fool. He should have seen it coming. Spared himself the humiliation.

"Don't think of it like that, René."

"How else would I think of it?"

She started to speak, but he was lost in his thoughts, trying to process what must have been happening right before his eyes. How he'd ignored the signs.

"Aren't you going to check your phone?" she was saying.

Brought back to the present, he saw a new message on his phone. Michou.

He read the message. Gripped the zinc counter's scalloped rim before he toppled off the stool.

The waiter behind the counter looked up. "*Ça va*, monsieur?"

"Check, please," he said. He stood and reread the message, feeling perspiration beading on his forehead in the warm café. He punched in Aimée's number.

Voice mail. Yet again.

"What's the matter?" Leila asked.

"Boris has been charged with terrorism," he said, his voice quivering.

"Your neighbor?"

"It's impossible. Crazy."

"Boris, a terrorist? It's certainly a mistake." Leila took his hand. She was always cool and calm in an emergency; this, he would miss. "It's either office politics or they're scapegoating him."

He had to think.

"What were you saying about your union rep?"

"That my job offer's perfect, since . . ." Leila paused with her cup halfway in the air. "Why?"

"Your union rep would have fought for you, *non?*"

"Yes. That's what they do."

He had to find Boris's police union representative. Now. He hurried out of the café, Leila calling after him.

BELLAN PRESSED A clicker and dark-green metal gates opened to a grassy courtyard: rose gardens and religious statues surrounded on four sides by limestone buildings with arched walkways.

Birds twittered and a church bell pealed on the right. Two nuns, their blue habits sweeping the cinnamon tiles, disappeared under the archway. Aimée followed Bellan down a gravel walkway to what appeared to be a small gatehouse.

"Bet you didn't know places like this existed," he said.

"Au contraire." The ministry had enclaves like this all over Paris, and taxpayers like her footed the bill.

Inside the gatehouse, Bellan gestured to a window seat in a warm, country-style kitchen. At the table, a man sat wearing headphones, intently watching several screens. Bellan busied himself ladling something steaming from a pot on the stove.

"Georges, our tech, comes from Dordogne and cooks a mean cassoulet," he said. "Eat first, and then I'll introduce you to someone."

He set a bowl on the counter and handed Aimée a spoon. She caught a whiff of tarragon and realized how hungry she was. Hadn't eaten at all this morning.

She spooned a bite. Delicious.

"Ready?" he asked Georges.

Georges nodded. Swiveled one of the screens in her direction.

"Meet Johan Selles, a fugitive who turned himself in to us."

A man with deep-set eyes, thin ash-colored hair, and hollow cheeks stared at something off camera. He wore a hospital gown over his withered frame and had an IV hooked up to his arm leading to a drip bag of clear liquid, but the room didn't appear to be a hospital room. Tattoos ran up his arm and disappeared under the gown. She noticed a faded red C but didn't catch the rest.

"Johan disappeared after the Action Directe bombing of Interpol in 1986—went to ground."

The case of her father's that Bellan had tipped her off to—she was still surprised it had been for an insurance company. "How did this tie to the skip trace my father did on Interpol's Iranian guard after the bombing?"

"It didn't. Did I say it did?"

"You implied the Action Directe message spelled revenge."

"At the time, in Iran, the Ayatollah Khomeini's Revolutionary Guard funded proxy terrorists. We . . ."

"We? Weren't you in short pants then?"

A muscle in his cheek quivered. He bit back a grin. She imagined him smiling, how his eyes would . . . what?

Concentrate.

"My boss, then part of an anti-terrorist team, suspected Iranians were bankrolling Action Directe's Interpol bombing. But the team had no proof."

"So all Iranians are terrorists?"

"*Zut* , did I say that?"

"Like all Islamists support 9/11?"

"*Pas du tout*," said Georges, readjusting the headphones to around his neck. "The Ayatollah Khomeini's Revolutionary Guard weren't the sophisticated, cosmopolitan Persian middle and upper class who flooded Paris in the sixties and early seventies bringing petrodollars. This Persian *first wave* entrenched themselves buying apartments, investing, setting up their children for

French university. We're talking the top business class, educated elite, intelligentsia, the crème de la crème. Their pervasive presence with Persian restos and specialty shops coined the quartier nickname Téhéran-sur-Seine."

She spooned another bite of cassoulet. How wonderful to have a multi-talented tech. "You're telling me this why?"

"*Alors*, after the Shah's overthrow in seventy-nine, a *second wave*, many who were political exiles, emigrated and made a life in France," said Georges. "Many blended into the Iranian community, or tried to. Some moved on. However, the ayatollah's reach stretched here. Still does. This second wave's underlying fear was of Islamist hardliners who'd exact revenge, settle scores or blackmail and steal their money. And it happened."

"So how does this connect with Action Directe?"

Bellan took over. "My boss has suspected an Iranian connection all along. Because of the note you received, we think they've struck again."

Then it was true.

"So Boris was at the wrong place at the wrong time," she said. "That means you're releasing him."

Bellan shook his head. "We rushed the evidence to the Lyon lab, who took over the forensic biological investigation. Their latest findings show traces of Semtex under Boris Viard's fingernails."

The words made her throat catch. "What?"

"I'm sorry." He averted his eyes. "Boris Viard's in custody at a secure military hospital. It's routine for suspected terrorists. After 9/11, we can't take chances."

She set down her spoon. Pushed the bowl away, her appetite gone. The GIGN had Boris.

"There are a million different reasons Boris could have explosive traces on him—his proximity to the explosion, flying debris, crawling through the site—"

"*Plastique* ignites in the explosion. Traces like this only appear with fresh contact."

She sat back against the window in disbelief.

"Why would Boris set a bomb?" She bit the inside of her cheek. "It makes no sense."

"Has he been acting differently lately? Did you or his friends notice anything?"

Her thoughts fled to the background search he'd asked her to do. How Michou suspected him of having an affair. How she'd promised Melac to keep Boris and Michou's relationship under the radar, for Boris's sake.

Would it add up to something? Should she tell Bellan?

Something made her hold back. She shook her head.

"We'll know more when Boris stabilizes and comes out of the coma. Meanwhile, two Action Directe members who participated in the bombing have never been accounted for, and Johan here is our only source regarding their whereabouts. He's in the last stages of terminal cancer." Bellan paused. "Well, our only source except you."

"If that means I can investigate this my way, then I'm interested," she said.

"My unit chief, Commander Tingry, suggested that you work for us temporarily."

So that was what Bellan meant by a new job.

"Suggested?"

"That's the polite term. It's more than a suggestion."

This was her way in. She followed their line of thinking— Action Directe had relayed their message through *her*.

"You want to use me as bait for Action Directe."

Georges averted his eyes and put on his headphones.

"Let's call it assisting in our counterterrorism operation."

"I thought you'd never ask."

OUTSIDE THE ARTIST colony of La Ruche, Hugo kicked a cobblestone that had been upturned in the explosion. Angry at his idiot grandfather and his crony, that bum Tonio, who was only interested in blackmail money. And Hugo was furious that Rasa the gorgeous sculptor knew he'd spied on her. On top of it all, they'd possibly prevented the authorities from getting to the bottom of an act of terrorism.

In the passage, he noticed a man he'd seen at the café with the reporters.

"You're a local, right?" said the man. He was young, wearing a black jacket and jeans, a bag slung over his shoulder. "I'm a reporter with *Le Parisien*. Got anything to say about the explosion last night?"

Wary, Hugo stepped back. "Why?"

"Bet you're happy to get out of school, right?"

"How do you know that?"

"Look, you came out of the apartment across from the lab. I'm writing a story on how this affects the neighborhood, a human-interest piece."

"Does that mean you'll write what I say? Quote me?"

"Of course."

"I'm not interested."

The reporter surveyed him with a searching gaze. "Or not. Up to you."

Hugo thought. "What about as a confidential informant?"

The reporter laughed, an eagerness in his eyes. "Why not?"

This could work, Hugo thought. First he'd have to get that videotape back from his grandfather.

Tonio, the despicable crony and hanger-on, was pushing his grandfather's wheelchair out of La Ruche's iron gate.

"Let's go, Hugo," called his *grand-père*.

Hugo turned to the reporter. "Okay, meet me by Monfort Théâtre in the park in two hours."

"I'm looking for a newsworthy angle, kid, or it's not worth my time."

Hugo glanced at his grandfather. Lowered his voice. "I saw a man run away from the explosion."

"I'M LOOKING FOR Paul," said Hugo's grandfather.

"Which Paul?" asked the stooped butcher, Monsieur Leban. His voice rose from behind the meat counter. "The redhead or dark-haired one?"

"Not the redhead," said his grandfather.

"What's he done now?"

"You tell me."

Leban laughed and his grandfather joined in.

"He in back?"

Hugo knew old Leban's *boucherie* well, with its vintage horse collars hanging from the ceiling and horseshoes tacked on the wall beside black-and-white photos of the old horse market. Leban's *boucherie* sold horsemeat. Old-school, and with a loyal clientele. More upscale butchers in the district sold beef from tan Limousin, white Charolais, and red-and-white Montbéliarde cows. Hugo's uncle had worked here, happy until he'd keeled over after a heart attack while opening the refrigerator door. His aunt Mimi shopped here weekly in a sort of pilgrimage. Leban still gave her an employee discount.

Clients surged at the front. Coins clattered on the counter. Busy as always.

"Hold on." Leban's crooked back strained under his bloodied butcher's apron. His cleaver hacked a beef joint with practiced aim. *Crack.* The reverberation sounded off the white-tiled butchery. Then another. *Thwack.*

Hugo stiffened.

Leban split the joint, wrapped the cutlet in waxed white paper, and tied a string around it. After his client paid, he joined them in the rear, rubbing his bloody hands on his stained apron.

"Redhead Paul's on deliveries. The other one . . ." He shrugged. "Who knows?"

"Come on, Leban."

"His mother lives on Passage Olivier de Serres. Tell her I've got his paycheck."

Another fruitless search, no doubt.

"Let's go home, *Grand-père.*"

Outside on the pavement in the bustling crowd, Tonio joined them. He held up his IOU with Hugo's *grand-père's* gambling debt.

"Where's the money?" said Tonio. "How're you going to pay me back?"

"*Grand-père's* tired. It's time for his nap, Tonio," Hugo said.

"I can't let the Germans get away," replied his grandfather.

Hugo shook his head. Lucid one minute and out to lunch the next. If he took a nap, Hugo could reclaim his tape and substitute it with another.

By the time he'd wheeled his grandfather home, Hugo's arms ached. He helped his grandfather into bed, and his loud snores filled the air within minutes. Quick as a wink, Hugo took the video cassette from his coat pocket. Riffled through his own tapes and swapped in another one.

The front door opened. His mother hung her coat in the hallway and shouted, "We need to have a talk, young man!"

Hugo grabbed his jacket and gave her a couple of quick *bisous*. "I'm meeting my friend Alain to find out about homework."

"What about dinner?"

"Later."

Then boom, out the door before she could stop him.

Monday • 4 P.M. • *Parc Georges Brassens*

AIMÉE SAT BESIDE Melac on a bench in Parc Brassens, watching Chloé in the sandbox. Bundled up in a blue wool coat, her daughter concentrated on dumping out her sand bucket and saying, "Look, *Maman!*"

"Bravo, *ma puce!*"

Melac had his arm around Aimée. Stroked her hair. "You're working with counterterrorism now? Knock me down with a feather, but that's so not you."

Aimée had arranged to meet Chloé and Melac here. She needed to see the park in daylight. The layout. Bronze bulls still guarding the gates. A large pavilion that was once the old abattoir now housed the Marché du Livre antique book market on the weekends.

"Tell me about it," she said.

For her, counterterrorism was the easiest way to investigate the case against Boris. She'd take advantage of their contacts, state-of-the-art gadgets, intel. If Toureau had set up Boris, she'd nail him with the GIGN on her team.

"*Pas de problème,*" he said. "You might like it. Just tell me when you're going operational."

Her stomach churned. "Tonight."

"Brilliant."

Surprised, she noted his pleased expression.

"I'm taking Chloé to Brittany. I'll pack her things and leave on the five-twenty P.M. train."

"But she's got school."

"*Ecole maternelle?* A few days won't matter. She's only three."

Already three years old, and it grabbed her heart. Chloé proudly lifted her bucket and laughed. The sand spilled and scattered in the box. Aimée reached over to help Chloé scoop it back in. Felt the granules run through her fingers.

Hadn't it been the right decision to accept the job from Bellan? She'd made the choice to vindicate Boris, who was unjustly accused of terrorism. The only way to do that was by finding whoever had really set the bomb. She kissed Chloé's rosy cheeks and looked up at Melac.

"*Non*, it's better we stay at Martine's."

She'd only been apart from Chloé for a night. Didn't know if she could stand longer.

"You're going to be on call twenty-four-seven. I've been there, Aimée." He sat back. Those blue-grey eyes Chloé had inherited looked down at Aimée's shaking hands. "Don't be nervous." He enclosed her hand in his. "As a novice, you're never frontline," he said quietly. "Think of this as your introduction. The world's crazy, and the new war zone's cyber counterterrorism. After this you could get a job anywhere."

How could he even think of this as a career move? Stifling her outrage, she took a breath. Another one. Why was she angry at this? It was par for the course.

"The government's contracted a computer facility in Brittany. Decentralizing computer surveillance," he said. "It's perfect, Aimée. You could work from the farm."

Not this again. She checked her phone. Nothing from René.

"I don't believe Boris is guilty."

"No one wants to believe that." He turned away. "But the proof exists. Things got to him. He must have snapped."

"Snapped and bombed his own workplace?"

They both stared at the laboratory ruins. A bulldozer's whine cut the afternoon air.

"What if Toureau planted evidence on Boris?" said Aimée.

Melac frowned at her. "Where did you get that crazy idea? He wouldn't do that."

So they were buddies now? The thought made her sick.

"I don't trust him."

"I accompanied him and his team last night."

"Why?"

"*Ecoute*, they followed procedure, believe me." Melac's voice sounded hollow.

"Rumors follow Toureau," she said. "Corruption." She didn't know that for sure, but she smelled rotten Roquefort.

"Old gossip. He had an affair with a colleague's wife. It got messy."

Melac knew something. She had to draw it out of him. "There's more to it than that."

Melac shook his head and stood.

Translation: *No one breaks the code; we always have each other's backs*.

"Chloé, let's go to Papa's farm."

A squeal from the sandbox. "Horses?" Chloé loved the horses on Melac's farm.

Aimée helped Chloé gather her shovel and pail. Hated again to admit Melac was right. It would be better for Chloé in Brittany. Healthier and with a routine.

A day or two. That was all.

"You'll feed the horses," she said, lifting her daughter up and hugging her tight.

"*Meelz Daveez?*"

Melac shook his head. But Aimée smiled.

"Him too, *ma chérie*," she said. "Let's get your things."

~

AT GARE MONTPARNASSE, Aimée kissed Chloé's rosebud lips, snuggled her little bundle. "*Maman* will come soon."

The train pulled away. Her eyes followed it down the platform under the ironwork glass roof. Melac held Chloé at the window, helping her wave, with Miles Davis in his other arm. Her heart tore in half. Stupid to agree to this, but she'd had no choice.

She could hop on the train, focus on her court work, and—

The phone Bellan had given her vibrated in her pocket.

One message.

Passage Olivier-de-Serres. Now.

RENÉ STOOD IN a long line at the closest *commissariat*. Ahead of him a man coughed, sneezed, and sniffled, continuously wiping his nose. All René needed was a cold or a case of the terrible flu going around. He hadn't gotten his vaccine yet. Why couldn't the line move faster?

Finally, his turn came. Careful to avoid touching the germ-laden counter, he tiptoed so his head at least reached above the neighborhood safety pamphlets.

"You want to make a report, monsieur?" said the young police-woman at the counter.

"I need to speak with a police union representative," he said.

"You're a member of the police union, monsieur?"

"It's concerning my friend who's a member. He needs his rep."

"Then your friend must request it himself, monsieur," she said, ready to beckon the next person in line.

"He's in a coma. Incapacitated."

"In the line of duty, monsieur?" she said in the same bored tone.

"You could say that."

"Either you say *oui ou non*. I don't read minds, monsieur."

"Technically, he's a victim."

"Then a report's been filed by the duty officer, monsieur. Next."

Parroting police procedure to him didn't help.

"*Bon*, can you verify that?"

"It's not a civilian matter, monsieur."

"But surely a family member can inquire. It's important."

"There are proper channels, monsieur."

He wouldn't get anywhere here.

Melac would know what to do. But he hadn't answered René's text or call.

He'd try Morbier.

Monday • 5 P.M. • *Parc Georges Brassens*

HUGO LOOKED AROUND but didn't see the reporter. He checked the time on the old abattoir's clock tower and belfry. The man was running late.

Hugo walked back and forth between the park and theater. Past the vineyard with four terraces of pinot noir grapes that produced Clos des Morillons, the local wine. His mother called it rotgut. Hugo grew up drinking watered wine with meals, which was customary in families like his. Hugo had first tasted wine at his christening party, not that he remembered. Family lore said his aunt massaged his gums with her wine-moistened finger for "good luck and happiness"—a provincial tradition from the Dordogne.

Now Hugo counted on his good luck to mean the reporter would show up. Back at Monfort Théâtre's entrance, however, all he saw was a grizzled clochard with matted white hair. The man swayed with a bottle in his hand, accosting pigeons on the grass. He was the one nicknamed "Bird Man" because he'd catch the ducks in the pond and eat them.

He shot Hugo a lopsided grin and approached him. "You here for the food?"

Apprehensive, Hugo wished the old coot would stay away. He shouldn't talk to him, or the reporter might see them and be scared off.

"Here's the thing, you don't look hungry, *bouboule*."

Fat boy. He heard that enough at school. Squirmed with shame.

"My luck's gone, can't even catch a pigeon for dinner," said Bird Man.

Disgusting. Hugo knew the campfires at the encampment behind the park where transients squatted in the tunnels of la Petite Ceinture's abandoned rail line. Until the seventies, crews unloaded lumbering horses from the cattle cars for slaughter here at the abattoir. His uncle had told him the horses' nostrils flared with fear at the smell of blood.

Nervous, Hugo looked around for the reporter.

The old rail line was the quartier's playground, his childhood haunt. Pine, sycamore, Mediterranean oak, and chestnut trees grew wild on the steep embankment. His frugal aunt picked wild-flowers such as *véronique*, a light-blue flower woven into "The Lady and the Unicorn" tapestry, and lacey white peonies, which she'd told him Pasteur, a local, had researched for its medicinal properties. Colorful weeds to him.

Again he wondered about the reporter. He'd seemed so eager for Hugo's story.

"Give me some change, *bouboule*," Bird Man whined.

Just his luck: no reporter and harassed by a drunk.

Hugo turned on him. "Get lost," he said angrily. "I'm meeting someone."

Weak afternoon sun pooled by the rusted grillwork. The Tour Eiffel rose above the distant rooftops. Puffs of dust erupted as the bulldozer's arm scraped up debris at the bomb site.

"Ooh!" The drunk grinned. "Would that someone be the reporter who pays for tips?"

The man sounded coherent now.

"What's it to you?"

He shot Hugo a knowing wink. "That reporter came around when we found the body by the tracks. He paid well."

Hugo remembered a law student's body had been discovered last month—a suicide, the paper said. A young woman, Delphine Latour, from the nearby branch of the Sorbonne.

"Paid you?" Hugo snorted in disgust. "For info on a suicide?"

Bird Man chugged his bottle. Tossed it on the wet grass. "Suicide?" He gave Hugo the side-eye. "Not according to Noiro."

That homeless *mec*. A junkie his mother called a disgrace. Ice ran down Hugo's spine.

"Noiro?"

"Noiro's in little pieces now, eh? Guess why, *bouboule*."

Hugo stepped back. Fear washed over him. Somehow, the running man, the explosion, Noiro, and this suicide all wove together.

"Want to know about the reporter? Give me ten francs, *bouboule*, and I'll tell you."

Hugo shook his head.

Bird Man cackled. "Anyway, you missed him. He's gone."

Why? Hugo wasn't late—why would the reporter have left without seeing him? Now who could he talk to without getting in trouble?

His bird was cooked.

Passage Olivier-de-Serres, down six worn steps off the street of the same name, held a history of some kind. Aimée couldn't remember it. She had no clue why Bellan wanted to meet here or what her "task" would entail. However it played out, though, she'd use it. Vindicate Boris.

Wouldn't she?

Her heel wobbled in the uneven cobble crack. *Merde*. Better step carefully in the Louboutins she'd spent far too much on and still felt guilty about buying.

Bellan stood at the warped ground-floor door of number six, an intent look on his face.

She'd better step carefully in more ways than one.

The short passage echoed with children's voices from the nearby *école maternelle*. She noted three-story maisonettes with bleached-out vanilla facades, crumbling stucco, and dirty white shutters.

"What's up, Bellan?"

"Later," he whispered and put a finger to his lips.

The door scraped open. A blonde woman wearing a black leotard and leggings gestured them in and through a narrow hallway.

It opened to a sunlit, open-plan living space. Chic, pale-wood Scandinavian furniture and a marble countertop kitchen with stainless-steel appliances gleamed in the light. Tall glass doors opened to a deck garden with tubs of olive trees, shrubs, and ivy.

Like a page from *ELLE Déco*. Stunning. She would never have guessed this from the run-down passage.

To live well is to live hidden. Or so went the proverb.

"You certainly took your time," the woman said.

"Where's Paul?"

"My son's gone straight."

Bellan glanced at his watch. He radiated calm authority. Her father had once said Bellan performed best when juggling several balls at once.

"That's not the point, Liane."

"The butcher called to warn me," she said. "My son's in danger."

"I'm here to make sure he's not," Bellan said. "But I need to speak with him."

"He's en route." Liane flicked her head at Aimée. Her eyes narrowed. "Who's she?"

Aimée wondered that herself. She also hated being referred to in the third person.

"If you both cooperate, she's his ticket out." Bellan checked his watch again. "You should get a fax right now."

On cue, a whirring sound came from another room. Liane slipped down the hallway.

Aimée took his arm. "What do you mean, 'his ticket out'?"

"Paul's my *tonton*."

Tonton, or uncle, was slang for informer. Like family. Sometimes it amounted to the same thing. Aimée's gaze caught on a basket piled with decorator magazines—all addressed to Liane Sénéchal.

"What's the setup here?"

"I'll explain later."

She was liking this less and less.

Liane returned and handed Bellan several sheets—enlarged photos in black and white. The quality left something to be desired. Still, Aimée recognized the scene of the bombing on rue de Dantzig: rubble, walls ripped apart and yawning open to the night, jagged brick, the *démineurs*, that *salaud* Toureau. Saw herself and René, faces in the crowd. She picked up several crowd shots. Studied them, lost in the memories of last night.

The glass *terrasse* door whooshed open, emitting fresh chilled air. A figure wearing a dark-green hoodie entered. Liane kissed him and rubbed his cheek. Paul Sénéchal.

"Were you followed?" she asked.

"Worse. Brigitte at the fruit stall saw me."

Bellan stuck a phone on top of the photos. "It's fresh," he said. "Stay at the address on the contact list. My number's programmed."

Paul shook his head. "So you'll follow me on GPS?"

"Don't need to," said Bellan.

Aimée noticed the ankle bulge in Paul's boot. A tracker.

"Look over these photos, Paul. Recognize anyone?"

Paul pointed to a man at the crowd's edge. Aimée saw the old needle tracks on his arm where his sleeve slid up. Former junkie and possibly a dealer. Low-hanging fruit turned into a counterterrorist informer?

"He runs Café de Dantzig," said Paul.

"Anyone else?"

Paul shook his head.

"What about him?" Aimée pointed to Feroze, the night guardian. His back was turned, but the lab logo was partially visible on his sleeve.

"Hard to tell."

It wasn't, if you knew what you were looking for. Or were a local, who would have seen Feroze routinely on his night beat. She recognized more faces in the crowd than he did. Didn't think much of Paul as an informer.

Who in this photo had put the article with Action Directe's message in her pocket?

IN HER DIMLY lit office, Aimée sent the updates for the trial to Dutot, then checked her email.

Ping. Bellan's email finally arrived with the police crime scene photos taken the night before on rue de Dantzig. A large file that took several minutes to download.

A quiet calm—almost too quiet—surrounded her. She heard only the occasional clanking and whistle from the steam radiator and the low hum of traffic outside on rue du Louvre. She looked forward to Saj's return.

When she worked alone late at night, she felt her father there with her, even years after his death.

She missed Chloé, her smell, her laugh, and those chubby, often sticky fingers. Too early to call and say goodnight now. She'd check in with Melac later.

She heard the alarm on the door deactivate, and René limped in. His unguarded look as he hung up his tailored Burberry coat showed a brow creased in pain, the lines clenching around his mouth. Her heart fell—the winter damp and cold exacerbated his hip dysplasia. He always tried to hide it.

"We need to talk, Aimée," he said.

The way he said it scared her. Good God, was he about to quit? Then she remembered he'd mentioned he was meeting Leila after the hospital. Maybe their relationship had hit a bump.

She could relate to that. Still, she tensed.

"About what? I'm listening, René." She rose from her chair, stepping on something that shrieked and jumped in the air.

Mon Dieu, a rat in the office! Already she'd made it halfway to the door when she realized René had erupted into laughter. "A little on edge, eh? That was Chloé's talking bear. If you could see your face right now."

"Glad you think it's funny. I almost jumped out of my skin."

But he was laughing, at least. His mood had changed.

Her shoulders sagged with relief. "Tea?"

He nodded. While she brewed his favorite Kusmi Russian tea and made an espresso for herself, she listened. Bad news.

"Morbier checked whether the police union rep had been notified about Boris's situation," he said. Standard practice. "According to Morbier, new counterterrorism guidelines supersede any union representation."

Her insides jolted.

"Therefore, as a suspected terrorist, Boris has no union representation."

They'd hung him out to dry.

"Can't the union appeal this?"

"Morbier says it's fuzzy. They've appointed him a lawyer."

Merde!

She poured René tea in his Sèvres cup. Caught him up on events since finding the damp *Le Parisien* article in her pocket, approaching Bellan, and getting pulled into working with counterterrorism.

"So you've joined them?" René snorted. "You're working for the very people putting Boris away?"

"It's not like that."

Or was it? No way. She opened the window to give herself time to think. Stared out onto the wet rue du Louvre, where headlights from passing cars cast shimmering reflections in the puddles.

"*Ecoute*, at first, Boris was a priority," René said. "One of their own, for God's sake. But now he's been labeled a terrorist. What will they do for him but throw him in prison, to the wolves?" René tugged his goatee. "I just can't believe he'd set a bomb. He's not part of Al-Qaeda, and this is no World Trade Center."

"Michou was afraid he was having an affair," she said, turning back to him. "Even you said they'd been fighting."

"A lover's quarrel. A tiff."

"And yet . . ." She hesitated before sharing everything. But René was her best friend, her partner. And Boris was fighting for his life. "Maybe it's something else."

"What do you mean?"

Thoughts rushed through her mind. Outside, the blare of a siren mingled with rain pattering on the pavement and the jingling of a bicycle bell.

"At lunch last week," she said, "at the Objets Trouvés canteen, Boris asked me to do a background check on someone."

René set down his cup. "He's part of the technical force and works with *flics*—why ask you?"

She'd wondered then, too.

"I owed Boris a favor, and he asked me to keep it *entre nous*."

Silver streams of rain slid down the windows. Lost in thought, she searched for a detail that kept slipping away, eluding her.

"Don't keep me in suspense," said René. "A background check on who, Aimée?" Peeved, René prodded.

The thought she'd been trailing evaporated. She snapped back to the office. Sat down at her computer and pulled up a file.

"I did a background check on a Marcus Seghers from Lille. A dockworker."

"Let me see." René scooted his chair over to her desk, its wheels skittering on the parquet floor. He took a look at her screen. The booking photo wasn't kind; stringy hair framed the face of a man with a black eye, prominent nose, and strong jaw.

"He's Boris's sister's ex-husband," she said. "Out on parole. Easy to see why Boris wanted this off his coworkers' radar. A stickler for rules, he'd never think of abusing the police database like everyone else does."

"You mean this Marcus Seghers is a dangerous former felon?"

Aimée shrugged. "His sister had a restraining order placed on him."

"*Et voilà*, the bombing's solved; Seghers, the ex-brother-in-law bent on revenge, plants a bomb and attacks Boris since he can't get to his ex-wife."

She wished it were as neat and tidy as that. "That's stretching it, René. They told you they found Semtex under Boris's nails, right?"

René nodded.

"That bothers me. We need to talk to a lab scientist."

"Right now, his lawyer should be stonewalling until we do."

On the screen she pulled up the photos she'd downloaded. Started examining the clearer, un-pixelated shots of the crowd.

"Someone here in the crowd put that Action Directe newspaper article in my pocket. Bellan said it might be revenge."

"Revenge for what? How does that make sense?"

"It doesn't."

René leaned forward, scanning the photos. "It's random. Boris was in the wrong place at the wrong time, *évidemment*." He leaned back and sipped his herbal tea. "Us showing up there, also random. No one could have known in advance that we would be there."

"Agree." Aimée nodded. "Assuming it's true, if Action Directe are claiming responsibility, why do it by putting that article in my pocket?"

"Because you'd report it. It would go public."

"It didn't have to be me for that."

René's brows knit as he thought it over. "What if it was simply grabbing an opportunity?" He put his steaming cup down. "You spoke up at the crime scene. Your name's been in the paper. People know who you are, Aimée."

"I wouldn't say they know who I am."

"Know *of* you," René corrected. "You stood in the crowd and gave the police your name, said Boris was your friend. You demanded action. And thank God for that, or he could have lain there for hours. He might not have survived."

True. And it could be just that simple. She cataloged the possibility.

"But my father also investigated Action Directe's bombing of Interpol in eighty-six."

"*Attends*, hadn't he left the force before that?"

She nodded. Studied the leftover foam ringing her demitasse. "It was a private case, for an insurance company."

"*Et voilà.* It's a coincidence."

"Papa used to say there are no coincidences."

"Look, even though you can find the instructions and materials to make a bomb on the net," said René, "this type of attack requires organizing and access for execution. It doesn't happen on the fly. But our appearance at the site, that was a coincidence. Unplanned, agreed?"

She nodded again.

"Where's the proof your father investigated them?"

She gestured to the box under her desk. "I found the file. He did a simple skip trace on one of the security guards."

She remembered her father saying most criminals he dealt with were driven by greed, anger, and jealousy. Sometimes passion. Showed little impulse control and were reactive. Hotheads. Few were criminal masterminds; even in his long career, he'd only known two. Both were dead.

"Bellan hooked you line and sinker," said René, sighing.

"We've got clients and a calendar full of court work. It's not too late to get out of this."

But it was. She pulled out the contract she'd signed with counterterrorism.

René stared at it openmouthed. "Count me out. You're on your own."

Worried, she grabbed his hand. She needed him. "Don't say that. For this to work, I have to be able to count on you. Boris needs us. Being on the inside lets me know all the details of the investigation firsthand."

"Sounds convenient."

"We'll use their resources, René." She squeezed his hand. "Bellan's got access to more than I can find on my own. I'd be dogging him for information, but this works better."

René was half right. Bellan had played her. The difference, though, was being aware of what he was up to—and how she would use it to help Boris.

She let go of his hand. Opened her palm. On it she'd written a long algorithm with numbers, letters, and symbols.

"What's that?"

If anyone could crack this, it was René, a hacker extraordinaire.

"That's for you to find out. I copied it from the GIGN tech's screen at one of their safe houses."

René took in a long breath. But she could tell he saw her logic. "If I do, what's to say we can vindicate Boris?"

"We'll just have to find out."

RENÉ GOT TO work on the algorithm. Aimée studied the fifteen photographs of the crowd. Realized she'd been so caught up with finding Boris, she hadn't noticed the police photographer. Why hadn't she remembered the first rules of crime scene investigation at a fire or bombing location?

Survey the crowd. Photograph the bystanders.

The photographs, taken with a high-end Canon EOS D30 digital, held time stamps. After printing them out, she put them in chronological order and tacked them on their whiteboard. With a marker, she drew a time line. Then remembered to check René's video of Chloé's birthday party to ascertain what time Boris had left.

Half an hour later, René gave a low whistle. "I'm in. Thank God they're still behind on patching firewalls. That's the first thing counterterrorism should have done. Give me time to explore the architecture before I figure out how to sync this up with our systems and your computer."

"Genius, René."

By the time he'd joined her, she'd had another espresso. Her brain whirred. She rubbed her eyes, tired from examining the photos. They all blended together.

"Nothing jumps out at me," she said.

"Step back, Aimée."

She did.

"Look again."

Why had she thought she could find whoever dropped the paper in her pocket in that dark crush of people?

And then she saw the next best thing. Her pulse raced.

"Maybe someone else saw it," she said, pointing to the last photo showing windows in a building on rue de Dantzig. "Look, René. Here."

"I see what you're talking about." He'd gone back to his desk and clicked something on the keyboard.

"Can you pull up the tenant information for that building?"

"On it," he said.

A minute later the printer spit out several sheets.

"You're brilliant, René. Let's go. I'll drive."

Monday • Early Evening • Villa Santos-Dumont

HUGO NEEDED TO think, and his best thinking always happened over a cigarette. He beat it over to Alain's before the drunk popped up again. With the reporter a no-show, Hugo would have to edit out the peep show earlier than he'd planned. And Alain had access to his father's editing equipment.

Alain, small and frequently taunted as an *avorton*—the school runt—was on the fringes, like Hugo. They'd struck up a sort of friendship studying together on the astronomy project. Alain's family lived in the home once belonging to the iconic postwar singer Georges Brassens, after whom the neighborhood park was named. The house even had an exterior plaque displaying this information. A winter rose trellis climbed the rust-and-milk-colored brick facade with colorful mosaic tile inlays under the eaves. Best of all was a big garden in back where they could smoke.

"*Bonsoir*, Hugo," said Alain's mother, answering the door in a mist of perfume.

Long blonde hair, tight black leather skirt. Rumor had it she'd modeled for *Vogue*.

And she remembered his name. He pinched himself before he drooled or blurted out something stupid. He managed a nod.

"Alain's in the kitchen." She smiled. "Come in!"

He followed in the wake of her scent. So heady he missed a step down and stumbled. A warm, blue-tiled kitchen greeted him. Alain stood near the sink munching a tartine slathered with Nutella. Hugo's stomach growled.

Alain grinned, showing braces laced with the chocolaty hazelnut paste. "Problems with the telescope again?"

"You could say that." Hugo shot Alain a nervous look and wiggled his pinkie finger—their code for a cigarette break.

"You boys up to something again?" said Alain's father, coming into the kitchen. He winked at Hugo.

Hugo shuddered. The man was a bigwig producer at Radio France and thought he was funny.

The radio was tuned to a news station where a commentator droned about 9/11 and the supposed links to the Toulouse bombing.

"Conspiracy theories," said Alain's father, shaking his head. "If Al-Qaeda did blow up the plant in Toulouse, you think the government would tell us?"

Alain's mother turned to Hugo. "We thought about you and your family after the lab explosion. Everyone okay? Is your mother all right?"

Hugo almost melted at her concern. He struggled to answer in a normal voice. "We're fine, merci."

Alain's father tapped his expensive watch. "Don't forget, you've got a piano lesson in ten minutes, Alain."

"Oui, Papa." Alain opened the door to the garden. Jerked his thumb.

Alain pulled out his cigarette pack behind the azalea bushes. Offered one to Hugo. He scratched a match and lit them up.

Both paused, inhaling and exhaling blue smoke into the early evening air.

"Why didn't you come to school today?" Alain asked after a moment. "Sasha asked about you."

The smartest girl in the class had asked about him? Surprising that she knew he existed. But he couldn't think about that now.

"You can't tell anyone what I'm about to tell you. Promise, Alain?"

Alain nodded. He looked bored. "Course not."

"I mean it. Swear on your life."

"Quit the drama, Hugo."

Hugo perspired in the chill air. Puffed hard, sending smoke clouds into the azalea.

"Swear you'll tell no one. Even if the *flics* come."

Alain's eyes widened. "O—okay."

"I synced my telescope to the video camera—"

"Like you're supposed to," Alain interrupted. "Today, Madame Sisich asked me when we'd turn in our astronomy project."

On top of everything else!

"The lab on my street got bombed. The telescope's angle had slipped and the video was still on."

Alain grinned. "You mean on the naked lady?"

"*Non*, well, I mean yes, but—"

"What's the matter then? You need to show me."

Alain was no help. He'd have to spell it out. "I will, but we have to edit that out. Let me work on it while you're at your piano lesson."

"*Désolé*." Alain shrugged. "But the editing program on my father's computer is gone. His computer crashed."

"*Comment?*" Hugo asked in panic. "We need that program. Now we'll get in trouble."

Before he could ask more, Alain's father's voice rang out, "Alain, your piano teacher's here."

His father was walking toward them.

They stubbed out their cigarettes in the dirt and furiously waved away the smoke.

"Didn't we talk about this, Alain?" his father asked.

"Don't tell *Maman*, please."

"Pretend I'm not smelling what I'm smelling?" Alain's father shrugged. "But for the last time, boys. Your grandfather called, Hugo. He said you've got a visitor."

Visitor?

Hugo walked home, avoiding Parc Brassens, and hurried on shadowy rue des Morillons. His fingers tightened on the cassette tape in his pocket. Every step he took caused him to fall two steps back.

His grandfather had been running his mouth again. Hugo expected another loan-shark lowlife from Café de Dantzig. Or worse, Hugo had come to the attention of the *flics*.

The number 89 bus, like a brightly lit blue-green caterpillar, let passengers off on the corner. It would be so easy to jump on that bus and run.

Monday Evening • Rue de Dantzig

"Let me see your ID," said the woman in the doorway of the apartment on rue de Dantzig.

Aimée flashed the GIGN card Bellan had furnished her with. Handy and the legitimate entrée she needed. The middle-aged woman, wearing a frayed sweater under an apron, took her time inspecting it. Aimée glanced past the woman's shoulder down the small hallway lined with family photos alongside vases of stiff, artificial flowers. Jackets, scarves, and an umbrella hung on the coatrack. Every nook and cranny bulged with decorations and knickknacks, leaving not a spare space along the walls.

"There's nothing more to say," the woman said. "I told you people already: We were asleep. Saw nothing."

Time to get official sounding.

"Madame, as you know, last night, suspected terrorists bombed the police building across your street. We need your help to catch them and prevent another attack. We would like to see the view from your rooms facing rue de Dantzig."

"Where's your search warrant?"

Another one who watched too much *télé*.

"I appreciate you've been inconvenienced several times already, Madame," said Aimée, holding her ground. "Forgive our intrusion, but we need to see your apartment. Since 9/11, the Republic's gone into high alert and operates under anti-terrorist legislation with no search warrant required."

She hoped that was true.

"You've thrown private citizens' rights out the window, that it?" said the woman, bristling.

Also not the type to back down. She sounded angry, but Aimée detected fear, and perhaps more: the woman was hiding something.

"Are you refusing, Madame? I can wait and summon a search team."

The sound of radio news came from down the hallway.

"It's dinnertime. I'm busy. Come back tomorrow."

Tired of the woman stalling, Aimée pulled out her phone.

Heavy footsteps sounded in the hallway. An old man with a video camera hanging by a strap around his shoulder appeared, holding what looked like a long telescope.

Now Aimée understood. This was the telescope lens reflected in the window that showed in the photo. Of course. The old man had seen something.

"Monsieur, were you watching from your telescope last night?"

He shook his head. "Have the Germans attacked again?"

Worry shone in the woman's eyes. "*Non, beau-père.* Go to your room."

He was her father-in-law.

"Hugo took the tape," the old man said in a whine.

Aimée's gaze rooted on the video camera. Had the explosion somehow been filmed? "What tape, monsieur?"

"Hugo, my grandson, stole it from me," said the old man, clearly agitated.

"*Non, Grand-père,*" a trembling boy's voice said behind them. "We have to tell the truth."

THE RADIATOR GROWLED in the corner. Bellan sat by the hospital bed in the curtained bedroom. The bag of clear liquid morphine dripped via the IV needle taped into Johan's vein. Bellan knew he had little time left.

"Ready, Johan?"

The man gave a grunt of assent.

Bellan looked at the camera, knowing Georges was capturing this, and nodded. He hit the record button on his micro recorder. Never hurt to have a full confession at his fingertips.

"Johan, you were saying the last two members of Action Directe were alive. That you would have heard through the 'grapevine' if they weren't."

"Grapevine? I never said that."

Bellan bottled his frustration. "That's what you meant, non? You need to identify who you heard this from and how to contact them."

Johan's eyes fluttered.

"Johan, I need their names."

Johan sighed. His pale tongue tried to moisten his parched lips. From the table, Bellan took a Q-tip, dipped it in petroleum jelly, and dabbed it onto Johan's mouth.

"Better?"

Under pressure from above to find the Action Directe bomber

or bombers before they struck again, Bellan forced himself to remain calm. Coax the details out. Lives depended on it.

Not to mention his job.

Johan grunted. "I'm tired."

"We're almost done, Johan. Who's the contact?"

The monitor showing Johan's vitals beeped. A nurse appeared. "Blood pressure's falling."

"The name, Johan."

A long breath escaped him. "Promise . . . promise me you'll tell Coco I tried . . ."

"Where's Coco?"

The beeping on the monitor got louder. Johan's eyes wandered. "Her funny little house, Labrador."

What did that mean? A dog?

"Talk to me," Bellan said. "Come on, Johan. We made a deal."

The beeping went to a steady hum.

The nurse grabbed the paddles and delivered an electric shock. Then another. After a few minutes and no response, she called it.

"He's flatlined. No pulse."

Johan had come so close, and still Bellan had gotten nothing. He'd kept his end of the deal, but Johan hadn't. Couldn't.

Poor old *mec*, he'd surrendered too late. But there was something in Johan's last words.

Coco. I tried. Her funny little house. Labrador.

Bellan searched his memory. Came up blank. He'd spent hours reading Johan's file. Now he'd have to comb through it again, dissect every detail.

His phone beeped. Georges from the communication center in the convent.

"Don't tell me," Bellan said. "Too late, I know."

Any moment, Tingry would call and read him the riot act; going over budget to cater to the old terrorist and gaining nothing.

Georges cleared his throat. "Yes and no."

Bellan felt a stir of hope.

"Meaning?"

"I've digitized Johan Selles's file. I could do a word search and see what comes up."

"What are you waiting for? Try 'Coco,' 'house,' 'Labrador.'"

The nurse unplugged the machine, removed the tubes from Johan's lifeless tattooed arm. Bellan's eye caught on the design, faded but distinct, embellished with roses. It spelled Coco.

He punched in Georges's number.

"Still looking, Bellan."

"Can you open the physical file? There's a list of the women he's been involved with. Start at the beginning."

Anxious, he waited while papers rustled on the other end.

"There's a Catherine Roussel, interviewed in 1989," said Georges. "A person of interest. She admitted to a former relationship with Selles. Cleared of any ties to Action Directe."

"Does she have a nickname? Was she called by something else?"

More rustling of pages.

"Not that I see in the file."

"What's her address?"

"In 1989?"

"Now. Look her up. Hurry."

A minute later Georges came back on. "The same as in 1989. Twenty-four Impasse du Labrador."

Labrador.

Bellan breathed in. This could be it. Anxiety knotted his throat. Every hair on his neck rose.

"I'm calling a code three. Have backup meet me . . ." He tried to picture where that would be. "What's the cross street?"

"Rue Camulogène," said Georges. He paused. "It's right across the park from the police lab on Parc Brassens. Not far from Porte de Versailles."

What if Action Directe had holed up there? Cooked up another bomb? He imagined the quartier in flames, buildings blown up, children crying.

The bodies.

Following protocol, Bellan left a message for his boss and reported to Berliot, chief of the *démineur* squad, requesting their presence at Impasse du Labrador.

"What you've got is a little thin, Bellan," said Berliot. "I watched the feed. Ever see Orson Welles in *Citizen Kane*? Rosebud?"

Thin was what he had, but as a *flic* he'd learned to pull these threads. Nine out of ten times it was just that one detail that led to the whole thing unraveling.

"Understood, sir," he said. "Didn't know you were a cinephile."

"That film's a classic, Bellan."

"Worst-case scenario, sir, if we don't prepare, it could blow up in our faces. Literally."

"Always a risk." Pause. "Find Action Directe's link to our suspect Boris Viard. Not only did the Lyon lab trace the explosive to him, he had opportunity and access to the area."

"True, sir, but then why would he have been injured?"

"Tell me, was Boris Viard a bomb expert? *Non.* The ones who think they know what they're doing are usually the ones to blow themselves up."

This caught him in his tracks. He detected pullback. Was this Berliot under pressure from above to end this and nail Viard?

Meanwhile, his own boss, Tingry, wanted proof Action Directe was linked to the lab bombing.

"Can't argue with that, sir, but if Action Directe links to Viard, it's a risk we need to cover."

"For now, I'll put the *démineurs* on standby alert."

Better than nothing.

BELLAN TOOK HIS armored vest from the car trunk and put it on under his leather jacket. A tight fit. The matchbook-sized, glazed-ceramic crossed fingers made by his son in art class rested in his pocket, as always—a talisman to accompany him as he walked into the unknown.

His backup team stood in the shadows, where two narrow streets angled in a V. The team wore black outfits, helmets, and night-vision goggles. Uzis draped across their chests. He motioned to their commander, who nodded and signaled to his men. They moved soundlessly behind him.

Old, whitewashed walls, peeling to reveal stone, lined the narrow Impasse du Labrador. A dead end. Bellan didn't like dead ends unless he was the one controlling them.

Adrenaline coursed through him. He'd been terrible at analytics on the ministry desk job. Being operational was when he felt most alive.

Once a *flic*, always a *flic*.

When his ex-wife finally realized he'd never change, the marriage had ended. But he missed his children. He fought a hard road back to be a part of their lives. Best thing that ever happened to him. He'd learned ways to cope with his guilt and loved his boy to bits.

A toffee-colored cat slunk across the street. Hissed, then ignored them.

His breath frosted in the air. Ivy spilled over the impasse walls, enclosing small gardens. Skeletal trees fretted the moonlight shadows on the uneven cobblestones. Still like the village it had been with two- and three-story houses in a maze of lanes abutting the long-gone fortified wall and Porte de Versailles' toll gate, dismantled in the twenties. Beyond it lay the heliport, a military helicopter on standby.

The intermittent streetlights cast a yellow sodium glow, illuminating the odd fence. One of the men would be videoing their progress and the license plates of the few parked cars. Standard procedure. They'd run the plates at HQ and send any flagged car registrations immediately. If Bellan found evidence of explosives, the chopper would be winging here within seconds.

Bellan put his palm up, signaling to stop. Peering through the red metal bars of the gate to number 24, Bellan viewed a garden covered in brown leaves. Set back lay a little white house with a red door, straight out of a fairy tale. *Charmant.*

Lights shone in the windows. He searched for vehicles, a garage or shed. Saw only a bicycle near the door.

The team knew what to do. Within minutes they'd unlocked the gate with a key drill, spread out, and kept to the edges of the garden with two men circling to the rear.

If Action Directe members holed up here, the team would arrest or neutralize them. He waited until all units were in place and one man with an Uzi flanked him at the door, covering him. He counted down, *three . . . two . . . one.*

Then knocked.

A woman wearing a purple kimono held a wine glass as she opened the door laughing, her red hair wild and frizzy. "Did you forget something again?"

Her eyes widened at Bellan's pistol. The wine glass dropped and shattered on the floor.

"Johan's dead, Coco."

Monday, • 9 P.M. • *Rue de Dantzig*

AIMÉE SET DOWN the china *tasse* of lukewarm tea on a table in Madame Dombasle's small salon. On the walls were paintings of the saints and a cross. René sat on a sagging couch and she on a stiff-backed chair that bit into her spine.

Hugo, Madame's son, cast his eyes down as he recounted what he'd seen and how he'd mistakenly left his video camera on.

"I meant to tell the *flics*. I wanted to. But *Grand-père* got involved."

She sensed Hugo still wasn't telling them everything.

"Hugo, I think there's more to it than that," Aimée said. "Please look at me."

He looked up, batting his eyelids in fear.

"For now I'm only interested in the footage on the tape, okay?" Thank God Madame Dombasle had left to deal with her agitated father-in-law.

"Please, I don't want to go to prison," Hugo said.

She debated telling him the penalties for withholding information about terrorists. But he was only sixteen. Right now, he looked like the scared overgrown child he was.

"It's good you're cooperating," she said. Smiled. "That's important. And important that you tell me everything so I can help you."

René had brought his laptop from the car and hooked the video camera feed onto his screen.

"Ready?" René played the video. The video caught a woman undressing in the window.

"Who's that?" Aimée said.

Tears dripped down Hugo's red cheeks.

"Maman said I'd go to hell if the priest knew. The telescope's only supposed to be used for my astronomy report."

"We don't care about that," she said. "We want to catch the man you think might have set a bomb, a bomb that's put someone in the hospital fighting for his life."

Hugo wiped his cheeks. Nodded. "I watch her sometimes. She lives at La Ruche. But they'll jail me for being a voyeur."

Aimée doubted this woman was the only one Hugo watched.

"Look, that can be wiped. All traces gone."

"*Vraiment?*"

"René's a genius at this. He'll even match up the time stamps."

René shot her a dirty look.

"We need you to tell the truth, Hugo. What's important is catching a terrorist. You could be a hero."

Hugo brightened.

René fast-forwarded the tape to 11:55 p.m. "About here?"

"That's him. See. There."

"Pause it, René."

He hit pause. A dark figure wearing black clothing froze at the door of the police laboratory.

"Now slo-mo," she said.

Shooting flames, a crack of thunder. Then the figure was running. The toe caps of his shoes caught the light. His head was down.

"But there were two explosions," said Hugo. "The first one woke me up. I looked out the window and saw him. Then we heard another and left the apartment."

So Feroze had been telling the truth about the second bomb.

Aimée kicked herself for not already getting Bellan to cough up those details.

In the meantime, she'd need to dissect this frame by frame.

"Okay, let's rewind and look for Boris."

René did. Now that they were looking, he was easy to find. She spotted the taxi, Boris hopping out. A streetlight illuminated his face, no fear or worry visible. Her eyes brimmed with tears. Stupid. She couldn't get emotional now.

Hugo's window overlooked rue de Danzig.

"Do you recognize the people who work across the street?" she asked him. "I mean, do you know them well enough to say hello at a café?"

Hugo nodded.

She pointed to Boris. "Do you know him, Hugo?"

"Not really *know* him, but he's on the badminton team at the gym."

Boris and badminton? "How's that?"

"It was our coach's idea. Kids team versus the police lab."

René was shaking his head. "It will be more efficient to use my equipment and editing program at the office."

True. An all-nighter ahead of them. Good thing Chloé was in Brittany.

She felt guilty at the thought. Had forgotten to call Melac and now it was too late.

René unhooked the video camera while Aimée went with Hugo to his room. He set up the telescope so she could survey his view. Next she searched for her Moleskine, but remembered Bellan had it. She found an old to-do list on an envelope and used the other side. Hugo gave her a running commentary as she sketched the scene on it. Later she'd fill in the sketch with Hugo's observations.

"Hugo, we're going to edit out the first part of the tape. But you need to trust me. Is there something else?"

"Are you going to tell the *flics* where the video came from?"

She shrugged. "I doubt it. Let me work on that, okay?"

He was still holding back.

"That man Boris, the one we saw in the video, he's fighting for his life in a coma. Yet the *flics* are treating him as a suspect. Talk to me, Hugo."

He blinked rapidly. Frightened. "Maybe it's nothing."

"Go ahead."

"It's what the old drunk said today in the park. I was waiting for a reporter who never showed up."

"Reporter?"

"A reporter from *Le Parisien*. I was going to show him the video."

He'd show this to the media before the *flics*? Aimée stuffed down anger. She needed this kid to spill.

"Why tell him? Was the reporter going to pay you?"

Hugo slammed down his fist on the desk. A box of paper clips rattled. "*Non*, I'm not like that drunk or *Grand-père*."

"Wait . . . your grandfather wanted to sell the tape?"

Hugo explained his grandfather wanted a new leg, one of the lightweight ones, but insurance wouldn't cover it. He'd supposedly recognized Paul in the video running away before the bombs exploded. In essence, his plan was to "expose" Paul unless he coughed up.

Blackmail.

Aimée remembered Bellan's druggie informer in the quartier was also named Paul—could they be the same?

"You mean Paul Sénéchal?"

"No idea."

She filed this away for later. Everything would be important.

"But that didn't happen, *non*? What did the drunk say that bothered you? Did he see something?"

Hugo blinked again. Frightened out of his skin.

"We call the drunk Bird Man because he's a disgusting idiot," said Hugo. "He kills the ducks in the pond. Eats them."

Disgusting all right. "Go on, Hugo."

"Bird Man said the homeless *mec* who slept in the lab got blown up because he saw the suicide in the park."

"A suicide? When?"

Hugo shrugged. "A few weeks ago?"

"What's the connection?" she said.

"The Bird Man said it wasn't a suicide."

IN THE CHILL night air, Aimée followed René up rue de Dantzig past the bulldozers parked behind the yellow tape. As she passed the rubble, she couldn't help picturing Boris on the videotape. Her phone vibrated in her pocket. Bellan's name flashed.

"Where are you now?"

Her shoulders ached with tiredness. "Near Parc Brassens, about to go back to the office," she said.

"Good, you're close."

"I have to show you something," said Aimée. "But it won't be ready until tomorrow."

"Put that on hold. Meet me at twenty-four Impasse du Labrador. Walk by the park. Hurry."

Click. He'd hung up.

What now?

She caught up to René. At the car, she looked on the map. It was close. Crazy to drive with all the one-way streets.

"Can you start editing the tape without me, René?" She pulled her gloves from her pocket.

"And where will you be?"

"That was Bellan."

"So you're at his beck and call," said René, his voice tight. Angry. "Even at this hour of the night?"

Basically true. But she didn't want to explain. Didn't even know why he wanted her there.

Still, she had to mollify René, have him get this valuable tape to the office, make a copy and start editing.

"Right now, Bellan's my only in to Boris."

"You believe that? Get real, he's hooked you in. He's just using you."

"And I'm using him back, René. You know that."

This was the worst time to argue, standing on a cold street corner, stressed over Boris. She should be processing what Hugo had told her. Studying the videotape.

"We've got to analyze that tape. I'll come as soon as I can."

René pulled his goatee. "Let me drive you."

"It's just over there. See?" She pointed to the lights visible through the trees. "Get a head start on the tape, okay? I'll taxi to the office."

"What did the boy cough up when you talked to him afterward?"

Suddenly, the *thupt-thupt-thupt* of a helicopter reverberated overhead. Closer and closer. The unmistakable dark-blue and silver-striped body of a Ministry of Defense helicopter.

It headed toward the bright lights shining up in the sky beyond the park.

Her gut told her something was coming down.

"Tell you later," she called over her shoulder before breaking into a run.

Monday • 10:30 P.M. • *la Petite Ceinture*

BIRD MAN'S HAND quivered. He held the spruce branch with the pigeon he'd skewered over the flickering flame. His other hand clutched a bottle of Napoléon cognac. Excellent.

He'd drunk half the bottle. Now queasy, his stomach churned. Maybe the cognac was a little rich for him.

Running into that tubby kid had turned into luck for him. Not only had he caught the pigeon—though he'd wanted the mallard in the pond—but he'd also found the bottle of cognac on the tracks. Only an idiot would have left it lying there.

His vision blurred. Premier cognac all right. He'd kept it hidden from the others in the tunnel. A superstitious bunch who never minded the bats but avoided this spot where the poor girl fell.

He guzzled more cognac, felt his gut wrench. He needed to eat, that was all. His comrades in the desert hadn't called him Iron Stomach for nothing. Him, he'd fought in Algeria, a hellscape where a comrade fell and you took his gun and fired the next shot. Moved on with the unit. In battle no one cried in front of others.

The other tunnel-dwellers had left flowers as a memorial where the girl had died. Not a suicide, according to Noiro. Bird Man had kept his mouth shut, except for blabbing to *bouboule*. But that wouldn't happen again. He knew how to keep quiet.

His insides were seizing up. Gasping and choking, he tried to breathe. Wracked by pain, he dropped the pigeon into the fire.

The cognac fell in the weeds. Everything around him clouded, went black.

The pigeon's feathers flamed as the carcass burned black, emitting a stench into the night air. A man stepped out of the bushes. With gloved hands, he picked up the cognac bottle. A moment later he was gone.

AIMÉE DOUBLE-KNOTTED HER scarf against the chill. Her breath fogged in the darkness. Leaves crackled and caught on her ankles. She hurried along the damp street, which crested the dark park below. On her left a chain-link fence bordered the steep embankment to la Petite Ceinture and the park. To her right loomed one of the other apartment buildings Hugo spied on with his telescope.

Her gaze caught on several limp floral bouquets, grouped like a memorial, tied to the chain-link fence. A *Résistance* memorial from the war? There were so many in the quartier.

On closer view she saw a plastic folder encasing a photo of a young, smiling woman, the name Delphine Latour written inside a red heart. In the photo Delphine wore glasses and a ponytail, and her arm was in a cast. Aimée remembered the suicide Hugo had mentioned. The suicide that wasn't a suicide, according to Bird Man.

Tragic.

She saw the helicopter hovering beyond the park over what had to be Impasse du Labrador. She broke into a run again. She was late.

A dog was barking. She thought about Miles Davis with a twinge of guilt.

Pounding footsteps followed her. Something was nipping at

her ankles. She tripped and fell, sprawling in the bushes. Yelped in pain.

She rolled on her back and saw the stars swim above. A figure loomed over her.

"WHAT DID THAT old fool Johan say?" Coco asked.

"He called you the grapevine," lied Bellan.

Coco shook her head. Downed the last bit of red wine in her second glass. Her bloodshot eyes spoke to several drinks already. "Only my friends call me that."

A kerosene heater sputtered in Coco's cluttered kitchen, emitting dry heat. Bellan perspired under the weight of his jacket and armored vest.

Two team members entered the living room behind her. One made the all-clear signal. The other held a poster for Action Directe. Coco turned and shook her head.

"Not this again," she said. "Leave me alone."

"We found canisters of kerosene, gasoline, and other unidentified liquids," one of the men said, pointing to the cellar door.

"Where's your search warrant?" Coco asked.

There were no search warrants in France but he wasn't going to waste time and explain.

"9/11's changed that," said Bellan. He turned to his team. "Get them analyzed."

"For God's sake, get real," she said. "The kerosene's for my heater, and the gas is for my old moped."

"That the wine talking, Coco? There's only a bicycle here."

"My moped's in the shop. Always in the shop. What's with

you? I'm not cooking bombs. Or dope." She sighed and looked to the ceiling. "I need more wine."

In the kitchen, she uncorked a half-full bottle of Beaujolais Nouveau. Poured herself a glass. "I'd offer you a glass, but I didn't invite you in."

Not that Bellan would drink that rotgut. Coco was passive-aggressive, not a sloppy drunk. He put her down as a functional alcoholic.

"Two wanted terrorists have gone active again." Bellan gestured to the Action Directe member photos he'd put on her kitchen table. Pulled a chair out for her to sit down. He moved away from the blast of heat. "Tell me about these two, Anna Soulages and Nicolas Pantin." The photos from the original wanted poster were placed beside age progressions of how they would look today. "*Dites-moi*, how do you contact them?"

"Contact them? I haven't heard from Anna in ages. Wait, she sent a postcard from Morocco a while back. It's on the fridge."

Bellan put on gloves, removed the postcard and turned it over. *Having a great time, miss you!* he read.

"Code for something, Coco?"

"What do you think?"

Bellan slid it into a clear plastic evidence bag.

"When did you last have contact with her?"

"Contact? Years ago. She's my cousin. But you know that."

He should have known that. It would have been in her file. But in the rush of the operation, he hadn't had the time to read it. He was playing catch-up. Hated it.

"She's sent postcards from places around the world. That's how I figure she's alive. But that postcard came two years ago."

"Where's Nicolas Pantin?"

Coco shrugged. "They're a couple. Or were. No clue."

"You answered the door saying, 'Did you forget something again?' Who did you think it was?"

"Not you. Or any of these monkeys tearing my place apart."

"I need an answer."

"Veronika, from next door. We'd had drinks and—"

Bellan motioned to one of the crime team. "Check that out."

"Look, you tore my house apart in 1989. There's nothing left of Action Directe here but an old flyer I forgot about. Why do it again?"

"Action Directe claimed responsibility for bombing the police lab. Don't tell me you didn't hear it last night."

"Hear it? It would have to have been nuclear, since I was in Marseilles. Got back this afternoon. Check my train ticket, it's in my bag."

A prepared alibi.

Her kimono sleeve showed wine spots. Underneath she wore a black camisole and paint-spattered jeans. He figured her for forty, give or take. Not in bad shape, but the empty wine bottles in the bin said more.

"I'm a graphic artist," she said, noticing his gaze. "I work in my studio except when I visit clients in the south."

He'd check that himself. Meanwhile, inside her studio, a glass-windowed sun porch with a white-painted wooden floor, he saw a rectangular worktable with an open sketch pad. He glanced at the sketches: scenes of spidery olive trees, pines bent in the wind off a rocky promontory framing an aquamarine spread of sea. He could almost smell the salt, feel the wind. Striking and recognizable as the Mediterranean. All done with vivid, economical strokes of color.

Talented, he thought. Above the worktable ranged neat shelves of old sugar tins holding calligraphy pens, colored markers and pencils, watercolor sets, brushes and paint tubes from Sennelier, the century-old art store on the Left Bank. He reached for a folder,

which revealed work orders from Savon de Marseille, known for
its iconic olive oil soap, and a menu design for a Michelin-starred
seafood bistro along the Corniche.

Her tools of the trade rang a bell. What was it?

Still wearing his gloves, Bellan picked up a marker, sniffed it.
Did the same with a calligraphy pen.

Now it made sense. He'd found the thread.

Back in the hot kitchen he spoke to an arriving crime tech.
"Take the calligraphy pens and markers in evidence," he said.
"Put them on the next police dispatch to Lyon. Priority."

"What the hell?" Coco reached for her cigarettes. Her hand
trembled as she flicked a pink Bic lighter. She took a long draw—
long enough to make the burning paper crackle. She exhaled a
plume of smoke. "I need my materials to work."

"Everything will be returned to you," he said. Took an ashtray from the counter, set it on the table. Tempted to join her in
a smoke, but he held back. Plenty of time post-interview. He'd
relish it.

"You left your cousin, Anna, a key, *comme d'habitude, non?*
She'd stay here while you went on work trips."

One of the crime techs lifted up a rock so Bellan could see.

Ash dropped on the table. Bellan pushed the ashtray closer to
her. "You left her a key in that fake rock. Silly, the first place a
burglar looks."

"That's for my neighbor. And you're crazy. It's been two years
since Anna was in touch." She stabbed the half-smoked cigarette
out in the ashtray. "Why does all this old garbage matter now? It's
old news. Anna played at politics, radicalizing because it was cool.
It was a fad."

But it was more than that. Action Directe had bombed and
murdered. Anna Soulages was a fugitive terrorist, high on the
wanted list.

"Knowing my cousin, she got tired of it. And then she couldn't come back. An exile."

There was pity in Coco's tone. As if Anna deserved forgiveness for her youthful folly and mistakes. As if she shouldn't pay for her crimes.

"Johan didn't think she was in exile anymore."

Coco sighed. "Another one. All political big talk. You know"—she took a sip of wine—"once he was rock-star pretty. A brooding rebel. I fell for him big when I was sixteen. Lasted until he got sucked into the ugly side."

"Ugly like gunrunning, bombings, and robbing banks to fund their sprees?"

"Rob banks, no way. Why?"

Her question threw Bellan. Interested, he leaned closer, centered his focus.

"Answer your own question."

"The idiots were funded. They used to buy cases and cases of champagne. Or didn't that come up in your reports?"

Intelligence had never been able to pin down who funded them. Or gather enough information for arrests.

"Right now, it looks better if you cooperate."

"If I do, you'll help me out?" Her voice came out pleading.

"I'll do my best." The stock answer.

She downed her wine, considering this. "There was a shop on rue des Entrepreneurs," she said at last. "Johan picked up packages there, or Anna did. That's what I heard. At night it would be champagne. Party time."

Rue des Entrepreneurs had a strip of Iranian shops and restaurants known as Téhéran-sur-Seine. The area had been home to Iranian exiles before and after the Shah's downfall. Later, dissidents targeted by the Islamic Revolutionary Guard moved there as well.

Still rankling in the ministry was the embarrassment of the

Shah of Iran's former prime minister, Shapour Bakhtiar, having been murdered while under French protection. Bakhtiar had been the exiled moderate's hope to bring about a secular Iran. Well respected in French diplomatic circles, he worked tirelessly to negotiate with the ayatollah's government. In 1991, under guard, outside Paris at his home, Bakhtiar's throat was slit and his secretary stabbed to death. The investigating magistrate uncovered an extensive network that had helped the assassins carry out the murder and escape from France using forged passports. A trail was suspected to lead to Hezbollah, whom allegedly Department 15— the Iranian government's enforcer arm—had contracted for proxy kidnappings and murder. MOIS?

Another well-funded operation. They'd never been caught. Bellan's boss, Tingry, then a junior officer on the team, had suffered the fallout. His career had stalled, and he'd nursed a years-long campaign—still ongoing—to find the Iranian culprits.

"Which shop on rue des Entrepreneurs?" Bellan asked now.

"Next to a bead shop. It's the one famous for good halvah. But that was years ago." She paused, eyed him. "That's all I know."

Bellan stared at her. Her red lipstick bled into the fine lines around her mouth. Her hennaed hair was darker at the roots. An artist on the radical fringes, always close to the fire.

"Would you turn in your cousin?"

"Why should I? That's her job—don't put it on me. Like I told Johan, give yourself up."

"What? When did you tell him that?"

Coco thought about it. "Last week."

Only now she was telling him this?

"You said you were in Marseilles."

"Before I left, he called out of the blue. Didn't sound well. He was in Paris. I agreed to meet him at a café. But before I could, he appeared at my door."

Bellan read people. Old Leduc, his former mentor, always said go with your gut when reading body language; pick up on the tells, the inconsistencies, the sweat on their palms. This Coco kept him guessing.

"*Ecoutez*, Johan and I talked sometimes, but it was more than fifteen years since I'd last seen him face-to-face. He was a wreck, ravaged and weak. Still, after all this time he wanted my help. He'd been my first boyfriend, but the gall he had, demanding I nurse him. I let him stay one night on condition he leave and turn himself in."

That, Bellan believed.

"End of story."

That, he didn't.

Bellan's boss, Tingry, had stood listening at the kitchen door. Shot him a glance that meant one thing: time to haul her in.

And where the hell was Aimée Leduc?

Aimée struggled, turning away from the hot breath and wet tongue licking her face. Her eyelashes stuck together, blurring her vision. Was that . . . ?

"*Arrête!*"

She felt a hand grab hers. Pulled and lifted her up. She shoved down the metallic taste in her mouth.

"I'm so sorry. He got away from his leash. Sit, Sami. Bad dog."

The old basset hound sat. Whined as if in apology and pawed the ground. His drooping ears and sad eyes made it impossible to be angry with him.

"We meet again, monsieur." She accepted the man's proffered handkerchief and wiped her face. Hoped the dog hadn't licked his own private parts before slobbering on her.

"*Mon Dieu*, I'm so sorry." Regret shone in his eyes. "Are you hurt?"

No skin broken. "I tripped. I'm fine."

"But he nipped at you. Forgive me, he's out of sorts. Crazy since the explosion."

She remembered Sami and this man, a professor type wearing a wool cardigan, whom she'd run into after she left the hospital. Lived in the quartier, he'd said.

"Can I offer you a coffee, a place to clean up?"

The bright lights from the direction of impasse du Labrador

glowed through the branches. This man might have seen or noticed something. But she didn't have time to talk.

"*Merci*, but I'm late. Let's have that coffee and talk tomorrow. Here's my card."

She took off.

AIMÉE HAD FLASHED her GIGN card multiple times to various *flics* on the scene but she still hadn't caught a glimpse of Bellan. Crews searched the garden of a dollhouse-like white maisonette, and a woman was being escorted out of the red front door. The house and garden were lit up like a rave gone wrong.

The hovering helicopter whipped up damp leaves and gravel. Deafening. She shielded her face with her scarf.

Her phone beeped. She answered.

"Where are you?" Bellan shouted.

"Right here."

One of the men accompanying the arrested woman turned. Bellan.

He clicked off. Muttered something and joined her, taking shelter from the updraft behind a tree.

"Did I miss the party?"

"Recognize her?" He pointed to a woman with red hair, a wool coat over what looked like a purple kimono.

"Should I?" she asked.

"Did you see her in the crowd? Maybe she slipped the newspaper in your pocket?"

"Her, I'd remember. Why?"

Bellan passed her a wanted bulletin with photos. A "then and now" with photos of a woman—not the one she'd just seen, though they shared some features.

She wanted to study this, but the noise and buffeting grit dust made it difficult. "Not sure."

"This woman's her cousin. We're treating her home as a possible hideout for terrorists. An explosives manufacturing site."

Her hopes rose.

"Is this Action Directe? Then you're clearing Boris Viard off the suspect list?"

"I didn't say that."

"What are you saying, then?" she said, raising her voice above the insistent *thupt, thupt, thupt* of the helicopter propellers.

"Doesn't look good for him."

A man was gesturing for Bellan.

"Study these photos. Get back to me."

Frowning, Aimée started down Impasse du Labrador past rundown two-story houses. Years of neglect had nibbled away at their roof tiles, peeled away the paint, and weathered the shutters.

Ahead she saw traffic. She found a taxi on rue Brancion letting off an elderly couple. Reined in her impatience while the man paid. Jumped in.

"Extra if you get me to rue du Louvre in fifteen minutes."

The driver, a middle-aged man wearing a wool cap, nodded. "In a hurry?"

"You could say that."

He ground into first gear and shot down the dark street. A man after her own heart.

She punched in René's number.

"I'm en route, René. Any luck?"

She heard him suck in his breath.

"Not on the phone." He clicked off.

If René answered that way, it meant someone was in their office or the line was tapped.

Not good.

All the way, the evening played in her head: Hugo's tape, Delphine, the suicide that apparently wasn't a suicide, the slobbering dog, the woman in the purple kimono, and the armed team response at the light show. Whatever trail Bellan was following, it was moving fast. Too fast to get things right.

AIMÉE TAPPED IN the office door alarm code, one hand gripping her Swiss Army knife. Ready in her pocket was a portable jammer to scramble hidden microphone transmission and another to detect wiretapping on their landline. She wished her Beretta weren't sitting in her desk drawer.

René sat at his desk, the lamp illuminating the three screens. One ran a continuous feed of Hugo's tape. Shadows filled the office.

"René?" she whispered. "You all right?"

He swiveled his chair. Jerked his thumb. "He's not."

She hit the light switch and spun, knife raised.

Morbier, her godfather, was sprawled on the recamier, a pack of frozen *petits pois* held to his temple. His jaw swollen.

She expelled air.

"*Putain*, you scared me to death. What's going on here, Morbier?"

"Your partner found me."

She snorted in disgust. "Fighting at your age?"

"Put the knife away and sit down, Leduc."

She'd let him down once already. Guilt and anger rose up, but she pushed down those childish feelings he always elicited in her.

She pulled out the portable jammers. "Do we need to use these, René?"

He shook his head. "I swept the office and phones two hours ago. Clean."

Satisfied, she slid them in her desk drawer. Flicked the knife blade back.

"Bar brawling, Morbier? A woman?"

He sighed. "Much as I'd like that to be true"—he grunted and sat up—"and I'm flattered you think it might be—there was a welcoming committee at your elevator."

"What?"

"He wouldn't let me call the *flics*," said René, unhappy. "Or a doctor."

"No need. I'm fine."

"Someone attacked you and we shouldn't notify the *flics*? But that's not safe."

"Don't worry, I made a call. Your building's safe."

"Just like that?"

She shook her head. Exhausted, she wanted to go home and curl up. But with an attacker on the loose, her cold, empty apartment didn't seem like a good idea.

"You made a call, Morbier? To whom?"

"I've still got friends in the force, Leduc. It's taken care of. Surveillance 24-7."

The old brotherhood again. Where had that been when her father had needed it?

Morbier blinked and rubbed his swelling jaw. "But they weren't waiting for me."

"How do you know?"

"Came up from behind. Last thing I remember is someone saying, 'Where is she?'"

She shuddered. Who'd target her?

Things were spiraling out of her control. Right now, she just had to make sense of what had happened in the video. Secretly relieved Morbier had called in surveillance, she'd shelve this for later.

"You never come here, Morbier. Why the surprise visit?" He'd hung up on her during their last phone conversation.

"You shouldn't be doing whatever you're doing, Leduc. Someone's after you, and you've got Chloé to think of."

She hoped the first part wasn't true.

"GIGN made me an offer I couldn't refuse, Morbier."

He set down the bag of *petits pois* and ran his fingers through his hair. "No wonder my hair's gone white. Make me some tea, Leduc."

Tea? Normally a whiskey drinker. This really must have shaken him.

After she made tea, she handed him Doliprane tablets from her bag. "*Tiens*, pop these."

She kicked the radiator. Twice. Heard an answering rumble and hiss as it came to life. She slid off her boots, grabbed one of Chloé's wool blankets, and draped it around Morbier.

"Start at the beginning, Morbier. What happened?"

"I'd like to know, too." René shook his head. "You haven't told me a thing. You're lucky I heard the elevator alarm and found you before things got worse."

"Didn't you ask me to check on Boris Viard's legal representation, René?" said Morbier. "That's what I've been doing. Came here to tell you, and . . . *bon*, never saw it coming. I'm getting rusty."

"Who's Viard's attorney?" Aimée asked.

"Poincaire. He's good, they say. Respected. Hasn't returned my calls."

"That's what you came to tell us? What about Boris's condition?"

"No change as of an hour ago. He's still in an induced coma, according to Michou. His surgery's on hold until the swelling in his brain subsides."

"What else, Morbier?" She could tell he was holding back.

"Got any biscuits, Leduc?"

This was Morbier's way of drawing things out. He'd reveal in his own time, as usual. And it would cost her.

She brought out a packet of MarieLu, Chloé's favorite butter biscuit, and passed him several.

"Let's watch this video René's working on," said Morbier.

That's why he'd come here, the old fox, to glean their information. He'd gotten beat up for his effort. Or had it been to warn her to stay out of trouble? She'd known him since birth and still couldn't figure him out.

René swiveled back in his chair. "Movie night without the popcorn. I've copied Hugo Dombasle's original two-hour videotape. As boring to us as it is titillating to a sixteen-year-old. Then edited a second copy down to an hour. From that, I've refined a third copy to about thirty relevant minutes. I kept the original time stamps at each relevant segment to provide a timeline."

René, always meticulous, had surpassed himself.

He projected the videotape on the white wall.

"The best way is to watch this backward from the explosion. Self-explanatory as I run it, but you'll know who to watch for that way."

She hadn't savored going back to a cold, empty apartment. Now, hunkered in the office, a warm cocoon with Morbier and René, she felt safe and relaxed for the first time in . . . well, a long time. They could watch the video, bounce ideas off each other. She might even get along with Morbier for once.

They passed the biscuits back and forth. The edit had done little to illuminate the shadows in the video. An explosion blew up the building, a figure ran, and before that, another explosion. The figure handed Noiro a bag.

"Pause it, René," she said. "So two explosions. This figure

might have handed Noiro a bag containing explosives. Hugo's grandfather named the figure as Paul. I met a Paul Sénéchal, Bellan's informer. Had tracks on his arm."

"A druggie informer?" asked René.

"So they're scraping the bottom of the barrel," said Morbier. "Maybe this Paul is Noiro's drug connection."

René hit play. Alarms sounded next door, and the *démineurs* and police responded quickly. Boris exited a taxi and went inside the doors.

"Boris never comes out," said Morbier.

"Except on a stretcher," said Aimée. "Theoretically, could he have set a bomb in that time?"

"The prosecutor will argue he'd set the bomb up already and only activated it then," said Morbier.

"Then how did he get hurt?"

"Easy. Amateurs blow themselves up all the time. The prosecutor will pull out statistics."

They watched more. At 5:30, workers left. Drunken sports fans spilled onto the pavement from the café, and amidst them a figure broke off, a car passed, blocking the view, and then a bus. Then a figure was at the lab door for a second before entering. Twenty minutes later the figure left, weaving in the shadows down the street.

René paused the tape. "Thoughts?"

"He's my number-one candidate for the bomber," said Morbier, brushing crumbs off his sleeve.

"Sure it's a he?"

Aimée pulled out the photos from Bellan: the crowd scenes on rue de Dantzig post-explosion, the wanted poster for Action Directe member Anna Soulages—the original and the age-progression image rendered by a police artist. René got out his magnifying glass to study them.

Something about Anna Soulages was familiar. Aimée searched her memory.

"That's it," she said. "I remember her now. These WANTED posters were everywhere—the post office, Métro. I'd see them on the way to school. But the terrorists evaporated like a whiff of smoke."

"Our investigation was as successful as braiding soot," Morbier agreed. "Making it more complicated as usual, Leduc?"

She told them about her appointment with Bellan on Impasse du Labrador, the woman escorted from her house so they could scour it for bomb-making materials, and Bellan's conviction of Anna Soulages's connection to the 1986 bombing.

René rubbed his eyes. "No way I could identify this Anna Soulages in the crowd from these photos."

"After evading discovery for years, would she really use her cousin's house to manufacture bombs?" said Aimée. "Involve Boris somehow, show up and mingle in the crowd, and slip Action Directe's claim in my pocket? And why me? It feels off."

"Let it go. Leave it to those GIGN cowboys."

"I've got to show Bellan the video," she said. "But we're missing the motive. Why target the lab when a bigger target would be HQ? More bang for their franc."

Morbier yawned.

"Why indeed." René stood and stretched. "The wrong building? A mistake?"

"Not necessarily," said Morbier. "The lab gets crime scene samples of blood, fingerprints, fibers, hair, to test and analyze. Those analyses go in our reports."

That gave her pause. "Evidence used in trials for a conviction. Or to prove innocence. And they keep the samples in the lab, right?"

"Nowhere else to store them. Le Tribunal's archive space is full."

Before she could further her thought, her phone beeped. Melac.

"How's Chloé?" she answered.

"Asleep. We both miss you."

Her heart thudded. "Me, too."

"It's good that you're getting experience with the GIGN. Golden opportunity."

She gritted her teeth. Still completely insensitive. She forced herself to take a deep breath.

"Why wasn't Toureau up front with me? There were two explosions, and it's doubtful Boris would have set either."

"Don't waste your time. God knows why, but Boris had Semtex under his fingernails. There's no getting around that, Aimée. Face the facts."

"That slime Toureau probably put Semtex there."

René and Morbier stared at her. Great. She had an audience.

"That won't stand up in court, Aimée. Look, I don't like it either."

"Fine way to show it. What's up with you and Toureau?"

As if he'd admit anything. That damn code. "Toureau's unlucky in love. I'm getting to know the feeling."

Her line clicked with an incoming call. Bellan.

"Got to go. Kiss Chloé for me." She'd deal with his snide comments later. She switched lines.

"What is it exactly you want me to see?" Bellan said, his voice cracking with tiredness. Never forgot a thing.

"Tomorrow, Bellan."

"New location. I'll send the address in a message."

"*Attends*," she said.

Hugo's earlier comment about the suicide had reminded her of the wilting flower bouquets she'd passed on the chain-link fence at Parc Brassens. With all the resources at his disposal, Bellan could do something practical and see if this tied in.

"Can you check out a recent suicide at Parc Brassens? A woman named Delphine."

"Why?"

"According to the homeless *mec*, Noiro, it wasn't a suicide at all."

"He's dead. Did his ghost tell you?"

"See you tomorrow."

"At seven. Sharp." He clicked off.

Merde. That was only a few hours away. Weary, she stood and grabbed a toothbrush and makeup remover cloth from her desk drawer. She'd curl up here. Miles Davis and Chloé were away—why go home?

"I'd suggest a slumber party, but you both need your beauty sleep. Go home, you two."

Morbier growled. Pulled Chloé's blanket tighter around himself. "I'm fine here."

"Me, too," said René, eyeing Chloé's cot in the corner.

Too tired to argue, she brushed her teeth, rinsed her mouth with Evian water, and spat in a demitasse. Wiped her makeup off, reclined her office chair, and snuggled up with an old wool blanket of her father's. The last thing she heard was Morbier's snores before she passed out.

GREY MORNING LIGHT filled rue Lecourbe, dense as old wool. Aimée parked her scooter, removed her leather gloves, and entered number 91's double green doors, wedged between a *parfumerie* and a lingerie shop. Once through the door she followed a cobbled walkway past former brick carriage houses to an open gate. Beyond loomed a sky-blue onion dome topped by a gold cross on the shingle roof of a structure resembling a long wooden chalet. She'd reached Saint-Séraphin-de-Sarov, the Russian Orthodox church founded by émigrés fleeing the 1917 Revolution.

A black-cassocked priest passed her. Voices floated in the brisk air, singing in harmony. An early morning service?

The priest paused and smiled at her. His dark hair was gathered in a ponytail, and keys jangled from the white cord around the waist of his cassock.

"Beautiful, *non?*" he asked, his Russian accent thick and warm as soup.

Aimée nodded, feeling moved in a way she couldn't explain. The notes lingered. A bird twittered from the greenery as if joining in.

"Our choir's practicing for the holiday liturgy service. It's only a month away." The priest gestured past a courtyard to a nineteenth-century faded-ochre mansion tucked behind greenery. Three stories high with a peeling façade, white trim on the windows, shutters, and a horseshoe-shaped double staircase.

"*Mademoiselle*, please go to the kitchen, ground floor. You're expected."

So Bellan had Russian Orthodox priests as well as convent nuns in his employ.

"*Merci*, Father," she started to say, but he'd already slipped into the church.

"PLEASE, TO THE table." The voice came from a grandmotherly woman with twinkling eyes, Slavic cheekbones, and a stun gun bulging from her apron pocket.

Were stun guns even legal?

The rectangular kitchen reminded Aimée of her grandmother's in the Auvergne. A cracked porcelain sink, enamel stove, open cupboards holding dishes, hanging metal baskets with onions. The onions were the only things that had been added since 1930.

At the fogged-up window, Bellan looked up from a bowl of something steaming. Like her, he'd had only a few hours of sleep. It showed.

The faint strains of singing seeped through the kitchen.

"Meet Faina," he said.

"*Enchantée*," Aimée said.

Faina smiled, revealing three gold teeth.

Aimée joined Bellan at the Formica table. Accepted a steaming bowl from Faina. White dumplings swimming in a rich bone-marrow broth and dotted with scallions. Aimée was a croissant-and-espresso morning person, but this hearty mix could make her change her mind.

She took a spoon.

A high trilling erupted from Faina's pocket. She pulled out a cell phone and spoke in Russian, standing in a soft slant of light by the window. She blew away a lock of hair that had escaped from her bun. Caught Bellan's eye and quickly ended the call.

"This one is complaining because he got caught stealing." Faina sighed. "Like we say in Russia, a bad workman blames his tools." She excused herself and disappeared.

"Since when do you work with a babushka?"

"All the time." Bellan set down his spoon and explained. Faina's White Russian grandparents had fled czarist Russia at its collapse to settle among other émigrés here in the neighborhood. The White Russians formed a community, built churches, taught the language and piano, ran shops and cafés, worked as taxi drivers and doormen at nightclubs. Their descendants lived here today. With studied reluctance, Bellan revealed that Faina ran a Russian expat network of informers. She worked for him.

Aimée covered up her surprise by scooping up the last dumpling. *Délicieux.*

"Faina teaches self-defense. Don't be fooled."

Great.

"If you're trying to fatten me up, it's working. Why'd you summon me here, anyway?"

"Faina's your contact. You two might go out sometime."

"You make it sound like clubbing at some *boîte de nuit.*"

Bellan laughed. His eyes crinkled and he looked younger, reminding her of when her father had trained him: boyish, eager, and carefree.

"Details coming," he said. "Show me what you've got."

She hadn't realized how tired she'd been. How hungry. On a full stomach, the world seemed a little brighter.

Except Boris was tucked away, fighting for his life.

She handed Bellan the CD René made from Hugo's tape.

"What's on it?"

"Didn't you want the bomber?"

Bellan blinked.

"You might recognize him on the video. Your informer, Paul Sénéchal."

He was already reaching for his bag and pulling out his laptop.

"It's just one theory," she said. She gave Bellan a brief version of how they'd edited the video due to privacy concerns of the source.

Bellan powered up his laptop. "I need to know your source. Proof."

She shook her head. "That's confidential."

He slotted in the CD. She heard a click. A whirr. He watched a short segment, hit eject.

"How do I know you didn't doctor this video? Spin a bunch of *mensonges?*" The stubble on his chin caught the light.

"Grow up, Bellan. I don't have time for this. You need to watch the whole thing. You'll see."

He powered down his laptop. Looked at his watch. Said he'd have a team analyze and dissect it with a lice comb.

"It's my turn. You owe me," Aimée said. "Plus, I'm your colleague now."

She put her hand on his arm. He turned, an intent look in his eyes. She inhaled the leather tang of his jacket, realized how warm his arm was through his sweater sleeve. The heat he generated just sitting there. She noticed the length of his eyelashes.

Idiot. Stop it. Heat flushed her neck.

Never get involved with a *flic*.

Especially a *flic* her father had history with.

Didn't she have enough trouble with the only *flic* she'd ever broken her own rule with, who was now the father of her child? She'd vowed never ever again.

She pulled her hand away. Tried to hide her embarrassment.

"It's stifling in here," she said.

He cleared his throat. Had he noticed how she'd looked at him for a moment? Read her mind somehow? *Flics* were trained to read people.

Had he felt the same?

Laughter came from the hallway, the moment broken.

"Owe you what?"

"Details on the suicide that might not be a suicide in Parc Brassens."

"I don't work in the *brigade criminelle*. Ask your contact there. Melac, right?" he said, his tone stiff.

Faina entered with a basket covered by a red-and-white cloth.

"Piroshki, hot from the oven," she said, slapping the basket on the table.

Great. More weight on her hips from a stun-gun-toting babushka.

"Feels like all take and no give with you, Bellan."

He glanced at a message on his phone.

"Got to go. You'll have fun with Faina."

She suppressed the urge to kick him.

Tuesday • 8 A.M. • *Leduc Detective*

RENÉ FLOATED ON a cloud. Slowly, layer by foggy layer, he grew aware of his alarm tinkling a Brahms sonata. His consciousness returned.

He situated himself. In the office on Chloé's big-girl cot, the one he'd bought her for her birthday. Yet his body felt rested, his limbs warm from the radiator. No ache in his hip for once.

Morbier had gone. Aimée had left a note inside a bag with a still-warm croissant: *Please keep going where the GIGN algorithm takes you and tell me.*

He looked at the time. *Mon Dieu*, he'd overslept. Had a conference call in half an hour and the security dossier to complete.

Then an elusive algorithm, seductive and beckoning, to pursue.

Busy, busy day. He pulled a chair to the espresso machine, stood on it, and made himself a double—not his usual, but if it worked for Aimée, it should work for him too.

He changed into one of the handmade Charvet shirts he kept in a drawer in his desk, ran a shaver over his stubble, and, once caffeinated, felt back among the living. He rescheduled the conference call, then devised action steps to perform in the security dossier before surrendering to the algorithm he'd ached to do. Like returning to a lover.

Small recompense for the lover he could never have. Who regarded him as her best friend.

Long-legged, big-eyed Aimée.

Leila's breakup had bothered him. Yet not as much as he'd expected. Face it. *No one else could replace Aimée.*

René perched on his ergonomic chair at the computer and began his digital digging and burrowing, exploiting back doors in firewalls. He'd never have Aimée, but this was the next best thing.

Tuesday • 8 A.M. • *Rue Lecourbe*

AIMÉE CALLED HER friend Marie-Pierre at le Tribunal, which she should have done sooner to set the wheels in motion. Her Tintin watch showed she had just enough time to make it to court for her testimony.

In the cobbled courtyard near the church her phone rang. An unknown number.

"*Oui?*"

"I'm sorry to call this early," said a man.

"Who's this?"

"*Désolé*, but my Sami knocked you down last night. You gave me your card. May I offer you a drink later to apologize?"

Now she recognized the voice of the man in the park with the cute dog. The man who might have witnessed something. She pushed open the gate with a dewy spiderweb.

"*Bien sûr*," she said, "just give me a moment." She wanted to know what he might have seen. She checked her agenda: She'd be in court most of today giving testimony. "Five P.M.," she said to the man. "Where?"

"How about Café Florian at Square Saint-Lambert?" he said. "My classes and meetings will be over."

An academic, as she'd thought.

"Again, I'm so sorry, and thank you for letting me make amends."

Her phone beeped. Bellan. His message popped up.

Re: suicide on October 26 by Delphine Latour at Parc Brassens—later ruled indeterminate, then homicide.

Tuesday • 8:00 A.M. • *Rue de Dantzig*

HUGO WANTED EARPHONES to block the ceaseless scraping of metal against concrete; to drown out the jarring whines of the digging bulldozers. Something to settle his nausea from the burnt odors invading his room.

Last night's shame lingered like a bad taste in his mouth. Tired, he wished for his cigarettes, but his mother had confiscated them. Forbade use of his video camera. And his grandfather had gotten up and started running around in the middle of the night, grabbing pots and pans to repel invading Germans. For once glad to go to school, he hurried to meet Alain and cadge a smoke.

But Alain didn't appear at the bus stop, nor did Hugo see him on the street. Finally, Hugo spotted him. He stood in a crowd looking down at la Petite Ceinture. Firemen lumbered down the steep embankment with a stretcher.

"It's him," said Alain, as Hugo joined him. "Bird Man."

"What happened?"

"A jogger found him. He's dead." Alain pulled at Hugo's sleeve. "Keep walking."

Hadn't he talked with Bird Man yesterday afternoon? Now this homeless *mec* died just days after Noiro?

He spotted Paul, whom his *grand-père* had recognized in the video. Paul stood by the old resto, a hole-in-the-wall. His uncle had boasted presidents and politicians had dined there on his freshly slaughtered meat from the abattoir.

"Did you hear, Hugo?" Alain tugged his sleeve harder.

"Murdered?"

"You saw him before you came over yesterday, *non*? How did he seem?"

"He was mean. He called me *bouboule*."

Alain stopped. "What if you were the last person to talk to him, Hugo?"

Hugo clenched his teeth. Paul was gone. But there was that man again, the one with the twitching eye. He was always easy to find in the crowd. Just standing. Watching.

Beyond the crowd, he saw the chain-link fence on rue des Perichaux. The flower bouquets, dried now, tied on the fence where that student had committed suicide—or hadn't, if Noiro was to be believed. Right above Bird Man's body.

AIMÉE ATTEMPTED TO exude professionalism and confidence in her testimony, despite the fact that she'd had so little sleep. She prayed her Dior concealer did what it promised to on the dark half-moons under her eyes. Her throat felt dry as sandpaper. Almost two years now giving expert testimony. Its impersonal language of facts and evidence appealed to her, and her work more than paid the bills. Nothing ever disappeared on a hard drive, unlike in the porous Internet ether.

She illustrated her final point in the cavernous courtroom, where voices echoed off the marble and the heating had died last millennium. In her summary of the land-mine charity's financial records, she remapped the trail of progressive embezzlement with digital proof.

Maître Dutot, clothed in the judicial ermine collar and black robe, thanked her. Now free to step down, she gave an inner sigh of relief and glanced at the time.

Late.

Outside the leather-padded soundproof courtroom doors, she hurried across the patterned, liver-colored marble squares and rectangles. She broke into a run at the *cour d'appel*, the appeals court, passing the niched statues along the limestone walls between the stained-glass windows and finally the scale of justice before exiting through a large wooden door.

She shouldered her Vuitton bag and descended into the

cafeteria below le Tribunal—the subterranean cavern for *préfecture* workers on the Ile de la Cité. Took a breath. Not her place of choice for coffee.

She knew the clubby ambience among the huddling judges, lawyers, and firemen stationed in the old Conciergerie and the Brigade de Recherche et d'Intervention, who hunched in blue with their black gun holsters over tiny gold-topped tables. Always on call in the oldest part of Paris, *le centre*, the historical ground zero of France.

Conversations hummed under the gothic columns supporting the vaulted ceiling. Burnished honey light from leaded mullion windows warmed the tiles. Her friend Marie-Pierre, the head court clerk, waved from the maroon velvet seventies modular seating.

"About time, Aimée." She gave a harried smile, making room for Aimée by a potted palm. Pecked her cheeks. "My break's almost over."

"I came as fast as I could. My testimony ran over." Aimée accepted the small demitasse Marie-Pierre pushed across the tiny table to her. Plopped in a brown sugar cube, took a sip. Still the same piss-brown excuse for coffee here. She unscrewed the bottle cap of a small Evian and drank it in several gulps.

"*Merde*, he's seen me," said Marie-Pierre, ducking her head.

Aimée glimpsed an older man eyeing them from the corner.

"*Don't look*," hissed Marie-Pierre. "It's that judge I clerked for in Nantes. The one who tongued my tonsils and pledged eternal devotion."

Aimée suppressed a snort. "The married grandfather?"

Marie-Pierre made a gagging sound. "Can you believe it? He said, 'I'll wait, Marie-Pierre, it will happen with us. I'm patient.'"

"What a dreamer."

A blonde, vivacious forty-year-old who looked thirty in her

miniskirt, boots, and floating scarf, Marie-Pierre always had men dropping at her feet. How did she do it?

Marie-Pierre loved attending the latest exhibitions, art openings, and runway shows, just as she loved trekking in Bali. Girls' nights out, which Aimée had foregone since Chloé's birth—those last-minute tickets and tearing her hair out to find a babysitter never worked.

"What's the news on rue de Dantzig?" Aimée asked.

"I'm not supposed to know this. *Mais bien sûr*, here on the island everyone knows everything. A village."

The Ile de la Cité—home to le Tribunal, the police *préfecture*, and Notre-Dame—all sat on this spit of an island in the Seine.

Marie-Pierre's job in *le greffe*, the judicial department, was to authorize payments to experts and specialists like Aimée, and for laboratory tests and analyses. She controlled the purse strings, cut the checks, and supervised a budget. Her head clerk position entailed knowing all the court intrigue; the behind-the-scenes of law enforcement and who owed whom a favor or a step up. *Liberté, égalité*, and certainly a *fraternité* that hadn't changed since the Revolution.

"*Et alors*, you accessed what I asked for, Marie-Pierre?"

Marie-Pierre looked around, then leaned into her ear. "I tried comparing my invoices against the payments. Quicker that way."

"And what did you find?"

"When the lab is done with testing and analysis, they send the evidence and report back to the police unit. I either file it in operating expenses or pay up, like I pay you sometimes as a consultant," she said. "However, the tally of the evidence samples sent in for analysis last week isn't complete. Several didn't come back. We assume the case evidence was completely destroyed in the bombing."

Aimée's fingers clutched the maroon velvet of her seat.

"It's a bureaucratic mess," said Marie-Pierre. "A legal land mine."

Aimée figured as much. "So can you help me?"

"*Moi?* I'm just a cog in the machine. *Mais regardes*, I stretched my neck out . . ." Marie-Pierre paused.

"Can you send me the info?"

"And leave a trail? Never." She slid something under the table into Aimée's waiting hand. A thick folder with several dossiers inside. Smiled. "And I never gave you this."

Aimée returned the smile and slipped the file into her Vuitton bag under the table. "Gave me what?"

The grandpa judge's insistent gaze caught her eye. The man waved. She nudged Marie-Pierre. "He's patient, all right. Wave back or he'll come over."

Marie-Pierre kissed Aimée again on both cheeks. Whispered, "He's watching me. I'm a woman, and he's on the hiring board. Have you forgotten what it's like here in the trenches?"

"Never," she said. "I owe you. But remember, this is for Boris, okay?"

Aimée peeked into her bag at the first sheet from the dossier. It was a long shot, but she had to try.

"I want to talk to this defense attorney, Soubrette. He's here, *non?*"

Marie-Pierre pointed to a man near the wall. "I'll introduce you."

Aimée followed Marie-Pierre past the burly BRI group drinking espresso, deep in intense conversation. Sounded like deals being made.

"Maître Soubrette, meet Aimée Leduc," Marie-Pierre said. "She heard I knew you and would like to talk. Ah, I've got to go. My break is up." With a quick wave Marie-Pierre skipped up the steps.

"Talk fast, my deposition's in two minutes," said Soubrette. His lawyer's robe and ermine collar protruded from a stylish leather Hermès case. Chiseled chin, piercing black eyes, and a rich tan.

"I'm exploring connections between crime scene evidence and the recent lab bombing—"

He raised his hand. "Connections? I thought the bombing was political."

Aimée lowered her voice. Showed the GIGN ID in her palm. "No one's saying it's not."

"Fishing for info, eh?" Soubrette glanced at his watch. "What's in it for my clients?"

"First, does the laboratory bombing indirectly affect them and their case?"

"*Oui*, you could put it that way," he said. "Only thirty minutes ago, I found out the evidence from not one, but two of my clients was destroyed in the incident."

So the file Marie-Pierre had given her was up to date.

"Don't the *flics* have backup evidence samples?" she said.

Soubrette shook his head. "As it often happens, the samples weren't large enough to divide. Proving my clients' innocence hung in the balance."

"Can that point in your clients' favor and help get their trial dismissed?"

"Not necessarily. The actual perpetrators that evidence could point to are still walking free." The lawyer shrugged. "Maybe it's an internal conspiracy. Destroying lab crime scene evidence for the sake of a single case would be overkill. I've never seen anything like that in my career."

THE LAWYER'S WORDS lodged in her brain. Rang a bell, but from where?

What she needed was sleep. An hour to turn off and wake up refreshed.

As if.

She was late to meet the bystander whose dog had rushed her last night. She wove along the quai on her scooter in the late-afternoon throng of traffic. School was out, people were getting off work.

Her phone rang, and she answered.

"Aimée," Michou said. "We need to talk."

Aimée's heart pounded. Panicked, she pulled over to the sound of horns and shouts. "Has something happened to Boris?"

"In person, Aimée. Now."

What did this mean?

"Is Boris okay?"

"He's still in a coma. They won't let me visit or tell me where he's hospitalized. It could be days—that is, if he makes it through just to be branded as a terrorist."

"I'm working on that, Michou," she said. Phone wedged against her shoulder, she stuck out her hand to signal, accelerated, and squeezed back into a lane on the quai. "Right now I'm meeting someone who might have witnessed something," she said.

"The *flics* demanded Boris's computer," he said. "But they're not going to find it, *compris?*"

"Michou!"

But he'd clicked off. Aimée swerved just before a bus clipped her sideview mirror.

She found the café near the oasis of Square Saint-Lambert in the pedestrian zone. Children rollerbladed in front of the café, which was filled with women with shopping bags at their feet, teenagers drinking *diabolo menthe* like she and Martine would do after a day at lycée and feel grown-up. A man read a newspaper and rocked a stroller with his foot. The ambience of the neighborhood café felt as local as hers did on Ile Saint-Louis.

Aimée recognized Sami, asleep under the café table, before she spotted the man. He seemed younger in the daylight.

He stood up and shook her hand. "Forgive me, Mademoiselle Leduc, for not introducing myself earlier. I'm Benedict Cléry." He gestured to his dog. "Sami, you of course know."

Sami's ears cocked up.

She joined him at the table. Leaned down to pet Sami, who licked her hand. "He remembers me."

"Red, white, or mulled wine?" he said, his tone formal.

"Actually, a *diabolo menthe*, like those girls are having. I love mint *sirop*."

Cléry smiled and handed her an envelope containing a Monoprix gift certificate. "To replace what Sami dirtied. I wasn't sure about your style."

How thoughtful. Yet she'd come across him twice in the past two days. A worm of suspicion niggled in her mind.

"*Merci*, but that's not necessary."

"*Non*, please, it's the least I can do," said Cléry. He looked at her for a moment. "Now I know who you are! I've read about you in the newspaper. You're a detective. Famous."

Infamous was more like it. She waved her hand, embarrassed. Would he turn out to be one of those stalker-like superfans who sometimes waited for her outside le Tribunal after a case? Was that what this was about?

Her eyes wandered over him. Corduroy jacket, cashmere scarf, designer loafers. Left Bank intellectual look. No wedding ring— not that all married men wore one. Was this meeting a ruse, some sort of excuse to befriend or pursue her?

She had to head that off and enlist his aid.

"You can be of help, Monsieur Cléry."

His brows arched in surprise. "*Moi?*"

After they ordered, she showed him the crime scene photos.

"See, you're there on rue de Dantzig in the crowd."

His jaw dropped in amazement. "Police photos? It's like on the *télé*. But I was just passing by. I didn't even have my glasses on."

In the photos, his profile was visible and, like he said, no glasses.

"I forgot them in the rush, blind as a bat."

"But looking at the crowd now, do you see anyone familiar? Maybe a neighbor?"

The waiter set down her drink. The emerald green swirled around her straw. She took a sip, feeling sixteen again.

Like Hugo.

At sixteen, the world had been simple; her father set rules that she broke, while her grandfather's disciplinary system was laissez-faire.

"Of course I want to help. Hold on," said Cléry. He pulled out a case, removed his glasses, and wiped the lenses with a handkerchief before putting them on. A man of precision and order, yet his head in the clouds. Hopefully this meeting would work to her benefit. "I still feel shaken. Don't you? I mean, he was your friend, *non?*"

"What do you mean?" she asked, suspicious.

"You told the policeman your friend had gone to the lab and you were worried. We all heard it in the crowd," he said. "Thank God you said something, or they wouldn't have known to look for him. I hope he's all right."

She nodded. "You live in the quartier, you mentioned? Whereabouts?"

He was a professor at the Sorbonne campus. Had sublet from a friend on rue Brancion. Sami had come with the sublet.

"Sami's in his golden years," said Cléry, ruffling the dog's neck and stroking his fur. "Part of the arrangement is that I take Sami to Saint Rita's for the blessing."

Stupid. Why hadn't she organized the same for Miles Davis? She'd promised Chloé they'd take him for the yearly animal church blessing.

This Professor Cléry appeared observant, even though he'd been shaken up. She hoped he might remember something that would spark an epiphany of her own. Or was he hiding something?

As her father often said, suspect everyone until you have evidence to the contrary.

"Where were you, Monsieur Cléry, when the bombing occurred?"

"*Chez moi*," he said. "But I heard it—who didn't? The concierge, he's an insomniac, heard it, too. Came to my flat. You can ask him. He lived through the war so . . ." A shrug.

Two lonely souls who kept each other company?

"But why haven't they caught the terrorists?" he asked. "There was a helicopter, lots of hubbub last night. You're working with the *flics*, right?"

"That's why I'd appreciate anything you can remember. Anything that might have struck you, however small."

"I'll try," he said, studying the photos.

"Something that I find might help is to visualize the night as if you're there again. The sounds, those awful odors."

"Him." His finger pointed to the man she recognized. Feroze Hooshnan.

"The guard?"

"I see him at night when I walk Sami." He looked closer at the photos. "But that's right, I remember now. He was somewhere near you in the crowd."

Perhaps he had seen them talking before Feroze had rushed off.

She leaned closer to him. "Why does the memory of his being there strike you in particular?"

Cléry hesitated.

"*Eh bien*, you asked," he said, shrugged. "He was in uniform, which meant he was on guard duty that night, but as far as I understand, he wasn't injured. I'm no expert, but it did get me thinking later."

"You think he was involved in the bombing?"

Cléry lowered his voice. "He had access, and who would suspect the one hired to protect the place?"

Tuesday Afternoon • Rue de Dantzig

HUGO HUNG HIS jacket on the hallway peg. The apartment was quiet. Usually his grandfather would have the radio blasting the horse races by now.

"*Grand-père?*"

No answer.

Hugo checked his grandfather's room, the kitchen, and even the bathroom. No sign of him.

The folded wheelchair sat in the hall. Yet his grandfather's crutches were missing. And his wool coat.

Of course, he was just off playing the horses and running his mouth at the café . . . wasn't he?

Unease climbed its way up Hugo's neck. He hadn't felt safe since seeing Bird Man's body on the weed-choked rail tracks.

The *flics* had dismissed it as another homeless alcoholic death. But it wasn't. In his bones, Hugo knew Bird Man had been murdered. And Hugo might have been the last person to talk to him.

The front door opened. *Grand-père* at last. But his insides jolted when his mother came in, dragging her wheeled shopping cart behind.

"Your *grand-père* was supposed to help me shop," she said, unwinding her scarf. "Such a lazybones. Tell him to help me in the kitchen, eh?" His mother shook her head. "He's your responsibility."

"He's not here."

His mother blew air from puffed cheeks. "Go find him. You know what he's like when we don't get him in time."

He would gamble and start fighting the Germans.

Hugo pulled his scarf and coat back on and opened an umbrella against the rain. He hurried up rue de Dantzig, past the bulldozers chomping in the now pelting rainstorm. He stepped into Café de Dantzig. Loud horse racing sounded on the *télé*; the bettors shouted and cheered, blue cigarette smoke spiraling toward the ceiling. He didn't see his grandfather.

Finally, he located gap-toothed Tonio. "Seen my grandfather?"

"Your old man?"

"This isn't a test. Just tell me, Tonio."

"Got into a black car, a fancy one—what do they call them, all long and shiny?"

"You mean a limousine," said the old codger next to him at the counter.

"That's right. With a chauffeur type."

"What?"

"Very secretive. Wouldn't tell us anything."

"Are you sure? When?"

"This morning, sometime after the *panier* took the Bird Man away." *Le panier à salade*, "the salad basket." What everyone called the police van that took bodies to the morgue.

Hugo's hands trembled.

"Do you know where he was headed?"

"Ask him," said Tonio

Hugo wanted to shake Tonio, if only to get some reason into him.

"We can't find him, that's why I'm here."

"Call his cell phone, Hugo."

"*Grand-père* doesn't have one. Doesn't know how they work."

"Well, he had one today. And certainly knew how to use it."

His grandfather had used a cell phone and gone off with someone in a limousine?

More importantly, no one in the family had seen him for the last twelve hours.

Tuesday • Twilight • Leduc Detective

RENÉ TURNED DOWN the volume of Radio Classique's symphony hour. Twilight fell outside the window, coating rue du Louvre in a dull pewter. He realized it had been hours since he'd started on the algorithm. Something was buzzing under a dossier.

His cell phone.

Merde, why hadn't he paid attention? He answered quickly.

"René, it's Michou."

"How's Boris?"

"Open the door and I'll tell you. I've been ringing the bell for five minutes."

Lost in the Schubert sonata and working on the counterterrorism firewall, he'd tuned everything else out.

He scooted off his chair. Stiff-legged and needing to crack his neck, he tapped in the alarm code. "*Désolé*, Michou."

"Where's Aimée? She's supposed to meet me here."

"First I've heard."

"Then you've got to help."

René watched Michou, in jeans and a sweater, unload a roller bag's contents on the Louis XVI chair.

"You moving in?"

"I may have to. Boris was having an affair, and now this." He gestured to the bag. "This was in the back of our closet. I've never seen it before, or the clothes inside. Or this laptop." An older model, still in good condition.

René's teeth clamped. "You think it's Boris's?"

"Well, everything reeks of Eau Sauvage, his favorite cologne. Who else would it belong to?" Michou's eyes crinkled in pain. "I thought I knew Boris." A sob came out.

René shook his head. "I'm so sorry all this happened, Michou."

René popped the laptop open. It was password-locked, but the wallpaper was unmistakable: a smiling Chloé wrapped in Boris's arms.

Tuesday • Twilight • Left Bank

AIMÉE MOUNTED HER scooter as the rain let up. Took off down the narrow street. Pale silver light reflected off the puddles and glinted in the cobble cracks. Small gusts of steam floated from the Métro grills in the pavement.

Humid air, freshened by the rain and laced by butter from the boulangerie, filled her lungs. Her stomach growled, longing for a *pain au chocolat*. That was for later; now, she needed to catch Feroze before she hit the office. Get some answers.

"Feroze, the *gardien*?" said the receptionist at the Laboratoire Central de Police HQ. "You must ask *la directrice*. But she's gone for the day."

Great.

Aimée flashed her GIGN card. "I need to speak with him immediately. Any chance you could help me?"

The young receptionist shook her head. "Everything must go through *Madame la Directrice*. *Désolée*, but you need to call and make an appointment."

Aimée would get nowhere with this one, who clearly had a rod up her behind. She caught the eye of one of the *démineurs* passing by with a gym bag. She followed him out the lobby door to the pavement.

"She always like that?"

He shrugged. "Things have gotten tense since the explosions."

No kidding.

"Grab a quick coffee?" She gestured towards the café up the street.

"I'm off caffeine," he said.

"It's important that I find Feroze, the guard, if you can point me in the right direction."

"*Desolé.* I'm in a hurry."

Another helpful one. But she'd play nice.

"Monsieur, my job is to investigate the bombing. I'd really appreciate your help."

He hesitated. "I play on Feroze's team at the gym," he said at last.

"Good," she said, patting her scooter seat. "Hop on, it's faster if I drive you."

"But he'll only have a few minutes before our big badminton game."

Aimée stopped herself from laughing. A potential terrorist and intramural badminton player? Well, it would be a good cover, at least.

She wondered if any animosity might exist between Feroze and Boris. She slid the key in the ignition. "Don't expect me to swing any rackets," she said.

Riding on back of the scooter, the *démineur* introduced himself as Stéfane, and expressed concern over Boris. Aimée parked and realized how close the gym was to both the laboratory and Hugo's apartment. It sat directly atop the old rail line embankment.

Stéfane gripped his sports bag. "I shouldn't say this, but . . ." He hesitated again.

Aimée let the silence linger. Her father taught her that people felt uncomfortable with silence. It worked best to let them fill it.

"Terrorism's random," said Stéfane. "That's what gives it power—it could be anyplace, anytime, any target."

She nodded. "But you don't buy it."

"It's hard to buy Boris as a suspect," said Stéfane. "None of us want to believe it. I've worked with him for six months." He paused, and Aimée saw hurt in his eyes. "Yet he tested positive for explosives contamination."

Alert, she asked, "Do you think the site could have been cross-contaminated in some way that left traces on Boris?"

Stéfane edged away. "Not my area of expertise. I find and defuse explosives. Handle the robot. Scientists and lab technicians handle the other part."

Even though Aimée knew Boris's work, certain areas remained hazy to her.

"But wasn't that part of Boris's job?"

"Boris rarely handled samples in the lab. He ran the department."

"Are you saying it's unlikely, but possible in theory?" she said, hitching her bag on her shoulder. "That Boris could have handled a sample of explosives that remained on his fingers?"

Stéfane turned and started walking to the gym. "Sorry, I've got to go. I'm late."

Aimée ran after him, her steps crunching on the gravel. "Wait. Is it possible?"

"This is putting me on the spot," he said. "I really don't know." Then he hurried inside.

FEROZE AND HIS teammates wore navy-blue jogging pants with white stripes down the side. A cheering section sat in the bleachers, equally divided between the *démineurs* and lab techs, each segment holding banners.

She waved at Feroze, and a moment later he joined her at the gym door.

"Feroze, we need to talk."

"I remember you," he said. "You're Boris's friend."

"Just five minutes, please," she said.

"I've got nothing more to say," he said, picking up his racket. "We've got a game."

"I'm not leaving until we talk, Feroze. Do you want me to make a scene?"

He stared at her, then at his teammates warming up with stretches. "This means a lot to everyone. Good for the esprit de corps." His gaze flickered to his teammates again. "It's awful losing a colleague on top of having your workplace destroyed."

"Feroze, you haven't lost Boris. He's fighting for his life," she said, angry at his defeatist attitude. "*Regarde*, I'm fighting for his innocence. I think evidence could have been planted."

Feroze pulled her aside and into the hallway.

"What do you want from me?" he hissed.

"I checked your schedule. Why weren't you on the rounds you were supposed to be when the bomb exploded?"

It was a guess. She wanted to throw him off-balance—an allegation that serious could put Feroze under suspicion.

"You don't know that," he said.

"Try me. You're going to be investigated, *comprends?* Count on it, Feroze."

His eyes batted in fear. His whisper came out in a tight rasp. "I didn't set the bomb. Or do anything wrong." He tugged her further down the hallway. "Please, you must promise not to tell anyone."

"Tell anyone what?"

"Please understand. Boris made me swear not to tell."

It felt like ice water thrown in Aimée's face.

"What do you mean?"

Feroze, a cold fish when she'd spoken to him the night after the bombing, now brimmed with emotion. His eyes teared.

"Boris and I . . . years ago, we dated," he said in a halting, whispered voice. "It was brief, a fling, and it's long over."

"When was this?"

"Before he met Michou. But someone's been blackmailing me." His dark eyes darted around the hallway.

Surprised, Aimée leaned closer. "Did they have proof?"

"They claimed to. It was enough—my family's traditional. This would ruin me if it came out."

Did this connect to the bombing?

"Tell me what happened on Sunday."

"By chance, I ran into Boris Sunday night at the lab. He saw how upset I was, and—stupid me—I told him about the blackmail. He wanted to talk it over, to help, but said he had to get something from his office." His throat caught. "He didn't come back for a while. So I left on my rounds, then took my break. I figured Boris had gone home and we'd talk another time."

She believed him. "But why didn't you tell anyone?"

"I'd lose my job if they thought . . . you know . . . it's the culture here. No one is openly out," said Feroze. "Boris's partner, that Michou, would be jealous, even though it was over long before their relationship. That day, Boris told me not to tell anyone. That he'd talk to the person blackmailing me and take care of it."

Her heart hammered. "How would Boris take care of it?"

"I don't know."

"Who's blackmailing you, Feroze?"

Feroze's teammates were shouting for him. Fans in the bleachers were stomping their feet.

"This has nothing to do with the bomb."

"Let me decide that. Give me a name."

A pre-game buzzer went off.

"I need to know, Feroze."

He wrote something on a receipt from his pocket. Scrunched it into her palm. "Call me later."

Tuesday Evening • Rue de Dantzig

HUGO COULDN'T STOP his knees from shaking. Where had his grandfather gone? Why didn't anyone know or care?

He'd quizzed *Grand-père*'s cronies in the café and gotten no further than what Tonio had relayed. Hugo didn't know where else to look.

If he went home, his mother would raise the alarm and get his aunt involved. Distrustful of the police, she'd insist they make the rounds of the hospitals or comb the streets.

Hugo sensed this time it would be beyond him to fix whatever idiotic thing his grandfather had done. He pulled out the cigarette pack Alain gave him. None left.

He crumpled it, the cellophane wrapper crackling in the night air. What he wouldn't give for a smoke. Or for his grandfather to come thumping down the street.

The dark winter night draped like a blanket over the bomb site and the misting park beyond. The acrid tang mingled with the scent of damp grass and the fetid smell from the sewer.

He walked around the corner to rue de la Saïda, where his aunt Mimi lived. But his aunt's windows were dark. He'd forgotten that she played belote with her friends on Tuesday nights. No way his grandfather would be there.

Shivering in his light coat, he turned back around the corner. Hugo noticed a delivery van on the narrow impasse by La Ruche. The artist colony's gate lay wide open.

Instead of returning to his mother empty-handed, he'd check La Ruche for Paul, Rasa's boyfriend. The one who his grandfather insisted was in the video. Had his grandfather blackmailed Paul successfully, hence the limo and new cell phone? A cold day in hell for him if Hugo's mother or the *flics* found out.

Grand-père had raised him with his mother and Hugo couldn't let anything happen to him. He feared his grandfather was lying injured in a gutter. Or worse. What if his grandfather wound up dead like the Bird Man, Noiro, and that student whose death might not have been a suicide?

A little voice told him that the big-eyed agent with the impossibly long legs was the one to call. To ask for help.

Yet he'd given her the video—shouldn't the *flics* have arrested Paul by now? If that was even him? His mother had taken Hugo's phone away last week after he'd missed curfew.

Out of other options, he followed the deliveryman inside the overgrown entry to Rasa's atelier. He'd ask to use her phone and call that Aimée Leduc.

"Ahh, my little voyeur," Rasa said, raising a shot glass of clear liquid. "Come to model for me?"

Hugo's eyes popped at her outfit—a leopard-print bikini under a clear plastic raincoat. In this weather? A kerosene heater kept the studio humid and the glass fogged up.

"Can I borrow your phone, Rasa?" he said. "My mother took mine."

"First, we drink." She poured him a fingerful in a jam jar like the one that held *Maman's* homemade confiture at home. Handed it to him, clinked cups, and said, "*Santé.*" She downed it in one gulp and gestured for him to do the same.

It tore down his throat like fire. He spluttered, coughing and squinting. His eyes teared. The aftertaste left a thick warmth.

"You like it?"

He nodded—a lie. He crinkled his nose. A curious botanical flavor lingered.

"Duty-free Żubrówka. Polish vodka, famous for the flavor of the herb that the bison chew on the steppes." She grinned. "A gift from Paul."

"He's here?"

A shake of her head. "I'm tired of him. He's been a bad boy lately."

"What do you mean?"

"Mean?"

"Why's Paul a bad boy?"

"Shhh . . ." She winked. "He gets paid for dirty work. But me, I didn't want to know. But he left papers with me. Call it insurance."

He noticed plaster splotches and blue paint blobs on her raincoat, looked around and saw a naked bust of a woman. He recognized a man's denim shirt. Must be Paul's. No phone in sight.

"I'm celebrating. Big sale." She grinned. "You're here, so you celebrate too. Now take off that shirt. I want to see that model figure."

He felt his cheeks go hot.

"Please, Rasa, it's serious. I can't find my grandfather."

"You think I know where he is?"

He didn't know what to think. "All I know is how crazy he gets, and that homeless *mec* died on the tracks this morning," Hugo said. "I'm worried. Maybe Paul knows where *Grand-père* went."

She poured more Żubrówka. "You seem like you need another drink."

He shook his head. He shouldn't.

She pushed it in his hand. "Life goes down better with a few sips. You'll think more clearly."

Hesitant, he clinked glasses with her again. "*Santé.*"

"Shirt off."

How could he do that? She'd see how fat he was. And his grandfather was missing.

"You're still a boy, eh?" A wistful look crossed her face. "If I were your age, I'd make you a man, little one. But you need a girl. A real one. Forget this voyeur business."

It was true—peeping had only gotten him in trouble. He felt his head clear. Thoughts flowed with the warmth.

"There's a student in my class, Sasha. She's smart, beautiful."

She poured him a third shot of Żubrówka.

"It's healthy. Drink, little one."

They clinked glasses again. Rasa hit the button on a tape deck and music blasted. Something from the seventies.

"ABBA." She laughed. "'Dancing Queen.' You like? It's my favorite."

Then Rasa was twirling around in her studio, her silly rain-coat over her bikini, laughing and singing along in the floating colors. Her braid had come undone, and her hair flew in the air. He didn't mind the humid smell of plaster, or that her sculptures seemed alive.

"Dance with me, little one."

Hot, it was so hot.

He didn't struggle when she unbuttoned his shirt. Or when she pulled him close to her. Didn't fight the beat moving his body, his legs, his arms. And then he was flying.

Tuesday Evening • Leduc Detective

AIMÉE CHECKED HER phone. No message from Dr. Joly, the head tech chemist who specialized in forensic explosives. She wanted to speak with him about the bomb report—she had to know how Semtex had been used for the explosion. If only he'd return her calls.

She punched in his number. Got voice mail and left another message.

Aimée had circled her office building on rue du Louvre twice. Normal foot traffic, evening buses, and no orange tip of a cigarette in a parked car or a pedestrian idling on the street. Still, one could never tell.

They'd gotten in last time.

She parked on a back street. Rang the closed boulangerie door and was let in by the owner, Rodolpho, a middle-aged man in a flour-dusted apron. He and his wife had come to an arrangement with her father years ago for all-hours access to their courtyard, which opened to the rear of Aimée's building. The baker refused when she'd once offered to pay him for the service. "Your father helped me, so I pay him back this way, d'accord?"

She thanked him. Sped to the rear, past the wood-burning ovens and welcome heat and through the dank courtyard, finally reaching the small lobby. No one waiting to spring, only a pile of junk mail and the out-of-service wire-cage elevator.

Just what she needed—a hike up the stairs to make a dent in the extra kilo she'd gained.

Her stomach growled, her legs numb with the cold from riding her scooter. On top of this, she was dying to speak with Chloé, but Melac hadn't returned her most recent call. She looked at her watch and realized it was bedtime. She'd think about that later. Right now she needed to face down Marie-Pierre's evidence lists and gather her notes from the day.

No word from Faina. Or Bellan. She remembered the warmth, his closeness, and pushed that aside, too.

Not now. Not *ever*.

So far, all the messages she'd left for the lab director and head tech chemist had gotten her nowhere. Serge, her friend and medical pathologist at the morgue, was due to return tomorrow from a medical conference in Budapest. Still no further update on Boris's condition.

René deactivated the alarm and buzzed her in.

Grateful, she swiveled her hip, managing to get by boxes in the entryway. "What's this, René?"

"Toner, paper, office supplies."

About time. She'd expected the delivery last week. Panting, she hefted the Indian takeout order from René's favorite resto and ran right into Michou.

"*Désolée*, Michou." Her thoughts flashed for a moment to Feroze.

Michou stood, hands on his hips in his platform boots. The parentheses creasing the outside of his mouth had deepened. Without makeup he looked older. Forlorn.

"Tell me the truth, Aimée," he said. "I can take it."

He burst into tears.

Tuesday Evening • Rue du Commerce

BELLAN GREETED HIS two daughters and son with customary *bisous* in his ex-wife's apartment. He headed to the freezer and pulled three frozen gourmet pizzas out. Hit the panel on *le micro-ondes*.

Voilà. Doing dinner wasn't as difficult as his ex made it out to be.

"Wash your hands, then *à table*."

A resounding chorus of three answered. "Pizza *again*, Papa?"

Teenagers.

"You love the truffle pizza *à Corse, non*? And we'll toss a salad."

"Not every night, Papa."

Had this been dinner every night?

"Maman does takeout on a school night when she's got a meeting," he told them.

And cooked every other night, they reminded him.

"How about Thai takeout from the place by the Métro, Papa?" said Guillaume. "Yummy prawns."

"Guillaume's right," said Lina, his older daughter. "It's quick *et délicieux*. Maman approves."

Of course she did. He stuffed down the resentment. His ex, a nurse, always finished her shift in time to pick up the children from school. Except for the occasional meeting, like tonight.

He bit his cheek. This wasn't a competition, he knew. If he wanted the arrangement to work, he needed to stay on the same page as them. Choose his battles.

"Why not?" he said. He searched for a menu in the drawer. Only finding old keys, a Hello Kitty pencil, receipts from the dry cleaner, an old checkbook with his and his ex-wife's names in it. A wave of pain hit him. He caught himself before emptying the drawer onto the floor.

Bellan supervised a continually unfolding counterterrorist investigation—ran complex analyses, reported to the ministry daily—and yet he couldn't find a damn takeout menu.

He was still waiting for news from the facial recognition specialist and the video analysis team on the bomb video. And no results yet from the lab's analysis of explosive chemical mixtures, much less on any found textiles, cordage, and toolmarks at the scene.

He wanted to hit something.

Guillaume's warm hand took his. His son smiled up at him. "It's okay, Papa. I can help."

His son, a gentle bundle of love, always made his anger evaporate. Softened life's rough edges.

"May I order, Papa?" Lina offered. "We've got them on speed dial."

"Brilliant, Lina, *merci.*"

He hugged his son. Held him tight. It mattered less now that he hadn't written up today's notes for the briefing. Hadn't reinterrogated Coco or obtained results from the overwhelmed Lyon lab.

He'd figure it out. Get it done. Compartmentalize.

Now the most important thing was to focus on being with his children, discussing their day. Follow the tips he'd learned in his parenting class, what he'd vowed to practice. Be present in the moment. Not worry that he had a Down syndrome parent support group tonight or that the girls needed help on a class project.

He'd make this work.

Forget Aimée Leduc's floral scent, her electric touch on his arm, her kohl-smudged eyes shifting from vulnerable to hawk-like in seconds—and how she'd wolfed down that soup with pure animal instinct. How he hadn't been able to get her out of his mind.

Tuesday Evening • Leduc Detective

"Glad you decided to join us," said René. His pained look told Aimée he'd dealt with Michou long enough.

"Were you followed?" he asked.

A quick shake of her head. "I came in the back way."

"Morbier called. He confirmed that his contact is watching our building."

For the second time in days, she felt glad of Morbier's help. She also doubted it would last. Nothing from him was ever free.

"Michou, any word on Boris's condition? Or from his lawyer?"

"Not a peep. But look what I found." Michou pushed a suitcase in front of him. "Packed! Proof of his secret life!"

"You don't know that," said René.

Conflicted, she debated telling Michou what she'd learned about Boris's dating history. But how could she hurt him further? She didn't know if it was even relevant. She needed to deflect Michou's pent-up frustration, fear, and anger. Put those to good use while she figured out what the hell to do.

"I'm glad you're here, Michou," she said, kicking off her heels and placing the takeout bag on her desk. "I need your help."

Michou shook his head. "He's not the man I knew," he said.

For a second, Aimée wondered if that was true—had any of them really known Boris? She averted her gaze and spread out the curry containers in front of her.

Michou checked the time. "I'm on in thirty minutes. *Mon*

Dieu, I have to go. You were so late, but I wanted you to see Boris's suitcase. He's a liar, a two-timer." Michou's lip trembled. "Why do I still love him?"

"We don't know anything for sure until he comes out of his coma, Michou. We have to keep doing everything we can."

Aimée opened the suitcase, which was jam-packed with clothing. Found a card in the inner pocket. Boris had filled out a goods donation card for *la Croix-Rouge*, the Red Cross shelter. Scribbled on it was, *Must ask René to scrub hard drive.*

"This explains it, Michou," she said. "He was donating and hadn't had time to organize it all."

Tears welled in the corner of Michou's eyes. His jaw quivered. "I'm just evil, thinking the worst of him, is that it?"

She had an idea.

"Tomorrow, I want you to speak with a man named Professor Cléry," she said. "He lives in the neighborhood and knows a few people who work in the lab building."

"Why me?" Michou asked, trying to hide his curiosity.

"I've already tried him, and there's something he's holding back about the night guard, Feroze. I think he witnessed something. Or Feroze did and told him. Check on his dog Sami, too. *Compris?*"

Three things about Michou she knew: He was sick with worry over Boris. He loved being busy. And he'd always wanted to be a PI.

AFTER MICHOU LEFT, Aimée went through the suitcase again while René ate. She didn't know what to think.

René set down the coconut curry, unfolded his napkin from his collar, and burped.

"*Excuse-moi*," he said. "So do you think this was Boris's escape suitcase? You lied to Michou?"

"*Mais non*," she said, "you can see he was donating all this."

"But you think he was actually having an affair?"

She had to tell René.

"I don't know about an affair," she said. "But I did hear something that would bother Michou. Feroze told me they dated years ago. Michou's the jealous type, so Boris never told him. Now, Feroze says he's being blackmailed. Boris had promised to help him deal with it."

"Eh?" said René. "But how does that make sense unless—"

"Boris was being blackmailed, too?" she asked.

"You think that's what this is about?"

"I don't know, but I smell a rat named Toureau."

"Aimée, you think Toureau's behind this like everything else. If he's corrupt—"

"If?" she interrupted René. "Everything he does smells."

She checked her messages. Found several left by Toureau. When she returned the call, she got voice mail. Reining in her anger, she left him a message in a flat tone, one that he'd respond to. Clicked off.

"*Alors*, Aimée, you think this has to do with the bombing?"

"I don't know."

"What about the video? Have they identified the person running from the lab?"

She hadn't heard a peep from Bellan or his counterterrorism team.

"It's all hurry up and wait, as usual," she said.

René stood and stretched before returning to his desk.

"For a minute, Aimée, let's go with the scenario of it being Action Directe making a political statement." He pointed at his screen. "I've cracked GIGN's algorithm, navigated my way but it's basic stuff. Reports, surveillance, all routine. To look through it will be time-consuming and tedious, but informative."

Merde. She'd been hoping for something sexier.

A pile of dossiers crowned the in-box on her desk. There was too much for just two people to stay on top of. The GIGN info would take time they didn't have. And she had to go through the info Marie-Pierre had smuggled her.

"We need help." Her gaze went to the wall clock. "Isn't Saj back from Delhi yet?"

"He landed three hours ago."

She said a silent prayer and punched in his number. "Saj? Welcome back. We need your good karma."

She slapped away René's hand, which was reaching for the coconut curry again.

"We've got your favorite curry here. It's still warm."

SAJ, LEDUC DETECTIVE'S part-time hacker, put his palms together in greeting, bowed his head, and looked up. Blinked.

"Your aura is severely disturbed," Saj said. "Too many chakras out of alignment, Aimée."

That bad?

René shrugged. "I could tell, too."

Long flight notwithstanding, Saj exuded calm and patchouli oil. Freshly tattooed and tanned a healthy bronze, he wore a white muslin shirt and pants and a string of Tibetan coral around his neck. His blond dreadlocks were tamed into a long braid.

Saj consulted with the government on the sidelines. The ministry had commuted his prison sentence for hacking the government, deeming his valuable hacking skills too valuable to the outside world rather than the inside. This year he'd spent longer than usual at the ashram in India. She had to admire his yoga-sculpted arms

"I don't know if I can work here, Aimée," Saj said. He waved his hand toward her. "These emanations are disrupting my peace."

"But that's why I need you, Saj. Positive forces, please!"

He closed his eyes. Swayed a moment. Shook his head.

She couldn't lose him. "Boris is in trouble, Saj."

Saj opened his eyes. "We need to cleanse."

This again? She hated incense. It made her sneeze.

"How long will it take, Saj?"

"With a series of deep cleansing asanas—"

"No asanas, Saj. We need to work now."

But in the end, it took what it took. After stretches and deep breaths, her mind did feel clearer and more focused. Not that she'd admit that to anyone, especially Saj.

SAJ SETTLED CROSS-LEGGED on his tatami mat, surrounded by several computer screens, and got going on the GIGN files René had downloaded.

Bellan had only told her so much. With Saj's help, she'd get a handle on counterterrorism's lines of inquiry and use those discoveries to clear Boris. At least she hoped she would. René sent Hugo's edited video to a specialist for another set of eyes while getting on top of the computer surveillance work for their clients.

Aimée started on Marie-Pierre's list of cases affected by evidence having been destroyed in the lab bombing. A daunting task, considering several hundred evidence samples were analyzed at the biological laboratory each month. Her mind reeled. Could she even make a dent in this?

"Why bother, Aimée?" asked René.

Her papa had taught her that every thread in an investigation led somewhere. It might not always tie the knot you needed, but you had to check or it could come back and strangle you.

"I just need to make sure there's nothing I'm missing."

"You're thinking like a *flic* who's got resources and a department to do the slog work," he complained. "What's that?"

"*Comment?*" she said. "Oh, this? Just the fascinating behind-the-scenes scoop from the head clerk at le Tribunal." She smiled.

She read him the explanation procedure sheet Marie-Pierre had enclosed: The evidence samples sent to the lab were sealed by a police or judicial stamp. When received at the lab's requisition desk, they gave *un reçu* for confirmation, which indicated how many samples the lab received, from which branch, and the date. Marie-Pierre had penciled in an aside that lab work for the police wasn't out of her budget—she just handled the paperwork. But if a judge requested forensic analysis, the lab gave a cost estimate, which Marie-Pierre would approve until she received an invoice for the actual cost.

Despite the boring bureaucratese, this was important. She just didn't know how.

Yet.

She suppressed a yawn. Her eyes glazed. She needed an espresso to stay awake, but she didn't want to stay up all night. She pinched herself and just kept reading.

Some samples that required low temperatures were kept refrigerated in the lab, since Marie-Pierre's office at the court didn't have refrigeration units.

René snorted. "Go figure, eh? The highest court in the land has medieval facilities for modern crime."

"There's more to it, René," she said. She went on to read how the majority of samples went to Marie-Pierre for storeroom deposit . . . in the fifteenth-century dungeons at *le greffe*. She provided *un reçu* for every piece. Others went to the *flics*, who brought them with the analyses and their own reports to *le greffe*. In that case, the *flic* signed *une décharge*, which indicated that he'd taken the samples with him, and also signed a receipt.

"In essence, everything's documented on both ends. In the lab's case, past tense. But Marie-Pierre's office has this record."

"What about info on their computers?"

"We're talking entries in ledgers," she said. "Nothing digitally input."

Saj piped up. "A lot of this lab info was corrupted, according to what I'm finding in GIGN downloads. If they find anything, though, I'll be seeing it, too."

She suppressed a sigh.

The list ran from mid-October until the Friday before the bombing.

It was a hunch but exploring for connections between the crime scene evidence and the recent lab bombing might lead somewhere. Or not. But like her father always said, put in the work or it haunts you later.

A returned lab report would generate a check by Marie-Pierre. Hopefully this way she could weed out which samples hadn't been returned—if any—and were likely destroyed in the bombing.

She had to start somewhere, so she'd take the most recent. By the time she'd made a grid, input the info, uploaded Marie-Pierre's chart for comparison, and hit sort to graph, she needed to pee. And check in with Melac about Chloé.

"*Oui, tout va bien*," said Melac, "We fed the horses, she ate two helpings of ratatouille, and we've started reading *Le Petit Prince*."

Chloé's favorite.

"Chloé loves it here, Aimée."

The implication was there: Why couldn't she?

"That's wonderful," she said. Would Brittany grow on her?

"*Meelz Daveez* wants to say hello."

The sound of sniffing came over the line. A little bark.

"Be a good boy, furball."

Aimée heard Melac yawn. Stifled one herself. "I've got to get back to work."

"Meaning you'll be done and coming up tomorrow?"

Think positive. Boris would survive and be proven the victim of a huge mistake. And maybe President Chirac would come pin *la Légion d'honneur* on her.

"Only if I get back to work," she said, determined to keep it light.

"I know it's hard for you, Aimée," he said. "Today Chloé asked where her birthday present from Uncle Boris is."

Her heart thudded. She clenched the cell phone. "What did you tell her?"

"I told her that friends and family are more important than presents," he said, his voice thick with emotion.

This surprised her. The recent events had hit Melac hard, too.

"Thank you for that," she said. Her throat caught. "Talk to you tomorrow."

No more stalling. She'd resigned herself to another night of sleeping at the office. As she sat back down at her desk to adjust the swing arm of the Anglepoise lamp, her eye caught on her screen. She sat up.

The sorted list went on for pages, but the graph she'd programmed showed only four evidence samples corresponding to non-returns at Marie-Pierre's court office for disbursement.

Had she done this right? How could that be? All were accounted for except these four.

Tuesday Evening • Rue du Commerce

AT THE DINNER table over lemongrass prawns, Bellan tried to ignore his phone. He'd muted it. But the fourth call came from the minister's own number.

"*Désolé*," he told his children. "I've got to take this."

"But you made the rule, Papa, no cell phones at dinner!" his younger daughter Clélia said.

His girl wouldn't let him get away with a thing. Like her mother. He made a face. "I'm afraid it's my job."

His eldest, Lina, narrowed her eyes. "Of course it's your job. That never changes. But what about us for once?"

She had been full of innocent wonder when she was little. He remembered blowing raspberries on her tummy when she was a baby. The resulting gleeful giggles, how she'd snuggle in his arms at bedtime.

Guillaume put down his chopsticks, blinking sadly.

"Aren't we important, Papa?" he asked.

"Of course you are. You're the most important."

Bellan grabbed Guillaume's hand and his younger daughter's. Squeezed them. His stomach churned. Did parenting have to be this hard? Hadn't he changed his ways so much that his ex had agreed to joint custody? But he always walked a tightrope.

More flashing from his phone.

Clélia noticed and followed his gaze. "Answer it, Papa. But you know it's going against your own rules."

He had the prime minister calling.

"I need to bend the rule just this once, Clélia. It's an exception."

"You said that last time." Clélia tore her hand from his. "Liar."

Lina rolled her eyes in disgust.

Teenagers.

"I'll make it up to you."

His thoughts were interrupted by the ringing of the door buzzer, accompanied by an insistent knocking on the front door.

Guillaume ran to answer it.

A second later, he returned with three men in camouflage and carrying Uzis. "We're instructed to bring you to the ministry. Now."

Lina's mouth widened in a speechless O.

"But we're eating dinner, and *Maman's* not here," said Clélia.

"Can you call a relative, mademoiselle? Your father's needed regarding national security."

Tuesday Evening • Leduc Detective

"LOOKS LIKE THE lab's testing and analysis was extremely efficient," said Aimée. "It still surprises me."

She'd redone her work. Checked again and again. And came up with only these four. So she asked René and Saj for their eyes on it.

Saj rolled his head counterclockwise, getting the kinks out after a long flight. "What surprises you, Aimée? What are you looking for?"

"Something that shows it's not political," she said, explaining how the GIGN's focus on Action Directe felt hollow. "Why would anyone set a bomb—two bombs—in a police laboratory to make a statement? It makes more sense if the purpose is to destroy evidence."

"A bit of overkill, *non*?" said Saj.

"Or a smoke screen," she said.

Saj nodded. "I understand your line of thinking. It's possible. But number one, how would the perpetrator know that evidence incriminating him or her was under analysis at this lab?"

"Good question," she said.

"Number two, how would the perpetrator know the lab layout and where to set the bombs?" said Saj. "That's a tall order, Aimée."

Aimée thought about her lunch with Boris last week. It felt like a lifetime ago. She'd visited his office afterward. Remembered

Feroze working on the building's electricity, but there was something else. What was nagging at her memory?

René had printed out the lab's layout from a building plan. Handed it to Aimée, who tacked it on the whiteboard.

"Don't ask how I got this," he said. "But if *I* could, couldn't someone else?"

True.

"Last week when I went to Boris's office, we entered this way, here." On the lab diagram she traced the route with her finger. "When I left, we took these stairs to the next level, and Boris had to stop and check on something in the lab."

René handed her a red Sharpie. "Make a mark there."

She did.

"I didn't pay much attention," she said, wishing she had. "I remember he said he'd walk me out a different way so he could check on the refrigerated units in the basement. There was a problem with them. We'd pass the lab's work in progress and the archives, he said."

René and Saj followed along.

"But en route, Boris got into a discussion with Claire, a tech I met at lunch. I ran late and had to go. He gave me instructions to follow the tunnel to exit out through the next building. Here."

Why hadn't she gone through this already? Had the memory been so painful that she'd pushed it away?

Aimée pointed to the parking lot abutting the fence of Parc Brassens. "The techs were working on the backup refrigeration mobile storage unit. There."

"In the parking lot?"

"The old refrigeration unit in the archive was giving out. Seems they were moving the stored samples to the mobile units."

"*Bien sûr*," interrupted Saj. "They need refrigeration to prevent samples from degrading, right? I'd say that's why staff analyzed and dealt with them so quickly."

Made sense.

"So if in theory the bomber targeted the lab to destroy evidence, he or she would have known that there were only four samples on-site," she said.

"That's another big if," said Saj.

"But getting back to Saj's point about knowing the lab's system and layout, that's big," said René. "Why spend time on what's probably not feasible?"

Aimée jumped up. "That's it!"

Tuesday Evening • Rue du Commerce

BELLAN GRIPPED THE phone to his ear with one hand, kissing a sad-faced Guillaume, Clélia, and Lina goodbye. He rushed downstairs so fast he almost fell. His other hand caught on a seam in his leather jacket sleeve.

"Give me an update," he said, struggling with the damn sleeve.

He heard a loud rip.

"We've been calling nonstop, Bellan."

Merde. A torn sleeve and eight missed calls on his phone.

"I'm en route, but I need details."

"A Métro worker recognized Anna Soulages from the photo. We've apprehended her."

"You're sure it's her?"

"She gave herself up. Admitted she'd been with Action Directe. Wants a deal."

They had her. Bellan could taste the impending interrogation.

"Where?"

"At Métro Porte de Versailles. She's in the patrol car."

Of course! The stop on Line 12 near Impasse du Labrador. Caught on her way to Coco's.

"Take her to field house three."

"You mean—"

"Not on the phone."

"You're both right," said Aimée.

"How can we both be right, Aimée?" René said. "I mean, who would even know when evidence samples were there in a 'secure' laboratory part of a police facility?"

"Only an insider."

She twisted her neck until it cracked.

"A purveyor, supplier. Technician for the refrigeration unit, the copy machine, a service that launders the lab uniforms." She thought of Toureau. "A *flic*."

"Like your biggest fan, Toureau?"

She nodded. "He's also the one who found *plastique* under Boris's fingernails."

"Okay, an insider," said Saj. "A person with a reason to be on-site, who wouldn't look out of place there. But why set a bomb?"

She thought.

"Loyalty, a hit, revenge, a cover-up?"

"Let's find the proof, then."

Aimée took another marker to the whiteboard. Wrote that down: *insiders, suppliers, techs, flics.* Below it: *loyalty, hit man, revenge, cover-up.*

Beside the lab layout diagram, she stared at the marker between her fingers. Her Terabyte-Teal fingernails had chipped. Bellan had said Sharpies didn't bleed. That meant something, but she wasn't sure what. She'd think about it later.

She needed to try Boris's lab colleague, Claire, whom she'd met that day having lunch with him. By the time she remembered Claire's last name and found her number in her contacts, she got voice mail. Claire's terse message was to the effect that she and all lab techs were transporting materials to work temporarily at the Lyon lab. Aimée left her a message, determined to talk to her and the director even if it meant going all the way to Lyon.

Right now, these leads were the only new ones she had.

Aimée pulled the four case dossiers from Marie-Pierre's heavy folder. Heartrending—the kind of cases she'd seen her father struggle with as a *flic*, wearied at the relentless, ugly side of humanity. She had to figure out how each of these four cases might link to the bombing.

Not rocket science, but straightforward police procedure. Each listing held the case number, crime scene location, description of samples recovered for testing and analysis, and crime scene photo descriptions. The print on the forms was the same as she remembered on her father's desk in the *commissariat* twenty years earlier. Old-school, as usual.

Case 4260 was a robbery at an apartment in the sixth arrondissement around the corner from Jardin du Luxembourg. Evidence submitted to the lab for testing and analysis included glass shards and wood splinters with blood, a broken tile labeled with possible virus contaminant.

Aimée remembered going with her father to a crime scene at a hospital waste site as a child when he was on call one night. Staying in the car wrapped in a wool blanket, hearing ambulance sirens, seeing the white plastic suits and masks everyone had worn when a corpse was discovered. A tech had whispered "contamination" to her papa, and he'd whisked her straight home.

She'd tasted the fear at the back of her throat. It had given her nightmares.

Case 4261 was an assault in the churchyard at Saint Rita's, blood and other DNA on clothing fibers. She knew Father Louis, one of the priests there. He was part of the ancient Galician order who'd broken from the Vatican and annually blessed pets and animals at the Mass where Benedict Cléry was taking Sami.

Case 4262: a possible hit-and-run or vehicular manslaughter on the quai across from the Maison de la Radio; shreds from the siding of a metal truck with blood on the victim.

Case 4263: a female suicide scaled up to a homicide on la Petite Ceinture at Parc Brassens; clothing, plant traces, broken eyeglasses. Traces of blood on jewelry at the scene had been under analysis. The jewelry was a man's engraved signet ring.

Her blood went cold. Proof of murder? But this ring—which she saw in the photo accompanying the report—had since gone up in flame, dust, and soot.

Tuesday Evening • GIGN Safe House

COMMANDER TINGRY STOOD out front of the safe house on the dead end, conferring with the lookout from Dehillerin. Everything about Bellan's boss, from his trim appearance in a tracksuit to his bullet-shaped head of white hair and weather-beaten complexion, said former military. Bellan joined him and lit up a cigarette.

Night birds twittered beyond the walls of la Petite Ceinture. Foxes and hedgehogs roamed the tracks, where Bellan had glimpsed a swooping of bats from the tunnel.

"You'll wrap Anna Soulages's case up nice and tight, Bellan," said Tingry. "We don't often get this kind of score. But I don't need to tell you that."

They all knew counterterrorism needed a win. They were constantly portrayed on the news picking up body parts or defusing homemade bombs in station lockers. "Late to the party" was their nickname given by the satirical *Canard enchaîné* rag and news commentators.

An amber glow fell from an upper mansard roof window, pooling on the cobblestones. Smooth like liquid honey, reminding him of an aged whiskey and how, somewhere, it was always midnight.

"The minister's pleased after last night's raid," said Commander Tingry. "We'll be executing a preventative strike to show our team's on the offensive."

Surprised, Bellan exhaled a plume of smoke, which he then

fanned away from his boss's face in the night air. He ground his cigarette out with his heel.

"What do you mean, sir?"

"Once you get the goods on Anna Soulages and her accomplice, Coco, we'll tie it to the missing Action Directe member, Nicolas Pantin, our lone bomber."

"Sir, we've got Boris Viard, the accomplice who's still in a coma."

"That stays quiet."

Quiet? Bellan felt the cold bite his neck. Damned himself for forgetting his wool scarf.

"Viard's not expected to make it."

But Bellan wanted Viard's statement to seal the deal. "Sir, there's still the video of the man running from the scene. He's a loose end, and Viard knows something."

"*Exactement.* After questioning Anna Soulages, call Leduc. It's time for her to work. Thanks to you, the minister's got a contingency plan."

Bellan nodded reluctantly. Why did this sit wrong in his gut?

Tuesday Late Evening • Passage de Dantzig

HUGO STAGGERED BAREFOOT from Rasa's atelier door into piercing glacial damp. He stumbled, knocking into a statue and what felt like a topiary tree. Pine needles scratched his chest.

He rubbed his eyes and realized he was standing in the overgrown garden.

Naked. Bathed in a frost of moonlight.

Dying to pee. *Mon Dieu.* He did so before his bladder burst.

Without warning, his stomach erupted with nausea. He heaved, splattering a statue. Losing his balance, he tripped on the slick paver and found himself grabbing a bucket. Stuck his head into the half-dried plaster, heaved again.

His guts were tearing apart. He heaved until nothing more came out. Dry heaved until his throat, raw with acid bile, burned.

Never. Never again would he even look at a bottle of Żubrówka. Sticky with his own vomit and muddy feet, he got up. A helpless mess.

What had he gotten himself into? How many sins had he just committed?

He looked up and saw his family's apartment window half lit. His *maman* would be pacing a hole in the carpet, frantic and wondering where he and his grandfather were.

And he'd failed to find him. Gotten drunk and . . . what had he done?

Still, he had to go home. Make up some story.

But he couldn't go like this. And if he didn't hurry, he'd freeze his ass off.

He followed a garden hose to the spigot. Turned the handle. Closed his eyes, took a big breath, and sprayed himself, yelling at the water, which felt like icy needles pelting him. He dropped the hose, picked it up, grit his chattering teeth, and sprayed every disgusting bit off. Rinsed his mouth, his face, and his matted hair.

The ice-cold water sobered him up. His whole body vibrated, alive; his brain cleared to crystal. He'd come here to use Rasa's phone, get her boyfriend Paul's number, and find his grandfather.

Then his plan faded into Rasa's laughter, dancing and . . .

He sniffed. That smell—something was burning.

White smoke drifted. He saw licks of yellow flames. Without thinking, dripping wet and naked as the day he was born, he ran back into the studio.

In the corner, Rasa lay crumpled among smoking sheets. He yelled, coughed as his lungs filled up. No response. He pulled Rasa up, grabbed under her arms and half carried, half dragged her outside. Then he looked around for a fire extinguisher or alarm. Saw nothing. Why wasn't there a fire alarm here? The studios and the whole wooden beehive would go up in flash.

Gasping for fresh air, he turned on the garden hose and ran back in to spray the burning atelier. The piddly stream of water only reached the area of the atelier by the glass door.

Merde.

The front of him was hot from the burning flames, his naked rear freezing. He grabbed the nearest things—Paul's shirt, Rasa's overalls—since he couldn't see his clothes. In the pocket he found Rasa's cell phone.

Thank God.

And then in the fire's light, he saw the blood clotted on her neck.

Tuesday Late Evening • Rue du Louvre

AIMÉE SAT CROSS-LEGGED on the Aubusson by Saj's tatami mat, waiting. At his urging, she'd tried to clear her mind and focus on an inner white radiance—wherever that might be—for clarity. So far, her thigh was cramping.

She'd reread case 4263, Delphine Latour, the suicide-turned-homicide found on la Petite Ceinture. One thing had struck her. Suicides who wore glasses, as this victim had, generally took them off before taking their life. According to the brief report, Delphine had kept hers on; they had cracked in her fall from the embankment. Only one brief line said: *Injuries sustained to the body were not consistent with findings of suicide.* She would need more info before she could theorize about the how and why.

She'd pulled away to think and to check on the GIGN's movements.

"Can't you decrypt more GIGN reports yet?" she asked Saj.

A dreadlock escaped down his neck as he readjusted his small painting of Krishna, a striking blue, which was near his mat, and hit print. Saj then turned his computer screen to display what he'd deciphered.

"Here's the latest," he said.

Her eyes locked on the screen: a verbatim transcription of an interrogation of Anna Soulages, fugitive Action Directe member, detailing Iranian connections.

Iranian connections.

She blinked. Her mind went to Feroze—why hadn't he gotten back to her after the game? She had rung him from her office line. Only voice mail, so she'd left him a message.

Her cell phone rang. Engrossed in reading the interview, she reached and answered it.

"*Allô?*"

Nothing. The ringing continued. Trilling from somewhere under her desk.

It was the other phone. The one Bellan had given her. She glanced at the time. It was late. She found the phone deep in her bag and answered. "*Oui?*"

"*Bonsoir* to you, too," Bellan said. "Check your email."

She stood, pivoted, sat at her desk and opened his email. It had just come in. She read it quickly, then again while walking over to the printer.

"What's this?" she said, playing dumb.

She positioned the sheets Saj had just printed out against the screen.

Bellan's email matched only the text of the first three paragraphs of the several-page transcript Saj had extracted from hacking the GIGN account. No more.

"This looks incomplete."

Pause. She heard Bellan's intake of breath. Imagined his long eyelashes.

Stop it, she told herself.

"Why do you say that?"

She blushed. Good thing he couldn't see her over the phone. Or what she'd read.

She checked the subject heading. "It says, 'Transcription of Anna Soulages interview.' There's not much here. I doubt this is all she said."

Saj looked up. Pointed to his screen and mouthed, *There's much more coming in.*

"For now that's all you need to know. I believe her."

Aimée chose her words carefully.

"In essence, the lone fugitive Nicolas Pantin, aka Warnek, invited Anna Soulages to a photo exhibition showcasing eighties radicals. Somehow he's meeting with the Iranians there? How does that make sense, Bellan?"

She'd read the transcription already but wanted his take on it.

"It's what we know. Faina's infiltrating—"

Her mind clicked into gear. "If the exhibition's happening now, I'll grab a taxi."

Pause. "You sure, Aimée? Could be dangerous."

"Tell Faina I'm en route," she said.

"I'll message you the details."

She threw both cell phones in the bag along with two burners and ran to the back of the office. At the armoire, she swung the hangers aside, racking past her green street-cleaner overalls, beaded opalescent mini, blue postal uniform, and a vintage little black Chanel dress until she found her black leather catsuit.

Parfait.

Behind the armoire's carved-wood double doors, she changed into the catsuit, pulled the Beretta from her drawer, plus a box of cartridges, two of René's bugs, and a balaclava.

René looked up in alarm. "What's going on?"

"Nicolas Pantin, an Action Directe fugitive, is at a *vernissage*. I'll find out more when I get there." She stuffed red high-tops in her bag in case there was roof work. Stepped into black suede pointy heels.

"You're going out like that?" René said.

Did the extra kilo show?

"For a hell-on-heels look." She hoped René and Saj didn't hear the false bravado in her voice. Martine called it "androgynous chic."

"You're crazy," René said. "Let the GIGN handle this. It's what they're trained for."

She grabbed her warmest wool scarf and her leopard print coat with faux-fur lining. Donned her black leather gloves. Ready.

"You and Saj should go home."

"Not a chance," said René. "We should go with you."

It wasn't fair to pull them into this.

"Boris means a lot to me, to all of us," said René. "I want to do something, not just sit here and crunch numbers."

Aimée looked at Saj pleadingly. He took the hint.

"But that's what we're good at, René. What we're doing is vital for helping Boris."

René looked down, then at Saj. "I know." His voice broke. "I just don't know that it will be enough."

Tuesday Late Evening • *Rue du Louvre*

ACROSS FROM THE Louvre in the rue de Rivoli's arcaded shadow, she hailed a taxi. The driver's dog, a fluffy mix of cocoa and dirty white, perched in the front passenger seat, copilot-style.

She couldn't believe it had only been Sunday when Miles Davis licked her toes and made them sticky with frosting. How his furball self had curled on the duvet, playing with Chloé. She missed Chloé with a physical ache: her sweet smell, those trusting eyes, how she would clutch Aimée's hand with her chubby fingers. She could almost hear Chloé's laughter and inquisitive questions. Her little three-year-old, who was so proud of her big-girl bed and zebra boots. A little fashionista who'd inherited good taste—she took after her mother, as Martine would say.

Doubt crept in. Was she acting *folle*, as René said, racing across the city at counterterrorism's call with a Beretta in her pocket?

Mais non. She had this one shot to vindicate Boris before the GIGN screwed it up. She didn't know how yet, but she had to make the most of it.

Only she could do this.

As the taxi sped along the quai fringed by globe lights, she pulled out her makeup bag and got to work, applying mascara to her lashes, smudging kohl on her lids to a smoky effect, swiping

Chanel red across her lips. Dabbed a fingertip on her lips and rubbed it in her cheekbone hollow.

By the time she'd overtipped the taxi driver and ruffled the pooch's fur, she had a plan. A valet opened the taxi door to a red-carpet museum reception.

Tuesday Late Evening • La Ruche • Passage de Dantzig

HUGO DIDN'T WEIGH his options or worry, as he usually would have, about how his body would bulge out of Rasa's overalls. It was clear that he couldn't contain the fire with the garden hose. The smoke burned his lungs and began to choke him. He could hardly see, and still no one had sounded the alarm.

Where were the fire extinguishers? Smoke alarms? Was there no sprinkler system in place to protect this historic landmark?

Flames engulfed Rasa's studio. Sparks flew and sputtered around his wet hair. And if they didn't get the hell out now, forget about leaving at all.

Grunting, Hugo squatted down and shook Rasa. No response. Panicked and driven by adrenaline, somehow he swooped her up in his arms, shielding her with his wet, dripping body. Prayed as he somehow fought his way past the jumble of statues and onto the path without tripping. He rushed, shouldering his way through the garden's bushes. Yelled "Fire!" again and again, hoping to God a tenant would hear him and call the fire department.

Then he smacked into something hard—so hard that it made him spin in the dark.

How could that be? Why was he dizzy? And falling, still holding Rasa as if his life depended on it?

A figure in the choking smoke looked familiar, but the thought disappeared as his head hit the concrete.

BELLAN POWERED ON his digital recorder for Anna Soulages's questioning. *Bien sûr*, Georges was recording from offsite
as well, but Bellan was counting on this to put a nail in Nicolas
Pantin's coffin and needed his own version to comb through.

Two hours of questioning later, fatigue ate at him. If he'd
thought she'd soften, or open up, *au contraire*. Bellan had resorted
to bringing up Johan Selles's terminal illness. That they were in
the very room where he'd died.

The minute he'd said this, her edges hardened. To him, she
appeared to be a middle-aged rocker chick, tired of hiding under
aliases, but still a die-hard authority hater.

Years on the run showed on Anna's face. Her skin bore a
leathery tan. Her hair was a limp blonde. Knotted, sinewy arms
and thin, muscular legs spoke to an active lifestyle. Henna designs
didn't quite cover the age spots on her hands. She'd kept herself
in shape but suffered sun-damaged skin.

"Where do you live?" asked Bellan.

"Like I told you, I run a resto south of Marrakech," she said,
voice weary.

"What time were you meeting Coco?"

"Haven't seen Coco in years. Got to Paris today. What a mistake."

She rubbed her eyes, which were red-rimmed from tiredness.
"But I already told you this," she said. "Hours ago."

He needed it again. And again. And again, until she cracked and told him the truth.

"Skip to the part about rue des Entrepreneurs," said Bellan, listening to his boss's questions in his earpiece. "How did you make deliveries and pickups?"

"Again?"

"Yes, again. This time with the names and addresses of the shops," said Bellan.

"Names? No names. We didn't even use them back then—only our own code."

Bellan watched closely to discern whether she was lying. Years in the field told him she was hiding something.

"Anna, let's go through the process. You entered the shop, and who did you ask for—the owner, a clerk who you picked deliveries up from?"

"Eh? That's more than fifteen years ago. I don't remember."

"*Vraiment?*"

He struggled to muzzle his rising impatience. Normally, he could maintain his professionalism and would have her talking by now. But nothing, even on his second round of questioning.

Maybe after twenty hours, with not even a bite of dinner, he wasn't on point. Why had she cooperated with the *flics* after being identified but chosen to pull back now?

Instead of battering her with scorn—which he certainly wanted to—he needed to rein in his frustration. His job was to extract information and convince her that it was smarter to own up. To confess and negotiate a deal. Like Johan, only Johan hadn't lived long enough to finish the game.

Otherwise, she could kiss Marrakech goodbye forever and say *bonjour* to the notorious women's prison in Rennes—one of the foggiest, wettest parts of France. One of the harshest prisons in the system.

"Do you want to drag Coco down with you, Anna? Get her locked up, too?"

Anna looked down at her feet. "What do you mean?"

"Coco remembers well how you, sometimes Johan, would go to the shop on rue des Entrepreneurs and throw parties. Champagne."

Bellan looked for a reaction. He got a blank stare ahead.

"Don't you remember the shop with the famous halvah, Anna?"

"I took a lot of drugs back then," she said. "It's all hazy."

"Not an acceptable line of defense in court," he said. "A judge will throw it out. But cooperate and maybe you can help yourself and save Coco."

A long pause. She chewed at her thumbnail.

"Nicolas knew the Iranians," she said, finally.

"We established that earlier," he said. "But I need more details, Anna, *comprends?*"

"Nicolas made the initial contact. We just did delivery and pickup."

Bellan pulled out several photos of street shots. "Explosives and money?"

She nodded.

"Can you point out the shop if it's still there?"

She put her finger on one right away. "Looks the same from the outside. Inside it was long and narrow."

Bellan showed more photos of the interior.

"Looks right. There were always people waiting for halvah. But we'd go to the back, didn't talk to anyone. Nicolas had prearranged it."

Bellan nodded. "You'd pick up the materials, like you did for the Interpol HQ bombing, then take them to Coco's to wire the explosives."

She took a breath. "Yes, but you missed one thing."

"What?"

"Coco never knew. I kept her in the dark."

"She's an accomplice. We found the right chemical traces in her basement." The report hadn't come back, but he had no doubt.

"Liar," she said, showing emotion for the first time. "Those would have degraded by now. Everything we made was low-tech, improvised from the shelf, you know, but—"

Bellan opened a much-thumbed file in front of him. "We know you constructed pipe bombs and stole linear explosives in eighty-six." He quoted from the file. "Stolen from a nearby construction building site at Porte de Versailles." Neglected to say the construction site was now part of the Parc des Expositions, and slapped the file closed.

"No one died, did they? We were always careful."

"So you got on the cleaning crew at the construction site, and Coco provided—"

Anna pounded her fist on the metal table. "You've got no proof against her. Listen, that's how we operated, never let the inno-cents—"

"Innocents?" Bellan interrupted.

"Coco had no clue what we were doing. No one did. It worked out. Kept us and them free for years. No one except us knew. That's why the Iranians used us—hippies who kept our mouths shut."

"And it's still happening," said Bellan. "I'm talking about this week. The explosion with your signature and the note claiming responsibility. We even have the proper chemical traces."

She shrugged it off. "Copycats, wannabes, I don't know or care. It's nothing to me now."

He slid the front page of *Le Parisien* with the phrase *We have struck again* toward her. Then the black-and-white photos of the crowd scene on rue de Dantzig, the destruction.

"Look familiar?"

She shook her head. Snorted. "Not our style."

Bellan controlled his surprise. From the way she said it, he believed her.

"Why isn't it your style? Convince me, Anna."

She pursed her lips. "First, we make a deal."

He had her where he wanted her. Or where she'd been headed all along. Time for negotiations.

"I can't promise you anything, Anna, but I'll do my best if you tell me about the Iranians. Give me something I can take to my boss, okay?"

Her lined and weathered face sagged. She'd once been quite something, he imagined. Now he saw lines of regret.

"My granddaughter's on life support," she said, her voice low. "Dying. That's why I came here. Nicolas sent me a ticket. I want to say goodbye."

Tingry's high-pitched yelp in Bellan's earbud made him jump.

"Tell her yes. Make a deal and get her talking before another bomb goes off!"

AIMÉE HAD ONCE visited Musée Bourdelle on a school trip. It had seemed ancient then. The nineteenth-century sculptor Antoine Bourdelle resided and worked here in a quiet warren of crooked streets alongside the Montparnasse station. Then a cheap place to live, the area had held small-industry manufacturing—ironmongers, blacksmiths, and commercial draft horse stables.

Even now, Bourdelle's atelier evoked the past, as though he'd just stepped out to smoke his pipe in the middle of his bronze-casting. His atelier—untouched, as his widow decreed—was lit by bright shafts coming through old tall windows facing a garden furnished with his statues. The atelier's chipped grey plaster walls and sepia tones seemed like an old photo coming to life. The herringbone wooden floor creaked at her step. A stand nearby held a bust in progress. The patina of age lay over everything; she could practically smell a century of dust. The old charcoal stove with its funny-angled flue pipe reminded her of her grandmother's farm kitchen in the Auvergne.

She wished she could spend a minute here, but her destination lay beyond. She needed to get to that photo exhibition and locate her target.

Soft ambient music drifted as she walked into the courtyard, swirling with aqua-indigo light over age-blackened pillars and dried-out hydrangea bushes. Inside a set of Belle Epoque rooms, she expected to find *les bobos*—bourgeois bohemians, Left Bank art types mingling with the *aristo*-chic. She hoped she'd dressed right and wouldn't attract attention.

She joined the crowd under the plasterwork curlicues along the edges of the ceilings and gilded mirrors. The *vernissage* was a grand opening reception showcasing black-and-white photos of civil disobedience, street demonstrations, protests in the seventies and eighties. Demonstrations with bell-bottomed protesters and hovering tear gas.

"Just the usual acts of destruction and resulting chaos," said a woman of *un certain âge*. "Revolution and business continue, no different today." Her long white-blonde hair was a seventies look that stood in contrast with the woman next to her, whose geometric punk-pink hair screamed the eighties. Both seemed slightly déclassé to Aimée. Wannabe rebels.

In fact, much of the crowd, men and women with ironed jeans and skin-tight leather jackets and snakeskin boots, shared this vibe. It seemed her target mingled with radicals who were still celebrating their greatest hits decades later.

Aimée scanned the faces for a look-alike that matched the age-enhanced projection she'd seen of Nicolas Pantin. She'd search for the eyes. Eyes, her father always said, even altered by plastic surgery or colored contact lenses, couldn't fundamentally change.

Anna Soulages, Action Directe member and most-wanted fugitive, had finally spilled about Nicolas Pantin. Anna had broken their longstanding silence by seeking his help to come to Europe. Pantin offered to hide her, insisting Anna meet him at tonight's *vernissage*. A dangerous agreement, Anna knew, but desperate, she'd agreed. Since Pantin loved attention, she knew he'd show. He prided himself on outsmarting the law.

Pantin had married a German heiress while on the run. His wife loved the fact that he was on an international wanted list;

she used that to give the finger to her family, former Nazi indus-
trialists. She'd insisted Pantin take her surname. People suspected
his past was shady, but with his wife's name, he moved in circles
that wouldn't dig too deep. His current abode was in Monaco, "for
tax purposes," according to Anna.

So the big radical had flipped his ideals and joined the über-
wealthy. *La jet-set.*

The perfect cover.

He had no qualms about going out in the open, in public.
Seemed he didn't watch the news, read the paper about his old
comrades, or even care where they were. He must presume no
one would recognize him after all these years, even in a crowd
like this, where there had surely once been some Action Directe
devotees.

Nothing to worry about. Protected—or so he thought.

Pantin was the only member of the Action Directe group who'd
bombed Interpol HQ who was still at large. Tingry had worked
the case and pursued him feverishly ever since 1986. Ached,
according to Bellan, to corroborate his ties to Khomeini's Iran. To
prove the state had contracted Action Directe to bomb and take
hostages by proxy in France.

But why would Pantin bomb the police lab and stick a warning
in Aimée's pocket? Or had he passed that task to someone else?
From the new generation? She'd soon find out.

People who'd had too much plastic surgery always stood out in
a crowd. The tightness, the immobility of their facial expressions,
screamed out to her. Like the man ahead with thick eyebrows and
a cleft chin. Nicolas Pantin?

Heureusement, she already knew what she was looking for. She
studied the eyes. It was indeed him.

Now the former radical could advertise the wonders of a Bra-
zilian face-lift and an all-over Ipanema tan. Laughing and acting

every bit the bon vivant with a woman Aimée figured for his wife, who'd had as much work done as him.

Aimée navigated through the crowd to get closer. It appeared someone was giving a speech and had asked Nicolas to say something.

His wife angled toward the waiter bearing wine glasses on a tray. The crowd, engrossed in their own conversations, paid little attention. What was going on? There was a rippling movement of persons standing by the door; for a minute it looked like a scuffle.

A man in a black suit and chauffeur's cap argued with a bouncer.

"He stiffed me!" the chauffeur shouted. "I'm not leaving until he pays me his fare! Him." He pointed to Pantin.

Not only on the wanted list but a tightwad, too.

If he had been pointing at her, Aimée would have wanted the earth to open up and swallow her. But Pantin, without missing a beat or changing his expression, joined his wife and beckoned the chauffeur over. His wife, wine glass in hand, reached into her clutch purse and withdrew some bills.

Had that really just happened? A few people seemed to notice. Aimée was surprised he hadn't made more of a scene out of it, given how much he apparently enjoyed attention.

Maybe he'd wanted Anna Soulages, his old comrade here, to witness his prosperity.

How shallow and sad, she thought. Aimée almost pitied this aging radical with too much plastic surgery on the leash of his heiress wife.

An older man with kinky, dull silver hair who had been announced as the artist stood drinking an Aperol spritz by his photos. Many of the shots were artistically blurred group scenes shrouded by clouds of tear gas. She couldn't pick Nicolas or anyone else out.

She walked up, clinked glasses with the photographer, and smiled. "Bravo!"

"*Merci.*" He eyed her catsuit before letting his gaze drift upward.

"Do you know them?" she asked.

"Know who?" he said, suspicious.

"The couple over there." She widened her smile. "I presume they're the benefactors of this collection. I'd like to compliment them on their choice."

"You can talk to me, then," he said, puffing up his chest with pride. "I took these photos."

Pretty full of himself. She'd prefer to sand his ego to a smooth finish. But more flattery would gain her entrée to Pantin.

"Ah! Your work's amazing," she lied.

He shrugged, trying not to look pleased. "My photographs are in galleries all over the world."

Maybe they had been once.

"My photos documenting the era represent . . ."

She tuned him out. Couldn't care less about this man and his passé photos. She tried again.

"A real testament to the time," she said. "So I was right, yes? That the couple sponsored your show. Collectors from Monaco?"

He raised his eyebrows. Displeased she'd pivoted the subject away from him.

"The Warneks," he said. "Nicolas and Petra, close personal friends."

If she wasn't mistaken, Nicolas Warnek, né Pantin, had a tell-tale rectangular bulge in his tailored jeans pocket. A knife.

Aimée's palm clasped the Beretta in her pocket and smiled. "Introduce me."

Tuesday Evening • La Ruche

HUGO CAME TO, head pounding, throat scraped raw. It hurt to breathe. Permeating clouds of acrid smoke made it impossible to see.

Where was he?

Then he remembered.

With his left hand, he began crawling his way through the cold mud. He tried dragging Rasa with his right hand, but Rasa, inert and bleeding, was heavy as a stone. The hissing flames spitting smoke that burned his throat. He would give anything for air.

A flaming timber fell on his thigh. Sputtering and sizzling on his muddy overalls. Hot, so hot; he was burning.

Somehow in the thicket of flames, he heard Rasa moan.

She was alive.

He wanted to give up. So easily, he could just let go.

From somewhere came sirens. Shouts. Everything in him screamed to keep crawling. *Don't stop.* He had to use whatever strength he had to get to safety.

Just when his muddy fingernails scraped the stone pavers and he couldn't pull his body or Rasa forward, he felt strong arms grab him and hoist him up. Other arms were grabbing Rasa. A powerful stream of water drenched everything around them.

"You're some kind of hero, kid. Good job."

Tuesday Evening • Musée Bourdelle

AT THE MUSEUM'S side door, shielded by a long, blue velvet draft curtain, Aimée spoke into her phone, keeping an eye on Pantin the whole time.

Her directive was to locate and engage Pantin, get his initial reaction on the explosion, then usher him outside to Bellan's waiting car.

She was calling Bellan to confirm he'd be waiting. "He's here. Ready for him outside?"

"Not going to happen. Stall him."

"What?" She suppressed a flash of annoyance. She had no desire to babysit this former criminal.

"Change of plans. Intel says he's meeting someone."

"Your intel's off. The *vernissage* is full of—"

"Look around, Aimée," Bellan interrupted. "He's not just expecting Anna. He's meeting someone else, too."

"*Mais oui*, old white hippies reliving their pasts as pseudo-revolutionaries."

"We need time. Faina's delayed."

She was on her own.

She rejoined the photographer, feigning more interest in his photos. Took his elbow and steered him to Pantin, who was sipping an Aperol spritz and chatting with an older rock critic she recognized from an eighties rockumentary. His name escaped her.

"Your friend promised to introduce me," Aimée said, aiming a beaming smile at Nicolas, then leaning in to give him *bisous* on both cheeks.

"You're a legend," she whispered. "Can we talk in private?"

She took him for a narcissist who'd lap up the flattery, keen on having his ego stroked by a woman young enough to be his daughter. But she had also shown her hand. A huge risk.

And a tactless one. Would Pantin run?

He gripped her wrist. Tight. His eyes bore into her.

"I'VE BEEN WATCHING you," Pantin said. His hand was like a steel vise.

Her instinct was to pull away, make a scene if she had to, but it would be better to use this to get him alone.

"Caught your eye, then?" she said flirtatiously. "I just love a good party. Don't you?"

His grip relaxed.

Her next suggestion would be to talk in the courtyard.

"Yes. And so does my wife." The woman had joined them and kissed Aimée's cheeks a beat too long.

She cringed, wondering if they were into drugs, threesomes, swinging, quickies in the hallway, or all of the above.

Wasn't he on the lookout for Anna? Didn't seem like it. She needed an excuse to ask about the explosion.

"There you are, Nico, *et bien sûr*, surrounded by beautiful women, as always," said a dark-haired man, a pronounced, harsh *r* in his accented French.

"*Bonsoir*, Bijan. You did bring me the Caspian Sea caviar, *non?*"

Her mind raced. An Iranian man. This was who he was meeting. Were they speaking in code?

Good thing her go-to kit had those tiny listening bugs René liked.

The man's thick black eyebrows and his high-ridged forehead under a widow's peak accentuated his ashy pallor. He could be anywhere from thirty-five to fifty-five, but his suit looked large on him. He was too slender. Unhealthy.

She suppressed a shudder at the spider tattoo snaking up Bijan's neck.

"*Enchantée*," said Aimée. She stepped forward to give him air kisses, avoiding his cheek. She used the moment to drop a bug into his jacket pocket.

Excusing herself and promising to return, she made it out to the courtyard. The temperature had dropped. She wound her scarf tighter and called René.

"Remember those extra bugs? I just planted one. Can you hear anything?"

"The green one?"

"*Exactement.*"

Over the phone, she heard René clicking his keyboard.

"Did you power it on?"

"*Bien sûr.*"

Pantin and Bijan were coming out the door into the courtyard, the space flooded with azure light. The two spoke in low tones, heads together. She stepped behind a column.

"Anything yet, René?" If he couldn't get reception, she'd have to try and listen in.

"Working on it," he said.

"Call you back."

She silenced her phone, backed up, donned her balaclava, and slid behind trailing ivy. Still couldn't hear their conversation. But she remembered passing a staircase and an EXIT sign, which led to the upper floor and balcony.

By the time she'd slipped inside, up the staircase and to the balcony, her great idea had hit a wall. The balcony ran along the other side of the building instead of the courtyard. Still no text from René.

She suppressed the urge to kick something.

She slid her heels off, laced up her red high-tops, and propped up the fire ladder, required by all buildings with skylights, to the ceiling. Turned the latch, popped open the bubble-top skylight, and climbed out onto the roof. Out of breath, she slithered across the slate roof tiles and looked down.

Pantin and Bijan stood right below. Their voices were raised. Still, she only caught every few words. Bijan sounded upset, but she couldn't tell if he was angry, demanding, or—

She rang René. No answer.

Worthless bug.

She crawled closer to the roof gutter, leaned close to the edge of the tiles.

Bijan was speaking. "What happened, Nico? We didn't give you the funds for this."

Aimée gripped her fingertips on the tile, inching herself forward to hear better.

"Who said you did?" said Pantin. "We haven't worked together since the eighties."

"But your people claimed responsibility for the lab bombing. Who should I hold accountable but you?"

"My people?" he said.

"Explain why Action Directe took credit for this."

"I'm as shocked as you. I would never have wanted this to happen."

"You must know what's going on, Nico."

She could see the tops of their heads now, their shoulders in the glow of the courtyard lights. The mist was settling, heightening visibility.

Bijan turned, and she ducked. Her neck muscles knotted.

She waited a minute, then edged her head back up.

"I have no idea." Pantin stamped his feet in the cold. "When you called and insisted we meet, it was the first I'd heard of it."

"This is not good for us. Here in France, we're very careful now."

For decades, Iran's covert state intelligence agencies had funded radical groups and terrorism in France, according to Bellan. Hadn't Martine written exposés and won an award for reportage on the Revolutionary Guard?

"We try other avenues," said Bijan.

Did he mean Hezbollah? Hamas? Lebanese Marxists?

"Nico, is *that* lab security guard involved?"

"What lab security guard? You can't mean—from eighty-six?"

Bijan interrupted. "Feroze Hooshnan. A local."

Was Feroze the link? She thought of her father's interview with Chatham from Interpol, who'd gotten to the site right after the bombing in 1986. That reference to "the guard."

But how did that make sense now?

"I don't know who you're talking about," said Pantin. "Action Directe's over. Kaput. It has been for years."

Aimée knew now that Action Directe wasn't behind this. If they had been, Bijan would have paid Nico for a deal done and they would've walked away from each other without a word more.

The two men smoked. Others joined them. In the mix of laughter and conversation Aimée crawled back up the tiles, alerted Bellan, and perched on the roof waiting for his team. She wrapped her coat tighter against the crisp chill. Under the soli-tude of the sky, she sat overlooking windows across the street, watching an old man feed a green parakeet in a cage. A few stars pockmarked the sky over gauzy clouds on the horizon, where the Tour Eiffel shimmered in a bright haze.

Not five minutes later she saw an unmarked van pull up. Black-suited men in balaclavas padded out, soundless, and approached the museum's entrance and around the back to the exits.

Slightly disappointed that it was Bellan's show now, she felt guilty. Why wasn't she happy she'd kept Bellan's quarry busy and could go to Brittany now to see Chloé?

But Pantin and the Iranian were clueless about the bombing. Which meant Boris was still in the crossfire of accusations.

Not only had she not gotten her answers, but she'd done counterterrorism's grunt work.

Aimée climbed down from the skylight and at the bottom of the ladder heard a noise behind her. Felt her wrists being grabbed. Bag torn off her shoulder, coat pulled down.

Then a knife to her ribs, piercing her catsuit.

Her heart stopped.

Pantin rasped into her ear. "You two-bit spy. I knew right away. Now you're my way out."

She felt the sharp nick and gasped.

Stupid to think she'd pulled this off. Why hadn't she stayed alert?

She had to ask questions. Stall.

"Why did you set up Boris?"

"Who?"

"The man Action Directe supposedly worked with to bomb the lab."

She could feel his hand sweating through the sleeve of her catsuit. Smell his Hugo Boss cologne mixed with perspiration.

"No idea who that is."

Keep pivoting.

"Then who did? He's my friend, and he would never do this."

Where the hell were Bellan and his team?

"It's a copycat, nothing to do with me."

He needed her as a hostage to escape—didn't he?

"You must know something. Action Directe claimed responsibility."

"Shut up and quit wasting time. Go back up the ladder."

A line of blood trickled down the side of her catsuit.

That did it.

"Do you know how hard blood is to remove from leather?" she said between gritted teeth. Her one hand gripped the ladder rail, the other sliding to her pocket.

He kept the knife to her rib. "That's the least of your problems. Climb. Now."

Her finger found the Beretta's trigger.

"And if I don't?"

He never answered, since she fired the Beretta through her catsuit pocket straight into his kneecap. He cried out in pain. The shock loosened his grip on the knife. Elbowing up and out, she knocked his hand away, ducked, and shoved him against the wall.

The knife had fallen to the floor. She grabbed it. Pantin groaned and clutched at his bleeding knee. She looked up to see Bellan and two others of the BRI team arrive, their Uzis drawn.

"You're late, Bellan."

Wednesday Mid-morning
Italian Cultural Institute • Left Bank

AIMÉE WOKE UP late and checked her phone. No messages. Worry tingled at the back of her neck. She took her double espresso outside on the terrace of the Italian Cultural Institute. The pewter sky and swollen clouds promised rain. She wrapped Martine's silk robe tighter around her. The lush flower beds, dormant in November, were covered with straw. Spindly branched plane trees arched over the green grass and metal lawn furniture.

The shaking hadn't hit her until late last night. She'd sought refuge at Martine's under the duvet in her spare room. But her nerves were so frayed she couldn't sleep. The scenario played and replayed in her mind: how she'd acted rashly and put herself in danger. How her daughter could be motherless if she didn't get her act together.

Never. She'd never put Chloé at risk.

Yet this was how she was wired. It was in her DNA.

Why couldn't she figure out how to be who she was *and* a good mother?

Martine joined her, clipping tarragon and chervil from pots on the terrace. She'd gone cooking-crazy after falling in love and moving in with Gianni, the cultural liaison who lived here. Snip, snip, and the clean, fresh herbal scents wafted up to Aimée.

"Did you really shoot him in the kneecap, Aimée? I thought that only happened in Mafia films."

"He was about to gut me like a fish."

Martine dropped her basket, herbs tumbling to the floor. She gathered them and looked up, pride in her eyes. "Bravo!"

A fine drizzle drove them inside to the kitchen. Martine rinsed the herbs from her basket in the porcelain sink. "That terrorist's wife's got a fortune, so he can afford a knee replacement in Switzerland."

"All the lawyers in the world couldn't get him off. Bellan's boss has been hunting him and his Action Directe pals since 1986. They're terrorists with an impressive body count. One of their bombings alone took thirty people."

Martine looked up. "They're like your mother," she said softly.

The hurt Aimée had thought she'd gotten over rose up, raw and searing. Her mother, Sydney Leduc, had radicalized in the seventies, had left Aimée and her father, who'd raised her alone. A few years ago, Sydney had reappeared—now a CIA freelancer, a claim Aimée didn't know that she believed—to be present in Chloé's life.

"She sent a check for Chloé's birthday. Not even a card."

"What else is new?" Martine reached for a bottle of Sicilian olive oil. "But more importantly, the GIGN captured the long-sought fugitive Pantin thanks to you. On top of it, Pantin was having a tête-à-tête with Bijan Ali. Huge, Aimée. Bijan Ali's been behind Iranian-funded terror groups since the eighties. Two for one."

Aimée nodded. Sipped what was left of her espresso. "But Pantin's old. No longer in charge."

"But he's a coup for the GIGN," said Martine, watching Aimée's face. "You're unhappy. Why?"

"Nothing's changed for Boris." She suppressed the urge to burst into tears. "He's still a suspect, still in a coma. And we're still stalled in the investigation. Why would someone have targeted the lab? The news has started claiming it's linked to the Toulouse explosion and tied to 9/11."

Martine set the herbs to dry on a dish towel. Took out a cigarette, lit it, and set it in a saucer.

"Be practical, Aimée. That knife swipe and bullet hole ruined your catsuit. Corrosive gunshot residue ruins leather. *Mon Dieu,* demand compensation!"

"Already done, Martine."

She'd demanded Bellan replace it, as well as strike her name and any tie to the bullet from her Beretta. He owed her that, since she was technically on GIGN's payroll.

Martine lifted a Le Creuset pan from the pot rack hanging from the high ceiling. "But wasn't *plastique* found under Boris's fingernails?"

"Either Toureau, who we know is a dirty *flic,* planted it to get back at Boris, or the contamination happened in the explosion— maybe he saw something and tried to stop it."

Martine inhaled. Aimée wanted to snatch the cigarette out of her mouth and take a puff.

"Good luck proving that, Aimée," she said.

"Boris has no motive," said Aimée. "Why blow up his own lab?"

"Totally agree," said Martine. "But he's the primary suspect because they've got no one else."

"His being there was totally random."

"*Exactement,* Aimée. Wasn't I there at the party? Listen, you've got to look at each angle separately," said Martine. "It's what I'd do if I were writing this story. How I'd pitch it to Pierre, my editor. Which, by the way, I will. He wants to meet for coffee."

Martine always liked to keep Aimée in suspense.

"*Et alors?*"

"I'd ask, why there? Why then?" said Martine. "Put 9/11 aside for a minute. Who benefits if it's not a political statement?"

As Aimée took the saucer with Martine's discarded cigarette to the sink, she grabbed the still-smoldering remains—just a bit left on it. Took a long drag. Felt the smoke hit her lungs. It used to help her think. Now she suppressed a cough.

"This could have to do with destroying evidence," Aimée said. "There are four evidence bags gone—I've got the list of the cases they're for."

"And now you pursue each of those," said Martine, reaching for a jar of capers. "Rule them out one by one. In the meantime, I'll make puttanesca." Whore's spaghetti—Aimée's favorite.

Boris's lab tech friend, Claire, still hadn't called. Aimée rang again. Voice mail. Disappointed, she left another message.

Aimée used Martine's extra laptop to access the file she'd sent herself of the four crime-scene evidence samples. Claire could help to make sense of this—maybe then Aimée could feel less like a dog paddling in the water. Yet doing the slog work, pounding the cobblestones, and checking up on tedious details was what got answers, her father always said. She recalled her grandmother's words: *You bake with the flour you've got.*

She got to it.

Fifteen minutes later she'd reached the burglary victim, a Danish art dealer whose apartment lay around the corner from Jardin du Luxembourg.

The man sounded suspicious. "Who did you say you were?"

"I'm with counterterrorism," said Aimée. "I'm just checking on the crime scene evidence from your apartment of the robbery that—"

"*Pwah,* don't you people talk to each other? The burglar got caught robbing the building next door. Can't believe he came back to the neighborhood."

One down, three to go.

At Saint Rita's church, her call went to voice mail. She left a message for the priest, hoping he'd take time out from blessing house pets to respond.

She began rereading the next case, 4263, and searched for the police officer's name this time. There it was: Gauchat.

Her phone trilled. Unknown number.

"*Oui, bonjour,*" she said.

"Aimée Leduc?" said a woman's voice Aimée recognized as Claire's. Her appearance came to mind: chin-length brown hair, worry lines around her mouth and eyes, paprika-red lipstick.

"Thanks for returning my call," she said. "I know it's a crazy time for you—"

"I can't talk about Boris Viard," she interrupted. "So if that's what you want, I can't help."

"Claire, I've been contracted by the GIGN—"

"That changes nothing."

Prickly. Was she nervous? Scared?

"My job's to collect intelligence, Claire," she said, her voice firm. "I need information on the four evidence samples that were either destroyed or went missing in the bombing."

Pause.

"To refresh your memory," said Aimée, "*le greffe*'s list shows your lab had them for testing and analysis on Friday before the bombing."

"Two of those cases were solved," Claire said after a moment. "One confessed and the other was caught in the act."

"Can you elaborate?"

Aimée took notes as Claire spoke. The cases were the apartment burglary and the assault at Saint Rita's—the burglar had been caught in another attempt, as the art dealer said, and a man had confessed to the assault in the churchyard. The two remaining cases—the vehicular manslaughter on the quai and the suicide-turned-homicide in Parc Brassens—were still ongoing.

"The actual crime scene photos weren't kept with the evidence, right?" Aimée hoped it didn't sound too amateur for her not to know.

An expulsion of air. "No one's that unprofessional," Claire said.

"Claire, I think your lab was bombed to destroy evidence—"

"I'm really not supposed to talk to you, *vous comprenez?* I have to go."

Merde. "You don't have to discuss anything confidential, but—"

"Look, this isn't my choice," Claire said. "We were instructed to say nothing to anyone. I don't want to lose my job."

That was her worry?

"*Mais non*, you're needed, Claire. They're desperate to keep skilled staff like you. Don't you manage a department? Put legality aside for a minute. Boris is your friend."

Aimée hoped it wasn't too late to reach her. "It was just last week we were all laughing at lunch," she went on. "Remember how Boris mimed assembling your IKEA shelves in your new apartment? It's *Boris*, Claire. He'd never in a million years plant a bomb."

An intake of breath. Silence.

"Boris left my daughter's birthday party to get her present at his office. Now he's in a coma," said Aimée. "So for me it's personal. And it's wrong he's a suspect."

"I'd like to help, but everything's upside down," Claire said, her voice low.

"Off the record, between you and me," Aimée said, not pausing for breath, "did you notice anything odd at the lab? On the Friday before? Or maybe that week? New cleaners? Or laundry workers, technicians, someone you didn't recognize?"

"Hold on."

Aimée heard voices. A door open. Then shut.

"Sorry, we're overwhelmed. Struggling to test and analyze and everything's backed up. This Lyon facility's inadequate for getting our work done. Can you believe we're housed in these archaic *bains-douches?*" A public bathhouse.

No wonder Claire sounded so on edge. An already difficult job in less-than-ideal conditions and others always within earshot.

"Today they tasked us with added testing and analyzing more of the biological components from the bombing. We haven't found anything conclusive yet."

A door opened. Voices.

"Sorry, I've got to go."

Disappointment flooded Aimée.

But she had to try one last angle. If only she could defog Claire's memory from that day.

"That day we had lunch, Boris stopped to talk with you about a portable refrigeration unit, some problem," said Aimée. "Did that get fixed?"

"Now that you mention that, it *was* odd. Those portable refrigerator units were to temporarily hold our samples, but one of the installers made a mistake with the generator. Like they were new at the job." Another pause. "Boris noticed and raised hell."

"What happened?"

"We're always having trouble with our refrigeration units, but this got fixed. Or at least one did. The other constantly malfunctioned."

Aimée wrote down the name of the company who contracted with the lab.

"One last question. Had you tested case 4263 before the explosion? The female suicide-suspected-homicide found in Parc Brassens?"

A pause.

"Close to home, right?" Aimée continued.

"She was found just beyond the parking lot," said Claire. Another pause. "I tested the man's signet ring with blood late in the day on Friday."

"Wait. How did you know it was a man's?"

"How? It was just like my brother's from university. Too chunky for a woman, and certainly wouldn't have fit the victim. As far as I know, the swabs weren't sent off yet. My colleague had a family emergency, making us short-staffed. Or at least the DNA results weren't in. Now we'll never know if we could match the blood to the victim or—"

"Gold or silver?"

"The ring? Gold alloy."

Aimée wrote that down. "Anything else?"

"Engraved."

Aimée found herself holding her breath. Hair raised at the back of her neck. "Could you read the engraving?"

"Hard to read since much of it had worn off. No idea." Another door and someone calling Claire's name. "Sorry, I really have to go this time. *Bonne chance.*"

Claire hung up.

A man's signet ring with a worn engraving.

Claire had tested the DNA on the ring. Had the swab by some miracle been sent off-site for analysis in time? An opening, slim and tenuous as it may be. Something to follow up on.

Aimée looked up the refrigeration unit company, Tout Frigo, in *les pages jaunes.* Their advertisement listed sales, services, servicing, repairs, and portable unit rentals for markets and food fairs. If the lab's cooling storage broke down frequently, how had that affected evidence?

Before she'd gotten her finger on the keypad to call Tout Frigo, a call came in from Directrice Bécard of the police lab. Finally. She had new questions after speaking with Claire.

"You've left me several messages now, Mademoiselle Leduc," said Directrice Bécard. "I'm sorry, but this must remain brief."

"*Bien sûr*," she said. "In my present capacity with GIGN I'm requesting the report of the *démineurs*'s preliminary findings from the bombing."

"That's a work in progress."

"Understood." The bomb squad technicians could take days, even weeks to write their report. "What I need to know right now is if a man's ring has been found in the detritus. A ring that was being tested in the lab. It was part of an ongoing investigation."

Directrice Bécard sighed. "Impossible to say with certainty, but if the ring didn't melt or degrade, it could have survived. Partially intact if it was protected, say under a shelf, behind a window frame."

"Could you check if anything has been found? Informally, of course."

"I'm sending an email as we speak," said Bécard.

"Also I'm requesting Feroze Hooshnan's, the *gardien*'s, employment file."

Background clicking on the keyboard stopped. "I need chain of command on that. For you to follow procedure, Mademoiselle Leduc." And she hung up.

Strange. Was someone higher up protecting Feroze?

She jotted that down in her notes. Feroze did seem connected, smoking with the *flics*, captaining the badminton team. His fear of blackmail came from somewhere else.

Hadn't Bijan Ali mentioned to Pantin that he thought Feroze was involved? Not a culprit, per se—maybe an informer? But for whom?

She made a column and put it under *Ask Bellan*. Next she rang Tout Frigo, who were closed for lunch. Smells of garlic and basil drifted from Martine's cooking in the kitchen.

She rose to set the table. Stopped. That officer's name on the hit-and-run—Gauchat—erupted from the recesses of her mind.

If this was the Gauchat she remembered, he'd been on her father's last case. He had a sweet tooth, and they both shared a love of violet pastilles. He'd remembered her birthday, and even after her papa was drummed out of the force, he sent her a box of Flavigny tins for years.

"Aimée, *à table*," Martine called out.

"*Un moment*," she said.

Turned on her heel and sat back in front of the laptop.

Wednesday Morning • Hôpital Vaugirard

"SMOKE INHALATION, A third-degree burn, and bruising," said the doctor, who, with his white hair and wire-framed spectacles, could've been Hugo's great-grandfather. "You're one lucky young man," he added, consulting Hugo's chart.

His mother stood beside him at the hospital bed, fingering a rosary, the beads clacking as she prayed. Dull grey slants of light patterned the worn linoleum in the hospital room.

"What does that mean, doctor?"

"He'll be fine, madame." The doctor smiled and winked as if that would reassure her. "We'll keep him hydrated, keep his burns under sterile dressings to prevent infection, give him something for the pain. If he rests and lets his vocal cords recover, I'll release him tomorrow."

"*Merci, docteur*," she said, her voice quaking in gratitude.

Hugo was afraid his mother might kiss the doctor's hand like a peasant would their lord and master in medieval times. Like she'd done at church after mass, asking the priest for a special novena. Hugo had wished for the church pavers to open up and swallow him alive.

The doctor and nurse, both reeking of disinfectant and wearing rubber-soled clogs, left on their rounds.

Hugo was dying to find out about Rasa, but his mother would ask questions. Demand to know why he'd been in the fire in the first place.

Was Rasa alive? Had he really saved her life, as the fireman told him? Been a hero?

Why couldn't his mother just leave for work? She was playing with a strand of hair that had fallen from her bun. She had on the same clothes as yesterday.

"What happened to *Grand-père*, Hugo?" she asked.

So his grandfather had never returned? Hugo shook his head, wincing.

She held up her hand. "No talking. Write your answers here."

Not this. Not now.

His mother thrust one of his school notepads in his unbandaged hand. This was like being in school.

She'd set down a copy of *Le Parisien* featuring the fire at La Ruche. Hugo took in the front-page article:

The historic landmark was saved by firemen responding to a neighbor's call. But there were tragic consequences for renowned Lithuanian artist Rasa Leonas, about to join a major exhibition when she died from injuries and smoke inhalation.

This was much worse than school, he realized, his eyes tearing up.

AIMÉE'S DAMAGED ONE-OF-A-KIND leather catsuit had gone to the "dress hospital"—a former haute couture seamstress Martine's mother and sisters swore by. Thank God. She'd borrowed Martine's black velvet cigarette jeans and a mohair blouson sweater to wear over a YSL silk shirt, which kept her warm under her leopard-print coat. To top it off, she donned Martine's Roger Vivier leopard-print ankle boots.

She strode through shoppers thronging the outdoor market before it closed. Even the shopkeepers on rue Charles Michels got into it, hawking their seasonal produce from frontage stalls; one had an old barrow cart once peddled by what her grandfather would've called a *marchand des quatre-saisons*, reminiscent of the carts on every corner even in Aimée's father's time.

Any moment it would pour. She hurried, turning onto rue Linois and reaching the *commissariat* just as she felt drops on her head. The ugly modern-steel affair was confined between the construction of the upcoming Beaugrenelle shopping complex.

"Officer Gauchat?" said the police receptionist. "He transferred to the *commissariat* at the *mairie* a month ago."

Great. Why hadn't anyone returned her message asking if he still worked there?

No way would she get the details of case 4263 unless she used Gauchat's leverage. She needed to appeal to him in person and use his old ties to her father. Ask a favor.

The hall reeked of fresh paint as she sheltered from the rain, phoning the *commissariat* at the *town hall off rue Lecourbe*. She was put on hold twice before a bored voice answered.

"Officer Gauchat's in the field."

Aimée gave her GIGN spiel, insisted on meeting Gauchat in person, and was put on hold. Again. Then the bored voice said Gauchat could spare her ten minutes at Square Violet. He was there now.

Her phone went dead.

A bus stop away. The rain had halted and the air smelled fresh. Clean.

She caught the bus and hopped off at Square Violet in time to see a fire engine pull out from the high crimson doors of the *caserne de pompiers*, sirens blaring. This elegant fire station with the limestone façade bracketing the park's gates was part of the old Château Violet. As she entered the square, she registered the sprawling lawn, banked shrubbery, pines and plane trees, and playground comprising a tucked-away park. Once the private garden of the château. A quiet jewel.

She looked around and trod the wet gravel path. Gauchat was nowhere to be seen. Baby strollers and children were filling the playground post-downpour. Force of habit made her scan the faces for Chloé, to see if Babette had brought her a *goûter*, those apple treats she loved.

Stop.

Chloé was in Brittany. Safe.

Aimée had stayed in Paris for a reason. Needed to finish this. But the ache of missing Chloé hit her.

Merde. Had she already missed Gauchat?

"Mademoiselle Leduc?" said a young policeman in a blue uniform. Pale blue eyes, Gallic nose, and stubble. About her height and checking his phone. "You said it was important?"

"I'm meeting Officer Gauchat. Who are you?"

"François, his son. Also Officer Gauchat."

Surprised for a moment, she stepped back. All this runaround and now she'd have to pull some other strings to convince him to talk to her.

"My father's retired," he said. "But he used to talk about your father."

No smile on his face. Or warmth. *Here we go.* Another wasted trip, another *flic* oozing resentment and corruption like Toureau. Who'd readily spit in her coffee.

Her shoulders tightened.

But she wasn't here to defend her father. She was here to pick a *flic*'s brain about the two cases he'd investigated. To help Boris, she reminded herself as she gritted her teeth and prepared to get information.

"A good man, your father," he said. A sad smile now. "That's what mine told me."

Phew.

"*Merci,*" she said. "I appreciate it."

Birds twittered in the bushes. Sunlight filtered through the trees over the wet grass, speckling glints of light. Sheltered from the wind, the park felt almost warm, the air soft like an October afternoon.

"Papa had a stroke. He's in a care home, talks about the past most of the time."

"*Désolée,*" Aimée said. "I remember your father, too. He used to give me violet Flavigny sweets."

"Still his favorite." Another small smile.

"I was going to ask him about one of his cases, but it looks like it's yours. Can you help me?"

"That's my job," he said.

"Well, it's a little beyond that."

She wiped off the rain on a nearby bench with the *Le Parisien* from her bag. Gestured for him to sit. "I just need ten minutes."

AIMÉE NEEDED TO brief René and Saj on what she'd learned from officer Gauchat on the two cases. He'd given her new avenues to explore. Gauchat's vehicular manslaughter investigation revealed the distraught driver, Alfred Latour, who'd identified his niece at the morgue, had suffered a heart attack after insisting his niece wouldn't commit suicide. Driving home, in the midst of his attack, he lost control, crashed into the wall along the quai. After the initial inquiry, his death had been ruled accidental. Gauchat investigated further and had become doubly suspicious about Delphine Latour's suicide. He'd routed the evidence to the lab, alerted *la proc*, and figured *brigade criminelle* had taken it from there.

Latour. Delphine and Alfred were related. Aimée could've kicked herself—she'd noted Delphine Latour's name at the memorial above the park. How had she missed their connection?

A double tragedy for the family.

But there wasn't much time. She couldn't dwell on this. She needed answers.

She also needed to visit Tout Frigo. Too much to do. Her mind spun.

Prioritize.

Just as she was about to hail a taxi, her phone trilled.

Hugo Dombasle's number showed.

"*Allô?* Hugo?"

"Please . . ." his voice rasped. "A fire . . ."

Had another bomb gone off and caused a fire? Her knuckles whitened as she gripped the phone.

"Where are you, Hugo?"

"In Hôpital Vaugirard. It's an emergency . . ."

Fear clamped her insides.

She hailed an approaching taxi. "I'm close."

But the line had already gone dead.

Wednesday • Mid-afternoon • Leduc Detective

RENÉ TURNED DOWN the volume on Radio Classique and answered his phone.

"Where are you, René?"

"At the office, of course. There's a new job." René paused at the keyboard, lifted his steaming cup of green tea. His tone implied she should be there too. "Aren't you coming in?"

"Do me a favor. I sent you a message. Go to that address."

René set down his teacup and looked at his text messages.

"Tout Frigo? What the hell, Aimée? My job isn't to handle your fridge on the blink."

"I'll explain later. Ask these questions, sniff around."

"What questions?"

Saj looked up from his keyboard. Struck a match and lit a stick of incense.

"I'm sending them now. Look, it's important. I'm in a taxi to the hospital."

René blinked. He imagined the worst.

"*Mon Dieu*, has Boris gone into cardiac arrest?"

"It's the kid, Hugo. There's been a fire."

"Fire?"

"More when I know. René, please. Ask Saj to go through what I just sent you. It's the investigating *flic*'s notes on the two cases."

His ego bristled. "But that's my job."

In the background, René heard horns blaring. The low throb of news from the taxi's radio.

"You want to find the culprit, René?" said Aimée. "The person who's put Boris on the edge of death? Isn't *that* your job?"

"Tell me what to do," said René, putting his phone on speaker.

Saj set down his copy of the *Bhagavad Gita* and looked over at René, alert.

René opened Aimée's email and shot it to Saj.

"Get Saj on what I'm sending you," Aimée was saying. "He'll understand when he reads it."

Saj had opened the email, clicked on the attachments. Gave a thumbs-up.

"He's on it."

René stood and grabbed his Burberry raincoat and car keys. Opened his desk drawer, found his knuckle dusters and a retractable whip. "So am I."

RENÉ DOWNSHIFTED WHEN he caught sight of the warehouse. Hard to miss with its old-fashioned logo: white icicles dripping against bright blue on the words TOUT FRIGO.

An odd location, René thought. It practically overlooked the nearby Vaugirard cemetery. He parked the Mercedes along the cemetery's stone wall.

Driving here, he'd rehearsed the questions he'd been given and focused on his goal. *You can do this*, he told himself. Still his shoulders knotted.

He locked the car. On the pavement he felt his breathing return to normal. His shoulders were looser now.

He made his way into Tout Frigo, whose reception office was the size of a small bakery. Old glass partitions separated two desks, a long, scarred wooden service counter, aged, brown wood paneling, and milky-glass lamps with display cases of refrigeration units. It even smelled like an old bakery with musty corners.

Apart from a thirty-something man with thinning hair who was sitting at the counter over a coffee, the place was lifeless. Out in the courtyard stood a single van. No staff except this man in overalls, who dunked a caramel cream pastry known as a nun's fart into his cup. He looked up, cream bracketing the sides of his mouth.

"You the one p.m.?" he asked René.

What did that mean? "I'm here to speak with Monsieur Sénéchal."

"Oh, him?" The man chewed. "He's off today."

"Then perhaps you can help me, Monsieur . . ."

"Tardi," he said, dunking the pastry again then swallowing it.

René noted the museum-like display cases with historic photos, from horse-drawn carts hauling blocks of ice from the ice factories on rue de la Glacière to a full thirties kitchen with an icebox. Butchers with bloody aprons at Les Halles piling carcasses into refrigerated units and trucks. The summit of a once thriving business, he imagined.

"Who besides Monsieur Sénéchal worked on servicing a unit on rue de Dantzig on . . ." René paused to check his notebook. As if he really needed to—the date was burned in his mind after reading Aimée's message. "Friday, November ninth?"

"Why?"

"Routine. Can you check your call-out sheet or service log, please?" René smiled. Showed his PI card. "I'm René Friant, and I'd appreciate it."

René sensed this lackluster office, with its outdated office equipment and lone employee, limped by as a front for money laundering.

Tardi pulled a tissue from his pocket and wiped his mouth.

Missed a spot of crème. The wall phone rang. Tardi ignored it, lit up a cigarette, and stood at the counter. Glared.

"What's it to you?" said Tardi.

René sighed. "Sir, I'm polite until I sense noncooperation. Then I'm not so polite."

"Polite?" Tardi snorted. "What's a little detective like you nosing around for?"

"I think you know, Tardi."

"Get lost, little detective." Tardi laughed. A harsh, guttural laugh that came from his throat. Waved his thick-fingered hand dismissively. "Think you're some *petit* Poirot?"

René looked around. The place was definitely a front. He sniffed.

"Smells like money laundering in here. You know, tax men like to jump on that right away."

"What?"

"Would you prefer accusations of illegal earnings, off-the-books work, sloppy accounting? A letter of denunciation sent to the tax office?"

"Like hell you will. You've got no proof." Tardi had clutched a ledger with his hand.

"Why not cooperate? Then you'll have nothing to worry about."

"I don't like you, little detective," he said, coming around the counter, the ledger under his arm. "Get lost. I don't want to hurt you."

René heard the snick and saw a switchblade in Tardi's hand.

"You don't have to worry on that score." He pulled out a yellow tape measure and pressed the retractor button. The concealed leather whip uncoiled. His latest gadget.

Tardi laughed again. "What kind of toy's that?"

Eyes locked on René's, he feinted to the left, then right. Then lunged, swinging the blade.

René flicked his hand. Cracked the long, black whip at Tardi's wrist. Tardi howled in pain and dropped the ledger and the knife. René scooped down and picked up the switchblade, his heart pounding.

"You won't get away with that," Tardi yelled and grabbed a cell phone from his pocket with his other hand. Punched in some numbers.

Calling for reinforcements?

René's breath came in short bursts. He cracked the whip again against the man's other wrist. Another yell of pain. Tardi's phone crashed to the floor.

"What the hell?"

René extended his leg and slid the phone away with his foot, careful not to scuff his handmade Lobb loafer.

The phone face had cracked. But a voice was saying, "What's going on? Another complaint?"

The bluster had gone out of Tardi.

"Why didn't you do the service calls . . . ?" the voice was saying. Distinctive and raspy.

Tardi looked scared.

René whispered, "Shall I tell him?"

Shook his head.

René picked up the phone. Noted the number calling. Then held it up to Tardi, speaking quietly.

"Say you'll call back. Then hang up."

René hit speakerphone, and Tardi complied.

He ended the call but couldn't reach any wires or rope in the back without leaving Tardi. Hating to do it, he took his spare silk ties from his inside pocket and tied Tardi's ankles together, then his wrists.

"Ouch, that hurts," he said.

"Talk to me about that work log," said René, "or I'll have a nice chat with your boss."

"He's not my boss. He's the owner."

"Better for me. Worse for you."

Despite the whip burns smarting on his wrists, Tardi's eyes blazed. "Fat chance. He's running this place to the ground as a loss for a tax write-off."

René couldn't help but ask. "Why?"

"Tout Frigo's an inherited family business, owned by the spoiled son who never learned management skills. He regards himself as an intellectual. Smart, thinks he is, anyway. Too good for running the business, even though he used to wear overalls. I couldn't care less. He can't touch me."

Tardi's tone regained a jagged bluster. He had something on the owner—that much was clear.

"Can't touch you because . . . ?"

Tardi's lip trembled. He hesitated.

"Well, what is it?" said René. "Embarrassing details, faulty equipment, false billing, or what?"

Tardi's eyes widened. Almost there. But still he said nothing.

"I didn't come here to hurt you," said René. "But I need that information."

René kept his distance but picked up the ledger and paged to the date.

"You did several service calls to the rue de Dantzig *laboratoire de police*. Documented right here on the page. An invoice for repairs, one for installation of a portable unit. Was that where you put the bomb?"

Tardi's eyes welled in fear. His shoes skittered on the wooden floor as he tried to push himself away. "What? Me? *Non*."

"Who paid you to set the bomb?"

"I never set a bomb." A shaking sigh. "You can't tell the *flics*," he whispered.

"Why would I? This is between us."

"*Vraiment?*" His chin wobbled. He winced. "My wrists hurt."

"Let's get this over, then."

"All I did was diagram where the refrigerator units are . . . were. The lab's layout. Locations of offices."

"Why you? How did someone know you worked there?"

"No clue."

"That doesn't make sense."

"I'm telling the truth. Someone contacted me. Anonymous, you know. I left the plans. Found my payment."

"Where?"

"Here in the mailbox. It happened twice."

"What about the owner?"

"He never comes here."

"Aren't there other employees?"

"It's down to me now. One retired, and the other's on disability."

Tardi looked worn out. René believed him. Mostly.

"What about Sénéchal? Where's he?"

Tardi expelled air in disgust. "Him? Odd duck. Young. Don't know why the owner hired him. He only does part-time work. Odd jobs."

Odd jobs like setting bombs?

René took down the information for Sénéchal and the other two.

"Where are the layout and plans you drew?"

"Why would I keep copies?"

René left Tardi nursing his injured wrists on the floor, and walked around to the back of the reception counter. Old ballpoint pens, invoices stuck on a nail. Prehistoric bookkeeping, he thought. No fax machine. Computer. Printer. Only yellowed notepads with Tout Frigo's logo and a black rotary dial phone with the old phone prefix, Lecourbe 0193.

An idea whispered at the back of his brain. He walked out to the warehouse yard past several hand trucks and refrigeration units looking reconditioned. Beyond the yard's fence, the view took in the cemetery's simple crosses of the fallen from World War I. Several of the graves had fresh flowers. Blooming rosebushes.

Think. What had he missed? He knew Aimée would have pushed Tardi harder, gotten more out of him. But what?

Walking back in, he saw more invoices on the unpainted warehouse wall. Carbon copies for work orders.

Weapon still in hand, he walked back to where Tardi sat on the floor.

"Tell me where you put the carbon copies and I'll let you go."

RENÉ STUCK THE key in the Mercedes's ignition. Rued the damage to his silk ties and punched in Aimée's number.

"Aimée, I've got proof. I know how the bomb was planted."

Wednesday Afternoon • Jardin de l'Hôpital de Vaugirard

"KNOWING HOW THE bomb was planted doesn't exonerate Boris Viard," Bellan said.

Aimée paced in the long garden by the hospital, phone to her ear. Fallen chestnut pods crunched under her feet. After René's call updating her on what he'd learned at Tout Frigo, she'd set Saj to find everything he could on the failing business and Tardi and Sénéchal.

"Look, Bellan. It proves Boris Viard didn't plant those bombs. He already knows the laboratory's layout."

"I'm having trouble seeing how setting bombs in the laboratory links to a refrigerator tech."

"He repaired and—"

"Not that part," interrupted Bellan. "If it's true someone anonymously hired this tech to sketch the layout, why not have him set the bombs?"

"All I know is Boris wouldn't need a layout. He's worked there for eight years."

"Could be a screen. Boris knows the tech and uses him to plant evidence. Red herring?"

"Too convoluted."

"By the way, good work recording that conversation between Pantin and Bijan Ali," he said.

She couldn't believe that René had actually gotten it. Damning in scope, but usable in court?

She shook her head. Not her problem. Nor did it help Boris.

"Where are you?" Bellan asked.

"You've got my info, now it's your turn." She picked a rust-hued leaf from her hair. The leaf crackled, brittle and paper thin. Just like this investigation so far. "Where's Paul, your informer? He has some role in all this, Bellan."

Muffled noises came from the background.

"Got to go." Bellan's line went dead.

Well, she thought, putting her phone away, last time she'd share with him.

Wednesday Afternoon, GIGN Safe House

ANNOYED, BELLAN SLID his phone into his pocket. He joined Commander Tingry across a metal table from Bijan Ali. Tingry finally had the man he'd been searching for since the 1986 Interpol bombing. Ali, a former agent of SAVAK, the Shah's feared secret police—the Iranian Gestapo, as some called it—had shed his SAVAK skin after the Shah's downfall. But like a snake, he'd coiled into Iran's Department 15—a new name, same job—who financed French and proxy terrorists and foreign assassinations.

Deep-state chatter had it that Department 15 operatives were linked to 9/11.

The brightly lit salon used for interrogation hid a microphone and camera.

There the minister was listening in, as were assorted government and military advisors. Ali had repeatedly insisted he carried diplomatic immunity.

"Your embassy post ended in 1999," said Bellan. "No immunity now."

Commander Tingry nodded to Bellan. Time to play Aimée's recording. Georges had cleaned it up for sound quality. Bellan made a show of standing up and walking again to the door. Whispered an aside to the guard to throw Ali off balance.

Ali, an old pro at this, seemed less than intimidated.

Bellan returned with a digital recorder. Set it on the table and hit play. A dangling metallic sound came through, then Ali's and Pantin's conversation. Bellan read Ali's posture: the shoulders stiffening, his almost imperceptible quick intake of air, a blink. Then a shrug wrinkling his spider tattoo.

Got you, Bellan thought.

"Eh, so what?" said Ali.

"There are photos of you and Pantin having this conversation."

A lie.

"Pantin's cooperating," said Tingry.

Another lie.

"Says you funded the 1986 Interpol bombing." Something Tingry had tried to prove for years. "And the rue de Dantzig bombing."

All untrue. Pantin had demanded an attorney, refused to speak, and now sat in a cell.

Ali's eyes shuttered, then looked down.

He didn't look well. His taut skin stretched over his cheekbones. There was a hollowness around the eyes; his suit looked large on his bony frame. Bellan hated to think Ali would cheat them and die before his trial. Avoid prison as Johan had.

Ali looked up. "My brother's here in prison."

"Correct. An identified agent from the Revolutionary Guard."

"Release him and I'll make a deal."

AIMÉE WONDERED WHY Hugo Dombasle had been taken here instead of Hôpital Widal near Gare du Nord, known for its burn unit. Approaching the nurse for a gown and gloves—required to visit burn victims, who were prone to infections—she recalled visiting Boris here. It felt like a lifetime ago.

The nurse waved her on. "He's being discharged soon."

Hugo's bed was empty. What the hell?

Then a toilet flushed, a door opened, and Hugo stepped out in a hospital gown and blushed. His arms and one hand were bandaged, along with his forehead, and he smelled like soap. She'd expected the worst—his body covered in third-degree burns—and should have felt relieved. Instead, she was exasperated.

He gave her a little smile. Whispered, "I'm fine."

Somehow that infuriated her more.

"You said this was an emergency. Now you're saying you're fine? I dropped everything just now, Hugo. Put my life on hold."

The nurse stood behind her. "It's called being sixteen years old, mademoiselle." She winked at Aimée.

Hugo got back into his hospital bed, and the nurse arranged his covers over the bed frame so they didn't touch his skin.

"He's quite the hero. He dragged a woman from the fire." The nurse held up a water cup with a straw and angled it into Hugo's mouth. Hugo blushed a deeper red. "He'd tell you about it, but he's supposed to rest his vocal cords."

The nurse fluffed up his pillows and, with another wink, left.

Aimée had calmed down. His injuries did warrant concern, even if he'd made them sound life-and-death.

"Hugo, tell me what happened," she said.

He mouthed *I'm sorry*, then pulled out a notebook from under the sheets. Pointed. She sat beside him and paged through several pages of close handwriting.

"This is what happened last night?"

He nodded. The sheets crinkled.

She read it all, but only about half of it made sense to her.

"But you saved Rasa's life, didn't you?"

He shook his head and pointed to the issue of *Le Parisien*. The artist hadn't made it.

"*Désolée*," she said. "I didn't mean to get angry." She took his good hand. "Please forgive me, Hugo. I've got some questions, and then I need to go, okay?"

Hugo watched her. She sensed he'd left things out. There was more.

"Look, the personal details don't interest me. But did you see Paul?"

I think so, he wrote. *But it happened so fast.*

"Any idea where he went?"

Hugo looked around. The nurse wasn't in the hall or at the reception desk. He leaned close to Aimée and rasped, "He was there before me. I saw his shirt."

"Could he have set the fire?"

Hugo shook his head.

"So someone else did? Thinking you were Paul there with Rasa?"

"I think Paul told Rasa what happened with the bombing."

Aimée hadn't thought of that.

He pulled her jacket sleeve. "My grandfather's missing. You have to find him, please."

That explained his urgency. But something else occurred to her. What if Hugo was the target?

AIMÉE LEFT THE hospital and checked her phone. Surprised to find Michou's message that he'd made a new discovery in the case.

Her heels clicked across the path as she hurried through the hedge-lined garden stretching to rue de Vaugirard. Behind the garden, the Sorbonne building with its limestone façade and round oeil-de-boeuf windows stared down on her. She punched in Michou's number.

"Discovery, Michou?"

"I hope you're sitting down, Aimée," he said.

Like she had time for that?

Staggered hues of pewter filled the sky. The warm dribble of sun had disappeared.

She leaned against the limestone wall, buttoned her leather jacket tighter, and checked the time. Hoped the "job" she'd given Michou to keep busy proved worthwhile.

She pulled out her notebook. "*Et alors*, Michou, tell me."

"It's those kids you need to talk to, Aimée. Find them."

"What kids? Weren't you asking Professor Cléry to clarify his suspicion of Feroze? Dig into that?"

"He's busy with the school's tribute to the dead student— her life celebration. He'd been at a conference when she died. Anyway, he's about to get promoted to head of the law school faculty. But his secretary was more than helpful, even though she was busy organizing the reception."

"Hold on, Michou, what—?"

"It's that murdered girl in the park, the suicide that's a homicide, the one you and René were talking about."

"How does this tie in to—"

"I'm getting there," interrupted Michou. "The victim was a student in the law school. A suicide, the school was told at first, but things do happen in the park at night she said. Maybe it had to do with the bombing."

"How's that?"

"She'd heard disturbing things."

"And the secretary just told you that?"

Pause. "I might have said I was an undercover investigator."

Her irritation rose. "So this secretary is your big lead?"

"The boys saw it."

A tingle went up her arm.

"I'm listening, Michou."

According to the secretary, her godson, who attended the Lycée Autogéré next door, a non-traditional school—no principal, no grades—had confided in her.

Aimée knew of this school, started by alternatives in the seventies for difficult kids who, if they didn't go here, wouldn't go to school at all.

"He and his friends witnessed something in the park," said Michou, "but wouldn't talk to anyone after the bombing."

Aimée's ears perked up. "Go on."

"Two nights ago, they said the Iranian guard—that Feroze—was by Parc Brassens . . ." He paused. "Where the homeless man's body was found."

Homeless man. The one Hugo called Bird Man.

"Isn't the park closed at night?"

"*Exactement.* These fourteen-year-olds climb over the fences and go drink. According to them, the homeless *mecs* see a lot. Might have known who set the bomb."

That tied in with Hugo's observation—what he'd heard from Bird Man. "What if Noiro and Bird Man—"

"Who?"

"The homeless men from the park," she said. "Noiro slept in the lab and died in the explosion. Bird Man was allegedly killed near la Petite Ceinture. But what if they'd both witnessed a murder of a young woman?"

That idea had pulled at her since she'd read the details in Hugo's notebook. He'd written two pages on Bird Man and their encounter. A man who cooked pigeons to eat.

She thought back to the flowers and photo of the young woman, Delphine Latour.

Were these incidents related? Her father always said there were no coincidences, only mistakes.

Michou connected her to the secretary. It took another ten minutes to convince the secretary it would be in her godson's and everyone's best interest to talk with her.

Now.

FIVE MINUTES LATER she met them in the park near the hospital. Neither the boy nor his friend looked happy to see her. She wasn't thrilled to be dealing with teenagers twice in one day either.

Félipe, the gangly godson with tight blond curls, wore jeans and a vacant stare. His pal, Yann, stocky and surly with stringy brown hair, eyed her up and down.

"Look, I don't care about your parties in the park," she said. Flashed her GIGN card. "I'm undercover. Plainclothes."

That got their interest. She figured it would. And it was true for once.

"Whatever you tell me goes no further," she said. "Not to the *flics*, your parents, or your godmother."

"That's supposed to what, make me trust you?" said Félipe, a sneer on his face.

"What did you see in Parc Brassens on Sunday night?"

"Nothing."

"I'm waiting," she said.

"Nothing, because we don't go on Sunday nights," said Yann, the dark-haired one.

"Why?"

"It's not cool."

Félipe grinned. "He means the girls don't meet us on Sunday nights."

She believed that. A school night. So they wouldn't have witnessed the bombing. She flipped open her notes on the suicide case. "So you go on Fridays, then?"

"We always party on Fridays," said the dark-haired one. "What about it?"

"A woman was at first thought to have committed suicide in the park on a Friday a few weeks ago. October twenty-sixth," she said, consulting her notes. "Did you see anything?"

"We're not involved," the blond said, his tone surly. "It's got nothing to do with us."

First Hugo, now these two. Why did people refuse to speak up about the crimes they'd witnessed?

"Your godmother promised you'd cooperate," she said. "So if you saw something, I need to know."

"I've cooperated. Time to go."

"Go?" She pulled out her phone. "Fine, I'll get a car to take you to the *commissariat*. Then I'll chat with your parents. Her death's been ruled a murder."

They looked at each other.

"It's against the law to withhold information in a homicide. Up to you," she said. "Okay, time's up. I'll notify my boss and you'll go in for questioning."

Punched in a random number.

"You can't do that."

She sensed their itchiness. Ready to bolt any minute.

"Try me," she said. "If you run away, I'll bring in your god-mother for withholding evidence."

This time they exchanged worried glances.

"Okay, but leave her alone," said Félipe. "*Oui*, we were in the park."

Aimée clicked off the phone. Gestured to a bench in their empty schoolyard and sat down. The boys looked around and then sat.

In her pocket, she switched on her tiny digital recorder, hit record.

"We had a test and went to celebrate." Félipe's words came out slower. Hesitant. "Then we heard a car. And a scream."

She pulled out the diagram of the park. "Show me where you were, at what time."

At midnight the boys—Yann and Félipe—partied near la Petite Ceinture with girls from their class. But the girls didn't like hanging near the homeless encampment, so they'd gone toward the rear of the police laboratory. They hung around in the park along the fence on the grass. The neighborhood and park were quiet at that hour. Only a little light filtered through the trees from rue de Dantzig.

That was when they'd heard a piercing scream that sounded like a woman's. Shouting. Another scream.

Then some kind of scuffling. What sounded like some-thing falling through the bushes, branches breaking down the embankment. Headlights on the embankment above la Petite

Ceinture gleamed down through the tree branches, a spiderweb of light.

The girls took off, terrified. Yann and Félipe had grabbed the bottles and cleaned up the traces of their little party; by then, they saw headlights streaking away. A car shifting and a shout from the homeless man. Afraid of getting caught, the boys had hightailed it out of the park.

"Weren't you questioned?"

They shook their heads.

"Why didn't you come forward? Tell the *flics?*"

"Get real," Félipe said.

She understood. If these teenagers had revealed they'd broken into the park and partied on the weekend, they would've risked getting thrown out of the last school that would take them.

She walked with them to the red door of their school. "Let's make a deal. You write everything down as you told me. No names."

Félipe backed away. Yann followed his friend.

"Look, you two. If you witnessed a murder, even from a distance, you have to step forward."

"And if we don't?" said Yann.

"I just recorded this conversation," she said, pulling out her recorder.

"That's illegal!"

"It's not me who'll be at your front door talking to your parents or the girls' parents," she said. "Picture an angry homicide detective who's not nearly as nice."

Wednesday Afternoon • Cité Morieux

AT 5 CITÉ Morieux—the home of Madame Latour, the wife of the accident victim—the concierge was sweeping the cobbled entry.

"Gone. Madame Latour's staying with her sister for a few months."

The talkative concierge, a middle-aged woman with a greenish cast in one eye, started answering questions even before Aimée showed her GIGN card. It was difficult for Aimée to get a word in. To explain she was here to follow up on Monsieur Latour's fatal accident.

"So sad," said the concierge. "Terrible."

The small, cobbled lane, lined with one- and two-story houses, emanated smells of butter and baking. A radio played the jazz station. Familial. Everyday life in the quartier.

"May I get Madame Latour's contact information?" said Aimée, finally finding an opportunity to get the woman's help.

"Of course. But why now?"

"There's some questions we need to ask."

"Questions? Old Monsieur Latour suffered a heart attack while driving. Can you imagine that? He hit a truck and ran into the quai's embankment. Dead. They tried to label it a hit-and-run or even manslaughter at first, I don't know why. That truck barely grazed him. And just after his niece's suicide, you know—"

"Suicide, madame?"

"Two deaths in one family. Such a sweet young woman. You'd never guess how smart Delphine was—always on top of her studies, even with all her stays in the hospital. Brilliant."

"What do you mean?"

"Soft bones. There's a name for her condition but I can't remember." Sigh. "Poor madame doesn't want to relive this." Ten minutes later, Aimée had caught the Métro at Dupleix, riding above ground on Line 6. Her favorite line, which crossed the Seine. To her it was the best Métro ride, with its view of the river and the Tour Eiffel. It was also known as the "suicide line," where people threw themselves on the tracks after a terminal diagnosis or too early a discharge from Sainte-Anne's mental hospital.

At Place d'Italie she changed to Line 5, riding four stops to quai de la Rapée. The morgue. Her friend Serge, a medical pathologist and friend since her failed attempt at pre-med, met her at his office door.

Serge, with his black-framed glasses and matching bushy black hair, held an index finger to his mouth. He gestured down the tiled hallway. Always one for secrecy, he exerted hypervigilance, afraid of getting caught helping her.

Outside at the vehicle bay where the van unloaded corpses for autopsy, an attendant in white boots hosed off the pavement. Aimée didn't like to think of what. At least here, to the right, the brick wall sheltered them from the wind and the view overlooked the Seine.

"Non, Aimée," Serge said. "I'm just going to say non before you ask. Refuse to even hear the request."

She handed him a noisette capped with extra foam and sprinkled with chocolate powder, exactly the way he liked it, and smiled.

"Isn't next weekend your anniversary, Serge?" she said, knowing it was. "Why don't I take the twins to Brittany? They can ride horses and play with Chloé."

Serge's kinetic twin boys, whose forbidden gummy bear addiction kept them in her power, were getting too old for their grandmother to handle all weekend. Serge's wife and her mother ran his life. Aimée had never seen him happier, openly henpecked, a willing slave to his *belle-mère*.

Serge sipped the *noisette*. The foam caught on his upper lip. Pensive.

"Please, Serge," she said.

"School gets off early next Friday," he said. "Can you pick them up at noon?"

She groaned inside.

Smiled. "*Pas de problème.*"

Serge scanned their surroundings. Then nodded.

Aimée slipped the evidence dossier cases in his hands. "I need the autopsy reports on Alfred Latour and Delphine Latour."

"A couple?"

"Uncle and niece. Separate deaths within days of each other. The uncle's a car accident mislabeled vehicular manslaughter, and the niece's a suspected suicide, now a homicide. Did you autopsy either?"

"I perform a hundred autopsies per month. Teach. How can I possibly—" He stopped. Pulled down his glasses, thinking. Then pushed them back up on the bridge of his nose.

Aimée nudged him. "You remember, don't you?"

"If it's the one I remember, my colleague performed the autopsy on the female. Had a lot of questions."

His alarm buzzed on his watch.

"Got to go. Our director's here snooping around," said Serge. "Quality control."

Serge stuffed the dossier inside his lab coat. He reached for one of the morgue's double doors, built for gurneys. It pinged open.

Aimée's hand caught his arm. "I need this tonight, Serge."

"But I have to pick up the twins from their school this afternoon."

She wanted to scream. Stomp her feet. Yell to the rooftops.

Instead, Aimée smiled again. "Done."

The morgue's double door pinged shut.

AIMÉE LEFT THE morgue and walked along the quai. Seagulls cried. A barge chugged past, sending waves fanning in a V formation. Being close to the water cleared her head. She hadn't been home in two days. Her apartment's tall windows were shuttered, Miles Davis was taken care of, and Madame Cachou was collecting her mail. Her office armoire held enough clothes. Plus, staying at Martine's meant gourmet Italian food and a distraction from missing her daughter.

Aimée sighed.

The light faded in the twenty minutes she used to check in with René. Gave him an update on her findings from Cléry and the lycée kids. She also left a message for Madame Latour with the phone number from the concierge. She walked toward Notre-Dame under an oyster-grey sky with shifting, layered clouds. They resembled the coarse, grey Guérande salt her *grand-père* used to use in cooking.

In the nineteenth-century café-bistro Soleil d'Or, a *flic* hangout, she greeted the maître d', Louis. He'd been here since she was little. She'd once asked her grandfather if Louis was what people called "part of the scenery." Claude, her grandfather, had laughed and said, "He's more of a fixture." Louis, a trim, sixtyish man with slicked-back grey hair, wore a white towel over his arm and a spotless white apron that nearly dusted the ground. He grinned.

"*Ma petite mademoiselle*, a delight to see you as always," he said. He kissed her on both cheeks, his signature Vetiver cologne just as she remembered. "Where's *mon petit chou?*" His "little cabbage," as Louis referred to Chloé.

"Up in Brittany." How she missed bringing Chloé in here for *un chocolat chaud*. "I'll see her this weekend."

Wouldn't she?

Louis pointed her to Morbier sitting at the back banquette under the wall mirror with desilvered edges. The 1930s brasserie hadn't changed. All dark wood, banquettes, and brass rails. How often had she done her homework here while her grandfather was upstairs with his mistress? The woman, a relative of the owner's, lived in the old family quarters above. Aimée had never wanted to know the mistress's story, and her father had adamantly pretended the woman didn't exist. Not her business.

"You sure about this, Leduc?" Morbier said.

The deep bags under his eyes were more pronounced than usual. What looked like béarnaise sauce stained his wool jacket. He rubbed his lined hands together as if cold, even though the radiator by the window sputtered, working overtime. It felt like an oven in here.

She unzipped her leather jacket. Took off her gloves. "You owe me, Morbier."

"What's this now? I'm no cash register."

She concealed her credit-card-sized recorder under the thick white napkin and placed it in front of Morbier's plate. "You're an old hand at this."

Morbier took a pull of his blond *bière alsacienne* and shook his head. "Human relations don't run like that. You need to learn to work with people."

She leaned in over the table, the marble cool on her wrists. "You know Toureau hates my guts. I need a hand with this."

"That's why we're meeting him, *n'est-ce pas*, Leduc?"

Louis set down *un chocolat chaud* topped by a dollop of crème. The dark drink was thick enough to float her spoon.

Exquisite.

A pre-*apéro* set scattered at the counter; an off-duty *flic* perched over a *ballon* of brandy. Two matrons with shopping bags at their feet sipped wine, deep in conversation; a pinstripe-suited lawyer whose black robe peeked out from his briefcase drank an espresso. Two animated men in blue overalls emblazoned with *Electricité de la Préfecture de Police* chatted over beers. Your typical late-afternoon crowd, a *chanson* playing in the background.

Aimée leaned back in her chair, savoring the velvety chocolate as it slid down her throat. Then Toureau slid into view.

"Good to see whose side you're on, Morbier," said Toureau. He signaled to Louis and pointed to Morbier's *bière*. "I'll have the same," he barked.

Already throwing around orders and he hadn't even sat down. Toureau hung his blue wool duffel coat on the nearby rack. Glared at Aimée. Sat and lit a cigarette.

"Quit the aggro, Toureau," said Aimée. "Let's have a little conversation."

"I'm here, aren't I?"

Did he want her to fall to her knees in gratitude?

She wished his very presence didn't make her see red. She tried to let this slide off her back, like her father would do.

Aimée shot Louis a look as he brought Toureau's beer. Discreetly, Louis pulled high velvet drapes across the ceiling, blocking their table off from the rest of the bistro.

"Why blackmail the guard, Feroze?" she asked him.

Toureau pursed his lips. "I don't know what you're talking about," he said.

"Truth bother you, Toureau?" Aimée drained her *chocolat chaud*. Licked the cup's lip.

"Who's blackmailing who?"

"Cut the act. You know about Feroze."

"Me? Why would I blackmail a *gardien?*" he said, dismissive. Threw a macho glance at Morbier.

Another one who needed his ego sanded down.

"You spit in my coffee to warn me off this investigation, so I can think of a few reasons."

Toureau slammed his fist on the table. The spoons jumped. "This was not your case."

Morbier put his palm up. "Both of you, stop it." His ridged fingernails, yellowed by tobacco stains, caught in the light of the wall sconce.

She nodded.

"*Bon,*" said Morbier. "Let's start over."

Aimée took a breath and related an edited version of what Feroze told her.

"Someone was threatening him with blackmail. Was it you?"

"Blackmail him? What would I possibly get out of that? He's already in police employ."

"All I know is that Boris ran out of my daughter's birthday party because he'd forgotten her present at his office, *n'est-ce pas*, Morbier?"

Morbier nodded.

"Next thing I know, you're calling from Boris's phone, refusing to identify yourself, and I hear a bomb go off." Indisputable facts. She needed him to agree so they could move forward. "Does that sum it up so far, Toureau?"

"How was I supposed to know who would answer that phone? I needed to know who it belonged to."

She took that as confirmation.

"I couldn't understand why Feroze, a guard on his rounds, hadn't seen Boris that night." She paused. "Later he told me he had."

Toureau took a swig of beer. "Did Feroze accuse me or someone else on the force of blackmailing him?"

"Not in those words." Her heel had jammed in a crack in the wooden floor. She wiggled it carefully, afraid she'd break Martine's stiletto. Leaned down to massage her ankle.

"*Et voilà.* He's exaggerating things. Blowing them out of proportion."

"What do you mean by that?"

Toureau expelled air, gave a large shrug. "Iranians start every story at the beginning of the universe," he said. "My ex-wife is Iranian. I know."

"Tell me what that means." So far it just seemed like he was chalking things up to stereotypes and a soured relationship.

Pause.

"Explain things so we can move on," said Morbier.

Another pause.

"No need to be lovebirds," said Morbier, "just communicate."

Toureau looked away.

Morbier drained his beer. "Fine," he said, "act like spoiled children. But not on my time."

Morbier pocketed his cigarettes and gestured to Louis for the bill. Toureau took Morbier's arm.

"*Désolé,* you're right," said Toureau. "My ex is Feroze's first cousin. They're a close-knit family. There are dynamics there I don't understand. Different cultural values. When I try to ask Feroze about my ex-wife and my child . . ." Toureau shrugged again. "He thinks I'm threatening to out him or something. I wouldn't do that. My ex thinks I want to demand custody. I never would. It's complicated, and the Iranian community's tight. Everyone knows each other. They talk."

So he did know Feroze's secret. But hadn't blackmailed him. For the first time she believed him. But did this connection fit in with the bombing?

"What's Bijan Ali's involvement?"

Toureau downed his beer. Reached out past the curtain and gestured to a watchful Louis for another round. "I heard you assisted in his capture." His words came with a grudging respect. Her jaw nearly dropped. Still, he didn't answer her question.

About to pose it again, she stopped herself. A muscle in Toureau's neck twitched. Wait, she told herself.

"My youngest called Bijan Ali a monster. Summers at the swimming pool he'd be there with the other Iranians. Everyone knew he was former SAVAK. That and his tattoos set him apart."

Aimée remembered the spider tattoo crawling up his neck.

Morbier nodded. "The elephant in the room, *c'est ça?*"

"But you're a *flic*," said Aimée. Didn't you ever go after him?"

"For what? Criminal masterminds don't do their own dirty work. *Bien sûr*, I kept my eye on him informally, but he's a specter. Operating behind the scenes."

Outside the window, a grey wash of sky over Pont Saint-Michel was alight with a lemon glow that heralded twilight.

"Why did you plant *plastique* under Boris's fingernails, Toureau?" Her fingers tensed on her mug handle. She watched for a reaction: another twitch, a telltale jerk.

"I'm not a dirty *flic*," he said. He looked pointedly at her. "Unlike some."

"*Attendez*, I cleared my father's name years ago. Tell him, Morbier."

Morbier slid the recorder out from under the thick white napkin. Clicked it off. "We're going to quit playing stupid games now, Leduc."

Her heart fell. He'd betrayed her. Again.

Morbier scratched a match against the edge of the table. A yellow-white flame as he lit his Gauloise.

"Same for you, Toureau. Tell her the truth. Off the record." He inhaled. Exhaled. Coughed.

Not good. He'd promised her he'd cut back on cigarettes.

"Or, *mes enfants*, I stop refereeing," said Morbier.

Louis, silent as smoke, served another round of beers and a *chocolat chaud* for her. Morbier slid a large franc note into his hand and he slid away. Metal clinked as he pulled the velvet curtains closed again.

She would need the sugar high for this.

"Why should I trust you?" said Toureau.

"Trust *me*?" Emotion rose in her chest. "I'm only here for Boris. He's in a coma because I let him go that night to get my daughter's birthday present."

"*Ça suffit*," said Morbier.

Toureau averted his eyes, narrow slits of suspicion.

He pulled out a small digital camcorder from his inside jacket pocket. Flipped on the power. Brought his chair closer to hers, the legs scraping over the tile floor.

"We documented everything, Mademoiselle Leduc," he said, a look she couldn't read in his eyes. "Ready?"

On the camera's screen, the horrific night unfolded. She could feel the soot and searing pain at the back of her throat; feel the drizzle on her skin. She watched as Boris's unconscious body was discovered by police search dogs in the rubble, the fire crew hoisting him onto a stretcher, a *flic* covering him with his jacket then a foil blanket, a team lifting him into the ambulance. Inside the ambulance, the medics worked on Boris's vitals—his bloody, dirty hands and bare feet bagged for later treatment. The gurney taking the stretcher into the emergency ward of Hôpital Vaugirard. The rush to the X-ray and scan, the operating room.

"Why did you film this?" she asked, breathless.

"Since 9/11, it's standard procedure to record everything in case we miss something and experts need to reconstruct the events at the scene."

Aimée took a deep breath. She remembered seeing the bags on his hands.

"So you're saying his hands were covered the whole time?"

For the first time, she saw hurt in his eyes. "Look, I didn't want it to be true either. He's one of us. A friend. I apologize for lashing out at you that night. I didn't want you doing something that might complicate his case."

Aimée stuffed down a sob. Tried to control the quivering in her throat. No one had planted the explosives on Boris.

Toureau fast-forwarded the camcorder for a few minutes, then paused it. "Boris came out of his coma an hour ago. I just picked up this tape from the hospital."

Aimée peered closer.

A still shot of Boris in a hospital bed. Bruises covered his swollen face. His head had been shaved. Bandaged and still intubated, his eyes closed. She felt her breath catch.

"Is he conscious yet?" she asked. Her fingernails dug into her palms.

"Not yet. The doctors say he could have motor impairment or brain damage when he wakes up."

She studied the grainy photo, noted the drips feeding into his arm. This was serious. This arsenal of machines meant they were afraid he'd code out any time. Would that be better for him? He'd avoid prison and shame. Wouldn't suffer life as a vegetable.

What the hell was she thinking?

Despite all this, she knew Boris hadn't set the bomb. It simply wasn't something he would do.

"Have you checked whether Noiro had Semtex traces on him?"

Toureau shook his head. "The results aren't back yet. I'll follow up." His phone beeped. "Got to go."

"Send me that last image of Boris in the hospital."

He frowned, then nodded.

"*Merci*, Toureau. Oh, and one more thing. I need a meeting with Dr. Joly, the scientist."

From his tensed shoulders, Toureau looked ready to veto this request.

Morbier sighed. "She's her father's daughter. Knows when to keep quiet. Right, Leduc?"

"*Bien sûr, parrain*," she said, using the more formal term for godfather. "Always."

Wednesday Afternoon
The Ministry of Interior · Place Beauvau

"BELLAN, THE MINISTER would like a word," said the commander.

"*Bien sûr*," he said.

He followed Tingry from the salon down a corridor in the ministry.

What now?

Bellan was burning to open the report he'd just received. A brief analysis of the evidence they had so far from the bomb site on rue de Dantzig. Hopefully, the notes the bomb technician had written up for him would clarify inconsistencies. Quick and dirty, he'd requested. Unofficial.

The commander paused in the corridor of the seventeenth-century building before entering the modern underground wing, part bunker and part strategic center.

"The minister's concerned. It's important to avoid political overtones concerning Farah Diba," said the commander. "He'll tell you himself."

Farah Diba? He searched his memory. Remembered. The widow of the former Shah of Iran.

Shown into the minister's office, Bellan contained his surprise as the minister smiled and handed him a recent *Paris Match* magazine with Farah Diba gracing the cover. She was a striking woman, couture-clad with her teenage children in exile on the Riviera.

In exile on the Riviera? The idea made him choke. But wasn't that where all the deposed leaders and their families settled? Baby Doc Duvalier and the Congolese dictators protected by the government and his ministry.

"Farah Diba's now living in Paris on quai d'Orsay," said the minister.

Millionaire's Row.

"Her father studied at the Sorbonne. Farah Diba continued the tradition by attending *l'école d'architecture*," continued the minister. "She met her husband, the Shah, in Paris. So she holds a special place in her heart for France. We treasure her family's deep ties with our country. She herself insists on being apolitical but is a force and unifier of the exiled Iranian community here. She does much good with exiles, and we regard her as a goodwill *ambassadrice*."

With a huge Swiss bank account stolen by the Shah. But that was just what Bellan's mother's *Voici* tabloid said.

Bellan had a premonition—or just a sinking feeling—that the minister was working up to having him guard Farah Diba or her retinue.

Ten minutes later, as a "reward" for his work, he'd been appointed to the Shah's family detail. Effective immediately.

Wednesday • Late Afternoon

FEROZE HADN'T RETURNED Aimée's messages, but nearly twenty-four hours later she finally reached him.

"I can't talk long," he said.

Like she had time for small talk either.

"I need to know who blackmailed you," she said. "It's not Toureau. Is it Bijan?"

"Bijan . . . which Bijan?"

"With the spider tattoo on his neck. Bijan Ali."

"*Comment?*" said a worried-sounding Feroze. "*Mais non,* Bijan Ali is family, a great-uncle on my mother's side."

"He funds terrorists, Feroze."

"But he doesn't mess with family."

Principles.

Aimée wanted to shake him. "Please tell me the truth, Feroze. Was someone really blackmailing you?"

In the background she heard children's voices. The creak of a swing. Laughter.

"I . . . may have exaggerated a bit. Boris always called me a drama queen," said Feroze.

"Does that mean you dreamed up a blackmail threat?"

"Stéfane's five years younger than me and he wanted to move in, but it's too soon with my family . . . well . . ."

Aimée's bus loomed at the corner. She had to hop on here or risk being late to pick up Serge's twins.

"Stéfane the bomb tech is your boyfriend? The badminton player? And he threatened to tell your family about his relationship with you, *c'est ça?*"

"We made up last night. I'm sorry I framed it that way."

Great. "Fingers have been pointed at you for the bombing."

He exhaled in disgust. "Being Iranian doesn't make me a terrorist."

"More like you had the best opportunity."

"Noiro's a dirty druggie," said Feroze. "My gut says he got paid but screwed up the bombs."

Aimée's mind returned to the figure in the video who'd carried the handbag into the lab and left without it.

"I don't get it. You say Boris is your friend, but you don't seem to want to help him. Even after he offered you his support."

For the first time, he seemed ashamed. "You're right. I'll be a better friend."

"Then find me some proof, Feroze," she said. "It's the only way we can help Boris."

AIMÉE MANAGED TO mount the crowded bus on the quai. Squeezed herself to the rear. Faint sunlight reflected on the Seine below, which flowed like dirty caramel.

Could Noiro have been the culprit? But who would have paid him to plant the bombs?

Her phone vibrated in her purse. Madame Latour's number. Finally. After all the messages she'd left.

Scrounging for her phone in the bottom of her bag took forever; her fingers first locating Chloé's hair scrunchy, a stub of Chanel lipstick, a software manual. By the time she'd found it, the call had gone to voice mail.

Merde.

Aimée pressed CALL BACK.

Madame Latour answered on the first ring. "I've got nothing to say if you're a journalist, Mademoiselle Leduc," she said, her voice low and scratchy.

A smoker? Or had she been crying?

"Not at all, Madame Latour," Aimée said, desperate to keep her on the line. She lowered her voice. "I'm with the GIGN." Serge hadn't gotten back to her yet, so she took a guess. "Madame, the autopsy reports of your husband and niece raise questions."

Several bus passengers turned to look at her.

Merde encore.

"Questions? *Now* you call them questions? What about when *I* raised questions?"

Had she just stuck her foot in it?

Aimée lowered her voice to almost a whisper. "What do you mean, madame?"

"Don't you people read each other's reports? Communicate?" Her grating, scratchy voice rose. "My niece would never have committed suicide. No reason. I said this to seven different people in law enforcement."

The bus jerked to a halt. People crumpled into her. Forget this.

Aimée struggled, jostling past the complaining passengers to get out at the stop.

"But not to me, madame. Can you tell me about her?" she said, hurrying as she pulled her collar up against the wind rustling the bare branches above.

Aimée thought of the man's ring in the evidence bag. "Did she have a boyfriend?"

"No one special or she would have told me."

But didn't every relative say that?

Aimée hurried on the busy street. Glanced at her Tintin watch. She could just make it.

"Delphine liked women," said Madame Latour. "Not that it

matters, but she was open about it. She had a job at an entirely woman-run law firm waiting for her after graduation. Meanwhile she was completing her journal article for a law review while interning at Paris Quatre." The Sorbonne.

Their law division ranked low. Odd place to intern.

"Why didn't she intern at the firm where she'd been hired?"

A sigh. "Delphine suffered genetic osteoporosis all her life," she said. "She's . . . she was top of her class. Studied during her hospital stays. So sweet, never complained, overcame every obstacle. In September, complications occurred when she broke her arm. She still had a cast on since her bones repaired slowly. It set her behind."

Finally she reached the school gate and waved at the twins. Caught their attention.

"*Un moment, Madame*," she said, "*s'il vous plaît.*"

She greeted the twins, took their backpacks, and guided them to the café terrace next door. Nodded to the waiter and ordered them Orangina and Coca-Cola Citron—drinks expressly banned by their mother. Thank God for small mercies.

She pointed to her phone, then to them and mimed a drink.

Big grins answered her.

She'd let them kick a soccer ball in the square to work off the sugar later.

Back on the pavement, she paced, keeping her eye on the twins.

"Madame, was Delphine depressed?"

A pause. "*Pas du tout*. Upbeat. Happy and relieved. She'd turned in her article. The last thing she said was—"

One of the twins called out to Aimée. She put up her palm in a wait-a-minute gesture. A bus blew its horn and drowned out everything.

"—meeting someone on the law review committee—"

"She was? Why call it a suicide so quickly if she'd made plans?"

"All I know is, they didn't find her body until a day later."

Aimée winced. That hadn't been in the report.

Sobs came over the line.

"What's the committee member's name?"

"I don't know. He was at some fancy law firm. I never got his name."

"Is there anything you can remember?"

"We told this to so many people, so many times. With 9/11 happening, Islamic terrorism, the Toulouse bombing, they just pushed my niece's case aside."

Still no excuse.

"I know it's difficult to speak about this," Aimée said, trying to empathize.

"Difficult?" Madame Latour's voice rose. "Quit patronizing me, mademoiselle."

Merde, she'd tried for tact but missed the mark.

"The stress gave my husband a heart attack," she said. "Now they're both gone. No one can bring them back."

Madame Latour stifled another sob.

"*Désolée*, madame," she said. "There's no one else, so I'm asking you for information. There might be links to a bombing."

"Bombing?" Madame Latour caught her breath. "The one on the news? *C'est ça?*"

"That's all I can say, madame."

"*Et alors*, I do remember she used to go to a lawyer's at la Motte-Picquet," she said. "I'm sorry, but that's all I know. Please don't call me again unless you can do something."

Click.

Aimée sat down across from the boys and ordered a double espresso.

Her own client Dutot's office was at la Motte-Picquet—he or someone in his firm might know who sat on the law review committee. She heard the twins' latest news from school, then bribed them with the promise of gummy bears if they kept quiet while she made two phone calls.

One to Dutot. Got voice mail.

The next to Melac, who answered with a brusque, "About time."

"I'm here with Serge's twins," she said. "They're coming to visit the farm this weekend."

"Wonderful. Chloé will love that. She misses you." Melac waited a beat.

"I miss her, too."

"Listen, I think you should come up to Brittany now. I know that Boris has come out of his coma. You've nailed Action Directe and a high-profile Iranian terrorist."

"It's complicated, Melac."

"The chain of command handles complicated. Not your job. You're done."

Why didn't she feel done? She missed Chloé. Wanted to focus on Melac and the future and next steps.

But did she want the next steps? Moving to Brittany, working for the ministry? Would it be such a bad thing?

"The boys and I want to say hello to Chloé."

Chloé's excited laugh greeted her. She loved the twins, and after slobber kisses over the phone, she sang them a song. How Aimée longed to be with her daughter.

AIMÉE DEPOSITED THE twins, angelic for once, at their grand-mère's and declined her apéro offer with regret. Found a taxi two blocks away, reapplied her lipstick and mascara. Made herself take a deep breath. After six attempts she finally reached the forensic bomb tech, who'd agreed to a short impromptu meeting.

She was late. And stuck in traffic.

René had already arrived—thank God—and messaged her to say that Dr. Laurent Joly only had twenty minutes.

No pressure.

She chewed at her chipped thumbnail. She had to prepare. Sequence the events from the night of the bombing to ask him the right questions.

In the taxi, she ran over the details: Boris leaving for the lab, the bomb explosion caught on Hugo's video camera, the nameless man—Paul?—running away, Action Directe's claim of responsibility, *plastique* under Boris's nails. Other possible players: Hugo's grandfather, seeking out hush money; Coco, Johan, and Pantin, the retired radicals from Action Directe; Bijan Ali, once Khomeini's fixer; Feroze, the guard; Noiro and Bird Man from the park.

She sensed that these threads intertwined but couldn't sort out how. Which leads brought her to the truth and which knotted into dead ends?

Aimée entered the Librairie Le Divan, a warm, inviting bookstore on rue de la Convention. Books everywhere, colorful nooks and crannies for reading. In the children's section, sitting on a sofa, was René; next to him Professor Laurent Joly, a man she recognized from the *démineur* crew.

They huddled in conversation, a large picture book between them.

"*Désolée*," she said. "Terrible traffic."

Dr. Joly's mouth turned down in a moue of distaste. Middle-aged, with a lean body and dark-blond hair, he seemed outdoorsy for a scientist. Then it occurred to her: he worked out in the field. "I don't have time for divas, mademoiselle."

Diva? She'd just picked up a friend's twins in return for autopsy reports—which Serge still hadn't sent. She worked herself to the bone. Certainly not a diva.

René shot her a look that froze her sharp retort on the tip of her tongue.

"Forgive me," she said, averting her eyes to appear penitential. "Please, continue."

René's eyebrows beetled together in worry. "Dr. Joly was just saying that, due to the recent anthrax attacks in the US and the train derailing outside Barcelona, they're overloaded."

Joly nodded. "It's all hands on deck. We're treating this as a global threat. My unit's still plowing through the chemical explosion at the fertilizer plant in Toulouse."

"Wasn't that just after 9/11?" asked René.

"Killed thirty and spread debris for kilometers. As you might have heard, it's the worst explosion in France since World War Two." Dr. Joly checked his phone and sighed. "Stretched thin doesn't begin to cover it."

"What can you tell us about this explosion?" said Aimée.

"Conclusively? We've been combing through the bomb-site detritus. Working backward to find where the bomb was set, what it was made of. The components. This takes time. It's like someone dumping a thousand-piece puzzle in front of you, but half the pieces are lost or burned."

He must know something by now.

"Toureau indicated you had preliminary results," Aimée said. A lie. "That you'd share with us." Another lie.

"Look, Sunday night, I walked into chaos. Shouts, horns, screaming."

Aimée nodded, remembering the smell of burnt flesh. The searing in her gut returned.

"When a bomb goes off, it sends residue everywhere from the main charge," said Dr. Joly. "Explosives aren't a hundred percent consumed, so if, for example, a bomb goes off in the street, I find nearby street signs and swab them for evidence, traces of powder, wire."

She hadn't exactly asked for a step-by-step *démineur* lesson. But she bit her tongue again.

"At the most rudimentary level, my team and I take a pair of tweezers and a sterile cotton swab and rub it over the surface area and collect soot," said Dr. Joly. "I take that back to a suite of instruments to test the extracts from the swab with water or maybe acetone to pull the explosive materials off. Then I run this through instruments to see what the bomb deposited. Part of what I'm trying to figure out is the main charge. To determine that, I use the residue that's left behind."

Dr. Joly picked up the children's book. Glanced again at the clock on the wall.

"Hope that helps," he said, about to stand. "I haven't been home in a week, and my kids are waiting."

He'd just wasted her time, revealing nothing about the case. Why had he agreed to meet just to give her the runaround? She wouldn't let him off that easy.

"But, Dr. Joly, the explosives were set *inside* the building. It's a contained site."

He'd gathered his briefcase, about to head to the cashier.

"Like I said, my preliminary report's not done."

"Two questions, please, before you leave. Could *plastique* or Semtex cause this kind of explosion? If not, what might?"

Dr. Joly looked around, then leaned in closer.

"Why?" he asked, seeming interested for the first time.

"My friend worked in the lab building and was caught in the blast. He had traces of Semtex under his fingernails."

"That's odd," said Joly, frowning.

"What do you mean?"

"First of all, Semtex is military. And I shouldn't say this, but the primary and secondary bombs were linear charges. Strictly commercial. Used for industrial purposes."

If that was true, it might be possible to exonerate Boris. "Then how—"

"You're the detective," he said. "You'll have to do the digging. But please, keep this information to yourself. It certainly shouldn't be leaving my office before it's official."

While René bought Chloé a book on horses, Aimée rang Claire, the tech who'd worked with Boris and was temporarily working in Lyon. She answered on the fourth ring.

"Claire," said Aimée, "do you remember telling me that Boris's colleague had a family emergency on Friday?"

Conversation and what sounded like water running from a tap filled the background.

"Hold on."

Voices receded. "You mean Neil?" said Claire.

For the life of her, she couldn't remember or maybe Claire had never said.

"Probably."

"Neil's father suffered a stroke and passed away. They had a funeral that weekend, so he's been incommunicado."

"How do I reach him?"

"He's coming back . . . hold on."

Claire came back on the line a minute later. "I just spoke with him. He's on the train. Terrible connection. After the storms, the cell towers are down."

"What's his number, please?"

NEIL'S VOICE WAS muffled like he was underwater. That, mingled with static on the line, gave his words a surreal quality.

"I had no idea about the bombing," he said, his words fading in and out. "My father . . ." The word blurred into elongated consonants ". . . the sample I left for him . . ."

"What sample, Neil?"

"Semtex . . ."

"Wait, why did you—"

She lost the connection. Kept trying but couldn't reach him. News bulletins on the car radio told of torrential rain, storms and flash floods up north.

"René, what if we're looking at this wrong?" She filled him in on the patchy call. "Let's get Saj looped in on this." She punched in Saj's number and put him on speakerphone. Together they caught Saj up while René drove.

"How would Semtex have entered this equation if the bomb was a linear charge?"

"*Attends*," said Saj.

The rain pattered like an insistent cat's paws on the car roof. Aimée turned up the volume on her speakerphone. The sound of Saj's fingers clicking across computer keys filled the car.

"I'm cross-referencing the GIGN data input for linear charge and Semtex," he said. "Both Semtex and *plastique* are military-grade, difficult to obtain. But a linear charge and blasting caps can be found at a building construction site."

René downshifted at the traffic light. Wind whipped at the tree branches. An umbrella flipped inside out and blew away from an elderly gentleman standing in the lines of the crosswalk.

"Looks like we need to check if there have been any recent reported thefts of explosives from building sites."

Saj clicked faster. "Matter of fact, that bit of detecting was already done by the GIGN. An earlier report stated linear explosives consistent with what the preliminary findings indicate . . . blah, blah, blah . . . were stolen from the Beaugrenelle apartment development on Sunday."

Her mind reeled. "That's here in the fifteenth arrondissement. Just a few blocks away."

René said, "So why did Boris's fingernails have traces of Semtex?"

"*Bonne question.* It makes no sense."

"I'm monitoring GIGN's recent data inputs," said Saj, "but a little research is showing me the advantage of linear explosives is brisance."

Damned rain. "What's that? Can you speak up, Saj?"

"Brisance means the shattering effect of an explosive that can cut pipe—it causes fire and subsequent explosions. A linear explosive can run off a simple circuit board, use an electrical timer on a nine-volt battery to set off blasting caps. In theory, it could be used to wrap around a gas main, blow it up and cause a massive fire. Very efficient for destroying papers and sample evidence. Whereas *plastique* causes severe damage when it explodes, but rarely causes fire."

"Say that again about the gas main," said Aimée. "Do mobile generators use propellant?"

She heard Saj clicking away.

"Fuel, gas, propane—whatever it takes to run a portable generator, you mean?" asked Saj.

"I saw generators in the parking lot powering the mobile refrigeration units," she said.

René added, "Those were installed and run by Tardi from Tout Frigo." He reached in his pocket. "Here," he said, handing Aimée a paper. "This is the info on Tardi, along with Sénéchal, the service man, and it has the phone numbers for the two other employees."

Sénéchal, Bellan's informer?

"Is his first name Paul, by chance?"

"No idea. Young with curly hair, from the office photo."

"Brilliant, René," she said.

"Say the bomber stole the linear charge and attached it to the generators or to the gas line inside the lab," said Saj, "but why?"

"Tardi's not the sharpest knife in the drawer," said René. "I can't see anyone trusting him to steal or set explosives. And he's definitely no mastermind."

"I'll contact Sénéchal and the other two," Aimée said.

"Say the goal of whoever orchestrated this was to destroy the samples. A man's signet ring was found by Delphine Latour's body." *Merde*, still no word on the autopsy from Serge. "Say that ring is the focus. The killer blew up the lab to destroy the one piece of evidence linking him to Delphine Latour."

"Wouldn't it be easier to just break in and steal the ring?"

"Like it's that easy?" she said. "Lab access doesn't guarantee you know where exactly samples are kept. Or their progress in testing and analysis. There are several floors and a basement with a huge number of archival dossiers containing their own samples. And a whole crew of scientists and lab techs buzzing around. Material was constantly shifting, at least when I was there, but they were on top of it. Boris called it a warren, but an efficient one."

René nodded. "So if the ring was in evidence and went missing, it would be noted."

"Bombing the lab to destroy the ring is still a stretch," said Saj. "But not impossible."

"But it had to be someone who knew it was there," René said.

"True," said Aimée, "and with some knowledge of the lab."

"But with that ring gone, there's no way to prove anything."

Aimée thought. Rain slid down the windshield like silver tears.

"It's someone who knew Tout Frigo would be there, bribed Tardi, and had access to stolen linear charges. Hell, it could be a building engineer."

"But why kill Delphine Latour? What's important about her?"

"Delphine's aunt last heard she was meeting a committee member of the law review over her article. That's all we have."

"Think of all the effort to make her death look like a suicide, plus blowing up the lab."

"It means he's run out of options and has everything to lose."

"Desperate," said René. "Maybe an affair? Say he murdered out of jealousy, or she was about to tell his wife. She might even have blackmailed him."

"According to her aunt, Delphine preferred women."

"So she could have blackmailed a *her*."

René hit the defroster to defog the windows. The fan whooshed, sending cool air over Aimée's ankles.

"An insider or . . . wait, there are all those apartments overlooking the lab's parking lot and entrance," said Aimée. "It would be easiest from the building right next door. Easy escape."

"So there are three questions," said Saj. "Why was Delphine Latour murdered? What's Semtex doing under Boris's fingernails when it had nothing to do with the actual explosion? And who had access to the lab?"

She hoped Delphine's autopsy report would provide some answers.

"Saj, keep monitoring the GIGN," she said, gathering her bag. "René, drop me here at the Métro, then zip straight to Gare du Nord and find Neil as he comes off his train from Lille. We have to know what he was trying to say."

"It arrives in twenty minutes," said Saj.

In the now-pelting rain, she got out of the car. René pulled out, tearing away from the curb and spraying puddle water on her boots. She hardly felt it as she ran into the Métro, clutching her phone. Serge answered.

"Got those autopsies, Serge?"

"My boss is still here."

"Serge, I picked up the twins, took them to your *belle-mère*'s, and if you're still wanting that anniversary weekend—"

"Meet me in the same place as before," said Serge.

Wednesday Evening • the Morgue

AGAIN, AIMÉE STOOD in the morgue's damp, protected vehicle bay. Rain slanted in sheets, pebbling the Seine's surface. From the *panier à salade* medics unloaded a body bag onto a stretcher.

Aimée averted her eyes. She opened the folder Serge handed her. Pulled out a decorator's brochure.

"What's this?"

Serge looked around. Smiled at a colleague meeting the stretcher. "I'd love your opinion on different wood samples. We're redoing our floors," said Serge.

He pointed to the papers under the color photos displaying samples. The autopsy reports.

"Apparently, it's all in the zigzag," said Serge.

"Meaning?" What was this code?

"See those parquet floors in a chevron pattern, *pointe de hongrie?*" Serge shot her a look that meant *play along.*

She looked at the pattern. The kind she had in her seventeenth-century flat in less than pristine condition.

"It's when the wood blocks run point-to-point and the ends are cut at an angle to create a continuous zigzag."

Aimée nodded. "I see." But she didn't. She nudged Serge in his ribs.

Serge pointed to a police report he'd clipped to the last page.

A brief glance at it disturbed her. She had to suppress a shudder. It showed a photo of crows picking at Delphine Latour's lips.

"Which one does your wife like?" said Aimée.

"She goes for the herringbone, where the wood blocks finish perpendicular to each other, resulting in a broken zigzag."

Like this whole investigation, she thought. A broken zigzag— but if she just shifted a piece, would it all make sense?

Wednesday • Early Evening • Gare du Nord

RENÉ BRAKED HARD, screeching into the delivery zone at the station door nearest the Eurostar entrance. He shoved his handicap placard on the windshield, which he hated doing, and scrawled Neil's name on the back of Chloé's horse drawing—a series of squiggles. The whole time praying he wasn't too late.

The cavernous station's blurred announcements, conversations, and roller bags clacking over the platforms were overlaid by the metallic clicking of the overhead departure and arrival schedule.

René craned his neck. Too many people were blocking his view. He strained on his tiptoes to see where the Lille train was arriving.

Platform 4. *Merde.* It had gotten there a minute ago.

René rushed forward in the streams of departing passengers, swallowed in the crowd. Not the best time to be a dwarf.

But was it ever the best time?

Huffing, he climbed on some scuffed wooden step risers used for loading luggage. Stood and waved his makeshift name card. Anxious, he scanned the hurrying departing passengers. No one looked up.

"Monsieur Neil Girard!"

No one paid attention.

He shouted, "Paging Neil Girard! Police emergency."

No response.

He shouted louder, his lungs heaving. The stairs jostled, he lost his balance and flew into the air. The seconds seemed like minutes before he landed hard on the platform, pain tearing at his hip.

WHILE SAJ SCANNED the autopsies and contents from Serge's folder into the computer, Aimée rang the Tout Frigo employees. After reaching both—one newly retired, the other out on disability—she found no reason to believe either knew of or had anything to do with the bombing.

The young part-timer Sénéchal's phone went to voice mail twice. She left no message. Debated. Worth it?

She was about to give it one more shot when her phone rang. "Sénéchal's calling back."

Saj looked up. "Paul Sénéchal, Bellan's informer who works also for Tout Frigo?"

She scanned René's notes. Idiot. She'd met him and his mother, it wasn't a common name. Why hadn't she put this together before?

She should have read René's notes.

"If I answer he'll recognize my voice. Can you answer and play along?"

"Me? Don't you want me to track him?"

"That, too."

"You mean lie? String someone along?"

"I do it all the time, Saj."

He hesitated. "But what would I say?"

"Find his location and get him to incriminate himself," she said.

"You're serious?"

"We're going to lose his call if we don't hurry. Look, we'll do a cleansing afterwards."

Saj picked up and hit speakerphone. "*Oui?*"

"About time." Paul Sénéchal was panting as if he'd been running. "I've been waiting."

Weird way to return a call. Who did he think it was?

But she mouthed "play along." With any luck Saj would get something out of him before he realized and hung up.

"You there?"

"*Oui.*"

"Small bills this time."

She caught Saj's gaze and mouthed *I'll track him*, as she slid over to René's desktop and opened a program.

"*Zut*, but I'm lost," Saj said. "Where are you?"

"Wait, who's this?" Sénéchal said.

She racked her brain for something half-convincing. She had to be quick.

Saj beat her to it. "Call me the fallback plan," he said.

"What do you mean?"

"Things have changed," he said nonchalantly. Disinterested, like he was just a hired hand. "Look, they looped me in late. Where's our handover?"

"Where's the boss?"

"No clue. Hurry up, I'm on my scooter. You're not my only delivery tonight."

She heard his sharp intake of breath. Horns. Rain plopping into what sounded like a clogged gutter.

"Small bills only. You know that much, *non?*"

A payment for services rendered—like setting a bomb? Aimée tested a hunch and scribbled a note to Saj. Lifted the paper so he could read it.

"*Bien sûr*," he said. "You told me. But it's funny for such a big job."

She grinned at Saj. He was getting the hang of it.

"What do you mean?" he said. "He told you what the job was?" He sounded terrified. "Who the hell are you?"

Keep it vague, she willed Saj. *Don't give him time to think.*

"The boss trusts me," he said. "Cooperate and you'll get a bonus."

"He owes me more anyway. Tell him I know things."

Greedy.

"They know about you. Better watch out."

"Me? I'm protected."

Aimée slid a finger across her neck.

"Word's out you're a suspect in a murder."

"*Mais non*, no one was supposed to be there." A pause. "Not my fault."

It never was their fault.

"Of course, and I know that. You do deserve that bonus. Now, are you going to keep me waiting here in the rain, or are you going to collect your money?"

Rain pattered in the background. Would he bite?

"Behind the Institut Pasteur, rue des Volontaires."

Click.

"Good job, Saj."

"We're going to have to do a major cleanse after all this lying, Aimée."

Great.

Aimée pulled up a visual on René's screen. "His nearest cell tower pinged from Pasteur." Pointed. "Here."

Aimée punched in René's number. No answer.

"He should have picked up Neil by now," said Saj.

Worried, she tried him again. Still no answer. She left a message.

Then Bellan. He answered after two rings.

"Get your team ready. I've found the bomber."

"We've already got him, Aimée."

"No, you don't. Your informer has admitted stealing the linear charges from the construction site and setting the explosives at the police lab."

Not in those words but she left that out.

"You don't understand—"

"Neil, the lab boss, will confirm the discrepancy," she interrupted. "Those Semtex traces under Boris's fingernails don't match the linear charge that blew the lab up." She really hoped all of this stuck. And that Sénéchal would lead them to his employer. "Bellan, meet me on rue des Volontaires behind the Institut Pasteur."

"I'm sorry, Aimée. We've closed the case. The minister's firm on this."

Where had his detective's instincts gone? She stifled a wave of frustration. Wouldn't argue with him.

"Fine. You don't have to bring backup, but come see for yourself."

For god's sake, Paul Sénéchal was his informer.

"Activate his tracker, Bellan."

His voice lowered to a rasping whisper. "The minister's stuck me on Farah Diba's security detail, so I need to—"

"Come to rue des Volontaires," she said again, "if you want actual closure to this case."

"I can't, Aimée."

She clicked off. Angry, disappointed. Something else lanced her heart. He hadn't even bothered to tell her they'd decided to destroy Boris's life.

She had to do something.

She picked up Delphine Latour's autopsy file again and read it the whole way through.

"According to Serge's autopsy note," she said, "Delphine Latour suffered broken bones, organ damage, and internal injuries consistent with a car accident. In other words, she'd been run over." Aimée shuddered. "More than once."

She needed backup. She dialed Julien, an old school friend who worked nights in the quartier for the Métro. They'd gone out a few times in lycée and kept in occasional touch. Aimée had once dragged Martine along to his infamous after-hours parties in the closed Métro—Julien knew every Métro line and track, abandoned or not. He agreed to meet her outside la Motte-Picquet–Grenelle station where he was supervising line equipment.

"So we rock-'n'-roll tonight, Aimée?" Julien said.

"You could say that," she said. "See you in twenty."

Saj pulled items from a drawer. "Aimée, you'll need backup and a wire." He grinned. "René doesn't like it when you go rogue."

She suited up in her blue Métro worker outfit, which provided space for a bulletproof vest beneath, plus her Swiss Army knife, a Kevlar paracord bracelet, and a tracker. Stuffed the orange vest with reflector tape in a side pocket with her phone.

THANKFUL THE RAIN had stopped, she turned the scooter key in the ignition and took off. The fresh, damp smells assailed her in the night air. She gunned her scooter across the Seine.

Aimée jumped the curb and idled the scooter by the Morris advertising pillar plastered by peeling posters. Above, the elevated Métro rattled from trains arriving at la Motte-Picquet–Grenelle station. René didn't answer and she kept getting voice mail.

Right on time, Julien emerged from a door, the old Métro workers' entrance carved into the pillar. Curly-haired, long-faced, and with a goatee. He gave her a thumbs-up.

"Volontaires in three minutes, right?"

His eyes sparkled. Always a daredevil—in fact, that was his

father's nickname for him. He handed Aimée a Métro cap, swung his leg over the seat, and gave a whoop.

"Let's go. If I'm caught, I want to at least enjoy it."

If he kept quiet, he'd be useful—right now she had no one else as backup.

"We play it low-key, Julien. A man's life's at stake, and this *mec*—"

"A real bomber?"

"*Shhh*, Julien." She revved the engine and took off.

Julien grabbed her waist to avoid going flying.

"I like your *grand-père*'s bike with the sidecar better."

Aimée parked near Métro Volontaires. It always reminded her of an Art Deco storefront, from its mustard-colored tiles with METROPOLITAIN over the sole entrance to its white stucco walls and yellow M encircled in a silver hoop.

"Odd place to meet," said Julien as they walked down rue des Volontaires. "You're sure this is it?"

Aimée nodded. But had they already missed him?

"This *mec* admits he's the bomber over the phone," murmured Julien, scanning the street, "without even knowing who you are?"

She'd wondered if this could be a setup too. But if Sénéchal was as desperate as he sounded, he would show up for his money.

Before them on the left was the small, darkened Hôpital Saint-Jacques and the Institut Pasteur looming behind it. On the right, the brick-façaded, brightly lit enclave of the Knights of Malta, and beyond that the *pension* Toscana and a resto that looked closed.

Aimée dialed Sénéchal's number. Got a busy signal.

She whispered to Julien, "Slow down." Their Métro work getups and orange vests—and with Julien carrying a lunch pail—provided the perfect cover.

No one on the street. Cars passed ahead at rue du Docteur-Roux. A dog barked. She heard a brief yell, a metallic thud, the sound of gravel spitting as a car pulled out down the street. A car with no headlights on. It took off around the corner before she got a clear view.

She didn't like this.

Before she could activate the tracker, her ear caught a faint something—a *whoosh* of the wind or footsteps?

"Hurry," Aimée said and broke into a run.

Julien thudded behind her. Inside the Knights of Malta enclave, Aimée shone her penlight over the gravel. No Sénéchal. Only tire tracks.

Merde.

He'd smelled something and taken off in that car. A siren's whine echoed in the street. A minute later they were running toward where the car had gone.

Wednesday Evening • Gare du Nord

RENÉ WARDED OFF help, embarrassment piling onto pain as he struggled to his knees. Throbbing pain seared across his hips and down both his legs. His hip had taken a beating this week. He needed Epsom salts and a hot bath.

"You're looking for someone, monsieur?" said a young woman with a clipboard. Petite and dark-haired with a pert, red-lipsticked mouth. Every inch the professional in her dark-blue suit. But what profession?

"Neil Girard, he's just come from Lille," said René, breathless. "It's an emergency."

"*D'accord*," she said. Gave him a warm smile and pulled out a portable microphone. Only then did he notice her SNCF badge. "I'll page him."

"Attention, Monsieur Neil Girard, come to platform three, *s'il vous plaît.*"

Five minutes later, Neil Girard and René sat over steaming tea in a station café. Neil had brown hair curling over his jacket collar, dark rings under his gaunt eyes. He explained that on the previous Friday afternoon he'd dropped everything at the lab to reach his father's death bed. He'd managed to say farewell, deal with his grief-stricken mother and sister, and arrange the funeral, lamenting how the recent storm had cut all outside communication.

"*Désolé*, Neil, but I have some very important questions for you," said René, pulling out his digital recorder. "Can you describe what you've told me about the Semtex sample? In detail?"

"It feels like years ago," said Neil, giving his account. "On Friday my team and I were tired after a big push to get the Toulouse samples analyzed and our reports submitted. That's been our priority. I'd just finished testing and analyzing specimens from two other cases—the victims had the same last name, oddly."

René pulled his goatee. Jackpot. "Would this be Delphine Latour and Alfred Latour?"

Neil took a sip of tea. Closed his eyes and breathed as if centering himself. "We go by case numbers—"

"4262 and 4263? A hit-and-run and suicide/homicide?"

"That's right!" said Neil. He took another deep breath. "We were about to work on those when a rush delivery came in—a ten-milliliter Semtex sample for analysis. But before I logged in the Semtex sample, our regular procedure—" he said, his breath catching.

"Take your time," René said, glancing at his wristwatch. It wouldn't help to pressure him, even if every minute counted.

Neil went on. "My phone rang, and my sister said my father wanted to say goodbye. He's been sick, and these were his final hours. If I caught the next train to Lille, I might make it. I threw on my overcoat without thinking. At the front door, I realized I was still wearing my lab coat underneath, plus my face mask. And I'd put the Semtex in my pocket like a fool. Boris's office was right there, but he was out. I left the coat and the sample on his desk with a quick note and taxied to Gare du Nord."

Neil gave an anguished look.

"I meant to call him from the train. But the doctors and my sister were ringing me the entire time I was en route. We had to decide whether to put my father on life support. It was my mistake. Legally, I'm required to log dangerous material into custody. It's my fault that Boris is a suspect."

Was it really that simple? A grief-stricken man had made a mistake? But it made perfect sense: Boris went to his office Sunday evening for Chloé's gift, found the sample on his desk, and handled it then. A deep relief settled over René.

"It's not your fault," René said. "You had so much going on."

The words Aimée had written on the board came to him: *insiders, suppliers, techs, flics* and *loyalty, hit man, revenge, cover-up.* He knew he had to push just a little further. Ignore the painful throb in his hips.

"Who would be capable of setting off explosives in the lab?"

"Apart from staff?" said Neil. "It honestly wouldn't be that difficult. So many people come through the lab. We have a laundry service that delivers, cleaning staff, service techs for all of our instruments and machines."

"Like Tout Frigo."

He nodded. "Tout Frigo serviced our old refrigeration units. A real pain." Neil paused. "Maybe it's silly, but . . ."

"Go ahead," said René.

"We got a call from a radio show not too long ago. The show was about crime: police procedure, how our lab processes evidence samples. Very basic, but the reporter spent a day with us in the lab. He did talk a little bit about our tech."

René put it together. "So if someone who listened to the radio show knew the kind of analysis that went on and knew where the lab was—not necessarily difficult information to find—they might be able to target that part of the building. It would be even easier if they saw that repairs were being made to those generators outside."

Neil nodded. "It's feasible. Difficult, but if you were determined, it's possible."

"You mean to destroy evidence?"

"Unless it's something I analyzed and recorded before I left."

"But your computer's destroyed. All the records were lost."

"What do you mean? Those last two results were picked up, signed for and logged in at the *commissariat*." He lifted his phone from his pocket and pulled up a message. "I got the notice just now on the train back from Lille. Factor in the weekend—plus, sometimes it takes a working day or two for results to get logged and recorded."

Adrenaline surged through René. He could have hugged the man.

Instead, he felt in his pocket to pay for the tea. Found the SNCF woman's card—Clotilde—and saw that she'd scribbled down her personal cell number. He would definitely come back to that later.

He wedged himself off the chair, ignoring the shooting pains in his leg. Smiled. "Thank you, Neil. You've just saved Boris."

Wednesday Evening • *Métro Volontaires*

AIMÉE AND JULIEN hopped on her scooter and took off down rue Blomet.

Julien consulting his phone. "Don't you need to call for backup?"

"No time. He's getting away."

"Sorry, I can't go with you," he said. "Just got a message. They need me back at work. Problem with the third rail."

"That's not like you," she pouted. He was always up for an adventure.

"I know. But a live electric rail can fry a worker, and I'm line supervisor tonight. Pull over when you can."

She dropped him at Métro Vaugirard Convention.

"Sorry. Another time," he said with a smile, waving as he walked off.

Her tired gaze took in the stretch of rue de Vaugirard, the longest street in Paris. Should she just go home? Wait for Morbier's call?

Then, in her rearview mirror, she caught a dark car nosing out from a passage. No headlights. And it was following her.

RENÉ CURSED AT the OUT OF ORDER sign on the wire-cage elevator. Did the damn tin can ever function? Why wouldn't Aimée consider moving to a sleek modern office instead of staying in this outmoded relic of her father and grandfather's time?

But of course he knew why.

Pain sliced his thighs. He pulled himself up by the bannister, one foot at a time. Pure torture. It must have been the fall earlier.

It took him forever to get to the third floor. Cranky and perspiring, he punched in the code. Straightened up as best he could before Aimée saw him.

"Neil's given a statement and has proof that Boris is innocent. Aimée?"

He expected a yell of victory. Cries of joy.

"She's gone," Saj said, poking his head around the corner. "But bravo, René."

A small consolation.

"We need to contact the GIGN and get Boris released."

"On it," said Saj.

"Where's Aimée?"

"She went to meet Sénéchal. Tried to reach you."

René set his digital recorder on his desk. Got into his chair, wincing, and hand-cranked it up.

"Let me transfer what I recorded. It's so simple, Saj. Stupid and simple." He powered up his desktop. "And obvious, if Toureau and the GIGN hadn't been so eager to blame someone and take the easy way out."

"*Et alors*, how did it happen?"

René explained.

"*Voilà*. And Neil had already tested, released for pickup, and sent a report for the two evidence samples back to the *commissariat*."

Saj looked up from his screen, hands poised on the keyboard. "You mean the man's ring?"

"*Exactement*." René smiled and turned to Saj. It was then he noticed the look on Saj's face. Alarm.

"We might have a problem."

Wednesday Evening • *Rue de Vaugirard*

THE RED SERVICE light shone like blood on her scooter. That damn spark plug again. Her engine coughed and sputtered.

Not good.

This Vespa, more temperamental than an Italian chef, spent as much time in the garage as on the *rue*. She looked for a place to ditch it. Eyed the empty taxi stands, bus stops. Closed cafés. Where was everyone?

She spied the red glow of the Métro ahead at the next station. Could she make it?

Phone in hand, she hit speed dial. *Merde*, why wouldn't Morbier answer?

The Vespa choked and gradually came to a stop. She struggled to push it over to the sidewalk, about to make a run for it.

She didn't even see the car before steel slammed her. Slung her lurching ahead, airborne against a bus shelter alight with a champagne advertisement and the relevant bus routes. She felt herself tumbling down, her arms yanked behind her. Then something hard cracked her head and everything went black.

"YOU LET AIMÉE go to meet a *bomber?*" Horrified, René looked at Saj. "Alone?"

"She's got the tracker on her, and said she'd call Morbier and Bellan for backup. Julien, the *mec* from the Métro, was definitely with her too."

"He's crazy," said René. "Not backup. So where is she?"

Saj pulled up the tracker's program. Not activated. Slack-jawed, he stared at the dark-green screen with a stationary blinking white cursor.

"Either she forgot or—"

"She couldn't activate it." René picked up his phone. Tried Morbier. No answer.

Then he looked up Bellan's number on Aimée's computer and rang him. No answer there, either. Could be good or bad.

"This is Aimée's partner. I'm sending you a recording, Bellan," he said, leaving a message. "It's proof Boris Viard didn't set the bomb. Call me."

René hung up with a sinking feeling. His insides churned. And his damn legs were locking up, going numb. At any moment he might go stiff and be unable to move again.

"Saj, we've got to find Aimée."

Wednesday Evening • Hôpital Vaugirard

HUGO WATCHED THE nurse put sprigs of fir and wild mint into a vase on his hospital table. Inhaled their fragrance. That familiar smell he remembered from walking along la Petite Ceinture.

Who'd bring this to a patient? Weird. Like some kind of message.

"From your uncle," she said, smiling.

"*Comment?*" said Hugo. His only uncle was dead. Suffered a massive coronary in Monsieur Leban's butcher shop years ago.

Unease bristled at his neck. Hugo's gut told him to leave. He scanned the room for his clothes.

"How long ago did he bring these?"

"No idea," she said. "Something wrong?"

"Where are my clothes, miss?"

"We had to cut them off of you," she said. "Your mother's bringing fresh ones tomorrow. She didn't want you to get any ideas about leaving before the priest comes for your confession."

Of course she didn't. But she didn't know a killer was after him. His heart thumped so hard he thought the nurse might hear it.

He had to get out of here.

Wednesday Evening

AIMÉE'S TEMPLE THROBBED. She blinked, her vision pebbled with dark spots. Flex ties cut into her wrists and bare ankles—she was trussed like an animal for slaughter. Her mouth was dry as dust.

Where was she?

"You're a problem, Mademoiselle Leduc," said a voice to her left. A figure loomed over her. "A problem I don't need."

She recognized that voice. Its cadence. But it didn't sound so culturally refined or academic now.

Idiot. Why hadn't she seen what had been staring her in the face? Now that she thought about it, even Sami—a creature bred to be loyal—had seemed to prefer her to him.

She put the pieces together. Cléry attempted to run her down but had ended up slamming her into the bus shelter. She remembered bracing her arms to break her fall—she couldn't have been unconscious for long.

Too public to leave her for injured or dead, so he'd moved her.

Dizziness washed over her in waves. Her wrists felt slick with blood. Any movement brought sharp, cutting pain. Desperate, she wiggled her pinkie, feeling for the paracord bracelet. Winced at the resulting slice to her wrist. But it was still there.

She had to stall him.

"Pretty good plan," she said, rasping.

"You think so?" She heard pride in Benedict Cléry's voice.

Chloé's face flashed before her. How could she have been stupid enough to pursue this without backup?

If it took everything she had, she'd get out of here and back to her daughter.

"Outwitted me." She made herself push the words out. Ignored the pain. Moistened her mouth. "I had no clue."

Her vision cleared bit by bit. She noted the shadowy grey world of brick arches overhead; musty smells, faint odors of engine oil. On the dirt floor, her body vibrated from the Métro's rumbling. She glanced around for her belongings and spotted only her tracker in a pool of viscous oil. Ruined. Her bulletproof vest and fluorescent orange reflector vest were tossed to the side. Her Métro suit pockets were inside out and empty. Not even her Swiss Army knife was in sight.

"Always stay informed," said Cléry. "Know your history, listen to the news. Adapt. It's what I teach my students."

His corduroy jacket and cashmere scarf gone, he now wore an oil-stained mechanic's jumpsuit. He knelt on the dirt floor pounding out dents in a blue Renault's bumper. The gentle *tac, tac* of a hammer followed by whizzing as he smoothed out the surface with a handheld sander.

"So you planted evidence involving Action Directe," she said. Took a breath. "Because an old radical fugitive had recently given himself up?" She forced herself to keep talking. "You took advantage of the situation. Kept pointing the finger at Feroze, too."

"It worked, *n'est-ce pas?*"

For a while, yes.

"Why? Who would link that suicide-turned-homicide to the bombing?" Her pinkie caught and loosened the Kevlar paracord.

"That's the beauty of it," said Cléry. "Who would think anyone would go as far as to bomb a government building to cover up a smaller crime? Only terrorist radicals would execute something so risky and complex."

She could practically feel the smugness radiating from him.

He set the sander down and rummaged in a toolbox. Metal clinking against metal.

"I've always enjoyed Agatha Christie's work," he said, his tone conversational. "You could call this a small homage to her. Two completely distinct crimes with no apparent links—I doubt even Poirot and his little grey cells would've gotten this one."

Was this just a game to him? Some intellectual exercise?

René loved Agatha Christie. Too formulaic for Aimée. The criminal was always the one you were meant to suspect least, the sympathetic character. Benedict Cléry: dog owner, professor, helpful citizen in the quartier. But she'd suspected Cléry at first, how he'd showed up conveniently.

"But why?" Aimée caught a ragged breath. "You almost burned down La Ruche, killed two homeless men, the artist, and Delphine."

"Don't call me a murderer." His tone rose in denial. "It wasn't supposed to happen. None of this was." He waved a mallet in the dim light. "I tried explaining to Delphine, but she wouldn't listen."

"Listen? I don't understand." Her forefinger worked the knots to unravel the bracelet.

"It was an accident." He straightened up. "She jumped out of the car. I couldn't stop and ran her over accidentally." His voice broke. "My god, then it hit me. *What had I done?*"

A simple car accident? But the autopsy showed multiple fractures and broken bones, concluding she'd been run over several times.

Liar.

"That must have been awful," she said, soothing her voice. Swallowed. "But why not get help? Report an accident?"

"Involve the authorities and ruin my tenure track in the department? Everyone knew I was going to a conference and I would have if Delphine hadn't hounded me."

So it was all about him.

"This was Delphine's fault, she started it," he said. "You must understand, she made me do it."

Blame the victim. Sickened, Aimée worked her bloodied fingers harder. Cléry straightened up and found another tool chest. Pulled out a tray of screws. "Delphine fancied herself the hot lawyer, but she wouldn't listen to reason."

"How so? I heard she was brilliant."

"Brilliant?" He shook his head. Snorted. "Mediocre at best. But I didn't mean to kill her. It wasn't like that. I just had to stop her."

Stop her? Delphine's arm had been broken, and she'd already suffered from severe osteoporosis. Not exactly a pillar of strength.

Aimée's fingers worked, tugging on the bracelet. With enough tension, the Kevlar paracord would saw through wire, pipe . . . and a flex tie.

The dirt ground under her rumbled again.

Desperate, she needed to keep him talking until she could . . . what? No one had responded to her calls, no one knew her location. She kicked herself for not turning on the tracker earlier.

"Was she blackmailing you?"

Benedict Cléry took out a soldering rod. Plugged it into a wall outlet. "You're fishing, Mademoiselle Leduc."

"What did she have on you? Was it sexual harassment?"

"Still fishing." So he did regard this as a game—but she knew that the longer he talked, the better things would work out for her. She had to free herself without him noticing so she could escape.

"Didn't the *flics* question you?"

As if scenting a link, he leaned forward. "Why would they?"

Fair. The *flics* only expended so much energy looking into what
was first deemed suicide. Her father would call that shoddy police
work.

"She was meeting a law review committee member about her
journal article, according to her aunt. That was you?"

Her wrists burned, but she kept picking and loosening the
cords.

"I always supported Delphine," he said, shaking his head.

He picked up his cellphone and checked for a message. Put it
down and picked up the soldering rod.

"I even went out of my way to suggest her for the law review,"
he said. "It shocked me when she wouldn't give me credit in her
article. She claimed I'd stolen her ideas and put them in my lec-
tures. It was the other way around."

Now Aimée understood. He'd had to stop Delphine from
exposing him before he got his big promotion.

"So it all came to a head when she threatened to accuse you of
plagiarizing her work, *c'est ça?*"

His slap stung her face. Then he slapped her again. Harder.
Everything fizzed with pain. She'd just bitten her own tongue
bloody.

"That little *salope* told me I was a dinosaur. So ungrateful. Put
my professorship at stake. Can you imagine?"

Blood ran from the side of her mouth.

"It's so simple to mislead *les flics*," he said, his tone matter-of-
fact. Aimée saw the pale band of skin on his pinkie finger. Where
he'd once worn a signet ring. "I merely took advantage of the situation, like you said. I should thank you for opening your mouth in
the crowd. Identifying you made it so easy."

She spat blood on the ground.

"You ran over Delphine, threw her body down the embankment onto the tracks," she said, gasping. "That's when you lost

your ring. The homeless *mec* Noiro saw you hunting for it. When the ring was logged as evidence, you hired Paul Sénéchal to blow up the lab. Total overkill."

"But he already works for me," he said, "and it's quite simple since we've been doing installation work at the lab for a long time."

Her thoughts went to René's account of his visit to Tout Frigo: the ledger, the owner's call. And then it made sense.

"Your family owned Tout Frigo, a business you've run into the ground."

He gave a rueful smile. Nodded.

"I'm not a criminal," he said. "*Alors*, with Delphine, what's done was done—an accident. So I had to make things go away. But I wouldn't put anyone at risk. This would be a bloodless crime—a bomb goes off in a deserted lab. *Pouf*, everything up in smoke. No one would get hurt."

"It didn't work out that way," she said, gritting her teeth. Twisting and rubbing the paracord.

"That wasn't my fault. A worthless druggie slept there, and you want to blame me? He wasn't supposed to be there. Neither was your friend, Boris."

Blame everyone else.

Her phone beeped. Cléry took it out of his pocket.

"Let's see who's calling." He waited until her phone went to voice mail and then hit the speakerphone to play the message.

"*Maman?*" Chloé's lilting voice broke the silence apart from the *drip, drip* of water from the rusted wall pipe.

Her heart hammered.

"Chloé?" But of course, Chloé couldn't hear her.

Then Melac's voice: "Blow *Maman* a kiss and say you miss her, Chloé."

And then Benedict Cléry stomped her phone to pieces under his heel.

Aimée felt a moment of blind fury. She was ready to fight.

Cléry's own phone beeped. With a whoosh of damp air, he leaned down to answer. She couldn't make out his words before he'd clicked off his phone.

She kept working her fingers, slippery in her sticky blood, but loosening the paracord until it unwound.

Thanks to Julien's underground parties in the Métro, she knew where she was. Cléry had hunched back down, phone still in hand. She sensed he was waiting for someone or something. She was so close—just had to keep him talking.

"But why set a fire at La Ruche? Burn Paul's girlfriend to death?"

"*Rasa?* She knew too much. Paul's careless. Sometimes I have to take care of things myself. Like I'll take care of you. They'll never find you under the concrete at Porte de Versailles."

Her teeth clenched. Why couldn't her fingers work faster? "Paul's an informer. He knows about you."

Cléry shrugged. "Of course he does. Very efficient, frying that Noiro—a two-for-one deal."

His manner turned her skin cold. No wonder he didn't seem worried that Paul was Bellan's *tonton*. He'd known all about it—figured it protected him.

She fingered the loose paracord in her grasp. Pincered each end between thumbs and forefingers, with only a few centimeters of leeway. She tugged it back and forth, bit by bit.

If only her blood hadn't made her fingers so slippery. The sawing cut deeper into her wrists each time. Like knives slicing her skin.

Power through the pain, she told herself. Keep going.

"Paul's bringing Hugo by now."

"That sex-obsessed teenager?" She snorted. "He doesn't know anything. He's just a kid."

"Oh, you'd be surprised." Cléry headed toward a block-and-tackle pulley system near the dark arches.

Foreboding filled her.

The last strand of flex tie gave. She took a valuable moment to clench her fists as the numbness dissipated and her circulation returned.

Her ankles were still tied. Automobile parts and tools lay everywhere. Screwdrivers on benches.

She scooched ahead on her derrière, reached for a screwdriver and rusted crowbar by a tire. Tried to leverage herself up on her bare feet. Teetered off balance on her bound ankles.

Cléry held her Swiss Army knife. Pointed it at her. "Stupid move, mademoiselle."

She'd kept her hands behind her back. When he rushed at her with her own knife, she dodged and swung the rusted crowbar. Hard. Connected with his stomach.

He went down, moaning.

She whacked him again, knocking her knife from his hand. Gasping, she scrambled for it and quickly used the knife to slit the flex tie binding her ankles. He doubled over, groaned, and struggled to rise. Cléry caught the cuff of her pant leg, yanking her down.

Using her last bit of strength, she kicked him off and, stone by slick stone, pulled herself up the uneven wall. As fast as she could with bloodied fingers, she pulled the coiled chains attached to the pulley system and looped them around his ankles. Before he could get up, she'd unbraided her bracelet and knotted one strand of Kevlar paracord in the chains, then looped another around his wrists.

She found the pulley and cranked his writhing body up until he was dangling like a fish, his head a stool's height from the ground.

"*Non, non* . . . you can't leave me like this."

She took his cell phone. "Why not?"

"Kill me now."

"I'd like to." It was true. "You destroyed lives, broke up families. All these tragedies. And for what?"

"Everything got out of hand. *Alors*, I tried to stop and it just . . ."

"Escalated? To me, you're more useful alive and in prison."

In the dungeon-like darkness she searched for an escape, his shouts echoing around her. She had to get out and find Hugo before Paul did.

Wednesday Evening • Hôpital Vaugirard

IN THE HOSPITAL corridor, Hugo waddled sideways in his skimpy open-backed hospital gown. Under it he was "naked as a jaybird," as his *grand-père* would say. If Paul was here, if he'd kidnapped Hugo's grandfather, he needed the big-eyed detective's help.

He turned the handle of the first door labeled LINEN SUPPLIES and ducked in. He found white orderly attire and almost screamed while pulling on the trousers, which were too tight and scraped his burns. He found another pair so big he grabbed a tourniquet pack, broke it open, and used one as a belt. Foot-wise he ended up with surgical booties stuffed and lined with gauze.

He had no phone. No money.

Fear caught at the back of his throat.

Back out in the lit hallway, Hugo kept going. Head down, he passed the nursing station.

"But we don't transfer calls this late, mademoiselle," the nurse said. "It's lights out for the patients." A pause. "I'm sorry, Mademoiselle Leduc, but I can't disturb him."

Leduc. The detective.

Hugo turned around, about to yell out to the nurse when he saw Paul coming down the hallway in a white doctor's coat.

Wednesday Evening • Rue de Vaugirard

AIMÉE RAN, CLUTCHING Benedict Cléry's phone to her ear on rue de Vaugirard. It only showed one bar. His battery was almost dead.

"Hurry, René," she said, panting. "Hugo's in danger at the hospital and the nurse doesn't believe me."

"Where the hell are you?"

"A block away, but I don't know if I'll make it in time."

She clicked off.

She'd somehow managed to get Martine's heels back on, wobbling as blood trailed from her left ankle. A siren whined in the distance, as they seemed to at every hour.

Before she could punch in 17 for the fire department, she realized the siren was getting closer. Three fire trucks, red lights flashing, sped up the street.

Would she make it in time? Would they?

Wednesday Evening • Hôpital Vaugirard

THE FIRE ALARM whooped in piercing tones on the burn unit floor.

"Hugo?" Aimée said. Called his name again. "Hugo Dombasle? Where are you?"

She imagined him dead in his hospital bed or stabbed in another hallway. Too late. Always too late.

She ran into the next hall. Paul stood brandishing scissors. No tracker on his skinny ankles.

She slowed. "Just tell me where Hugo is."

"Same place as his grandfather," he said.

"Liar."

All of a sudden something giant and white whipped through the air. Caught Paul's arm, slapping it back. The scissors fell, clinking on the floor. And there stood Hugo, a hospital orderly's pants around his ankles.

Aimée dove and tackled Paul to the ground. Tied his arms with the tourniquet Hugo handed her.

"A hero for the second time today," she said.

"Technically, it's the first time today," he said, looking at her bleeding wrists. Blinked. "What happened?"

"I got tied up, then hung someone up. Literally."

His eyes popped.

"Now, let's go find your grandfather."

A doctor came running up, his stethoscope bouncing on his

chest. "Hold on, this patient needs care. He's in no shape to be out of bed, much less running around."

The *flics* arrived—late to the party as usual—and she looked for Toureau. No sign of him. No word from Bellan, either, whom she'd messaged. But there were Morbier and René, thank God.

"You okay, Leduc?" Concern showed in Morbier's tired eyes.

She wanted to give him a big hug like she used to when she was little. Smell the wet wool of his overcoat and know things would be all right.

Instead she took his hand—warm and calloused—and winced. The wrist and ankle bandages the nurse had applied smarted, and the antiseptic stung.

"Where's counterterrorism when you need them?" she said.

"Why?" said René. "Paul's been nabbed. Boris's colleague, Neil, confirmed he left a Semtex sample on Boris's desk—"

"What?" she interrupted. "I haven't heard any of this. Tell me."

"Poor Neil made a mistake," said René. "An honest one. Long story."

"Upshot's this, Leduc," said Morbier. "Boris has been cleared. Bellan's already got the audio of Neil's statement."

Aimée let her mind relax for a moment. Took calming breaths. Let herself savor the truth. Boris would be okay.

René nodded. "That's the good news. Bad news is, we still don't know exactly who bombed the lab or why."

"Yes, we do." She adjusted the adhesive on her wrist bandages. Winced. "Benedict Cléry's chained and hanging upside down in his viaduct garage below la Petite Ceinture."

"You hung him up?"

"Alive and struggling. He's a dirty piece of work—it's everyone's fault but his. It was him or me, René. And Hugo needed my help."

"You mean Benedict Cléry, the professor with the dog? That was *his* ring?"

"He'd plagiarized Delphine's work."

"Delphine, the student?" asked René.

"She confronted him and when she got out of his car, he hit her—an accident, according to him. Cléry tried to disguise her murder as a suicide but lost his ring when he pushed her body onto the abandoned tracks. It snowballed from there."

She related Cléry's plan of a bloodless crime to destroy evidence. How the lab bombing backfired, taking Noiro, injuring Boris, and then the bodies piled up.

"So he heard you in the crowd and used it as an opportunity to point to Action Directe." René expelled air in disgust. "Counted on a terrorist group getting attention in the Islamophobic climate."

A medicine trolley's rubber wheels squeaked on the linoleum as the nurse rolled it by.

"Cléry inherited Tout Frigo and used Sénéchal to set the bomb to destroy his evidence."

"But he didn't get to it in time," said René. "Neil sent the ring and evidence back before the explosion."

She blinked. "He did? It's not on the evidence logs."

"You'll see it on the updated one." René grinned. "Neil showed me."

Aimée looked around the hospital corridor.

"I need counterterrorism or BRI here to charge him. But since neither Bellan nor Toureau is answering my calls or responding to my messages, maybe the press will."

"Who needs another scandal?" said Morbier. Tiny beads of perspiration dotted his brow. "It's crazy to involve the press."

"People need to hear the truth, Morbier."

"The truth?"

She hated when attention was focused on the suspects, not the victims whose lives had been changed, perhaps forever. Like Delphine and Boris.

"The media and the press will make it a three-ring circus," Morbier said.

"Martine's not your standard press," she said.

"Print runs in her veins, Leduc. She's a bloodhound when it comes to news."

"I can't help that my best friend's a prizewinning journalist," she said, a little pride seeping into her voice.

"Willful and stubborn, as usual." He shook his head. "If I don't tell Toureau about this, he'll never speak to me again."

"Do what you've got to do," she said.

But she'd already decided. She borrowed René's phone to call Martine. Then Michou.

POLICE CAR LIGHTS bathed the graffitied garage under the overpass in vibrating blue and red. A surreal kaleidoscope, Aimée thought. Benedict Cléry stumbled out, handcuffed by Toureau's team. He squinted in the bright flashes from *Libération*'s photographer accompanying Martine.

Too caught up, Aimée never noticed the set of eyes watching her. Nor who tailed as René dropped her at home on Ile Saint-Louis. Or followed her up the worn marble sweep of stairs.

Thursday Morning

AIMÉE'S EYES SPLINTERED open under the sun's bright slant from her window overlooking the Seine. Loud, incessant knocking sounded from the front door. She pulled the pillow over her head. With a start she realized there must be an emergency. Chloé? Or had Boris suffered a downturn?

Her phone. She scrambled her fingers over the sheets. Where was her damn phone?

The memory sharpened into focus. Benedict Cléry had smashed it to bits last night when Chloé and Melac had called.

Merde.

She jumped up, tossed on her father's old robe, and ran barefoot to the front door.

When she opened it, Bellan stared at her. Circles under his eyes, a stubbled chin. "I tried calling, but your phone's off."

"It's kaput. Is Boris okay?"

"So far so good. You know he regained consciousness?"

She squeezed his arm. "That's wonderful." Smiled. "Now that he's cleared, maybe I'll even forgive you for not showing up last night."

"But I did."

He didn't look so good. She noticed his leather jacket on the floor. Crumpled, like he'd used it as a pillow.

"You okay?"

He looked away.

"What's going on, Bellan? Just spit it out."

"I slept here on your doorstep. I couldn't—"

Alarmed, Aimée lifted his chin to get a better look at him.

"Why'd you do that? What's wrong?"

"I was afraid you were in danger."

The dried blood on her wrist dressings showed from beneath her sleeve.

"And you were," he said, shaking his head. "You got hurt."

"I'm fine. Cléry's not."

"I know."

"You . . . do?" she asked.

His hand pulled her closer to him.

"I can't get you out of my head."

Then he was kissing her. His warmth, his leather-jacket smell. And she was kissing him back.

Then she was pulling him into the hallway.

AT THE *commissariat,* Officer Gauchat opened the cell door to reveal Hugo's grandfather lying on a bench. Hugo rolled his eyes.

What had his *grand-père* done now?

"Did you get arrested?" Hugo asked.

"There's been an alert out for him," Officer Gauchat said. "I informed Aimée Leduc. I've kept your grandfather here for his own protection."

"Protection? Where've you been? We've been worried sick about you."

"Deauville casino, *mon petit.*" His grandfather grinned and sat up.

Hugo blinked in surprise. "A casino? Gambling?"

"I won," he said. His eyes shone with pride. "Stepped into the big time. Can't let the Germans get my winnings, eh?" He pulled a receipt from the pocket of his new tailored Hugo Boss camel overcoat. "See? My new leg's on order. A custom model, titanium."

Turned out Paul had given him a phone and cash to place horseracing bets at the Café de Dantzig in order to keep him occupied until he was taken care of later. But Hugo's grandfather had given the cell phone to his friend, a limo driver, in exchange for a ride to Deauville. He'd gambled Paul's money and won, then booked a hotel room.

"Told you he'd pay for my leg, Hugo."

Thursday Morning • Ile Saint-Louis

BELLAN'S PHONE CHIMED as they tumbled onto the hallway recamier.

"Don't tell me you're going to answer that," she whispered in his ear.

He paused, running his fingers down her neck. Sighed.

"It's the minister. If I don't, he'll send an armed team to get me."

She started to laugh but caught herself. "You're serious."

"He's got a car waiting downstairs. *Merde!*"

Several hot and heavy kisses later, she saw him go down the stairs. They'd said nothing else. Made no plans. She was going to Brittany today.

This was just a one-time, spur-of-the moment incident, she told herself. They'd acted on a mutual attraction, and now it was over. *Phfft.* Finished. And it was a good thing.

She ran to the salon door, opened it and stepped onto the balcony. In the chill morning below on the quai, Bellan went to the waiting black car. If he looked up, it meant . . .

But he wouldn't.

Bellan opened the car door. Then he paused and looked right at Aimée. She hugged her bathrobe tight against the cold. He waved. She smiled and waved back.

Then the car drove off, disappearing toward Pont Marie.

It was then that she saw Melac standing on the quai by Chloé's stroller, staring up at her. Hurt on his face.

Oh my God.

She knew what this looked like. Her half-naked in her father's bathrobe, Bellan leaving first thing in the morning.

The next moment, he'd turned the stroller around, holding a sleeping Chloé, to leave.

"Wait!" she shouted.

He kept walking.

Acknowledgments

SO MANY GENEROUS people helped in my research: Betsy Glick, former FBI; Elvis Chan, FBI; Doug Lyle, MD; the ever-patient Dr. Terri Haddix, MD; Jim Maxwell, retired special agent bomb technician, FBI; JT, Susanna, cat *maman* Jean Satzer, Robyn Russell, Libby Hellmann, April Henry for the paracord, and Jaleh Hooshnan who introduced me to Téhéran-sur-Seine. In Paris, big *mercis* to Arnaud Baleste, former *brigade criminelle*; Jean-Marie; Simone Phaure on rue de le Saïda; the ever-generous and helpful Dr. Christian de Brier and Blandine de Brier Manoncourt; Naftali Skrobek, *ancien résistant*.

So much gratitude goes to Axel Bellivier, *ingénieur prévention incendie et permanence générale pôle mesure physique et sciences de l'incendie*, Laboratoire Central de la Préfecture de Police; Marie-Pierre at the Tribunal; the hospitality of Stephanie Nadalo and Afchine Dee; pals Ann Mah and Anne Ditmeyer; Julian Pepinster for the late night Métro exploration and Julie Macdonald, for those drinks at la Rhummerie.

More thanks than I can express go to Claire Menut, expert in DNA at laboratoire de police scientifique de Paris, now a friend, for the dinners, the many visits to her lab, and her staff at the Laboratoire Central Biologique de la Préfecture de Police, whom I bothered too much. Many thanks for the assistance of Sandrine Pereira-Rodrigues, *chef de cabinet du Directeur*, Laboratoire Central de la Préfecture de Police.

In the *quinzième*, thanks to Forest Collins of 52 Martinis and Jacques Leban of Boucherie Chevaline; at Institut Pasteur, generous Sarah Marsh Arnaud (and her mother, whom I met at the Tucson Book Festival!), project manager, Infravec2, Genetics and Genomics of Insect Vectors, who let me pick her brain even while picking up her daughter at the *crèche* in the Marais; Annick and Emma from the Institut Pasteur. So thankful to Bruno de Rotallier, my favourite flâneur, for his patience and long walks in the *quinzième*; to Jim former Interpol for accounts of the '86 bombing and Mick Moran's insights as former Interpol agents; to Dr. Nazanine Bayani for her courage.

Thanks to my agent, Katherine Fausset. And, as always, it's thanks to the wonderful Bronwen Hruska, publisher; Juliet Grames, who makes it all better; Paul Oliver; Rudy Martinez; Rachel Kowal; Amara Hoshijo; Janine Agro; super Steven Tran; *et toute ma famille à* Soho Press.

Nothing would get written without the encouragement of James N. Frey; my son, Tate; and Jun.

Continue readeing for a preview of the
first Kate Rees WWII Novel

THREE HOURS IN PARIS

Nine Days into the German Occupation of Paris

Montmartre, Paris | 6:15 A.M. Paris time

SACRÉ-CŒUR'S DOME FADED to a pale pearl in the light of dawn outside the fourth-story window. Kate's ears attuned to the night birds, the creaking settling of the old building, distant water gushing in the gutters. It was her second day waiting in the deserted apartment, the Lee-Enfield rifle beside her.

Will this really happen?

She moved into a crouch on the wood parquet floor in front of the balcony and winced. Her knee throbbed—she had bruised it on that stupid fence as the parachute landed in the barnyard. She smelled the faint garden aroma of Pears soap on her silk blouse, which was dampened by perspiration. The June day was already so warm.

She dipped her scarf in the water bottle, wiped her face and neck. Took another one of the pink pills and a swig of water. She needed to stay awake.

As apricot dawn blushed over the rooftop chimneys, she checked the bullets, calibrated and adjusted the telescopic mount, as she had every few hours. The spreading sunrise to her left outlined the few clouds like a bronze pencil, and lit her target area. No breeze; the air lay still, weighted with heat. Perfect conditions.

"Concentrate on your target, keep escape in the back of your mind," her handler, Stepney, had reminded her en route to the airfield outside London Friday night. "You're prepared. Follow the fallback protocol." His last-minute instruction, as she'd zipped up the flight suit in the drafty hangar: "Always remember who you're doing this for, Kate."

"As if I would forget?" she'd told him. She pushed away the memory that engulfed her mind, the towering flames, the terrible cries, and looked him straight in the eye. "Plus, I can't fail or you'll have egg all over your face, Stepney."

As dawn brightened into full morning, Kate laid her arm steady on the gilt chair on which she had propped the rifle. From the fourth floor her shot would angle down to the top step. Reading the telescopic mount, she aligned the middle of the church's top step and the water-stained stone on the limestone pillar by the door; she'd noted yesterday that the stain was approximately five feet ten inches from the ground. She would have been able to make the shot even without it—three hundred yards was an easy shot from one of the best views of the city. Next, she scoped a backup target, referencing the pillars' sculptured detail. She'd take a head shot as he emerged from the church's portico, fire once, move a centimeter to the left and then fire again. Worst-case scenario, she'd hit his neck.

With a wooden cheek rising-piece and a telescopic sight mount on its beechwood stock, the Lee-Enfield weighed about ten pounds. She'd practiced partially disassembling the rifle every other hour, eyes closed, timing herself. She wouldn't have time to fully strip it. Speed would buy her precious seconds for her escape before her target's entourage registered the rifle crack and reacted. Less than a minute, Stepney had cautioned, if her target was surrounded by his usual Führer Escort Detachment.

Her pulse thudded as she glanced at her French watch, a Maquet. 7:59 A.M. Any moment now the plane might land.

Kate sipped water, her eye trained on the parishioners

mounting Sacré-Cœur's stairs and disappearing into the church's open doors: old ladies, working men, families with children in tow. A toddler, a little girl in a yellow dress, broke away from the crowd, wandering along the portico until a woman in a blue hat caught her hand. Kate hadn't accounted for the people attending Mass. Stupid. Why hadn't Stepney's detailed plan addressed that?

She pushed her worry aside. Her gaze focused through the telescopic sight on the top step, dead center. Her target's entourage would surround him and keep him isolated from French civilians.

That's if he even comes.

The pealing church bells made her jump, the slow reverberation calling one and all to eight o'clock Mass. Maybe she'd taken too much Dexedrine.

But she kept her grip steady, her finger coiled around the metal trigger, and her eye focused.

A few latecomers hurried up the church steps. Kate recognized the concierge of the building she was hiding in. She'd sneaked past the woman yesterday, using her lock-picking training to let herself into one of the vacated apartments. An unaccustomed thrill had filled her as the locked door clicked open—she'd done it, and after only brief training in that drafty old manor, God knew where in the middle of the English countryside.

After the flurry of the call to Mass, a sleepy Sunday descended over Montmartre. The streets below her were empty except for a man pushing a barrow of melons. He rounded the corner. The morning was so quiet she heard only the twittering of sparrows in the trees, the gurgling water in the building pipes.

The wood floor was warm under her legs. On the periphery of the rifle's sight a butterfly's blue-violet wings fluttered among orange marigolds.

8:29 A.M. Her heart pounded, her doubts growing. Say her target's plans had changed—what if his flight landed tonight, tomorrow or next week? She wondered how long she could stay in this apartment before the owners returned, or a neighbor heard her moving around and knocked on the door.

8:31 A.M. As she was thinking what in God's name she'd do if she was discovered here, she heard the low thrum of car engines. Down rue Lamarck she saw the black hood of a Mercedes. Several more followed behind it, in the same formation she'd seen in the newsreels Stepney had shown her. She breathed in deep and exhaled, trying to dispel her tension.

She edged the tip of the Lee-Enfield a centimeter more through the shutter slat. Kept the rifle gripped against her shoulder and watched as the approaching convertibles proceeded at twenty miles an hour. In the passenger seat of the second Mercedes sat a man in a white coat like a housepainter's; in the rear jump seats, three gray uniforms—the elite Führerbegleitkommando bodyguards. She suppressed the temptation to shoot now—she would have only a one in five chance of hitting him in the car. Besides, that might be a decoy; her target could be riding in any of the cars behind the first Mercedes.

The second Mercedes passed under the hanging branches of linden trees. A gray-uniformed man with a movie camera on a tripod stood on the back seat of the last Mercedes, capturing the trip on film. She held her breath, waiting. No troop trucks. The cars pulled up on the Place du Parvis du Sacré-Cœur and parked before the wide stairs leading to the church entrance.

This was it. Payback time.

The air carried German voices, the tramp of boots. And then, like a sweep of gray vultures, the figures moved up the steps, a tight configuration surrounding the man in the white coat. He wore a charcoal-brimmed military cap, like the others. For a brief moment, he turned and she saw that black smudge of mustache. The Führer was in her sights now, for that flash of a second before his bodyguards ushered him through the church door. As Stepney had described, five feet ten inches and wearing a white coat. In her head she considered his quick movements, rehearsed the shot's angle to the top step where he'd stand, the timing of the shot she'd take, noting the absence of wind.

The church door opened. So soon? Kate curled her finger, keeping focus on the church pillar in her trigger hairs. But it was the woman with the blue hat, leading the toddler in the yellow dress by the hand. The little girl was crying.

Why in the world did the child have to cry right now?

It all happened in a few seconds. A gray-uniformed bodyguard herded the woman and child to the side and the Führer stepped back out into the sunlight. Hitler, without his cap, stood on the top step by himself. He swiped the hair across his forehead. That signature gesture, so full of himself.

The wolf was in her sights. Like her father had taught her, she found his eyes above his mustache.

Never hold your breath. Her father's words played in her head. *Shoot on the exhale.* She aimed and squeezed the trigger.

But Hitler had bent down to the crying toddler. Over the tolling of the church bell, the crack of the rifle reverberated off limestone. A spit of dust puffed from the church pillar. The child's mother looked up, surprised, finding dust on her shoulder. Any moment the guards would notice.

Concentrate.

As calmly as she could and willing her mind still, Kate reloaded within three seconds, aimed at his black hair above his ear as he leaned over, extending his hand to the little girl's head, ruffling her hair. The guards were laughing now, focused on the Führer, whose fondness for children was well-known.

Kate pulled the trigger again just as Hitler straightened. Damn. The uniformed man behind him jerked.

As the shot zipped by him one of the guards looked around. She couldn't believe her luck that no one else had noticed. She had to hurry.

Reloading and adjusting once more, she aimed at the point between his eyes. Cocked the trigger. But Hitler had lifted the little girl in his arms, smiling, still unaware that the man behind him had been hit. The toddler's blonde curls spilled in front of Hitler's face.

Her heart convulsed, pain filling her chest. Those blonde curls were so like Lisbeth's. Why did he have to pick this toddler up just then?

Killing a child is not part of your mission. This time, the voice in her head was her own, not Stepney's. Agonized, she felt her focus slipping away.

Now. She had to fire now. Harden herself and shoot. Ignore the fact the bullet would pass through the little girl's cheek. That the woman in the blue hat would lose her daughter.

The hesitation cost her a second.

The uniform slumped down the church pillar. A dark red spot became a line of blood dripping down his collar.

Hitler was still holding the child as she heard the shouts. She hadn't yet taken her shot when all hell broke loose.

A guard snatched the little girl from his arms. Guards forced Hitler into a crouch and hurried him to the car. In the uniformed crowd now surrounding Hitler a man pointed in Kate's direction. Through the telescopic sight she saw his steel-gray eyes scanning the building. She could swear those eyes looked right at her.

Le Bourget Airfield outside Paris | 9:00 A.M.

"THIRTY-SIX HOURS," BARKED the Führer, pausing at the plane cabin door. Despite the heat, he was wearing a leather trench coat. It was bulletproof, and after what had just happened at Sacré-Cœur he refused to take it off. *"Verstehen Sie?"*

"Jawohl, mein Führer." Gunter Hoffman blinked grit from his gray eyes.

Thirty-six hours to find the sniper.

The cabin door slammed shut and the Focke-Wulf taxied down the airstrip. Gunter was thirty-two years old, a Munich homicide detective in the Kriminalpolizei before he'd been folded into the Reichssicherheitsdienst, RSD, the Reich's SS security service. He sucked in his breath. He knew his job; he'd headed the southern Bayern section. But he'd never investigated solo in an occupied zone.

Beside him, Lange, the trim Gestapo agent, stood at attention until the plane's belly lifted off the runway. "Better you than me," Lange said, shielding his face from the hot engine's updraft. "I've got Berlin and Lindau's successor to deal with." He nodded to the stretcher carrying poor Admiral Lindau's corpse. The admiral had taken the bullet intended for the Führer. Lange would be accompanying the body to the troop transport plane at the refueling depot.

After the shooting, Hitler had instructed the guards to round up all the Sacré-Cœur churchgoers, as if any of them would know anything about the gunman—but of course the Führer's orders were to be followed. Gunter would have chosen to head the detail to comb the surrounding buildings for the sniper, but he had ordered him and his superior to accompany him to the airfield.

For the duration of the car ride, the Führer had issued wild demands: "Bring me that little girl, my good luck charm." "Take the priest and his parishioners to the church crypt and get the truth out of them, you know how." He raged at suspected traitors. "My suspicions were all correct. I knew it as soon as I saw those reports. This plot started in London. I'll pay them back."

After months on the job, Gunter had grown to distrust the man who led the Third Reich. At home in Munich, he focused on his work, kept his head down and avoided the Reich's inner politics. But today he had attracted the Führer's attention, for better or for worse.

"Better dig up a few suspects for the chopping block, eh?" Lange said.

The Führer's penchant for mock trials before the *Fallbeil*, a stationary guillotine, was well-known, but Gunter would conduct his investigation his own way—to the extent he was allowed to. "I'm still a Kriminalpolizei, Lange. We follow the law."

When he'd heard the shots fired at Sacré-Cœur, Gunter had caught sight of the glint of the rifle in a fourth-floor window. The sniper wouldn't get far. Chances were the squad had already apprehended the shooter and the Sicherheitsdienst, SD, the SS intelligence, had the shooter waiting for Gunter's interrogation.

Lange shook his head. "Our Führer's as slippery as an eel in the Elbe. How many times has he escaped death? But you already know all about that."

There had been eight attempts on Hitler's life on record since the National Socialists' rise to power, and Gunter knew that almost double that number hadn't been reported.

But he didn't voice agreement; he didn't trust Lange. After seven years under National Socialism, Gunter knew better than to comment on the Führer, lest Lange twist his words and backstab him Gestapo-style. How often had Gunter witnessed someone slip up and make an untoward remark, leaving behind nothing but an empty desk.

"My job is to bring the perpetrator to justice," Gunter said instead. The standard line.

As Gunter turned away from the still-smirking Lange, his boss, Gruppenführer Jäger, a broad-shouldered dark-haired man in full SS regalia, strode toward them from an airplane hangar.

"I'll be following the Führer," Jäger told Gunter. "He insists." His words were politic but his expression conveyed his chagrin. No man was a hero to his valet and no Führer to his security chief. "I'm leaving the investigation under your control, Gunter."

"Of course, Gruppenführer."

"The Führer himself requested I put you in charge, Gunter. Such an honor."

An honor, yes, but being on the Führer's radar was a double-edged sword. Life changed in a moment—just yesterday evening he'd been in Munich, checking decoded messages that reported a possible British parachute drop in France, when his assistant, Keller, took a call for him.

"Your wife told me to tell you she's frosting the *Kuchen*."

Gunter could still make it home in time. How often did his daughter turn two years old?

He'd slipped that evening's reports and his daughter's present, a Steiff teddy bear, into his case. Before he could make it any farther, though, Keller had brought him Jäger's telegram, which summoned him to the airfield immediately for a flight to Belgian HQ at Brûly-de-Pesche, to continue on to Paris early this morning.

Gunter could almost smell the Schokoladenkuchen. *Ach*, why on his daughter's birthday?

He blinked again, still trying to dislodge the stubborn grit from his eye, bringing himself back to the dusty runway. "A privilege, Gruppenführer."

"Make us proud, Gunter," said Jäger. "You excel at the hunt. No one assembles the pieces better than you, putting order to the chaos."

"*Danke*." He hoped his boss would leave it at that and let him get to work.

Jäger nodded. "Your uncle trained you well."

Gunter's mother had abandoned him as a child on his policeman uncle's doorstep. He'd never known his father. Gunter counted himself lucky to be raised by his uncle, who had made sure there was always a coat on his back and bread in his school lunch pail, even during the hungriest days of the Weimar Republic. His uncle, a stickler for order and detail, had provided young Gunter a sense of safety he'd never known with his mother. No wonder he'd followed in his uncle's footsteps. He'd found a great sense of purpose in police work, a world where his efforts produced tangible results.

"An honor to be of service," Gunter said, a repetition of what they'd learned to always reply at the police academy. "I'll assemble a team and report back to you as soon as I have news, and liaise with the SD at the Paris Kommandantur."

Jäger took Gunter's arm. "You will issue reports only to me. Am I clear? No information to SD, or anyone else. No assembling a team."

"*Jawohl*, Gruppenführer, but without contacts on the ground . . ."

"I'll see you're in communication with the right people." Jäger tapped his thick fingers together. "Your cousin Eva's biology professorship is up for tenure at Universität Bayern, isn't it?"

What business was it of his? Gunter's heart beat hard in his chest.

"My old friend Professor Häckl heads the science department," said Jäger. "He could smooth the way to tenure for her. But if that business with the Jew came up, well, it might be a bumpy road."

His silly little cousin Eva's affair, long since over, was a vulnerability that never went away. It had almost cost his uncle his police position a few years ago. Gunter, who had his own family now, had to be careful.

But Jäger had never put personal pressure like this on him before. His boss's job must be on the line. That meant Gunter's was, too.

Jäger stuck a cigarette between his thick lips. Lit it and inhaled. Gunter always thought those lips were mismatched to his otherwise long features. "You will keep me exclusively informed of findings."

Already Gunter didn't like this. He wondered if he was being set up to be the fall man. But what choice did he have?

He nodded. "*Jawohl*, Gruppenführer."

Other Titles in the Soho Crime Series

STEPHANIE BARRON
(Jane Austen's England)
Jane and the Twelve Days
of Christmas
Jane and the Waterloo Map
Jane and the Year Without a Summer

F.H. BATACAN
(Philippines)
Smaller and Smaller Circles

JAMES R. BENN
(World War II Europe)
Billy Boyle
The First Wave
Blood Alone
Evil for Evil
Rag & Bone
A Mortal Terror
Death's Door
A Blind Goddess
The Rest Is Silence
The White Ghost
Blue Madonna
The Devouring
Solemn Graves
When Hell Struck Twelve
The Red Horse
Road of Bones

CARA BLACK
(Paris, France)
Murder in the Marais
Murder in Belleville
Murder in the Sentier
Murder in the Bastille
Murder in Clichy
Murder in Montmartre
Murder on the Ile Saint-Louis
Murder in the Rue de Paradis
Murder in the Latin Quarter
Murder in the Palais Royal
Murder in Passy
Murder at the Lanterne Rouge
Murder Below Montparnasse
Murder in Pigalle
Murder on the Champ de Mars
Murder on the Quai
Murder in Saint-Germain
Murder on the Left Bank
Murder in Bel-Air
Murder at the Porte de Versailles

Three Hours in Paris

HENRY CHANG
(Chinatown)
Chinatown Beat
Year of the Dog
Red Jade
Death Money
Lucky

BARBARA CLEVERLY
(England)
The Last Kashmiri Rose
Strange Images of Death
The Blood Royal
Not My Blood
A Spider in the Cup
Enter Pale Death
Diana's Altar

Fall of Angels
Invitation to Die

COLIN COTTERILL
(Laos)
The Coroner's Lunch
Thirty-Three Teeth
Disco for the Departed
Anarchy and Old Dogs
Curse of the Pogo Stick
The Merry Misogynist
Love Songs from a Shallow Grave
Slash and Burn
The Woman Who Wouldn't Die
Six and a Half Deadly Sins
I Shot the Buddha
The Rat Catchers' Olympics
Don't Eat Me
The Second Biggest Nothing
The Delightful Life of
a Suicide Pilot

GARRY DISHER
(Australia)
The Dragon Man
Kittyhawk Down
Snapshot
Chain of Evidence
Blood Moon
Whispering Death
Signal Loss

Wyatt
Port Vila Blues
Fallout

Under the Cold Bright Lights

TERESA DOVALPAGE
(Cuba)
Death Comes in through
the Kitchen
Queen of Bones
Death under the Perseids

Death of a Telenovela Star
(A Novella)

DAVID DOWNING
(World War II Germany)
Zoo Station
Silesian Station
Stettin Station
Potsdam Station
Lehrter Station
Masaryk Station
Wedding Station

(World War I)
Jack of Spies
One Man's Flag
Lenin's Roller Coaster
The Dark Clouds Shining

Diary of a Dead Man on Leave

AGNETE FRIIS
(Denmark)
What My Body Remembers
The Summer of Ellen

TIMOTHY HALLINAN
(Thailand)
The Fear Artist
For the Dead
The Hot Countries
Fools' River
Street Music

(Los Angeles)
Crashed
Little Elvises
The Fame Thief
Herbie's Game
King Maybe
Fields Where They Lay
Nighttown
Rock of Ages

METTE IVIE HARRISON
(Mormon Utah)
The Bishop's Wife
His Right Hand
For Time and All Eternities

METTE IVIE HARRISON CONT.
Not of This Fold
The Prodigal Daughter

MICK HERRON
(England)
Slow Horses
Dead Lions
The List (A Novella)
Real Tigers
Spook Street
London Rules
The Marylebone Drop (A Novella)
Joe Country
The Catch (A Novella)
Slough House
Bad Actors

Down Cemetery Road
The Last Voice You Hear
Why We Die
Smoke and Whispers

Reconstruction
Nobody Walks
This Is What Happened
Dolphin Junction: Stories

STAN JONES
(Alaska)
White Sky, Black Ice
Shaman Pass
Frozen Sun
Village of the Ghost Bears
Tundra Kill
The Big Empty

STEVEN MACK JONES
(Detroit)
August Snow
Lives Laid Away
Dead of Winter

LENE KAABERBØL & AGNETE FRIIS
(Denmark)
The Boy in the Suitcase
Invisible Murder

KAABERBØL & FRIIS CONT.
Death of a Nightingale
The Considerate Killer

MARTIN LIMÓN
(South Korea)
Jade Lady Burning
Slicky Boys
Buddha's Money

MARTIN LIMÓN CONT.
The Door to Bitterness
The Wandering Ghost
G.I. Bones
Mr. Kill
The Joy Brigade
Nightmare Range
The Iron Sickle
The Ville Rat
Ping-Pong Heart
The Nine-Tailed Fox
The Line
GI Confidential
War Women

ED LIN
(Taiwan)
Ghost Month
Incensed
99 Ways to Die

PETER LOVESEY
(England)
The Circle
The Headhunters
False Inspector Dew
Rough Cider
On the Edge
The Reaper

(Bath, England)
The Last Detective
Diamond Solitaire
The Summons
Bloodhounds
Upon a Dark Night
The Vault
Diamond Dust
The House Sitter
The Secret Hangman
Skeleton Hill
Stagestruck
Cop to Corpse
The Tooth Tattoo
The Stone Wife
Down Among the Dead Men
Another One Goes Tonight
Beau Death
Killing with Confetti
The Finisher
Diamond and the Eye

(London, England)
Wobble to Death
The Detective Wore

PETER LOVESEY CONT.
Silk Drawers
Abracadaver
Mad Hatter's Holiday
The Tick of Death
A Case of Spirits
Swing, Swing Together
Waxwork

Bertie and the Tinman
Bertie and the Seven Bodies
Bertie and the Crime of Passion

SUJATA MASSEY
(1920s Bombay)
The Widows of Malabar Hill
The Satapur Moonstone
The Bombay Prince

FRANCINE MATHEWS
(Nantucket)
Death in the Off-Season
Death in Rough Water
Death in a Mood Indigo
Death in a Cold Hard Light
Death on Nantucket
Death on Tuckernuck

SEICHŌ MATSUMOTO
(Japan)
Inspector Imanishi Investigates

MAGDALEN NABB
(Italy)
Death of an Englishman
Death of a Dutchman
Death in Springtime
Death in Autumn
The Marshal and the Murderer
The Marshal and the Madwoman
The Marshal's Own Case
The Marshal Makes His Report
The Marshal at the Villa Torrini
Property of Blood
Some Bitter Taste
The Innocent
Vita Nuova
The Monster of Florence

FUMINORI NAKAMURA
(Japan)
The Thief
Evil and the Mask
Last Winter, We Parted
The Kingdom
The Boy in the Earth